Broken Promises

A CPS Novel – Book 1

Christy Wilson

Christy Wilson

Visit my website at http://www.authorchristywilson.com

Printed in the United States of America

ISBN-13 978-1979691819

I would like to thank my daughter, Katey, for encouraging me throughout this entire process and always pushing me to pursue this dream.

Our family dog, Tyson, is the real-life Bones; most of the antics that he pulls in this story line are based on his true-life antics that keep our home full of laughter on a daily basis.

Other Books by this Author

The CPS Series ~

Broken Promises

Amongst the Debris

A Balancing Act

Off the Deep End

The Ties that Bind

Crossing the Line

A New Beginning

The Romantic CPS Series ~

Promises

Debris

Visit Christy's website at http://www.authorchristywilson.com to purchase books, sign up for her newsletter, and stay informed of important information.

*She's a sarcastic and stubborn strawberry-blonde with
a red-headed temper, and an addiction to Olive Garden and
Dairy Queen Blizzards. She's sworn off men forever.*

*He's a green-eyed, rock-hard bodied Probation Officer,
that works 24/7 because he has no life outside of work.*

*When CPS worker Sadey Collins is sent to investigate
the abuse/neglect of a drug using mother, she has no idea
that this case will be the one to change her life forever. Being
run over by the drug dealer causes her to confront more than
she's willing to admit. For the first time in her life, she's
falling in love. But Chase Davis isn't just any man – he's the
soon-to-be brother-in-law of her best friend.*

*As if this doesn't complicate her life enough... her
family, this case and his job force her to confront the one
thing that's been haunting her most of her life – her strained
relationship with her father. Convincing herself to look to the
future instead of the past has her on an emotional roller-
coaster she's struggling to control.*

Table of Contents

Abuse and neglect of children is real and is happening every day in every neighborhood across the world. While Sadey's story is fictional, the situations she deals with on the job are very much real. This is just a reminder to always keep your eyes and ears open. Be ever vigilant where our children are concerned.

Children are not a distraction from more important work. They are the most important work ~ C.S. Lewis

There comes a day when you realize turning the page is the best feeling in the world — because you realize there's so much more to the book than the page you were stuck on.

Abuse and Neglect

"No! No!" I hear the screeching tires; I see the car coming straight at me, but I'm helpless to do anything about it. I see his eyes glow a devilish red right before I feel the searing pain of the car bumper hitting my right leg, bouncing me into the air and dropping me onto the asphalt several feet away. I feel my hand twist backwards as my head lands hard on the ground; then agonizing pain as I feel a tire roll over my right ankle.

I hear voices, but I can't make out the faces. It seems to take forever for my eyes to focus; the first thing I see is Chase standing over me. Why is he here?

The pain is intense. I can't breathe.

"Mark! No!"

"Sadey, Sadey; wake up! You're having a nightmare."

6 days earlier….

Tuesday, September 18th

The sun is shining brightly overhead, bouncing a glare off my windshield that requires sunglasses in late September. Colorful leaves of red, orange, and yellow create a spectacular view as I drive the winding roads of the Appalachian Mountains. Unfortunately, I have no time to stop and admire the scenery. I am on my way to investigate another allegation of abuse and neglect of young children, one of many I will respond to in the following days and weeks.

I've slowed down to a crawl, trying to find the blue house with white shutters that says "Sams" on the barely stable mailbox at the end of the driveway. Of course, this is the description given by the anonymous caller who has accused this mother of 'doing drugs and leaving her small children at home all night alone while she is out getting high'.

Another five minutes of roads snaking their way through the mountains, I finally locate the barely standing mailbox and turn down a driveway with potholes deep enough to swallow my little Hyundai sedan.

The "blue house with white shutters" is actually three shades of blue with only a couple of shutters actually attached to the house.

I raise my arm to knock, and the door is opened by a small-framed, tired looking woman who appears years older than her true age. She has the same long brown hair and beautiful brown eyes as the little girl who is hiding behind her, trying to get a look at the stranger at the door, and she's dressed in ragged sweatpants and a t-shirt that's probably a size or two too big for her little frame.

"Ms. Sams," I say, handing her my card. "My name is Sadey Collins. I work for Child Protective Services."

She doesn't show any emotion – not shock, or curiosity, or even anger. She slowly opens the door the rest of the way and motions me into the house.

Protocol says that I should interview the kids before the parent and somewhere other than their home, but since the caller didn't know the names or ages of the girls, that put a damper on my protocol. So, I just go about it backwards. Protocol, smotocol – it's all just technicalities.

"Ms. Sams, the reason I am here is because someone is concerned that you are doing drugs and leaving your girls home alone at night. I'm here to investigate those allegations, so I'd like to ask you some questions." She looks at the floor as though it has all the answers to the questions I'm asking.

"It's Mark's fault – he's bringing her pills now, too," says a young voice behind me. I turn around and face a girl of about 9 or 10 years. She appears cleaner than the younger girl, with light brown hair brushed and pulled into a ponytail. Her jeans have a sparkling butterfly on the left leg and a plain pink shirt that appears to be the right size and matches the butterfly, only without the sparkle.

"Who's Mark? And what pills?" I ask.

"Lacey's dad, and I don't know what they are", she answers with a shrug of her shoulders.

I look back at Ms. Sams to see a reaction to what her daughter just stated, but all I see is her continuing blank stare focused on some spot on the floor.

"I'm Kasey. Are you a social worker?"

"Yes I am. Have you had a social worker at your house before?"

She looks at me like I've just asked the dumbest question in the world.

"Are you new?" she asks me in a sarcastic tone that would give me a run for my money.

"Not really. I've been doing this job for a couple of years now. Why?"

"I figured all you social workers knew my mom. We've been dealing with this problem since before Lacey was born."

"We?"

"Look lady…"

"Sadey."

"Whatever! I know I'm only 10, but I'm very smart and I take care of everything around here when mom's high – she sleeps a lot."

"Ok, Kasey. Can I ask you some questions? Like, starting with, why aren't you in school?"

"Well, for one, mom was too high to take me to the bus stop, and two, somebody has to take care of Lacey."

This kid is wise beyond her years, and reminds me of myself – direct, to the point, and doesn't take any crap, especially from somebody who appears to be in authority. She seems to have no respect for social workers, and I obviously need to scan the computers for previous allegations on this family; something I probably should have done before I headed out here, but I was just busy and forgot. Now that a 10-year-old has made me feel completely incompetent, it's time to figure out what's really going on in this house.

"Kasey, would you mind to get me up to speed on everything in this house since I've never been here before?"

Again, she looks at me like I'm completely stupid. After a full minute of enduring an evil glare from this dark-haired devil, she finally came around the couch and sat down beside me.

"Do you want the long version or the short one?" she asks.

I sighed. This day is probably going to require an extra scoop of ice cream!

"Might as well start at the beginning."

She began to tell me a story. She said that her mom was only 16 when she was born, and she dropped out of high school; they lived with their grandma until she died about four years later. They got to stay in the house, but Deborah had to get a job. She started working at the Food Shop, where she met Lacey's dad, Mark. Apparently, that's when she started smoking drugs. Her mom started acting weird and would just sleep all the time instead of going to work. Wanda was their first social worker and she forced Deborah to attend drug meetings and Mark wasn't allowed over anymore. Kasey said that Deborah promised her that she would take care of herself and Kasey, but obviously she didn't keep that promise. Her eye-roll was impressive as she said, "Big surprise!"

She went on to tell me about Deborah getting back together with Mark, more social workers, Lacey being born, Mark bringing her pills and cigarettes, and more broken promises – the thing that bothered her the most.

I seriously could not believe this kid was only 10. She's definitely seen and lived a lot in those 10 short years. I knew at this point that this investigation was going to be a long-term case, one that was going to tear through my heart strings.

Kasey told me that Deborah has never left them home alone, and she wasn't the type to cover for her mom, so I marked off that allegation. I spent another hour talking to Deborah, who confirmed everything her daughter told me, although she was reluctant to add any more details. I had to pry out of her that the pills were Xanax, she didn't have a prescription for them, but she wouldn't tell me where she got them – I had a good idea where they came from since Kasey pointed the finger at Mark, but I had to prove it. She tried to convince me that she wasn't high right now and the last time she smoked weed was yesterday. Since I didn't have drug tests with me, I couldn't really prove that statement right or wrong, but I was betting on the wrong.

I attached my card to the fridge and left instructions to Kasey that she was to call me if she saw her mom smoking anything besides those Marlboros. Deborah promised me no drugs today, and I told her I would be back tomorrow, with a drug test, and I expected Kasey to be in school and for her to take care of Lacey, bath and all. She agreed, but I could tell that nothing was going to be easy with the Sams family.

I made her sign a safety form – I wrote out everything I expected of her before my visit tomorrow, including cleaning the trash up off the living room floor, and made her sign it; just to cover my own butt. The girls were not in imminent danger, so I figured I was ok.

As I got to my car, I looked back at the house and Kasey was standing at the door, hands on her hips, giving me a look that said, "You're wasting your time – nothing's going to change". As I drove back down that rough and bumpy road, I vowed to make sure this little girl didn't have any more broken promises – at least not from me.

As Kasey watched the Social Worker pull away, she thought to herself, "It would be nice if this time was different." But, in her heart she knew that nothing was going to change. Her mom was a drug addict, and this lady was just wasting her time trying to fix things. Before she left, the lady – Sadey - told her mom to clean up the house and take care of Lacey. She figured she'd better get started since she knew her mom wouldn't make the effort – especially since it required cleaning AND giving Lacey a bath!

In spite of what's been happening, each day is a new chance to change your attitude and do your best.

Bones

Well, for a Tuesday, it sure felt like a Monday – it royally
sucked! Forget dinner, I'm going straight for dessert! Yeah, I know
that Dairy Queen sells real food, but I didn't want real food, I wanted
comfort food. A Chocolate Extreme Blizzard (with whipped cream
on top) – to be exact. No, it doesn't come with whipped cream, but
if you're really nice to the teenage boy making your Blizzard… Ok,
it doesn't hurt that I'm a regular customer.

It didn't take long for the ice cream to begin working its magic;
I was feeling calmer already. Yes, it's an addiction, but the thing
that separates me from my clients is that my addiction is legal. I
love that the Dairy Queen is only 2 miles from my house; not great
for my hips, but on nice nights I can take my dog, Bones, for a walk
and then I can justify getting some ice cream for both of us because
we are going to walk it off on our way home.

Of course, Bones doesn't have to worry about ice cream going
to his hips because he's a dog, and he has big brown eyes and floppy
ears, and everybody thinks he's adorable no matter what. Then

again, I don't really need to worry about the size of my hips either since it's been a few years since they've been seen by a man.

Even though today started out pretty crappy, I'm expecting it to end on a better note. The Blizzard was a good start, but Leroy Jethro Gibbs is always a fine finish. Tuesday nights are reserved for sweatpants and NCIS. Gibbs is a fine piece of man candy and seems to get better with age! I know I'm only 27, and he's old enough to be my dad, but I would still be willing to try my hand at being his wife – whatever number that may be.

I figure while Bones is currently occupied with Dairy Queen's finest creation, that he snatched from me when I walked in the door, it's a good time to find those sweatpants. Now while I'm meticulous, organized, and borderline OCD at work, my house-keeping skills leave a lot to be desired –I'm not Martha Stewart. Typically, a smell test is in order when it comes to finding sweatpants. Basically, how this works is:

1. You locate any pair of sweats from among the piles of clothes,

2. You hold up the sweats and observe them for obvious signs of dirt, mud, or ice cream spills,

3. Seeing none, you proceed to sniff the sweats for any sign of an odor you can't tolerate,

4. And if there is limited or no odor, you put the sweats on your body – if the smell would deter a skunk, then you throw them back on the floor until laundry day.

Luckily my comfy gray sweats passed the smell test, so they win the honor of being worn while watching NCIS and the delicious Gibbs. I cleaned up Bones' cup pieces that were scattered around the living room and let him out back to do his business. I still have an hour before I become completely lazy in front of the TV for the night, so I gathered my laptop and the Sams' folder and figured I can start documenting my visit. Might as well be productive.

I opened the folder and began looking through the family information that was listed; there was a mention of a half-sister to Deborah – Karleen – that lives less than 10 minutes away. She's a DJ at the local radio station and works the 10a-3p shift.

Bingo! A relative that appears to be stable; definitely need to pay her a visit. Everybody needs a sane family member – sometimes you just have to dig real deep to find one.

My mom is a strong woman, but Grandma Daisy (Collins) was the sane person in my family. Going to her house was like a get-away retreat when I was little. There was always sweet tea and Swiss cake rolls, reading books on the porch swing, and catching lightening bugs after dark. That was my place to run to for sanity. Now that house of sanity belongs to me.

Grandma Daisy always called me her "Snow White Princess". My full name is Sadey Nevada Collins; Sadey means "Princess" and Nevada means "white as snow", which is kind of funny since the state of Nevada is really just one big desert mixed with casinos. I like to think she left me her house because I was her favorite, but the truth is that I was the middle child of her only son (who turned out to be an abusive, drug addict spending most of his adult years in and out of jail) and she always said it was her job to look after me.

That may be one reason this Sams case is pulling at my heart strings so much; I spent a lot of years dealing with broken promises from my own dad, who kept swearing that each time was the last time. At least I had my mom and grandma to lean on – Kasey has nobody. I guess I feel the need to try and fix that. First thing in the morning I'm going back to Deborah's house with Janice Keefer, my favorite drug addiction specialist from Western Health, and my favorite cop, Leland; there are most likely drugs in the house that need found and we are definitely doing a drug screen and evaluation. This lady has two beautiful girls she needs to be taking care of and, somehow, I'm going to fix this family.

Ok – snap out of it! Put this case out of your head and curl up on the couch with Bones for a night of mindless TV and the yummy Gibbs.

Never ask a woman who is eating ice cream straight from the carton how she's doing.

Clientville

Wednesday, September 19th

The clouds are rolling in for a day forecasted to be cool, filled with scattered thunderstorms, and probably leaves blowing all over my front yard. It pretty much matches my mood today. I think I just woke up on the wrong side of the bed this morning; not to mention I can feel the whole "cramps" thing comin' on.

Wavy, unruly strawberry-blonde hair in a ponytail, just enough makeup to bring out the green in my eyes, khakis with a ¾ length turquoise sweater that hugs just enough that I appear to have some perky boobs. I'm thinking tennis shoes, since my day is going to be spent in and out of my car. My boss prefers dressier shoes, but we have an agreement - she won't comment on my choice of shoes and I won't make fun of her 70's hairdo. Childish, I know, but seriously who wants to go in and out of icky houses in high heels. Get real! The only reason to wear high heels is a wedding or a funeral. And while some days my job feels like a funeral, it's really not – so tennis shoes it is.

When I first started out as a social worker, my boss told me that the worst thing I could do in this job was to get emotionally involved with clients. *"Keep your distance with your heart, work only with your head; otherwise, your heart will impede your judgment."* Words to live by in social work. So far I've done a good job, so why now am I letting a case get the best of my heart? Ugh – I'm a total downer this morning! As I pull into the parking lot of Western Health to pick up Janice, I tell myself it's time to check my attitude at the door and prepare myself mentally for the day ahead.

Children's Services works very closely with Western Health. They are a one-stop shop for a lot of the services my clients need: drug testing, parenting classes, anger management, counseling for children and adults, psychological and psychiatric services, and an in-house caseworker to put together a plan for the client. Janice is my favorite caseworker – she can "read" the clients, she has a great sense of humor that puts the clients at ease, and she totally gets my sarcasm – a rare trait in social workers.

Janice Keefer is on the front side of 40, black as the ace of spades, with the most beautiful curly black hair I've ever seen, that sits atop a body that's as round as it is tall. I've never seen her in anything but bright, colorful swinging skirts. Bright being the operative word. She doesn't do neutrals, or pastels, or simple navy blue – nope – her skirts are always a mixture of bright yellow, pink, blue, green, purple, or whatever scraps of fabric she found on sale and put together. She sews them all herself, and while I would never be caught dead in one of those skirts, I couldn't imagine her wearing anything else. I absolutely love her southern accent, a girl being raised in South Carolina, too far from the beach to enjoy the view, but just close enough to have to deal with the aggravation of tourists. She lost her husband a few years ago to a boating accident and decided to move north and get away from the ocean. She once told me that she packed her car, started north, broke down in the mountains of WV and decided to stay awhile. She's never left. And I for one, am very grateful for that.

As Janice rolls herself into my car, she says "Giiiirrrrllllfriend (which is actually an elongated word in the south), I hope you're feeling good today, 'cause we have an extra stop to make before we go see Deborah."

This is not what I wanted to hear, considering my need to feel grumpy. Apparently, that was obvious by the look on my face, because Janice suggested that we make a stop at Tim Horton's before we get started. "Ain't nothin' in the world that cain't be fixed by some honey glazed Timbits and chocolate milk." I'm pretty sure that "cain't" ain't a word, but there is no way I'm going to argue with that logic! So off to Tim Horton's we head.

Apparently, James Michaels missed his drug screening and counseling yesterday afternoon, so we have to stop by his apartment and do a random test before we can go check on Deborah and the kids.

Of course, quick in my world is not the same as everybody else's quick. The good news is that James lives in a small apartment in town, so it's easy access. The bad news is that he lives in the heart of "Clientville". Basically, I can head to the house of one client and see six more at the same time. This means I have to document my observations for each client. Saves money on gas, but requires time catching up on my notes. And of course, this was just that kind of morning – good thing I've had donuts!

As we turn down James' street, the view takes bleak and depressing to a new level. There is no color at all – just a long row of old brown brick apartment buildings on both sides of the strect. Very few cars are parked on the road. In any other neighborhood, this might mean that people are at work. But not here. Most of the residents of these apartment buildings can't afford a car. The ones that do have a job either ride the bus or walk.

As I scan the buildings for signs of life, out of the corner of my eye I see a curtain move, and an 8-year-old boy named Sampson looking out at me from behind that moving curtain. Looks like this will be my first stop of the morning – James gets a few minutes reprieve. Janice just laughs as she says, "Gonna be a long day – good thing Tim Hortons understands our needs." I pull over in front of building #2, pop one more Timbit into my mouth and head up the sidewalk. I only have to knock once before Sampson comes to the door.

"Hey Sam – what's up? How come you're not at school today?"

"Mom's not up yet", he replies.

"Have you eaten breakfast?"

"Yep – cereal".

"Ok – go get dressed in school clothes and brush your teeth. I'll go get your mom up". Good kid – lazy, drunk mom. I walk back the hallway and pound on Elaine's door. She doesn't get up to answer, so I just walk on in. She is laying on her stomach sound asleep, an empty bottle of vodka on her nightstand. Well, no need to be quiet.

"Elaine!" I hollered loudly. "Why aren't you up yet?"

"You don't need to scream".

"What's wrong – hungover again?" I keep prodding. "Looks to me like you had a little party last night".

"What? No! It was just me and Sampson here, I swear!"

"Really? Well, I guess that means you drank that entire bottle of vodka by yourself then, huh?"

She's awake now. The realization of what she just said seems to hit her, hard.

"Sampson is going back to your mom's, Elaine, until this stops – until you are sober. You are out of control again. You can't even get up in the morning to get your son to school because you drank an entire bottle of vodka last night. Janice is taking Sampson to school, and when she gets back, you're taking a breathalyzer. Now get up and get dressed. You're going to have a busy day."

I love the fact that Janice has all the cool stuff in her kit – drug testing thingamabobs, a breathalyzer doohickey, and lots of other neat toys. Of course, it's all serious addictions that we have to deal with; but sometimes you just have to laugh at the insanity and enjoy the cool toys.

Next stop – James. Only three apartment buildings down on the opposite side of the street. Of course, since they all look the same, I actually have to look for building #6. As I'm climbing the steps to his 2nd floor apartment, I am cheering on my decision to wear tennis shoes today, but silently cursing that last Timbit I felt the need to pop a little earlier. Janice is right on my heels the whole way – I have no idea how she moves so quickly. Two apartments on this floor; we are headed to B.

I give it my best cop knock and the door shakes and rattles. I could probably do a cop kick and knock it down – of course, knowing me I'd probably pull a hamstring in the process and end up on my butt looking like a complete fool. Wouldn't be the first time I looked like an idiot, but I definitely wasn't in the mood for it this morning, so I resorted to pounding loudly again.

"James! Get your lazy butt off that couch and answer this door. I'm not going away so you might as well just open up!"

I can hear him grunt and groan as he makes his way to the door. He opens it slowly, and the view was not great. His 5'8" skinny frame was only covered by a pair of sweatpants that had more holes in them than the story I was sure he was about to make up for our sake. His long blonde hair was in total disarray and his eyes were bloodshot – drugs or sleep – not sure which, but I was fixing to find out.

"Morning, James. You missed your appointment yesterday, so Janice and I graciously drove out here this morning to make sure you didn't miss your drug screen. Wasn't that nice of us?"

"Yeah, whatever".

"Ok, no attitude this morning because it's fixin' to be a completely crappy day for me, and I'd hate for that to be partly your fault. Not to mention I'm feeling a little PMS coming on which would legally give me the right to kick you in the nads and no judge in the world would argue with me." I give him my sweetest smile.

James has been a client for quite a while – actually since his daughter Kara was only 1 and James decided to leave her in the car while he walked down to the corner to buy some weed. Now she's 4 and I'm still working on him and his drug habit. His drug screens have been negative lately, but he's not out of the water yet. Bad thing is that he's not too bad of a father, just needs some help.

"Ok, James. Time to pee in a cup. Janice will then let me know if I need to kick you in the nads or just Gibbs slap you for missing your appointment yesterday. Now get to it."

In the meantime, a sleepy Kara comes slowly meandering out of her room to check on the commotion. She's so adorable! She has long blonde curly hair and the bluest eyes I have ever seen. She absolutely adores her dad, so I work really hard at keeping James out of jail and taking care of that little girl.

"Good morning, Kara."

"Morning Miss Sadey – why are you here?"

"Well, your dad missed his counseling appointment yesterday so I'm checking to make sure everything is ok. How are you doing?"

"Fine. Jimmy had a nightmare last night. (Jimmy is her raggedy old stuffed bunny that's missing an eye and part of an ear)."

"Oh no. What happened?"

"He dreamed he was being chased by a dog and it cut off his tail. Good thing I saw that his tail was still on his butt, so I calmed him down a little bit."

James and Janice come strolling back down the hallway and Janice is giving me a thumbs up – meaning he passed his drug screen.

"Nice job James. Now let's get that counseling appointment rescheduled and get you back into those parenting classes. Kara seems to be doing well, but she is supposed to be enrolled in pre-school. How come she's still here this morning?"

"I hate sending her to school already, man. She still so little and besides, she keeps me company."

"Yeah, I know. But you are supposed to be looking for a job. Your unemployment benefits run out in three months and then we're going to have problems."

Janice piped in. "James, when you come in on Monday for your appointment, talk to Jennifer at the front desk. She has a list of businesses that are hiring. Some of them are just part-time, but you could still get HUD assistance and provide for Kara at the same time."

"Ok, fine."

"Now, about preschool."

"Yeah, yeah. I know. Can it just be at the pink church on the corner? That way I can walk there and it's only 3 days a week."

"That's fine with me, but I want her enrolled before you show up to counseling on Monday or I'm going to be in a very bad mood. Comprende?"

"Yeah, I got it."

"Good. Now get your little girl some breakfast and then take her over to the park to play before the rain decides to set in. You need to get out of this apartment once in a while."

"Ok."

"Monday. Be on time."

"I got it! Don't get your panties in a wad!"

"Just so we understand each other."

"I understand. Now you can go bother somebody else. Kara and I are doing great."

As I walk out of the apartment, I have to admit that James and Kara are doing much better. He does take care of her physical needs, but a 4-year-old needs a little more and James just needs a little guidance.

Off to see Deborah.

Janice and I knocked on Deborah's door, but didn't get an answer. We knocked again and then heard some little feet padding across the floor. Lacey opened the door and she looked so loveable. She was wearing cute capris and her hair was pulled into a ponytail. I had hopes that my day was about to turn around. Then.....

Broken trust is like melted chocolate. No matter how hard you try to freeze it, you can never return it to the original shape.

You have the right to remain silent...

I saw Deborah sit up on the couch and it occurred to me that she was wearing the same grungy clothes she had on when I left yesterday. The living room was clean, Lacey had been bathed and looked very cute, so I was sure that this was the work of Kasey.

"Good morning, Deborah. I see you haven't ventured very far from the couch."

"Um, yeah, well…"

"I'm already having a crappy day, so please don't give me any excuses. I really want to work with you and your girls, but you are going to have to be a lot more cooperative than this. Since you are still in yesterday's clothes, can I assume that Kasey did all the cleaning last night?"

"Um…"

"Just give it to me straight up, Deborah."

Sigh. "I fell asleep on the couch last night after Kasey and I had an argument. I woke up this morning and all of this was done, so, yeah, I'm sure Kasey did it all."

"Ok, just please be honest with me. I can't do my job if you are always trying to skirt around the problems. Ok?"

"Yeah, ok. I just don't like social workers and people butting into my business."

"Well, I'm sorry, but you are stuck with me. And you are going to be stuck with me for a while because I'm bound and determined to make this a better home for the girls. So, you're just going to have to suck it up and deal with me."

"Fine. Whatever. I guess you aren't going to be like the other ones and just forget about us, are you?"

"Nope. I'm here for the long haul. So, we might as well get started." I'm the queen of sarcasm and attitude, so she might as well give up on that one. "Do you know Janice?"

"I don't think so."

"Janice works for Western Health, and I know you're familiar with them. She's going to give you a drug test and then we'll go from there."

Janice took Deborah back to the bathroom to do the test. I heard a single knock on the door and Leland walked right in.

"I've got a search warrant for the house. I specified that we were looking for drugs, so if we find anything else incriminating we're just out of luck. But drugs are the problem here, right?"

"Yep, I'm pretty sure she's going to show up positive for marijuana and Xanax. Maybe only one of the two, but she's definitely on something."

"Ok, I'll introduce myself and get started."

"Thanks, gorgeous – you're the best".

Leland is my favorite local cop and our county's Sheriff. He's engaged to my best friend, Cami, and he always treats me well. Not to mention he's easy on the eyes - sandy-blonde hair, blue/gray eyes, and 6-pack abs that were built from lots of time in the gym – something I do very little of! But on top of all that, he's a cop with a heart. When we're dealing with clients, he doesn't just come in guns-a-blazing. He always gets my opinion on the family and the situation before he takes over. Just common courtesy – that's why I always call him directly. Forget the rule book – Leland just uses his own best judgment, which works for me; plus, he's the boss, so nobody argues with him.

Janice came back in the room with Deborah, who had tears streaming from her face. Guess that drug test didn't come back in her favor.

"Well?"

"Positive for marijuana and benzodiazepine – commonly known as Xanax. She doesn't currently take any medications, so I'm guessing these were given to her by someone else."

Xanax is one of the fasting growing drug problems in our area. Because it's prescribed by physicians, people are getting the prescription and then selling them for a pretty steep price. When I first heard about Xanax a couple of years ago, I had no idea what it was or why people were abusing it, so I had to hit the internet to get some info.

The biggest problem we have with Xanax in the Mountain State is that people become addicted to them, and then they abuse the drug, which causes them to have no fear – of law enforcement, social services, or themselves. Basically, a person overdoses on Xanax and then just doesn't care what happens to them; they tend to steal, or vandalize businesses or houses, not caring about the consequences.

Coming down off that high often makes them sick to their stomach, have panic attacks, insomnia, and sometimes it even causes seizures. It's ugly – not only because it's easy to get, but also because it's legal if prescribed and used properly. That makes my job a little more difficult when it comes to drugs. At least with marijuana I can say "that's illegal". Period. No discussion. But with Xanax I actually have to make sure there's no written prescription, and/or it's being used as prescribed. However, in Deborah's case, this is what we commonly refer to as "you're screwed".

"Deborah, this is turning into a really crappy day for you. This cute little thing with a badge is my friend Leland. He is the County Sheriff and has a search warrant for your house to look for drugs.

Do you want to make his life easier and tell him where you have them hid, or let him search through every crevice in the house looking through all your Victoria Secrets, electronic items, and anything else that seems interesting?"

Deborah looked ultimately defeated. She sighed loudly and said, "3rd dresser drawer down, box is inside the blue t-shirt".

We all stood silently in the middle of the living room while Leland went on the hunt for the drugs. It only took about one minute before he returned with a small wooden box, painted purple, with the words "I love you mom" in bright pink stickers across the top. When he opened the box, there were two baggies inside: one with about two cigarettes worth of pot with paper to wrap it in, and ten pills – that turned out to be Xanax.

"Ok, first, I really want to bitch-slap you for hiding your drugs in a box that one of your girls made for you. But I'm going to try and move past that so we can get to the bigger problem – which happens to be the drugs themselves. So, do you want to continue to be cooperative and tell Leland here where you got the drugs?"

Deborah looked straight to the floor, tears started flowing, and she was visibly shaking.

"I c-c-can't."

"You can't or you won't?"

Leland piped in. "Deborah, you look a little scared to answer questions, so I'm going to go ahead and read you your rights and then you can choose to talk or not talk. Ok?"

Deborah just shook her head yes, and Leland started his best Law-and-Order version of "You have the right to remain silent..."

Deborah still looked stunned when Leland put the cuffs on her. I decided to give the question-and-answer bit one more try.

"Deborah, let me explain how this is going to work. Leland is placing you under arrest because you have illegal drugs in your house. I would really like to get you into rehab, rather than have you wasting your days sitting in jail – which doesn't help your girls at all. The problem is that you definitely aren't being honest with us and I'm pretty sure I know why. So, I'm going to make you a deal."

I had her attention. She looked scared but interested at the same time, so I continued. "You don't have to answer my questions out loud – that way they aren't 'on the record' for Leland to use against you. All you have to do is shake your head yes or no so that we can do everything we can to help you and your girls and keep everybody safe. Is that ok?"

She shook her head yes.

"Ok. Are these your drugs?" Head shake yes.

"Did you buy these drugs?" Head shake no.

"Did somebody give these drugs to you?" Head shake yes.

"Was that somebody Mark?" She hesitated, apparently weighing her options. Then she shook her head yes.

"Does he have a prescription for the Xanax?" She shrugged her shoulders – she had no idea. But she appeared to be visually shaken.

"Deborah? Are you scared of Mark?" Her head shot up quickly, she looked me straight in the eye, and then dropped her head just as quickly. Okey-dokey. I think that solves that problem. I've never met the jerk, but I already don't like him – for two reasons. 1. He apparently scares Deborah, and 2. Kasey doesn't like him. Good enough for me!

Leland's turn. "Deborah, I'm going to do you a favor. Not because I think you deserve a favor, because if it was up to me I would have let Sadey bitch-slap you for the drugs in the cute box. However, Sadey is also my friend, and she appears to want to help you instead of just locking you up and throwing away the key. So, because I have a little bit of a heart, and because Sadey scares the living crap out of me when she's mad, I'm going to recommend to the judge that you be released into Janice's care at Western Health's Rehabilitation Inpatient Unit. That means that you have to live in their homes, and go through their drug program, doing absolutely everything you are told to do – even if it means standing on your head and singing the Barney song. Understand?"

Deborah looked slightly relieved and shook her head yes. She still looked very shell-shocked to me, but she needed to be scared or she wouldn't succeed.

"That means," I butted in, "that if you screw up, or go against anything you're told to do, Leland has the right to throw your butt back in jail and leave you there. Got it?"

She shook her head yes, and then finally spoke, but in a soft whisper. "What happens to my girls?" It's the first time she's seemed to care about them, but it was a start, I guess.

"I'm going to talk to your sister, Karleen, and see if they can stay with her while you're in treatment. Is that ok?" Didn't really matter if it was ok or not, that's what I was doing anyway. But it made her feel better to think she had some kind of say-so in it.

She shook her head yes, so I just continued. "Janice and I will take care of closing up the house and making sure Karleen gets everything she needs for the girls. We will take Lacey with us now and have your sister pick her up at my office. Leland is taking you to jail. I don't know how long it will take before you can appear before the judge and get a bond set, but that won't let you out – it will simply send you directly to the rehab center so you can get started on treatment. Mark can have no contact with you, and I will make sure the girls are safe. "

To Leland I said, "Let her out of the cuffs for a minute so she can say good-bye to Lacey."

He looked at me and rolled his eyes, but then he uncuffed her. As Deborah ran over to hug Lacey and try her best to explain all the things that I'll have to explain in better detail later, Leland looked at me and said, "Some days I just don't understand you. You can go from bitch-to-motherly-instinct in 2.4 seconds. I just hope you know what you're doing."

"I hope so too. Now cuff her in the front, treat her good, but still do what you can to scare the crap out of her so she never wants to be in jail again. K?"

"Well, since you asked nicely…"

Our purpose on earth is not to get lost in the dark, but to be a light to others so that they may find their way through.

Baring My Soul

~~~~~~~~~~~~~~

Trying to explain what was going on to Lacey was just
impossible. Deborah knew that Sadey would take care of it, and she
hoped that Karleen wouldn't be too angry. She'd keep the girls and
take good care of them, but she'd never forgive her. Deborah just
felt kind of numb; this was all just a bad dream. The handcuffs were
tight, but they were cuffed in the front, so she thought that was
tolerable. The ride in the back seat of the police car with the super-
hot cop didn't even seem to bring her out of her stupor.

She was photographed, fingerprinted, sprayed down with an
extremely cold chemical that was supposed to kill lice and other
creepy stuff, and then thoroughly searched up and down, inside and
out, to make sure she didn't bring drugs into the jail in some strange
part of her body. She didn't utter a word, barely blinked, and never
shed a tear. They took her old, grungy clothes and traded them in for
an orange shirt and orange pants that were a tad too big. Still - no
emotion. She was given a plastic mattress and a pillowcase full of

stuff she needed, including a pillow half the size of her head. She was led down a long hallway by a Corrections Officer who finally took the mattress when he realized she could barely lift it off the ground.

Every few feet they would stop and a door would slide open and then close behind them with a clang. The officer led her through one last door – it was marked B3. She carried her stuff through the door as the Officer said, "Room 7". She barely heard his voice. She looked around the big room – a pod, the officer called it. Twelve women, all in the same orange clothes, stopped to stare at 'the new girl'. Concrete floors; concrete walls; two metal tables with four metal seats each bolted to the floor; a TV on a stand that required a ladder to reach; four cells on bottom with even numbers and four cells on top with odd numbers. Room 7 – that's what the Officer said – top of the steps and all the way on the end. The Officer said, "Welcome to your new home, Sams", and then he turned to leave. The metal door slammed shut with a bang and she heard a lock click behind her. She couldn't stop the flood of tears that now flowed freely down her face.

~~~~~~~~~~~~~~~~~~

Talking to Kasey at school was an easy task since I had an "in" with the teacher – my best friend. I found out that spelling was right after lunch, and since Kasey was an expert speller, it would be an ok time for her to miss. The principal let us use the small conference room for privacy. Kasey walked in and sat down like this was routine for her. "Ok", she said. "Let's get this over with."

~~~~~~~~~~~~~~~~~~~~~~~~~~~~

Kasey knew as soon as they pulled her out of class where she was going. Been there, done that. She knew the routine: name, age, birthday, family members, favorite things, why is your mom a bad mom, yada-yada-yada. She sat down with a huff. "Ok. Let's get this over with."

~~~~~~~~~~~~~~~~~~~~~~~~~~~~

I knew at that moment that this wasn't going to be a typical interview. I laid my folder and note pad off to the side, got out of my chair, walked around the table, and sat down in the chair beside Kasey. I turned my chair and Kasey's chair so they faced each other, and Kasey just stared at me in confusion.

"Kasey. I know that you know me as Sadey the social worker, but can I tell you about Sadey the little girl?" Kasey just kind of shrugged her shoulders.

"Remember when you told me how much you hated broken promises?"

"Yeah."

"Well, my dad made many promises to me when I was your age, and he broke them all. He kept promising we'd go on vacation, but then we never did, because he spent that money on drugs. My dad smoked pot like your mom, but he also used the drug cocaine. Do you know what that is?"

Kasey shook her head yes and I realized just how fast this little girl has had to grow up.

I continued, "My dad is in jail right now because he was selling those drugs."

"Do you ever go visit him?"

I answered reluctantly. "No, I don't".

"Why not?"

"I guess I'm still mad at him."

"You shouldn't stay mad at him, because it's not his fault."

"I disagree. He chose to do the drugs and then to sell them, and now he has to pay the consequences."

"Yeah, but he was addicted to them like my mom, right?"

"Yes, I guess he was."

"My teacher told us to never even try drugs because once you do then you're going to be addicted and then you start doing stupid stuff."

"Your teacher is very smart."

Kasey just beamed with pride after that because she could "teach" someone else what she learned. I could not believe how personal this conversation had become, but Kasey was opening up to me, so I just continued.

"When my dad was high, he used to just lie around in his chair and laugh. He wouldn't work or help my mom with us kids – he just laid around. But then when that 'high' feeling would go away, he would get mean and yell at my mom and hit my brother. He had to go to jail for that, too."

I could not believe I was baring my soul to a 10-year-old.

"My mom does stupid stuff too."

"Like what?"

Kasey hesitated, then she responded, "When she's smoking, she laughs a lot like your dad did. But she never laughed at stuff that was really funny – she laughed at things like somebody sneezing, or when Lacey had an accident, she would laugh but then she wouldn't get up to clean her up – I had to do that. And she wanted to eat junk food all the time – cookies and candy bars, stuff like that. Then Mark started bringing her pills – he said it would calm her nerves. All it really does is make her do more stupid stuff."

"Kasey – you are a very brave girl and a wonderful big sister. I want you to know that I'm not like the other social workers you have seen before."

"What makes you so different?" she asked with skepticism. "Nobody has really cared in the past."

"I'm different because I don't break promises."

Kasey started to roll her eyes, but then stopped herself and stared at me in disbelief.

"I just don't trust anybody," she said softly.

"You can trust me. Now, I'm going to need your help if we are going to help your mom. Are you up for it?"

"Yep."

"Ok, now some of this might seem scary at first, but I need you to be brave so we can help Lacey be brave."

"I can try."

"Ok, now for a little while I'm going to need you and Lacey to stay with your Aunt Karleen."

Kasey started to tear up, but then sat straight up in her chair, probably to show me that she could be brave.

"Sadey, will you promise me that you will always tell me the truth about my mom and what she's doing? I don't want to be treated like a baby. Please."

I just looked at this little girl, only 10 years old, but with an adult-like persona. I just wanted to cry for her. I opened my folder, took out a sheet of paper, and began to write.

I, Sadey Collins, promise to be honest with Kasey Sams about how her mom is doing in her treatments and will keep her updated as much as I can.

I signed my name to the paper and handed it to Kasey. She read the paper, clutched it tightly in her fingers, sat up straight again in her chair, and with her most adult-like voice said, "Lay it on me!"

I felt my heart just break, but I had promised to be truthful, and I was going to live up to my promises no matter what. So, I started from the beginning.

A bird sitting on a tree is never afraid of the branch breaking, because her trust is not on the branch but on its own wings. Always believe in yourself.

My phone call to Karleen Sams took only a minute. She wasn't surprised to hear about Deborah and said she'd be glad to keep the kids.

I arranged for the kids to receive a medical card and Karleen agreed to whatever medical care and counseling the girls would need. She told me, "This has been a long time coming and I really hope that you can give Deborah the help she needs. Kasey and Lacey are great kids, and they deserve a great mom. Deborah could be that if she got off the drugs and away from Mark. Thanks for doing this and I promise to take good care of the kids." That made me feel a lot better – at least the kids would be in good hands.

Cameron Lawson, Cami, is a 4th grade teacher at Fairlawn Elementary. Cami and I had grown up together and we are still great friends to this day. We were born a day apart, raised on the same cul-de-sac, right next door to each other, went to High School together, and then headed off to WVU where we spent 6 years as roommates working on our Bachelor and Masters degrees – it's a miracle we survived that! Cami lost her parents to a car wreck our freshman year in college, and my mom has attempted to fill that void for her, which was easy since she was always just considered the fourth kid in our family.

Cami went into Education and I went into Social Work, and occasionally our paths cross professionally as well. Cami is engaged to a great guy – my favorite cop, Leland – and I was still looking for one I could put up with. Cami, of course, had made it her life's mission to help me find just the right guy, always bringing along a new 'friend' every time we went out. Cami grew up to be beautiful with blonde hair, blue eyes, and big boobs. I grew up addicted to Blizzards and Swiss Cake Rolls.

But, luckily for me, Cami was Kasey's 4th grade teacher. We agreed to meet after school at Phil's Diner, an awesome little Mom & Pop place with the best Sausage Gravy & Biscuits this side of the Mississippi. Oh yeah, and don't forget the cookies and cream pie – homemade, of course.

While I finished up my last bite of pie I said, "Ok, enough small talk, give me the scoop on Kasey – all the details please – I think I really need to help this kid."

"Why? Because she's a little like you?"

"What's that supposed to mean?" I snapped back.

"Don't get all huffy on me Sade. I just think she's struggling with her mom's addiction the way you are with your dad's."

"Thanks Cam. You sure know how to aim straight for the heart, dontcha?"

"Oh, come on Sadey. We've been friends since before we could walk. We know each other better than we know ourselves."

I knew she was right, even if I didn't want to admit it. Cami always knew what I was thinking and could call me out on a lie faster than my own mom could. I remember that History test in 9th grade that I failed. I tried to pretend I got a "B", but somehow Cami saw right through me. And she was doing it again. Ugh!

"Ok, Sadey, spill it."

"I just see this sad little girl who is starting to resent her mom because of the drugs. She just wants a normal family."

"Nobody's family is normal."

"I know, but she kept telling me about all the broken promises from her mom, and I remember all those years of just wishing that one thing my dad said would come true."

I was worried that I may have just broken a confidentiality law, but Cami was bound by those same laws, so I just moved on.

"Alright, so aside from the fact that Kasey reminds you of me – what else can you tell me?"

The more we talked, the more I kept promising myself that I would do everything possible to help this child. A little more small-talk to catch up and then Cami started throwing out names of people she thought I should go out with.

"Enough about my love life, or lack thereof, and next time you're buying." I kidded.

"Well since you don't have a date for Saturday night, you might as well come over to my house for a BBQ. And don't even think of arguing. Be there around 6:00 and after dinner we'll get a bonfire going, roast some marshmallows for S'mores and make some strawberry daiquiris."

"Ok fine – I'll bring the S'mores stuff

I'm always told that the right man will come along, but I'm starting to think that my Prince Charming isn't coming on a white horse...he's obviously riding a turtle lost somewhere and not asking for directions.

Phone Calls & Paperwork

Thursday, September 20th

Phone calls and paperwork – the worst part of the job! Well, aside from having to dress up in order to be in the office, which seems utterly ridiculous to me – dress pants, nice shirts, dress shoes, make-up, and hair curled – just to sit at my desk and type all day.

Unfortunately, documentation is critical in every case, especially if the case ends up in court. If I want a judge to be on my side I can't just go in the courtroom and express my opinion, I have to have facts to back me up. That means writing down everything that happens, every step of the way. So, I set out to spend the morning doing just that – catching up on documentation.

Back from lunch = afternoon of phone calls. Western Health was first on the list. I set up counseling for Lacey and Kasey, drug counseling for Deborah in jail, and rehab and parenting classes when she was released. James was set back up with his drug counselor, who was told this was his last chance before going to jail and losing custody of Kara. That's not really my plan with him, but he needs to stay a little scared in order to stay drug-free.

Next was Sampson's grandma – he's doing fine but wants visitation. I added that to my lengthy to-do list, which continues to grow at a rapid rate. Then the call to the jail to set up an interview with Deborah for tomorrow afternoon. I always dread jail interviews: the search of myself and my purse, the amount of time it takes to get through each section of the jail to reach the interview rooms, and most of all, I hate the sound of those metal doors closing. They send chills up my spine and I wondered if those doors were partly to blame for the fact that I didn't visit my father in jail. Probably not – just another excuse.

Finally, I called the Prosecuting Attorney to set up a meeting for tomorrow morning to discuss Deborah's case.

"Galvin, its Sadey Collins."

Galvin Nichols is the Prosecuting Attorney in our county. He's good at his job and has good rapport with the judges and defense attorneys. He hates to hear from me because it usually means that kids are being removed from a home.

"Oh geez. Happy Birthday to me. I just always love hearing your voice."

"Oh, come on Galvin, I'm the Queen of Sarcasm; you can't take over my job. But Happy Birthday anyway. What are you – like 40?"

"Ok, now you're totally not getting what you want – 32 to be exact. So now that you've busted my self-esteem, what can I do for you?"

I went over the Sams case with him and what I wanted to accomplish with Deborah and the kids. He agreed to meet with me after staff meeting in the morning and gave me the usual spiel. I had to work out all the details before I met with Galvin – the outcomes were always more favorable if I was prepared, and Prosecutors hate loose ends!

I still had one more issue to deal with today – Mark Kinders. Leland came through for me with the Magistrate, and thankfully, he has my back.

I decided the easiest way to find Mark was to hit the Food Shop where he worked, apparently as a manager. A stake out in the parking lot for a few minutes proved to be successful. At precisely 4:30, Mark Kinders walked out the door and headed to his car – where I met him.

"Mark Kinders?"

"Yeah? Who are you?"

"My name is Sadey Collins. I work for Child Protective Services. Can I talk to you for a minute?"

"What for?"

"We need to discuss Deborah and Lacey."

"What about them?"

"Is there someplace we can go talk?"

"Whatever. There's a picnic table over there."

I headed to the side of the store with Mark and sat down at the picnic table. This guy was giving me the creeps for some reason, but I had a job to do.

"Deborah was arrested yesterday for drug possession."

"What's that got to do with me?"

His attitude was starting to get on my nerves. "I would think that your first question should be, 'what's happening to Lacey', but I can see that she's not on the top of your priority list."

"Look, you stupid bi…"

"My name is Sadey. And I don't recommend that you start spewing your threats to me. I'm here to tell you what's going to happen, not the other way around."

The veins on his neck were starting to stand out and I was now sure why Deborah was afraid of him. He was only about 2" taller than me, and I was sure he could easily kick my butt, but one thing I was never good at was backing down from a fight. Not to mention, I already didn't like this guy just because of the way Kasey felt about him, so he was not on my 'be nice to' list.

"Ok, fine. You talk. I'll pretend to listen."

"That's better. You get so much further when you're nice to me," I said with my cutest smile.

He didn't enjoy my sarcasm, but as the Queen I'm required to deliver as much sarcasm as I can in every possible situation.

"As I said before, Deborah got arrested for drug possession. Just in case you care, Lacey is staying with a relative. Don't worry - Deborah did a good job of protecting you. She refused to tell me where she got the drugs; but lucky for her, I'm pretty smart. So, you might as well just tell me that you gave them to her."

"I'm not telling you anything, you stupid bitch."

"See, there you go again, not being nice. That's ok, you don't have to tell me. My friend, Sheriff Davis, will be busy building a case against you. It will save me the trouble. I am here because I don't want you around Deborah or Lacey."

"You can't tell me what to do."

"Actually, I can – and I will. Remember my friend, Sheriff Davis? He has a protective order for you – courtesy of our local Magistrate. It states that you can't go near Deborah or Lacey. "

I held up my arm and Leland appeared out of nowhere – that's what friends are for.

"Mark – meet Sheriff Leland Davis."

"Hi Mark. As Sadey said, I have a protective order for you. You are officially being served. You cannot come within 500 yards of Deborah or Lacey. You are also under arrest for the distribution of prescription medication."

Mark had a stunned look on his face as Leland again gave his best Law & Order rendition of "You have the right to remain silent…" Now I know why he's a cop.

Mark went from stunned to instantaneously angry – and his anger was directed at me. My heart started beating a little faster, and I immediately knew that this guy was not going to let this go. He started to threaten me, and then Leland instantly shut him up with a warning that he would press more charges against him for threatening a state employee, which moves him straight from a misdemeanor to a felony. Mark shut up immediately, but his angry stares were boring a hole through me. I didn't take it lightly, but I was glad Leland was taking him to jail tonight!

The world is not full of assholes, but they are strategically placed so that you'll come across one every day. Every. Freaking Day.

Sadey Collins; that's a name I'll remember. I don't know who she thinks she is showing up at work and then having me arrested. The last thing I need is for my customer base to see this and think that it's not safe to shop here; this is my easiest place of distribution. She obviously doesn't know who she's dealing with; I own this side of town and I own Deborah. She'll get hers soon enough!

~~~~~~~~~~~~~~~~~~~~~~~~~~~~

Leland put him in the back of the cruiser, turned to me and said, "Watch your butt. I'll keep him locked up tonight, but he can make bail in the morning."

Then he hauled him away, I took a deep breath, crawled into my car and broke down into tears. I don't scare easily, but the look on Mark's face made my skin crawl. *Good grief. This is not the first bad guy you've dealt with or the first guy to threaten you. Get it together, go home, take Bones for a walk, and eat a Blizzard. And quit talking to yourself!*

Driving home I kept looking in my rearview mirror. It was absolutely stupid since I knew that Mark would be in jail overnight, but my paranoia had set in full force. I even drove around my block twice before I pulled into my driveway. Ridiculous, I know; blaming it on the PMS.

This isn't the first protective order I've dealt with in a case; they are pretty typical. So, I couldn't figure out why Mark was getting to me so much. I was acting completely stupid and couldn't wrap my head around any of it. I looked all around my yard and around my car before I got out. Then I practically ran inside my house, tripping over the loose board on my front porch, which propelled me through the air, thrusting me head-first into my front door, causing Bones to begin barking like I was an attacker. After my head made contact with the door, I promptly went down on my right knee causing me to say words that would make my mother blush and then smack me across the mouth. Good thing she wasn't here!

Although now I had a headache, my knee hurt, and I needed my mommy to take care of me. Except that I'm a grown woman who is supposed to take care of herself. After I picked myself up off the porch, that I keep meaning to get fixed, I yelled at Bones and tried to unlock the door without letting my hand shake too much.

I had promised myself a walk with Bones and a Dairy Queen Blizzard. However, after I lost the fight with the porch, I decided that some Ibuprofen and ice on my knee would be a better option. I never turn down ice cream, but the porch definitely kicked my butt. And here I was afraid of Mark; that was beginning to look pretty stupid on my part.

Just as I got comfortable on the couch in my sweatpants (which I'm not sure passed the smell test, but I was in too much pain to care), with an ice pack on my knee, Bones started barking incessantly. I started to yell at him to shut up, just as my doorbell rang; nobody rings the doorbell, they just walk right in and announce themselves – it's just how we do things in our family.

After I huffed and rolled my eyes, I began to slowly make my way off the couch. I started to roll to the side, and then realized I couldn't put my knee down to stop my roll. So, much to my dismay, I continued to roll, right off the couch and right into the legs of my best friend Cami. She was laughing hysterically. I was in no mood for her cheery personality, or for what I knew was going to be a snide comment about my lack of grace.

"Dang it, Cami. Stop laughing at me and help me off this floor; and why the hell did you ring the doorbell?"

"Because my hands were full, and I was hoping for some help. What the heck happened to you?"

"I tripped on that loose board on my porch, went head-first into my front door and landed on my knee. What are you doing here?"

"Leland said you had a stressful day and probably needed one of these."

I saw the most beautiful sight a woman could lay her eyes on – a large Chocolate Extreme Dairy Queen Blizzard. "Is that for me?"

"Yep. Leland said you were having a bad day, but it appears that it got a lot worse."

"Did he tell you why I was having a bad day? And hand that thing over. I'll just eat it down here on the floor."

"Yeah – he told me. Now let me help you off that floor because you'll either spill this all over you, or Bones will take it out of your hands. Either way, it will make your day even worse."

"You're right."

"I know. I usually am", she said with a chuckle.

"Stop laughing at me and get me off this floor!"

"No problem. Now, are you going to give me your version of what happened today?"

"Do I need to? I'm sure Leland told you everything. Besides, my version makes me look like a huge chicken, a big klutz, and a complete idiot."

"Ok. But you have to promise me that you'll be careful."

"Yeah – yeah – ok. Now hand over that Blizzard before I kick your butt."

"That'll be the day. Now – promise me you'll be careful."

"I will. I promise. Have you seen Bones?"

"Yeah – he's in the kitchen eating the Blizzard I brought for him."

"Have I ever told you what a great friend you are?"

"Yep – I'm outta here. See you Saturday. 6:00."

"I'll be there, and I'll bring the stuff for S'mores. Just like I promised."

God bless Leland!

Friends are the angels who lift you to your feet when your wings aren't able to fly.

Plan of attack

Friday, September 21st

Staff meetings suck! That's the only thing going through my mind as I gather my recent investigations and join my fellow suckers around the big conference table. Investigations are discussed, cases are transferred, and an hour-long bitch-fest ensues about having too many cases, uncooperative clients, pain-in-the-ass lawyers, and everything in between. They happen every Friday, promptly at 8:00 a.m., and attendance is mandatory – death is the only excuse for missing a meeting, and it only counts if it's your own death! The only good thing that comes from a staff meeting is the 2 dozen Dunkin' Donuts provided by my boss.

Three more investigations were added to my caseload, leaving a feeling of suffocation deep in my chest. Too many investigations, not enough hours in a day! Custody battles are the worst, and I refuse to get involved. Unless I can see obvious signs of abuse or neglect, my statement to parents is always the same: *'Custody cases are fought in court by lawyers – not by Child Protective Service workers. Your children are fine – their parents are the problem.*

And if either one of you files another report against the other then I will have you arrested and charged with filing a false report!'

Although I can't technically do that last part, I believe that putting the fear of God in these childish, selfish people is the only way to cut down on the number of these reports. I don't have time for their crap. Unfortunately, my tough attitude means that every custody case seems to land across my desk. On the plus side, these are usually investigations that can be wrapped up in a couple of weeks. Of course, there are those occasional cases that are legit and require more work, but for the most part these are just selfish parents trying to use their kids to get back at each other. They just need a 'Gibbs slap'. Too bad I can't use that!

Next on the agenda was a visit with Deborah.

Have I mentioned lately that I hate visiting the jail? Not only does it take me 45 minutes to get there, but I have to be thoroughly searched before I can go through the doors. I know its policy, and there are some strange people out there bringing some weird things into the jail, but I'm one of those people who just want to get in and out without them keeping me.

I made it through the search process with no problems; now comes the long walk through the metal doors – my least favorite part! A Corrections Officer escorts me to the visitation room. We walk down the first hallway, and then we have to stop so that the powers in the ceiling can open the door for us – it then shuts with a loud 'clang'. I HATE THAT NOISE!!! It's what nightmares are made of. It takes two more of those doors before I get to the visitation room. I called ahead to let them know I was coming, so they had Deborah already waiting for me. She looked terrible. As I sat down across the table from her, she looked up and the tears just flowed down her face. Her eyes were red and swollen from crying, and I couldn't tell if she'd lost weight in the last two days or if her new orange wardrobe was just too big, and therefore made her look even smaller than she already was.

"Deborah, are you doing ok?"

"Not really. This is awful. I don't want to stay here any longer."

"Sorry – your hearing isn't until Monday morning, so you're stuck here for the weekend." She broke down and just started sobbing. I tried to be consoling, but I had to also remember that she earned her way into this place by using and possessing illegal drugs. She finally calmed down a little and asked, "How are my girls?"

"They are doing ok. Karleen has them, and we got Lacey set up at daycare at the YMCA, so she'll have some other kids to play with during the day."

"What happens on Monday when I go to court?"

"You are going before the judge, and he will decide whether to leave you here waiting for trial, or if he's going to let you out into rehab."

"I'll do whatever it takes to get out of here."

"I know you're saying that, but I'm here because we need to talk about everything you are going to have to do before I can let the girls come home to you."

"Ok."

"If the judge lets you out on Monday morning, you won't get to go home. You will leave with Janice and go to Western Health into their inpatient rehab program. You will stay there at least 6 weeks – maybe longer depending on your progress – but 6 weeks is the least amount of time. You're looking at the first week of November, at the earliest. Ok?"

"What do I have to do in rehab?"

"That's up to Janice. You will discuss that with her on Monday. But basically, it entails being detoxed from the drugs – getting them permanently out of your system, and then doing some classes and counseling to help you so that you don't start doing the drugs again."

"Ok, I can do that. I'm already detoxing, but I promise I'll do whatever it takes."

"Deborah, we need to talk about those promises. I know it's easy to use that word, and you believe you can follow through with what you're saying, but Kasey is having problems with you and the word promise."

"What do you mean?"

"When she was talking to me, she kept using the words 'broken promises'. She says that you constantly promise to do something with her, but that you never keep your promises. That's what she's dealing with."

"Oh, man. Are you serious? I'm so sorry. She probably hates me, doesn't she?"

"No, she doesn't hate you. But she worries about you a lot. She's a kid, Deborah. She should be worrying about kid things, not whether or not her sister's had a bath in the last couple of days. You've gotta get it together Deborah. Your kids need a mom."

"I know, I know. I just, the drugs, you know – they help."

"Help with what Deborah? You can't take care of your kids when you are doing drugs. What's more important to you – the kids or the drugs?"

Deborah hesitated. "Are you serious, Deborah? You can't even give me an answer. That's pathetic. I'm telling you – this is your only chance. If you screw this up, you are going to jail, and staying there for quite a while. Your girls need you – it's time you get your act together! It's either rehab or jail – you choose."

This time there was no hesitation. "Rehab."

"Ok, rehab it is. But the results are up to you. I will be in court with you on Monday morning. I had a meeting this morning with the Prosecutor, and he's agreed to recommend to the judge that you be released into Janice's care at Western Health. But all it takes is one wrong move from you and its back to jail. Do you understand that?"

"Yeah, yeah, I got it. I promise!" I gave her a look of disbelief. "No. For real. I mean it. I'm going to get clean. I'm going to get my girls back."

"Ok. I believe you. But there's one more thing we need to talk about. Mark."

"Oh, man. Does he know I'm in here? He's going to be angry."

"Yeah, he's angry all right. But it's not at you – he's mad at me. There's a protective order out against him and he's not allowed near you or the girls. He also got arrested yesterday for selling drugs, but he has a court hearing right now, so I don't know if he'll be out on bond or not."

"How did he get a hearing before I did? That's not fair."

"His charge was a misdemeanor and he's going before a magistrate, which is quicker. You were in possession of more than the minimum of prescription pills that didn't belong to you; that's a felony and you're going before a Circuit Judge, which takes longer. Also, he didn't have any drugs on him when he was arrested, so right now his charge is just for known distribution and it's a misdemeanor so bail is likely."

"Oh, man. Can he get to me? He's going to be mad."

"No, he can't get to you. Like I said, it's me he's mad at. Not you."

"Keep my girls safe. Please."

"You know that I will. Now, the ball is in your court. You have a decision to make. It's the drugs or the girls. You choose. I was told that you were appointed an attorney – Timothy Weston. He'll probably be here later today or really early Monday morning to meet with you before the hearing. He can be a real horse's patoot, but the Prosecutor has already talked to him about rehab and what we're trying to do. He'll take care of you. His job is to get the best deal he can for you. But you have to be honest with him at all times. He can't do his job if you don't do yours. Ok?"

"Yeah, I got it. No problem. Just get me outta here. This place is horrible."

"Well, maybe spending the weekend in here will help you realize that you don't want to come back."

"Definitely. I hate it here and I don't want to come back. I'll do whatever it takes. And that's a promise I intend to keep."

I signaled for the Officer that we were finished. He told me he would take Deborah back to her cell and then be back to lead me out. I stood at the window and watched as the prisoners were lead down the hall. A long line of men stood down the hallway, all wearing their given orange outfits, waiting for the officer to allow them to go. It was all so organized; they walked so far and stopped. The officer would move along the line, wait for the metal door to be opened, the line of prisoners would move forward and stop. The door would clang shut behind them and the process would continue. A group of men started walking past the room I was waiting in, and every head turned to look at me. Not that I am something to look at, but I wasn't in an orange outfit; therefore, I was absolutely gorgeous to them. I was seeing them walk by, but I wasn't actually watching them carefully. Then they stopped. Right in front of the window, looking back at me through the glass, stood the last person on earth that I ever wanted to see.

One bad chapter doesn't define the rest of your story.

What now?

"Dad?!"

The word was out of my mouth before I could stop it. I was standing face to face with my father, separated only by a Plexiglass window. Bryson Collins - I haven't seen him in over 2 years. When mom called me on that July day, I was sitting on the beach with Cami, getting one of the best sunburns ever, talking over our plans for the rest of the week at Emerald Isle. One of only three vacations I've ever taken – the first being Kings Island with Grandma Daisy, and the second being a camping trip with Trey the summer before he left for college. I hung up the phone and started swearing like a sailor. I couldn't believe it happened again – arrested yet again for drugs. Only this time was worse, because he sold cocaine to an undercover cop. It was bad enough that he'd already been to jail twice for doing drugs, but now he was headed there for several years for a distribution charge. Just when I thought he had turned things around.

Now, two years later, here I was standing face-to-face with the man who spent years and years making promises to me, and the rest of the family, only to break them over and over again. What now?

The door opens, and the Officer senses something is wrong. "Ma'am. Are you ok?"

"What? Oh, yeah. Um, that man right there is my father. I haven't seen him in over two years, and I guess it was sort of a shock for me."

"Would you like for me to see if you can have a visit with him?"

What do I say now? Do I want to visit with him? What would I even say? Can I talk to him and be civil? Ugh!

"Um, well…" I'm here already; maybe I should just suck it up and do it.

"It's up to you ma'am. I can talk with his CO if you want."

"Yeah. Ok. I'm already here; might as well." I hope I'm making the right decision.

The line of orange suits kept filing past the window until, eventually, I was simply staring at blank, white concrete walls again. This place is so depressing; no wonder Deborah was so miserable. I haven't even slept here and I'm ready to bolt out the door.

Sometimes I feel so stupid. Why am I even questioning whether or not I want to see my dad? He is my dad, after all. Shouldn't I want to see him? Shouldn't I be excited? After all, it's been two years, right? So, why exactly am I questioning this?

Time to suck it up, act like an adult, and face my dad. Five minutes later, I was standing face-to-face again with my father, minus the window barrier.

"Hi dad."

"Sadey-bug." He immediately wrapped his arms around me and squeezed like he hadn't seen me in years. Well, technically it had been years – two to be exact. He peeled himself away from me and said, "When I saw you through that window, I thought I was dreaming. I didn't even know what to say. What are you doing here? I know you didn't actually come here to see me, right?"

"I was here to see a client."

"I'm glad you asked to see me. I've missed you guys so much."

"Dad. I really don't know what to say. I didn't exactly ask to see you. The guard suggested it, and I agreed. But this is not exactly how I want to hang out with my dad, you know."

"Baby, I'm so sorry. I know I've let you down, and I'm very, very sorry. I can't say that enough, but I'm sure you're tired of hearing me say it."

"Well, yeah, a little."

I didn't even know how to answer him. On one hand, he's my dad and I love him. On the other hand, I feel like a little kid, like Kasey, being let down by my daddy and only hearing excuses.

"Dad, I love you very much. But I would be lying if I didn't say this is very awkward. I definitely didn't show up here planning to see you. And now I'm kind of at a loss for words. I don't want to sound rude, but I just don't know what to say."

"Can we just sit down for a minute?"

"Yeah, I guess."

"Sade. I'm not going to make excuses for why I'm sitting here. I deserve everything that's been thrown at me. I've made some extremely bad choices, and I'm suffering the consequences for those choices. I know I've been here before, and I know I'm too old for this. I've had a lot of time to think about the stupid things I've done with my life. But, you kids, you're the best thing I've ever done. I know that I've let you down, all of you. There's probably nothing in the world that I can say that will change any of those feelings. Basically, all I can do now is try and move forward."

"I'm not going to deny that I'm still kinda mad at you for this. I really, honestly don't know what to say. I have this case right now where a little girl is dealing with this same crap from her mom, and it's reminded me of you so much. Dad, I just want this to stop; I want you to be home with mom, and have family cook-outs, and normal holidays where we sit around and torture each other, not think about the fact that you're not there because you're sitting in here. We've had too many Thanksgivings and Christmases without you; I'm not going to deny that it really, really sucks!"

"Oh, man. Sadey. I love you so much, and I'm so sorry that I've hurt you like this."

"Not just me, dad. Everybody. Mom, Noelle, Trey – even Blake and Abi. Do you know how hard it is to explain to a 3-year-old that her Grandpa can't be there to watch her open gifts because he's sitting in jail? I know that Noelle and I don't always see things eye-to-eye, but I wouldn't want to be in her position at the holidays when the kids are asking questions."

"I know. I know. I've let everybody down. But what do you want me to say?"

"I don't know what you can say. I just know that I'm angry and I don't know how to deal with it. I can't speak for everybody else, but this is getting old."

I'm starting to rethink my decision to agree to this visit. Arguing with my dad was not on my list of things to do today. Now that I'm face-to-face with him, it's like I'm tongue-tied. I can't even express what I'm really feeling. I can't help but hold back. I don't trust my brain to say nicely what my heart is feeling. That fuse between my brain and my mouth is running a little short today. I love my dad, and I don't want to end this on an angry note, but I'm not feeling all that loveable.

"Dad?"

"Yes, baby?"

"I don't want to have a fight with you, and I don't want this visit to end on an angry note. But I feel like I need to be honest with you."

"Go ahead. I deserve whatever it is you need to say to me."

Here goes nothing. "Broken promises."

"What?"

"Broken promises. That's what I'm dealing with. For the last 27 years, I couldn't believe a thing you said. Over and over you promised us trips and vacations. We never went. Why? Because you spent your money on drugs, or you ended up in jail because of drugs. It's always the drugs. I feel like if you had to choose between us and the drugs, the drugs always won. Honestly, it pisses me off!"

"Go on. I can take it. I deserve everything you're saying."

"I know you deserve it! That's why I'm so ticked off. I just want you to start choosing your family, not the drugs. You're too old for this shit!"

"Sadey Nevada – I've never heard you talk like that."

"Well, what do you want me to say? Its ok, dad? We don't mind that you're dealing drugs and sitting in jail, dad? You're my dad, and I love you, but you've done a great job of screwing things up!"

"You're right. I know you're right. I'm obviously completely clean since I've been sitting in here for two years. But that's not what you want to hear, is it? Drugs do terrible things to you. They've definitely done a good job of ruining my life, and yours, apparently."

"Apparently?! Seriously?!"

Ugh! I should have said "no". This was a stupid decision on my part. I'm not ready to deal with this!

"Dad, I don't want to argue. I've said my peace; you know how I feel. I'm going home now, eat some pizza and ice cream, and woller in my own self-pity, ok?"

"Sadey – don't leave. Please. I haven't seen you in so long, and I don't want to spend this time arguing with you. I love you."

"I know dad. I guess I just wasn't prepared to see you today. I came here to deal with a client, and I ended up dealing with my feelings for you. It wasn't on my plan for the day."

"I'm sorry. I love you and I'm so sorry I've let you down. I don't want you to leave angry, and I really want you to come back. Will you, please? Your mom comes every week, but I never see you kids. If it wasn't for her, and the fact that she loves me unconditionally, I would never make it through this." His eyes watered up; I've never seen my dad cry before, and I'd be lying if I said it wasn't getting to me.

"Look – all I can say is this: I love you, I'm angry with you, and it makes it hard to like you. I'm having trouble dealing with all these pent-up emotions coming to the surface so quickly. I just need time to deal with them, that's all. Can you accept that?"

"Of course – of course. I just want to see you guys. I want to make it all up to you. I know I've screwed up; I want to fix it."

"That's sounds easier said than done, dad. Things can be fixed; feeling and emotions take time."

"I accept that. I just want to see you again. Please?"

"We'll see. Please, don't push this, dad. I just need time to deal, ok? It's definitely easier to deal with this stuff when I'm not actually seeing you. I can be mad but not have to do anything about it because I don't have to see you. Basically, I can ignore the fact that anything's even happened. Does that make sense?"

"Yeah, it does. Ignore it and it'll go away, right?"

"Yeah, something like that."

"I understand. I don't like it, but I understand. Will you please think about coming back and seeing me?"

"I will. Just don't expect it to be an overnight fix, ok?"

"Fair enough."

"Dad, I love you. I just need some time to work through this."

"I completely understand. I just want to see you again. I'd love to see Trey and Noelle, too, but I'm probably asking way too much there. I'll take anything I can get right now."

"I'll think about it. I will. I promise. Just give me some time. I love you, but I really need to go now."

"Sadey."

"Yeah, dad?"

"I love you. I love you very much, and I'm very sorry that I've let you down."

"I know."

I left on that note. This was absolutely not on my list of emotions to deal with today. I knew walking into the jail that there was a possibility I would see him. But I put it in the back of my mind because I just didn't want it to occur. My best line of defense: ignore it and it will go away. I'm a pro. I wanted to get in, see Deborah, and get out. Of course, nothing ever works the way I plan it to. Not in my world.

The drive home was the longest 45 minutes of my life!

Things are great until God slaps you in the forehead, lands you on your butt and says stay down ~ I'm not done teaching you something.

Burgers & S'mores

Saturday, September 22nd

Sleeping until 10:00 a.m. is what Saturdays are made for. Of course, it doesn't hurt when you stay up until midnight watching movies and playing Solitaire on the computer. Luckily, Bones saw things my way and stayed cuddled up beside me until we were both startled awake by the screeching of the phone. I rolled over to check the caller-ID: mom. Guess I better answer and try not to sound groggy.

"Hi, mom."

"Are you up?"

"I am now."

"It's 9:00 already. I figured…"

In between yawns, I interrupted. "I know. I know. I shouldn't sleep my life away. But it's Saturday." And I was planning to sleep until ten. I didn't voice that thought out loud, though.

"Ok, well since you're awake, I thought we could go shopping and grab some lunch."

I resisted the rolling of my eyes since I clearly wasn't awake, but the words "shopping" and "lunch" got my attention.

"Sounds good. Who's having a sale? And where's lunch?"

"Kohl's and Olive Garden."

"I'm totally in. Let me shower and I'll be over. I have to be at Cami's at 6:00 for a cookout, and I'm in charge of S'mores."

"Wal-Mart it is. See you in a bit."

Bones did his best stretching routine, which takes up the majority of my queen size mattress, and then slowly crawled off the bed. He was on all fours on the floor and using his cold, wet nose to nudge my arm. That's my cue to get out of bed and let him out. I only get three nudges to get up. Well, technically, two nudges; on the third nudge he jumps back on the bed, straddles me, and proceeds to use his tongue to cover my entire face, including my ears, with dog slobbers. I can't decide if he just likes the taste of ear wax, or if after licking and polishing his "jewels" he just needs to get that taste out of his mouth. Either way, since I didn't feel like getting drool out of my ears, I decided to roll out by the 2nd nudge.

I actually had great intentions of staying in my sweats until time to go to Cami's, but Olive Garden is a weakness that gets me out of the house every time. I can already taste the breadsticks dipped in Alfredo sauce. Yum! Then the Black-Tie Mousse cake – better than sex. Well, right now anything chocolate seems better than sex since it's been a while since that's occurred. But I'm totally not letting that complicated relationship ruin my day of shopping and eating; it's been over three years since I've seen the biggest dating mistake of my life and there was no sense drudging up that nightmare when there was Olive Garden to think about.

First stop of the day – shower. Next stop – stare at the closet. Jeans are a definite for the day. T-shirt or nice girl shirt? Maybe I'll just do the 'Eeny-meeny-miny-mo' choice. I'm pretty sure it's the easiest way to make a decision, aside from 'rock/paper/scissors'; that's fairly successful as well. So, after this brilliant process, 'mo' landed on a cute tank top that fits just tight enough to make me appear to have a nice chest. Then I throw on a loose ¾ length cardigan over it, so I'm layered. Great for a day that will hit upper 70s and then drop to the lows 50s; of course, by that time I'll be in front of a bonfire with a daiquiri in my hand.

Next problem – hair. Ponytail sounds good; mom wouldn't approve. I opted for a couple of curls with it half pulled back. Make-up is required. Mom is a firm believer in always looking your best every time you step out the door. We don't really share the same opinion on fashion – I figure if you don't have holes in your pants or stains on your shirt, then you are ok to go out in public. But if I'm going to hang with mom all day, it's best to do things her way.

My parents have a nice 1 ½ story house with funky colored siding – not really tan, but definitely not yellow. But the dark green shutters make it look appealing. Their house is just one of five in a nice cul-de-sac just on the edge of town. Cami grew up right beside me, and we spent a lot of our childhood playing Barbie's in the grass and racing our bikes around that cul-de-sac – against the wishes of our mothers.

I picked mom up at 10:30. Even though my knee was still sore from that fight with my front porch, it's always best that I drive because my mom's "perfect" driving exhausts me. Although my mom spends a lot of time holding on to that "Holy Crap" handle at the top of my door, at least she doesn't complain too much.

Of course, mom comes out of the house in her nice khaki pants, flowered blouse, and flats. There is no way I could do shopping in anything but tennis shoes. But my mom is the exception to fashion comfort. Not to mention her hair is in a perfect bun, and make-up is on and well-blended.

Kadira Collins. Her name means 'powerful', and she lives up to her name. When she speaks, we listen. She's a forced to be reckoned with. 5'2", blue eyes and bright red hair that is always so unruly that she keeps it in a tight bun on the back of her head. She always dresses in the best clothes that she buys only at TJ Maxx or Kohl's because she has a rule that has never been broken: Never buy anything that isn't on sale! And don't let her find you doing any shopping when there isn't a sale or there will be hell to pay. I mean that in the strictest of terms – my mom spends every Sunday and Wednesday at church and made sure all of us were there as well –

active in everything! No matter what was going on with my dad, she never gave up on him and always told us that there was an Angel in there somewhere underneath the devilish exterior.

She climbed in the car, gave me the once-over, nodded her slight approval and said, "What are you waiting for? This sale isn't going to shop itself. I'm armed with Kohl's cash; let's go spend it!"

Shopping at Kohl's is an art form, and today it netted me two new bras, on sale, of course, one nice shirt for work, two hanging out in shirts (straight off the clearance rack), and a new pair of semi-comfy work shoes. And I saved more than I spent – mom's rule!

Olive Garden was awesome; not to mention, mom paid the bill. Yay! That always makes the food taste better. Oh yeah, and there were leftovers.

Wal-Mart made me want to slit my wrists as usual, but I managed not to cuss out loud. I got everything we needed for S'mores and stocked up on snack cakes since they were on sale for $1.00 a box. Very successful shopping trip in my opinion.

I gave thought to a short nap before heading to Cami's, but then I figured I wouldn't wake up, and I didn't want to feel the wrath of Cami if I was late. I did opt to pull my hair back into a ponytail – no need to fix the make-up because Cami and Leland don't really care what I look like.

As I pulled into Cami's driveway, I saw the most awesome car in the world – a '69 cherry-red Camaro. I'm not a big car person, but this one made me drool. I walked around the house to the backyard, since I knew this was where the food would be. The picnic table was already covered with a tablecloth and Cami was setting a bowl of fruit salad and dip on the table. I laid down my bag of S'mores stuff, grabbed a grape, dipped it in the fruit dip, and realized why I loved cookouts at Cami's house.

"Is there anything I can do?"

"Nope – just waiting for the boys to get the burgers on the grill."

"Boys? As in more than one?"

"Yeah. Leland's brother, Chase, was helping put up the fence so we just invited him to stay."

I immediately got a scowl on my face and made some kind of guttural sound that marked my disapproval with the situation. Cami read my mind as usual.

"Don't get your panties in a wad. I'm not trying to set you up. You and Chase would eat each other alive, especially since you both feel the need to fix everybody's problems but your own."

"Thanks Cam. I can always count on you to build up my self-esteem – twice in one week. What does he do?"

"Besides help Leland build a fence? He's a probation officer." Cami just chuckled. "See, you're too much alike."

I did my best sigh and eye roll.

"How have I not met him before? I mean, you and Leland have been together a while and I work with the probation officers enough to know them; I don't know his name."

"He's spent the last few years in Juvenile probation, and he's been working Wood, Wirt and Ritchie counties, so he's never home and he's a work-a-holic; like somebody else I know."

I stuck my tongue out at her.

"You'll actually be seeing more of him now, though, since he just moved to adult probation and he's handling drug cases, so you might be working with him with Deborah."

Then, just as I popped another dip-covered grape into my mouth, I started to drool again.

Walking out the back door, carrying a tray of burgers, was a 6' 2", blonde-haired, green-eyed, hard-bodied, down-right gorgeous human being. Chase? Wow! He was built just like Leland, but even hotter. Of course, it didn't hurt that he was barefoot and bare-chested, wearing a pair of Wranglers that fit just right. A barefoot, blue jean night – sweet!

"Sadey, you're drooling."

"What? Oh, sorry. You didn't tell me that he was drop-dead gorgeous."

"Well, he is the brother of my future husband, and you have to admit that I've landed me a man that's not hard on the eyes."

As Chase put the burgers on the grill, Cami proceeds to introduce us. "Chase, this is my friend Sadey." I'm still ogling over his rock-hard chest and wishing I'd fixed my hair and make-up. He's giving me the once-over and I'm not sure if it's because he likes what he sees or if I actually look like something out of a Friday the 13th movie.

"Hey, how are you? Leland's actually talked about you a time or two."

"Great. I guess that means you've been told about all my finer qualities?"

He just laughed. "Well, he definitely hasn't bored me with stories about you and Cami growing up together."

"Gee, I don't know if I should be happy about that or not? Leland? You want to enlighten me on what you've told your brother about me so that I can at least defend myself?"

"Nope. I'll plead the fifth on that one."

"Good move."

Cami jumped right in to create the peace – something she does well. "Ok, children, we are going to have a great evening with burgers and S'mores and daiquiris, and neither of you boys is going to ruin that. Got it?"

"Yes, mom", Chase said as he laughed. "But do I have to drink a daiquiri, because I've already started on my first Corona?"

"Fine. I'll let you drink Corona as long as you act like a man instead of a small child." Cami teased. "And by the way, Sadey is the Queen of Sarcasm so she doesn't need you helping her out."

"Well, every Queen needs a King," Chase answered.

"Not this Queen," I responded. "I haven't found anybody worth crowning yet."

"See, that's the problem with you Queens. You always think you have to find the right King. What's wrong with a King finding the right Queen?" Chase smarted back.

"Hmmm. Let me see." My Queen of Sarcasm was about to flow. "First of all, Kings aren't capable of finding the right Queen, because it would require them to make a decision, something men aren't capable of doing."

"And how exactly did you decide what to wear today? Eeny-meeny-miny-mo?"

"What the…?"

"So, I'm right, huh?" Ok, I was already beginning not to like this guy.

"Second," I continued.

Cami stepped in again. "Are you two planning on arguing all night, or can we eat sometime soon?"

That was the cue to get the food together, on the table, and everybody to gather 'round and eat. It also gave everybody something to do with their mouths besides argue. The burgers were

awesome, and I also ate way too much fruit – not normally
something I eat a lot of, but when there's cream cheese dip involved
it makes the fruit taste much better.

During the couple of minutes of silence while everybody was
eating, I saw Chase look up at me a few times. As much as I didn't
want to admit it, I wouldn't mind if Cami invited him over more
often when I'm around.

Leland and Chase built a fire in the pit and I fished out all the
stuff for S'mores – graham crackers, Hershey bars, and
marshmallows. I started roasting marshmallows while Cami made
us some strawberry daiquiris, with plenty of whipped cream on top!
Definitely a great way to spend a Saturday evening.

"So, Sadey, tell me about the porch catapulting you headfirst
into the front door." Leland started in.

"You know, I was actually praising you for sending Cami over
with a Blizzard that night, but since you've resorted to making fun of
me, I've decided I don't like you anymore."

"You know you love me. And if I stopped torturing you, then
you'd be worried. Not to talk shop or anything, but you know that
Mark made bail, right?"

"Yeah, I got your message. I was on my way back from the
jail."

"I heard. Are you ok?"

"I'll be fine. How about we change the subject?"

"Ok, as you long as you promise me that you'll be careful."

"I promise."

"Now, about that story where the porch kicked your butt?"

"Too funny, Leland. I'm totally not giving you the pleasure of laughing at my expense."

"Good thing Cami already told me the story."

"Thanks, Cam – I knew I could count on you to keep my little secrets."

"That's what friends are for, Sadey. You have to admit, you rolling off the couch was downright hilarious!"

"Well, I wasn't finding it all that funny at the time, but looking back on it…At least you were there to save the day with a Chocolate Extreme Blizzard."

"That's what friends…"

"Hey, what am I, chopped liver?" Leland interrupted. "I'm the one who sent her over with the Blizzard. Shouldn't I get some kind of credit for that?"

"Sorry, Leland. You are a God. I keep forgetting to bow to you."

"Now, see, that's better".

Chase was laughing hysterically. "Are you guys always this much fun? Dinner was great, but the after-show is even better."

"All of you can just bite me! Come on, Cam. Aren't you gonna help me out here? I know these are your boys, but you've known me longer. Doesn't that count for anything?"

Now Cami was laughing hysterically. "You're right Sadey. Leland, knock it off or I'm cutting you off."

"Only from the beer, I hope."

"Hey, Cami?"

"Yeah, Chase."

"Since you can't control me, can I make fun of Sadey?"

"Only if you don't value your life. She may be a strawberry-blonde, but she has a red-headed temper."

"Good. I love a girl with spunk."

"Spunk. Spirit. Determination. Call it what you want, Chase, but I'm pretty sure I can kick your butt." I chided.

"In your dreams, Sweet Cheeks. But, watching you try might be down-right sexy."

"See, there you go again pretending you are some kind of King." I never back down from a fight. This guy was really starting to get on my nerves. Or was he? Good grief – must be the daiquiri talking. "On that note, I should probably be getting home."

"Tell me you're not serious, Sadey."

"Why not, Cam?"

"Um, because it's only 9:30."

"Yeah, and because you like a good fight."

"Who asked you Leland?" I retorted.

"Nobody, but I thought I'd talk while I was still allowed."

"You mean, before Cami cuts you off."

Now everybody was laughing. I absolutely love Cami, and she's the best friend a girl could ask for. She totally has it made to have found somebody like Leland. I could only get so lucky. I have to admit that Chase was adorable and tons of fun to be around. So not the marrying kind; of course, I'm not really looking at getting married anyway.

Get those thoughts outta your mind Sade. He's about to be your best friend's brother-in-law; definitely not somebody you can go out with. And why would you want to go out with him anyway? Because he's cute? Because he's hilarious? All of the above?

"Yo, Sadey."

"Huh, what?"

"You were in another world again."

"Sorry, Cam. I was actually dreaming of all the different ways I could kills these boys and dispose of their bodies without getting caught."

"Good comeback Sadey."

"Thanks Leland."

"No problem. Just for the record, when you do leave, I'm having Chase follow you home."

"No! Why? I'm a big girl. I can take care of myself."

"Yep, as long as there's not a porch involved."

"Ok, I admit I lost that fight. But I'm fine. Bones protects my house just fine and I'm perfectly safe there."

"I wasn't worried about you when you got in the house – it was getting from the car to the door I was worried about."

"Hardy-har-har. You think you're so funny. Honestly, I'm fine."

"I know. But I can't afford to buy you a Blizzard every night because I'm worried about you."

"Gee, and I thought you were making the big money – Mr. Law-and-Order. Are you planning to follow me all through town while I'm working and then make sure I get home safely every night?"

"Nope. Just tonight. For one, it's the weekend and Mark has nothing better to do. And two, I've already fed you tonight, so I'm not providing another Blizzard."

"Man, just when I thought you were starting to care…"

"She really is the Queen of Sarcasm, huh?" Chase piped in. "I'll follow her home and I'll even wait until she's safely inside the house." Before I could argue, he looked at me and said, "Don't worry. I won't get out of my car and I'll leave before you get naked for the night."

"Boy, you guys sure are funny tonight. Good thing Cami is my friend, or I'd have to break bad on all of you."

"Again, might be sexy."

"Quit while you're behind, Chase."

"Got it Cam."

I tried to just drive myself home without an escort but arguing with my best friend and her cop boyfriend was more of a fight than even I can win. I drove home with an escort. I pulled in my driveway, got out of my car and started to walk to the porch. Against my will, there was a 6' 2", blonde-haired, hunk of muscle walking right beside me.

"I thought you were going to wait in the car."

"I thought I was too. But then I decided that if anything happened to you, Cami would be pissed."

"Well, as you can see, I'm home and perfectly fine."

"Ok, as soon as you step through the door and are safely inside with the dog, then I'll leave. I promise."

I did my best sigh, but Chase didn't seem to care.

"Fine. Whatever. Just watch your step." As soon as that came out of my mouth, that stupid board jumped up and tripped me again. And for the second time in a week, I was catapulted through the air, head-first into my front door.

Once again, Chase was laughing hysterically. "Are you ok?"

"Maybe you should ask me once you stop laughing. You don't sound so sincere when you're cackling."

"I'm sorry. But if you could've seen yourself fly through the air…"

"Quit while you're behind, Chase."

"That's the second time I've been told that tonight."

"Maybe you should start listening."

"I'll try. Let me help you up."

"I'm fine." And I'm extremely stubborn. I didn't want him to see the amount of pain I was in because I don't show weakness. It's part of the job – stay strong, never let them see you sweat. It's always been my motto. I'm lying on my front porch, head pounding, knee pounding, trying to act tough. Now, my only job was to get up off this porch without showing weakness; and before he notices how hard my heart is beating or the weird tingle going through my body. Good grief! What is wrong with me?

"Stop being a pain in the butt. You're hurt. You don't have to pretend that you're not, so lose the stubbornness and let me help you up and into the house."

"I'm fine."

"You've said that already. Now shut up and give me your hand."

"Fine. Ok. I keep meaning to get that board fixed. I really need to replace the whole porch. This was my grandmother's house and I really haven't done anything to it since I inherited it. Mainly, I'm just too cheap, but I guess I don't have a choice now, huh?"

"Well, since this is the second time in a week that the porch has kicked your butt, yeah, I'd say it's time to replace it. I can help if you want. I'm actually pretty handy with a hammer. I just spent the day building a fence with Leland."

"Thanks, but it'll be fine."

"Ok Miss stubborn, whatever you say. Can we at least get you in the house so I can go home to my own?"

"You might want to stand behind me, unless you like drool in your ears."

"Well, that depends on who's drooling."

"A 90-pound dog."

"Oh, in that case, I'll be right behind you."

Having plans always seems like a good idea...until you realize you have to put on pants and leave the house.

Court

Monday, September 24th

9:00 AM

Court – my other least favorite place to be. However, I need to be here for Deborah. The officers brought her in through the back door, handcuffed and dressed in her oversized orange outfit. The judge took the bench in his oversized black robe and we all rose out of a sign of respect (and because the bailiff told us to).

The hearing was short and sweet, and it went in my favor. Deborah was released into the care of Western Health Rehabilitation Program, specifically to Janice. Her conditions consisted of completing a six-week drug rehab program, as well as an evaluation from the Adult Probation office, and any other terms as requested by DHHR, at which time she will be seen back in court to discuss her fate. If she does not complete the program, she will immediately be sent back to jail to await her court date.

Deborah assured me that she didn't want to go back to jail and she would do whatever Janice and I told her to. Sounds good to me.

So, I told her that she had to complete 3 weeks of the program before I would set her up with supervised visitation with the girls. I emphasized that she not only had to complete rehab, but also participate in the drug counseling program, whatever Janice sets up for her. Then, I told her that Janice would set up the meeting with Adult Probation and she would have to be completely honest in all their paperwork. She agreed and I left her to Janice, who is great about keeping me informed.

Since the courthouse is only a couple of blocks from my building, I find it easier to walk to court, rather than fight to find a parking place in which I have to put money in their meter just for the privilege of parking there. Walking that two blocks would normally not be an issue in my tennis shoes, but because I had to appear in court, this required being dressed in nice, professional clothes, which includes dress shoes. I opted for a small heel this morning to accompany my black slacks and cream-colored short-sleeve sweater. This small heel was not comfortable for walking the two blocks back to the DHHR building. I got to the parking lot of my building, and then convinced myself it was only a few more steps to the door. The "Little Engine that Could" came to mind, and I found myself saying, "I think I can, I think I can." I'm pretty sure I'm a complete idiot, but since I didn't say it out loud it doesn't really count, right?

Being lost in my own stupidity, I didn't pay any attention to the sound of screeching tires behind me; after all, it's not unusual for people to be a little perturbed when they leave our building.

~~~~~~~~~~~~~~~~~~~~~~~~~~

Mark had been sitting in the parking lot of the DHHR for about an hour now, waiting patiently for Sadey to come out the door; a blitz attack of some sort sounded good. But, as luck would have it, she was walking down the side road on her way back from the courthouse. She was alone and in the perfect location for a drive-by; or a drive-thru.

Before she ever saw him, he had punched the gas, squealing the tires in the process. He was gaining speed as she locked eyes with him, screaming. He bounced her right off the front of his car like it was some sort of trampoline, and he couldn't have planned it any better as she landed right in front of the car in time for him to literally run over her.

"That should do it," Mark thought to himself. "Sadey Collins now knows who's in charge, and it's not her."

He was smiling as he tore out of the parking lot heading straight towards the house of his 'flavor of the month.'

~~~~~~~~~~~~~~~~~~~~~~~~~~

"No! No!" I hear the screeching tires; I see the car coming straight at me, but I'm helpless to do anything about it.

Just as I realize that the face behind the wheel is Mark Kinders, I feel the searing pain as the car bumper hits my right leg, bouncing me into the air and dropping me onto the asphalt several feet away. I feel my hand twist backwards as my head lands hard on the ground; then agonizing pain as I feel a tire roll over my right leg.

I hear voices, but I can't make out the faces. It seems to take forever for my eyes to focus; the first thing I see is Chase standing over me. Why is he here?

The pain is intense. I can't breathe. I feel like I'm standing outside my own body.

I was immediately surrounded by people, most of whom were screaming something about calling 911. Chase was trying his best to hold me still, and saying things like, "you're going to be just fine", and "hold still until the paramedics arrive", and "did you see the car that hit you?"

I was immediately jolted back into reality. There wasn't a single part of my body that didn't hurt at that exact moment, but I mustered up enough strength for one word: "Mark".

Of course, that sent Chase into an immediate fit of rage, and I could hear him on his phone talking with someone I could only assume was Leland, while trying to hold me still at the same time.

I heard sirens in the background, and the next thing I remember was waking up in the hospital surrounded by Leland, Chase, and my mother. I don't recommend this as a normal wake-up; I'm pretty sure I uttered words that made my mother blush, and I'm sure had I not been lying on a hospital bed in the emergency room, she probably would have slapped me across the mouth.

There was a nurse talking to me, but I'm not sure I heard everything she said. Apparently, according to Chase, who happened to be there so quickly because he was leaving a meeting in our building, I was hit by a car that never stopped, thrown through the air at a great rate of speed and landed squarely on my side, bounced my head off the ground and my right leg was run over by the car. I have a broken leg, broken arm, concussion, my shoulder was popped out of socket, and several cuts and bruises that were highlighted by my pavement rash. This combination means that I will not be walking on my own, driving my car, typing with both hands, or even staying alone for a few days. At least I can still write; the only plus side to being left-handed.

I figure this means I'm going to be a little bit grouchy for a while. On the plus side, they just gave me something in my I.V. that's making me feel all warm and fuzzy inside. Woo! Pain pills are the bomb. Hope they send me home with some of this good stuff! Good thing Leland got my statement before they put this stuff in my I.V. I don't think I could tell him my name right now.

Why did Mark run me over? Who called my mom? Why is Chase still here? Why am I talking to myself again? Maybe it's the good stuff they gave me.

So, how many people does it take to transport a 27-year-old woman to her home, get her out of the car and into the house, past a 90-lb dog with a super-slobber tongue, change her clothes, and lay her on the couch so that she's comfortable and not complaining? I really have no idea, because apparently, I was in and out of it all the way here, thanks to the wonders of modern-day medicine.

I will tell you that when I came to, on my pillow-covered couch, my living room was filled with Chase, Leland, Cami, my mother, my sister, and my dog, Bones, who was sitting beside the couch with his head on my stomach, whining. I can guess that Chase and/or Leland carried my helpless butt into the house, but I'm trying to guess who it was that changed me into my cut-off sweats with a t-shirt that I'm hoping passed the smell test. Only problem with that is, none of the people standing in my living room truly understand the concept of the smell test. They all believe in doing laundry frequently and putting their clothes away in dressers neatly folded. Well, I guess I'm making assumptions, since I really don't know anything about Chase. I'm just guessing that he's just like Leland. But then again, my sister would probably not appreciate people comparing her to me, so…

Bones is doing his best slobber routine on my face, leaving inches of drool in my ears.

My voice sounded gravelly as I asked, "Who changed my clothes?"

"You've been hit by a car, broken some bones, doped up on some good drugs, dripping in drool, and the only thing you can say is 'who changed my clothes'? Really?"

"Ok, Cami. You win. Why didn't somebody bring me a Blizzard?"

"Well, for your information, there's one in your freezer. Now, sassy pants, our instructions were to get you home, make you comfortable, and give you round the clock care for several days."

"You mean protection?"

"What?"

"Oh, come on Cami. I won't argue that somebody's gonna need to help me out a little for a while, but the real reason my living room is filled with "concerned citizens" is for my protection, not to take care of me."

I did the best imitation I could of the quotation marks with my fingers, considering the cast on my hand. But the movement of my fingers sent my body into immediate pain mode, and I made the mistake of wincing in front of my protection detail.

Leland jumped in. "You two can have a little girl fight some other time. Cami, get her some pain meds; we need to keep her pain in check, or she'll go into shock."

Then he looked across the room at me and said, "Sadey, he's on the loose. Mark. We haven't caught him yet. I have cops looking for him, and we'll bring him in, but right now, somebody is staying with you 24/7. Don't bother arguing with me, because I'm not going to listen. I'm putting you in protective custody, so you can either have somebody stay with you here in your own house, or you can move in with your mother. Your choice."

Ugh! "Ok, fine! I won't argue, but you are not going to hover over me like I'm some invalid."

"Sadey, sweetheart." It was mom's turn to put her two cents worth in. "Right now, you are an invalid. You can't walk because your leg is broken, and you can't use crutches because your arm is broken. You can't even just use one crutch because your shoulder had to be popped back into socket and you have a serious concussion. That means that you have to rely on all of us to take care of you."

"Mom. I'm fine." My stubborn side just won't give up. I was out to prove to everyone sitting there that I could take care of myself. So, I used my good arm to push myself up, trying not to wince at the pain in my shoulder, then I put my good leg on the floor, and proceeded to show them all how ridiculously stupid I can be. As soon as I went to stand up, I immediately fell on my good side. The entire living room, with the exception of my mother and myself, erupted in laughter. Now I was completely ticked off!

"Whatever! You guys win. Who's taking the first shift? Whoever it is needs to get my wobbly butt off this floor and get me that damn Blizzard!"

"Sadey Nevada Collins! I won't have you using that language!"

"Sorry mom. Must be the drugs talking." In my best sing-song voice I said, "Would somebody please get me that ding-dang Blizzard? Is that better, mom?"

"Yes, young lady. Much better."

It was Noelle's turn to pipe in. "I can stay the rest of the day. But I have to be home to put the kids in bed, so I can't really take the night shift."

"I don't need anybody to take the night shift. I can sleep just fine."

"Sadey Nevada Collins – enough of this crap, ok!"

That's the second time in two minutes that my mother has used my full name.

"You can't get yourself off this couch, which means you can't get yourself out of bed if you have to go to the bathroom. Now stop this incessant arguing. You will do whatever we tell you to until you are better, understand?"

Why argue with my mother; it hasn't worked in the last 27 years, why would I try now?

"Great. So now that my posse is here to rescue me, who gets to stay with me all night? Should we just make a calendar and post it on the fridge so everybody can sign up for their shift?"

"Sounds like a good idea."

"I'm the Queen of Sarcasm, Cami. Just because I'm all casted up doesn't mean you can ignore my abilities."

"Sure it does, sweetie. I'll take the night shift. I have to leave by 7:30 in the morning for school, so I'll need a replacement by then. Who's next?"

"I can do all day tomorrow," my mom added.

"I'll come after work and take the evening shift," Chase added.

"Why would you want to take care of me? You've known me for 2 days and you've already pulled protective duty twice."

"You're Cami's best friend, which means you're practically family. So, I have the same obligation as they do to help take care of you. Besides, it's your fault I have another case on my hands, so I figured if I can't torture you about it at work, I can just do it here."

"You're Deborah's PO?"

"Yep. So, you're stuck with me no matter what. We might as well learn to be nice to each other."

"Well, that might be a chore, but give me enough drugs and it might work. Now that we've determined my nursing schedule, who's going to get that Blizzard for me? And maybe some pain medication would be good. Oh, and who the hell changed my clothes?!"

"I've got her guys. Leland, go find that SOB that ran over my sister. Mom, I didn't cuss so don't give me that look. And Sadey would probably love it if you made some apple cinnamon muffins for her. Wouldn't you Sade?"

"Oh, man, that would be awesome! I love apple cinnamon muffins!"

"Ok you two, I get the hint. Any other requests while I'm at?"

"Are you being sarcastic or serious? Because if you're serious, then I also love triple chocolate fudge cake, lasagna, and pizza."

"I get it. But if you just sit here eating like that you won't be able to fit in your jeans."

"No worries, mom. I won't be wearing jeans for a while."

And with that, I was handed a Blizzard and a pain pill, probably just to shut me up before my mom slapped me silly. I got lots of hugs and kisses, and everybody left but Noelle. Funny how you don't really appreciate your friends and family until you truly have to lean on them. Right now, the only thing I can do is lean on them, because I sure can't stand on my own – thanks to a cast that goes ¾ of the way up my leg – oh yeah, and a pain pill.

Noelle Darlene Bradley – my older sister; the perfect one. Her name means "Christmas" and "little darling" – enough said. She's married to her college sweetheart, Dane; he's a loan officer at the bank, so she doesn't have to work. Although she does have a Bachelor's Degree in Psychology. She takes care of her kids, my niece and nephew – Blake is seven and Abi is three – and she's about four months pregnant. She has that cute little baby bump and keeps a perfect size six figure, even after two babies.

Noelle kept me comfy on the couch watching reruns of The Big Bang Theory. I'm pretty sure it's an absolutely stupid show, but Noelle laughed all the time. Probably because she's extremely smart and she gets it. I know I'm high on pain meds, but even then, I probably wouldn't understand this show. The only character I can relate to is Penny, and she's supposedly the dumb blonde, so that's not saying much for me.

I have discovered that Bones isn't really pleased about sharing his home with my friends and family. Apparently, he doesn't like having to "ask" everybody else to let him out. Not to mention, Noelle is great with kids, but not with dogs. She has no understanding of the fact that you only get three nudges prior to the tongue lashings. When I said on nudge two that she'd better let him out, she didn't believe me. She tried to just ignore him. My prim and proper sister then ended up pinned back against the chair, with big paws on her shoulders, and an extremely long tongue covering her in drool, and I'm pretty sure she said some words that would have gotten her slapped across the mouth from my mother. I laughed hysterically. She shot me that look that meant she'd withhold my pain medication if I continued laughing. I did my best to stifle that laugh.

"Not to change the subject or anything, sis, but nobody ever told me who changed my clothes."

"Good grief, Sade. I'm covered in drool and you're still worried about who changed your clothes?"

"It's a legitimate question."

"It was me. Ok. Me and Cami. Trust me, Leland and Chase didn't see you naked, if that's what you're worried about. Well, I don't know what all Chase saw in the hospital when they cut your pants off…"

"Stop laughing Noelle. I guess we're even now."

My next babysitter was Cami. She got there in time to put me in bed. Lucky for me, Bones is attached to Cami and when she put me to bed, he went to bed too. I'm pretty sure Cami gave me another pain pill when she put me to bed, because I don't remember anything between rolling into bed and the smell of my mom's apple cinnamon muffins.

In hard times, we must remember three things: friends are closer than we ever knew they could be, family loves us more than we thought, and we can be stronger than we ever imagined when we are surrounded by family and friends.

Babysitting

Tuesday, September 25th

Aside from waking up to the smell of apple cinnamon muffins, I'm not sure spending the day with my mother is going to be a great idea. I mean, I love my mother. I love to go shopping with my mother, and eating at Olive Garden, and doing those mother-daughter things. I do not, however, like being stuck in my house, not being able to move or do anything on my own, at the mercy of my mother. Spending my day watching the Today Show, and Rachel Ray, and the news, and soap operas, and doctor shows is not my idea of a great time.

On the plus side, I had apple cinnamon muffins for breakfast, grilled cheese and tomato soup for lunch, and a triple chocolate fudge cake was left on my counter. In order for that cake to be left on my counter, though, I had to allow my mother to help me with a sponge bath and put me in clean clothes. Not something that's happened since I was five.

I also had to consent to my mother washing every piece of clothing that was not already in a dresser drawer. Of course, that meant that my mother criticized every undergarment I own, folded all that clothing, and put it in the dresser drawers that she thought they belonged in. I actually felt sorry for my sweatpants. I mean, they aren't meant to be confined to a dresser drawer, right? They don't confine me, all that wonderful elastic that allows me to eat Blizzards, so why should I confine them to a drawer? I was not about to argue with my mother, considering I wanted that chocolate cake to be left on my counter, but as soon as I was able, I was freeing my sweatpants from their captivity.

Changing of the guards took place at approximately 4:40 p.m. I'm pretty sure that's because it only takes 10 minutes for Chase to get from the Probation Office to my house, and he obviously left at precisely 4:30 p.m.

He refused to let my mom leave the house until he 'secured the perimeter'. I told him that he was starting to act like Leland, and he just laughed and said, "Leland can kick my butt, but I'm more afraid of Cami. She told me that if anything happened to you that I was personally responsible. I was also instructed to cook dinner, and make sure the TV was on channel 13 at 8:00 sharp, because if you missed a new episode of NCIS you would be angry enough to physically hurt me, whether you were wearing casts or not."

"I knew there was a reason she's my best friend."

"Oh, yeah. I was also informed that if I left dirty dishes in the sink she would personally make sure I was never able to create children of my own. So, I was thinking we should order pizza. Whaddya think?"

"Pizza sounds good. I have a huge package of paper plates in the cabinet, because I hate doing dishes myself, and loading the dishwasher for one person seems silly, so I guess I can save you from the wrath of Cami on that one."

"That would be good. So, what do we have planned for tonight?"

"Besides eating pizza, watching NCIS, and eating triple chocolate fudge cake?"

"And making sure you are safe and not in pain? Speaking of pain, when did you have your last dose of medicine?"

"I don't know; didn't you ask mom before she left?"

"No, sorry. I guess I'm already failing at this nurse thing."

"I'm not really that great of a patient, so it's ok if you're not a great nurse. Find my phone and I'll call her."

"I'll call her. Maybe we should create some kind of chart or something so we can keep track of these things."

I punched him in the arm.

"Ouch. What was that for?"

"Suggesting a chart for taking care of me? Really? Are we gonna have a column for who gets to wipe my butt, too?"

"Yep; that's Leland's column."

"Ha ha ha ha. You are sssooooo funny. Just get the dang phone, call my mom, and then order some pizza. I had grilled cheese and tomato soup for lunch and I'm starving. So, either order that pizza or start cooking."

"Adorable AND demanding. How did I get so lucky?"

"There you go again - trying to be the Queen of Sarcasm."

A half hour later the aroma of pizza and breadsticks filled the air. Whoever invented the idea of picking up the phone and then some young kid brings a pizza to your house is a genius! Bones was doing circles in the kitchen. I'm glad I remembered to tell Chase to order an extra pizza for him; otherwise, I probably wouldn't even get a bite of my own. I can't exactly fend him off right now. Come to think of it, I can't do much of anything on my own right now.

Have I mentioned that I'm not a very good patient? Don't get me wrong, I like to be lazy. But there's a difference between wanting to lay around in my sweatpants being lazy, and actually HAVING to lie around because I physically can't do anything else. I don't like not even being able to walk myself to the bathroom without help. Good thing I don't need help IN the bathroom – that would be even more embarrassing. Although, there's no way in hell I'll ever admit that my shoulder still hurts when I move my arm in crazy ways.

"So," Chase started, "tell me all about Deborah. What do you want me to do with her?"

"Deborah? Oh crap! Deborah!"

"Sadey, what's wrong?"

"Does Janice know that Mark hit me with a car? What if he tries to go after Deborah, or Janice? Leland got a protective order against him for me and he still tried to run me over."

"I'll call Leland and have him check. And by the way, he didn't try there sassy pants – he succeeded. If you haven't noticed, you are sporting two brand new casts, a colorful bump on your forehead, as well as some road rash on your cheeks and arms."

"Thanks for the self-esteem booster. And here I was laying around in my cut-off sweatpants thinking I was downright sexy. Way to ruin it!"

"Hey, I'm only getting paid for your care and protection. Nobody said I was supposed to stroke your ego too."

"And what exactly are you getting paid to babysit me?"

"I get to continue hanging out with my big brother and his future wife."

"Does that mean that I'm some kind of ultimatum? Like, take care of her or else you're cut off from future family barbeques?"

"Something like that. But look, Sadey, I know you're miserable. It has to completely suck to be stuck in those casts and having all of us invading your privacy. I'm sorry. But you do know that you have some pretty great friends and family, right?"

"I know. I'm sorry. I'm just still in a lot of pain. And I'm laying here on my couch thinking about all the crap I need to do at work, and there's not a thing I can do about it. I'm just sorta stuck, and at the mercy of everybody around me. I can't even drive myself to see clients. Who in the heck is going to do my home visits?"

I just lost it. Tears were flowing down my face and I couldn't stop them. I looked like a complete idiot and poor Chase was just stuck with me and my emotional breakdown. He just looked down at the floor, like he had no idea what to do with an emotional basket case. I kind of felt sorry for him.

"Chase?"

"Yeah."

"I'm sorry that I'm falling apart on you. I'm sure you didn't sign up for this. You're here to help because I'm Cami's friend, and here I am being a big crybaby. You know you don't have to do this, right? Nobody really expects you to be one of my nurses."

"It's fine Sadey. Truth be known, I don't really have anything else to do. I'm kind of a work-a-holic. My clients probably hate me because I'm famous for making spur of the moment evening home visits. I've kind of been that young, ambitious kid trying to prove himself in the workforce, ya know."

"Yes. I do know. I'm the same way. I graduated with these grand delusions that I was going to save the world. I'm pretty sure I haven't really saved anything, aside from thousands of Microsoft Word documents. I really like my job though. There are times when I'm so frustrated that I could pull out all my hair or eat an entire box of Swiss Cake Rolls. But then a case like Deborah comes along, and for some reason my heart gets overly involved and I can't help but want to save the world again. Does that make sense?"

"Makes perfect sense. I'm sure that people see you as the enemy, as well. I know they do me. They cower when they hear my voice or see me coming. I try to help; I really do. I don't want to be the person that sticks them back in jail, you know. I want to be the one that steers them in the right direction and helps them never go back to jail. Now I'm the one getting all mushy."

"Your brother wears his heart on his sleeve, so I'm assuming you've been blessed with the same quality – or cursed, however you actually see it."

"Leland's great, isn't he? I've always been the little brother that's followed him around, and he never complained. Never tried to push me away; kind of took me under his wing and made sure I stayed out of trouble myself; he was the real father figure in my life. He's a good cop, too. I think it's because he cares about people so much. He's not a hot head; he's not on a power trip. He truly cares about people and tries to help them."

"That's why I'm such a thorn in his side. I never call central – I just dial Leland. He never comes blaring into one of my houses trying to be a badass. He can read me. He knows when I'm truly ticked off at a client and when I'm trying to help. Like with Deborah. He had all the right in the world to turn her house upside-down looking for the drugs; but he didn't. He got the search warrant, but then he followed my lead. Chase, I really feel like we can help her and those two little girls. It's going to be a big family affair, though."

"Yeah, I thought of that. It's Leland's criminal case, your CPS case, Cami is the teacher of one of the little girls, and now I'm the probation officer. But, if you're right about this lady, it will all turn out fine. We'll do it together. Maybe we can pull off that "save the world" thing we've got going on, huh?"

"Thanks for listening to me Chase. And I'm sorry I went all emotional crazy-girl on you."

"No problem. I think that nurses are supposed to listen to their patients, right?"

"Ha ha – you're pretty funny. Do you want the bad news now?"

"Lay it on me."

"I have to pee."

"I was afraid you were going to say that. I was hoping I could get all the way through my shift without having to do this duty. Ok, crip, let's get you off that couch. I only have to take you to the bathroom door, right? I'm not, like, responsible for anything else, right?"

I laughed so hard I was snorting. Then I was completely embarrassed, especially when I realized that he was kind of serious. "Just get me to the door, and I'll yell when I'm finished; then you can hobble me back to the couch."

"Ok, I think I can handle this."

I don't think he realized how much I actually had to lean on him in order to walk. He didn't complain, not even a word, but I sort of felt sorry for him. At least he wasn't being a jerk; I guess I should be thankful for that. Not to mention I just got that major tingling thing again when he wrapped his arm around me to help me walk.

We sat pretty quietly through NCIS. Shortly after we finished our triple chocolate fudge cake, courtesy of my mother, Bones started getting restless. I thought maybe he just needed out, but then he got this low growl going and took off for the door. He was standing at the front door, paws up on the door, the hair standing up on his back, barking madly.

~~~~~~~~~~~~~~~~~~~~~~~~~~

It didn't take Mark very long to find out where Sadey lived. He gave thought to just torching the place since he knew she was inside, but he figured that maybe instilling some fear in her might be a little more fun. He figured he could kill her anytime, might as well have a little fun, especially since she can't come running after him. He was actually upset when he found out that he didn't kill her with the drive-thru, but he broke a few bones so at least it wasn't for nothing.

Paint in an aerosol can is genius. It only took him a minute to paint 'Die Bitch' across the front of her car; she'll play hell getting that paint off.

He heard her dog barking like mad and figured that was his cue to disappear. He took off towards his car, which he'd parked about four doors down; far enough that he wouldn't be seen, but close enough that he could watch the fun.

What he hadn't anticipated was that she would have that cop that arrested him at her house. "Wonder if they have something going on?"

He focused his binoculars and then got a tad bit more confused. That's not the cop; looks almost identical to him. Son-of-a-bitch; he must have a brother and he's obviously Sadey's babysitter. Well that just means he has to be a little more careful while playing 'fear factor'.

He did a U-turn and headed back to Amber's house. Amber's a strung-out junkie that he freely supplies with whatever she needs; he in turn always has a piece of ass to do with whatever he wants, and she didn't have a kid in tow like Deborah, since CPS came and took her baby away right after it was born. She didn't need a kid anyway; she's a junkie – and a good screw that will let him hide-out at her house for as long as he needed.

~~~~~~~~~~~~~~~~~~~~~~~~~~

Chase immediately sprang to action. He ran to my back door, locked and chained it, grabbed the flashlight off my kitchen counter, and took off out the front door straight on the heels of Bones. I didn't even think I owned a flashlight; and I'm darn sure I don't keep one on my kitchen counter. Apparently, these people were taking crazy precautions I didn't even know about.

I couldn't get off the couch to see what was going on, not that I could have been any help anyway, but I don't really like it when Bones gets riled up. It's only happened a couple of times – once when there was a skunk getting into my trash, and another time when one of the neighbor kids was sneaking through my yard trying to get into his house through his side door because he was late for curfew.

As I sat on the couch freaking out, I kept hoping that it was the neighbor kid that had Bones all worked up. I didn't want to think about any other alternative at this point. I didn't have long to think, though.

Chase came flying back into my kitchen, with Bones on his heels this time. He was on his cell phone, obviously talking to Leland, running through my house checking doors, windows, and everything in between. I was turning my head every which way trying to follow him with my eyes, trying to figure out what he was doing. I heard him say, "It says 'die bitch' across the hood. The house is safe and secure, and I didn't see anybody. Bones was right with me doing circles around the yard, but he was gone before we got outside. Bones was standing at the door barking and going crazy."

I was trying hard not to cry. Somebody was in my yard – well, not somebody – obviously Mark. He was here. He knows where I live. My hands started trembling, I could feel my heart beating out of my chest, and tears were flowing down my face.

It's my house. I'm not safe in my own house. Why does this guy hate me so much? I was just doing my job. How did he know where I live? Why haven't the police arrested him yet?

I was crying so hard I could hardly talk. "Ch-Ch-Chase? Was he here? Was Mark at my house?"

"I think so, Sadey. Somebody spray-painted your car, and I can only assume it was him. Leland has put an APB out for him – they'll catch him, Sadey. They will."

He came over to the couch and sat down beside me. He put his arm around me, and just let me cry into him. I've never been so scared in my life. Bones was sitting at my feet, kind of like he was saying to me, "I've got this mom, I'm here to protect you." I love that dog! I was frozen stiff. I couldn't move.

"What if he comes back, Chase?"

"Then we'll nail him. You're safe now Sadey. I promise nothing is going to happen to you."

At that moment, my front door flung open and Cami and Leland came running in. Chase got up and Cami took his place. She just held me and let me cry. I heard Leland and Chase discussing what happened, and next thing I knew the rest of the posse was pouncing through my door – mom and Noelle. The gang's all here. Now what?

Group meeting.

"She can't stay here," Cami said.

"She can stay with me," I heard my mom say.

Do you ever feel like you're having an out of body experience? Yep, that's me, right now. I know I'm sitting in this room and my friends and family are having a discussion about what they are going to do with me, but I'm not really an active participant. They are just talking around me.

"She's going home with me. That's the only place she's safe."

Cami replied, "Chase, are you sure? You barely know each other. I don't want you to feel like you have to take on this responsibility. She can stay with me."

I heard Chase raise his voice, "Look guys, this is not up for discussion. She can't stay with Noelle because there are babies in that house. I'm not sending her to her mom's house. What happens if he finds her there before we find him? Not in a million years am I putting this lady's life in danger as well. I can work from home. I can do some phone appointments and do paperwork; I have plenty of it. Leland, you concentrate on finding that son-of-a-bitch." My mom cringed and Chase realized what he said. "I'm sorry ma'am. I just don't know what else to call him."

"Maybe an evil son-of-a-bitch would be more accurate."

The room just got eerily silent. My mother just cussed! I've never heard her cuss in all of my 27 years. It took a minute for everybody to jerk back to reality.

Chase continued, "Kadira, if you don't mind to come over in the mornings to help her bathe, I think I can handle everything else. I just don't think we have any other options. Until Mark is safely behind bars, Sadey stays with me. We can't put any of her family in jeopardy – it's just not an option. I have a security system. She'll be safe at my house."

Cami was still holding on to me – afraid that if she let go I would just fall over. I couldn't move; I couldn't quit crying.

"Why does he hate me so much? I was just doing my job." I said between sobs.

Now it was Leland's turn. "Sadey, I'm not telling you anything that you don't already know. But with all the crazies we deal with, it can turn bad on any given day. This one just appears to be crazier than either of us ever anticipated. Are you ok with staying at Chase's house? We need to keep you safe, and he's right, we don't want to put any of the rest of your family in danger."

"Whatever. Just find him, Leland. I don't want to be scared in my own house."

"Chase and I will get her in his car. Noelle, go home to your babies, make sure your home is secure. I don't want to scare the kids but show them Mark's picture and just tell them that he's a bad guy that's being mean to Aunt Sadey, just in case he would show his face around them. They need to know he's a bad man, but I don't want them scared. Understand?"

"Yeah, I got it," Noelle said.

"Cami - You and Kadira get Sadey's stuff packed up. Everything she might need. At least a few days' worth of stuff. Make sure you get her medications. What about Bones?"

"We'll take him too. As long as I feed him frequently, he seems to like me."

"Chase, are you sure you want Bones too?"

"Leland, I don't think you could separate them right now. If we took Sadey out of here without Bones he would go crazy worrying about her; either that or he would hunt me down. I will have to dog-proof the house, but they need to stay together. He's actually a good comfort for her."

I was slowly losing my fear, and it turned into anger. "It's not fair! He should be in jail and I should be safe in my own house!"

Mom sat down on the other side of me. "Baby girl, you listen to me. You have the best friends a girl could ever ask for. I don't want you thinking about this Mark guy, ok. I want you to work on healing up so you can get back on your feet. I don't really know Chase, and I'm not all that keen on sending you home with somebody I don't know, especially some cute man; however, one thing I've learned in the past day is that when times get tough you lean on friends and family. Chase is Cami's family and I trust Cami with my life and yours. I'll be over in the morning to help you bathe. Ok?"

"Yeah. I'll be fine. Chase had to take me to the bathroom this evening and he didn't run away then, so I guess I'll be ok at his house," I joked.

"Ok, baby." My mother then stood up, got within breathing distance of Chase, put her finger in his face, and very seriously said, "You take care of my baby girl, or you will not ever have children of your own. Got it?"

"Yes ma'am." Chase kind of chuckled and then looked at Cami. "Are you sure that Kadira's not your mom too? That's the second time today I've been threatened with future generations."

And on that note, I was carried out of the house, careful not to let me see my car, and I was loaded in Chase's Blazer and sent off to my new temporary home. I was very disappointed that I was not sitting in the front seat of a '69 cherry-red Camaro. I was informed that the cast on my broken leg would prevent me from fitting in the front seat of a Camaro. Major bummer!

God puts people in our lives for a reason ~ and when one finds that reason, those people become so much more valuable.

Basket case

Chase lives in a nice 3-bedroom house just on the edge of town. No cul-de-sac, and the nearest neighbor can't be seen from either the back porch or the front porch. Good thing the front porch only has 2 steps, because I was not good at leaning and hopping one-legged from step to step. He actually has a spare bedroom with a nice bed and dresser, which was currently being loaded with my clothes, thanks to my good friend Cami.

"Sadey, it's late. Do you need some chill time, or do you want me to put you in bed? I'm going to work from home, so it's ok if you just need to talk."

"Chase?"

"Yeah, Sade."

"Thanks. You didn't have to do this, you know."

"Don't go all mushy on me. But you're welcome. You'll be safe here, I promise."

"My leg hurts. And so does my head."

"You have a bad concussion – one other reason we can't leave you alone; you could actually pass out at the smallest thing. I'll get you some pain meds. Do you want a piece of cake to wash it down with?"

"Are you serious? You brought the cake?"

"Cami made sure it ended up here. She said you would need it."

"She's right. I love her. And I know I've already had a piece of cake tonight, but I would love another piece. Thanks."

"That'll just be our little secret," he said as he headed into the kitchen.

~~~~~~~~~~

"No! No!" I hear the screeching tires; I see the car coming straight at me, but I'm helpless to do anything about it. I see his eyes glow a devilish red right before I feel the searing pain of the car bumper hitting my right leg, bouncing me into the air and dropping me onto the asphalt several feet away. I feel my hand twist backwards as my head lands hard on the ground; then agonizing pain as I feel a tire roll over my right ankle.

I hear voices, but I can't make out the faces. It seems to take forever for my eyes to focus; the first thing I see is Chase standing over me. Why is he here?

The pain is intense. I can't breathe.

"Mark! No!"

~~~~~~~~~~~~

"Sadey, Sadey; wake up! You're having a nightmare."

I sat straight up in bed, disoriented, heart pounding out of my chest and I was having trouble breathing.

I felt Chase just pick me up out of bed and the next thing I know we are in the living room, tucked in the corner of his couch, and I am sitting on his lap with my head laying on his shoulder. He has one arm around me rubbing my back and the other holding my head against him.

"Breathe, Sadey; it's ok. Take slow deep breaths. You just had a nightmare, but you're safe, ok."

I tried to stop the tears, but they stubbornly slid down my face anyway.

"Wanna talk about? What were you dreaming about?"

"Mark. He had devil eyes; they were glowing. Then I was bounced off the bumper and landed on my hand and my head bounced and then the car ran over my leg. That's when I woke up."

I realized I was shaking.

Chase grabbed the blanket off the back of the couch, pulled out the recliner, propped up his legs and then covered us both up.

"You're safe now Sadey. It was just a nightmare, ok. I've got you. Just close your eyes, take deep breaths and relax."

Closing eyes; check. Deep breaths; check. Relax; there were still tears falling down my cheeks, but my body was tingling; and Chase, is he…no, I'm just certifiably crazy.

I woke up Wednesday morning to the sound of the doorbell. I heard Chase talking – to my mother.

"She didn't sleep well last night. I gave her a pain pill, but she was very restless."

The last thing I remember was being curled up on Chase's lap, covered in a blanket with his arms wrapped around me, and my body acting like a teenager. I woke up in my own bed – well, my bed at Chase's house. I just realized that I didn't hear him say anything about the nightmare to my mom.

"Hey mom."

"Morning, baby. How are you feeling this morning?"

"Very tired. Yesterday sucked, and I didn't sleep well last night; guess I just couldn't turn my brain off. Chase gave me a pain pill before I went to bed, but my head still hurts this morning."

"I'll get you something after your bath. I don't want you falling asleep on me midway through. Now let's clean you up and give you some fresh 'hanging out in' clothes."

"Thanks mom."

30 minutes later, I was clean and in a pair of shorts and nice shirt that covered the uncasted parts of my body quite nicely. The

color of my shirt matched the bruise that was forming on my head -
nice shade of turquoise.

"I left you some more apple cinnamon muffins. Is there
anything else you want?"

"Mom. Thanks."

"You're welcome, baby. Tell Chase to call me if there is
anything you need. Anything."

She kissed me on top of the head and left me sitting on the
couch. It was a nice couch, too. Comfy, actually. Big cushions and
several throw pillows. I'm thinking a girl decorated this house.

"What's her name Chase?"

"Who's name?"

"The girl who decorated this house."

"Why would you think a girl decorated this house?"

"Because no man goes to a furniture store and purchases a
comfy couch, with big cushions, and several throw pillows. Plus,
your spare bedroom is actually a bedroom, with a nice comforter."

"Cami."

"What?"

"Cami. When she and Leland first started dating, they were
over here for dinner one night and she said that she was not coming
back until there was real furniture in the house."

"That sounds like Cami."

"She told me to give her a budget. I cringed, and then I gave her the smallest figure I could think of that would sound reasonable. She laughed. Three days later I came home from work and had a brand-new house. Do you like it?"

"She did well. I like the couch."

"Good thing, since you're probably going to spend a lot of time on it."

"Yeah. About that. Is it ok if Janice comes over so we can work on some case info? I have lots of documentation that I could be working on while I'm sitting here."

"You can have anybody over that you want. Just tell me first so I don't go all Louisville Slugger on them when they come through the door."

"Fair enough. Can you set up my computer, like on a TV tray or something, so I can work?"

"No problem. But you have to be careful how much you try and work. Staring at the computer could make your headache worse, but just give me a few minutes and I'll get a whole office space set up. Is there anything you need from work? I can have Janice go get whatever you need."

"I'll call her. And Chase?"

"Yeah?"

"Thanks for not telling my mom about the nightmare."

"I didn't think she needed anything else to worry about, and you didn't need the stress of listening to her freak out and then spend the day hovering over you."

"Thank you; for all of that."

I think I fell back asleep on that comfy couch. I woke up to the sound of Chase and Janice talking about me, so I hollered at them, "Hey, guys, I can hear you talking about me."

"Go back to sleep Sadey."

"Too bad. I'm awake now. And guess what?"

"You have to pee?"

"How did you know?"

"I'm starting to read you like a book."

"Does that book tell you how long I can wait before I pee all over your comfy couch?"

Huff. "I'm coming."

A short time later I was back on that comfy couch with a workstation all set up around me. I've only known Chase for a few days, but somehow he's taken over the big brother thing; at least that's the vibe I seem to be getting from him. I had paper strung all over the couch and coffee table, a computer set up on a TV tray in front of me and a stack of files sitting on the end table beside me. Aside from the broken leg, broken arm, and nice bruise on my forehead, I definitely had the most comfortable office in the world right now.

Janice and I started going over Deborah's file while Chase fixed us some lunch.

"How did she do when you got her to rehab?"

"She was still pretty shook up from court and her weekend in jail, but she settled in ok. I took her by the house, and we packed her some clothes to take with her, so she'd be a little more comfortable. I told her about Mark yesterday. She started shaking and crying – she pretty well freaked out. I tried to console her and convince her that she was safe at the rehab center, but she kept her door locked. She came out for her sessions, but then she was right back in. I think she'll be ok, but she needs some time to figure out she's strong enough to live without him controlling her. We'll get her straightened out."

"I know. I've just been worried. If he's willing to do all this to me, I can't imagine what he'd do to her if he thought she turned him in. Or to Kasey. I don't think he'd hurt Lacey, but Kasey didn't like him, and he knew it."

"Does Karleen know what's going on?"

"I don't know. I haven't talked to her. I'll call her when she gets off work. Mark was only told that the girls were staying with a relative – he was never told what relative. I don't know if he even knows Karleen or not, but we'd better find out. And quick. If anything happens to those girls..."

"Ladies, chicken salad is served. Sadey, do you want it in there or do you want me to hobble you to the table for a change of scenery?"

"I'll take the change of scenery, please."

"No problem – you know I'm here to serve."

Janice looked at me and said, "Girlfriend, where can I find me a cute little servant like this?"

Chase just laughed. "If you were related to Cami, you'd do whatever she tells you to do. She threatened me with the lack of future generations if I don't take care of Sadey."

"I'll be related to anybody you want me to if it means I get a cute little blonde guy to wait on me hand and foot."

"Maybe you'll be lucky enough to have Mark Kinders run you over too."

"It might be worth it."

"Enough, you two. Somebody just get me off this couch and over to the table with food on it."

"She's so demanding, you know."

"You have no idea," Janice said. "You should work with her all the time."

"Well, unfortunately, even after she's all healed up, I still get that honor. I'm Deborah's PO. So, let's eat and then we can lay out a plan of attack for her."

I spent the rest of the afternoon making phone calls. Elaine was doing better, James got Kara into preschool at the nice pink church down the street, and I set up an appointment for Friday afternoon to interview a couple of idiots who seem to think that neither of them are capable of raising their children. Child custody case – makes me want to slit my wrists – only problem is that one of my wrists seems to be covered with a pretty little cast. Ugh!

I figure that since I somehow have to be in staff meeting on Friday morning anyway, I might as well try and be useful that afternoon. I finished up by calling Karleen and filling her in on the situation. She hadn't seen Mark, but she knew who he was. She wasn't sure what all he knew about her, but she was sure he had no idea where she lived. I told her that Kasey was safe at school, but she needed to show a picture of Mark to the YMCA and let them know so they'll be on alert for Lacey.

"Hey Chase."

"Yeah?"

"Any word from Leland about Mark?"

"Not yet. I'll give him a call and see what he knows though."

"Thanks. I've got a headache again. Why can't I get rid of this headache?"

"It's called a concussion. I'm going to get you some meds and put you in bed for a while. Maybe you've just been doing more than you're supposed to. When are you supposed to see the doctor again?"

"How should I know? You guys took care of all of that for me. Remember?"

"I'll check with Cami. I'm sure she knows. Get some sleep; I'll make some phone calls and see what I can figure out for you."

"Thanks. I keep saying that a lot these days. But thanks."

Thursday, September 27th

"Mom, I don't want to talk about it."

"Fine. You don't have to talk. You can just listen."

"Like I have a choice. You pretty much have me naked, under your complete control right now. Not like I'm going anywhere."

"That's right, smart mouth. Now listen. You can be mad all you want, but he's still your father."

"Doesn't mean I have to see him."

"I thought you weren't going to talk about it."

"Now who's being a smart mouth?" Sometimes my sarcasm gets in the way of common sense, like not talking back to your mother.

"Sadey, he loves you. He's always loved you. I know you're still angry with him, but you two can put this behind you and move on."

"I didn't say I didn't love him. I don't like him. And I don't want to deal with it. Seeing him at the jail was not really in my plan that day. It just sorta happened. I didn't want it to happen, it just did."

"It happened, and you can't take that back, so you might as well move forward. At least go see him again, write him a letter, something Sade. He misses you guys."

"Maybe he should have thought of that when he decided to sell drugs to an undercover cop!"

"You don't need to yell young lady. I'm not the one you're mad at. But I'm your mother, and I know that keeping all this bottled up inside of you isn't good for you. You need to talk about it – isn't that what you tell your clients?"

"I'm not one of my clients!"

"No, but you're struggling with some of the same issues they are. You make them get counseling, so why won't you do something for yourself."

"Mom, I'm not going to see a counselor. Why should I? I don't have the same problems as my clients."

"Ok, fine. But don't just leave him hanging. If you don't want to see him, at least write him a letter telling him how you feel and why you won't come. It's only fair."

"Fair?! Fair?! Why would I care what's fair for him? He didn't care about how fair it was for us when he made promises over and over and over again that he didn't bother to keep. All those vacations we were supposed to take. All those times he was released from jail and swore that he'd never go back. What about that? How was that fair to us? To you? Huh? Tell me that, mom. How's that fair?"

"I think you need to tone down the attitude problem a little, young lady," she said while giving me that mom glare.

Forgetting who I was talking to, I snarkily replied, "I don't have an attitude problem. You have a problem with my attitude and that is not my problem."

She gave a loud huff when she realized I wasn't backing down and said, "I'm not going to spend the morning arguing with you. I love you and so does your dad. Just think about it. He'd really like to see you again, but if not, then please at least send a letter saying why you won't. He at least deserves that from you."

"Actually, he doesn't deserve anything from me. I deserve some stuff from him, though. Like, maybe some lost family vacations, lost holidays, not seeing his children grow up, let alone his grandchildren; should I go on, or is that enough for you? I know you always see the good in him, but that doesn't mean I have to."

"I didn't mean to start an argument with you, Sadey. I'm going over to Noelle's and keep Abi so she can go to a doctor's appointment. I'll be back in the morning, but I don't want to leave here on a sour note. I just saw the sadness in his eyes yesterday when I went to visit; his eyes lit up when he talked about seeing you, and then he was on the brink of tears. He misses you kids, a lot. Just think about it."

On that note, she kissed me on the head and walked out the door. I was trying hard not to get emotional; not to let it show how upset I was, but apparently it wasn't working.

Chase was standing in the doorway, studying me closely. "Do you want to talk about it?"

"Nope."

"Ok. I'll be back here in my office if you need anything." Chase walked down the hallway, and I fell apart.

Why did she have to start in on me this morning? It's not like I'm not dealing with lots of other things - Mark Kinders, broken bones, can't stay in my own house, and I still need to work on my cases. Can't she just leave it alone?

I must have fallen asleep, again. It just keeps happening to me. I'm going to blame it on the pain meds. I woke up to heavy breathing on my face, and just as I opened my eyes, this long, wet tongue seemed to slime my entire face. Next came the paws – first the left, then the right – directly on my chest. Bones was standing on his hind legs staring me straight in the eyes, turning his head from side to side, like he was questioning whether or not I was still alive. I started to say, "Bones get off of me," but the only thing that came out was, "Bo…" At that point his tongue went straight in my mouth. Yuck!

"Do you guys need a moment?"

"Aren't you funny?"

"Well, I try to be." He was doing that lean against the door frame thing again. Blue jeans, t-shirt, no shoes – I was having flashbacks to Saturday night.

Get a grip Sadey. What's wrong with you?

"Why don't you get this dog off of me, and then help me to the bathroom."

"Sometimes I hate it when you wake up – it's like 'eyes open, must pee'."

"Just a regular comedian today. Get me off this couch."

"Yes, your highness. To your throne we go."

Have you ever noticed how your mother knows exactly how to push all of your buttons? That's because she installed them.

Fear factor – take 2. Today's goal was to find Sadey's dog, kill it, and leave it as a present at her front door. Mark figured the gods were on his side when he drove down Sadey's street and immediately spotted a Rottweiler that he was pretty sure belonged to

Sadey, although at this point he really didn't think it mattered much. A dead dog on her porch was still going to scare the crap out of her whether it belonged to her or not. Belonging to her, though, would be icing on the cake.

It only took a couple of Milkbones to have the dog climbing in the car. He was driving Amber's van today since it had limited windows and nobody on Sadey's street would recognize it.

He snapped the dog's neck and put a note around it; it took every muscle in his body to carry that heavy-ass dog up to her porch, but he finally made it and looked around one more time to make sure he wasn't spotted before taking off. He really wanted to stick around to watch the fun, but he wasn't taking any more chances today; right now, the cops had no idea where he was, and he intended to keep it that way.

~~~~~~~~~~~~~~~~~~~~~~~~~~~~~

Chase got me back to the couch, sitting comfortably amid all the pillows, and then he sat down beside me with a serious look on his face.

"What's wrong?"

"I need to talk to you about something. While you were asleep, I talked to Leland. You know he's been having officers driving by your house, just for safe keeping. This morning, they found a dead dog on your front porch with a note around its neck that said, 'you take from me, I take from you'. The dog looked a little like Bones."

I felt like I was going to be sick; I just sat with a stunned look on my face. I couldn't say anything; once again, I was frozen in place. After what seemed like an hour, with tears streaming down my face, I finally managed to say, "Why?"

He didn't say anything. He simply put his arms around me and let me cry. For the second time in two days, poor Chase was dealing with a basket case. I couldn't stop the tears; I was absolutely sobbing.

Why would anybody hurt a dog? He took somebody's dog and killed it – just to send me a message. What kind of sick person would do that? I approached him as a drug dealer; I have so underestimated him. What's next?

"I was going to tell you about it this morning, but after you fought with your mom, I just didn't think it was good to put more on your plate. But I don't want you to think we're hiding anything from you. This is serious; but my job is to keep you safe, and I promise to do just that – you AND Bones. Ok?"

I couldn't even speak. I just nodded my head. I was a complete wreck. I was living in the house of some guy that I didn't even know this time last week; I couldn't even take myself to the bathroom. But yet here he was, willing to do whatever it took to protect me. Some people are lucky to even have that one friend in their lives that would do something like this for them – let alone the 'soon-to-be-brother-in-law' of that best friend.

I finally whispered, "Whose dog was it?"

"He doesn't know yet, but he's trying to find out."

"If it's somebody's pet, I have to buy them a new one, ok?"

"Seriously? There's a sicko out there trying to kill you and you are worried about buying somebody a new dog. You're one of a kind, Sadey."

"I just don't understand."

"Nobody does. By the way, Cami and Leland are coming over for dinner tonight. Are you up for that?"

"Yeah, I guess. What I really need is a Blizzard."

That got a huge laugh from Chase. "I'll be sure to pass that word along."

"Chase? Can I ask you something?"

"Sure, whatever, Sadey."

"Are you sorry you ever met me?"

He started laughing again.

"I was being serious."

"I know. I'm sorry. Do you mean because I've been your bodyguard since the first night we met? No, I'm not sorry I met you. I'm just sorry it had to be like this."

"Me too."

"Let's get you cleaned up. I don't want Cami to see all those tears and think I've been abusing you again."

"Yeah, she just might take away your ability to have kids."

"No kidding. She can be scary."

"You have no idea. I met Cami at school one day after parent/teacher conferences to pick her up for dinner, and I saw her get in the face of one of her students' parents and tell him that if she ever heard him cuss at his daughter again, she would personally ensure that he never had any more kids. She's definitely not scared of anybody. Sometimes I wish I was more like her."

"The world can't handle two of Cami."

"That's probably true. But she's definitely a strong person."

"That she is. Now let's get your face washed and maybe run a brush through your hair before I have to endure that wrath."

With that, Chase actually washed my face, brushed my hair and pulled it into a ponytail. I was thoroughly amazed at this talent.

"Where did you learn to do hair?"

"When I was a teenager, my mom broke both her arms in a car wreck and Leland was too cool to do hair, so it became my job. Whenever he didn't want to do something, he would just claim 'seniority' and I had to do it. Didn't do me any good to argue with him. Maybe I should have been a hairdresser instead of a Probation Officer."

"You don't flame enough for that."

"Yeah," he said laughing, "I guess not."

That's the point when the party began. Cami and Leland came bursting in carrying cheeseburgers, fries, Cokes, and a Dairy Queen ice cream cake.

"Cami, I know you are marrying Leland, but I think I'm in love with you."

"It's just lust; you're actually in love with Dairy Queen. I'll settle for lust, though. How are you feeling?"

"Don't ask. It's not been a good one."

Chase decided to add his two cents worth at this point. "She started the day by arguing with her mom about her dad, then she slept for a long time, then she and Bones were tonguing on the couch, and then she sat and cried because of the dead dog."

"Thanks, Chase. Cami can read my mind, so my simple statement of 'it's not been a good one' was actually more than enough for her."

"Sorry. I opened my mouth and inserted both feet, huh?"

Cami decided to scold him, too. "Chase, that question wasn't for you, it was for Sadey. Now, when I asked how she was feeling, it wasn't so you could give me a play-by-play of the day's events. However, now that we've aired all her dirty laundry…"

I guess Chase didn't think he was in enough trouble, because at this point he added, "Oh, no, there's some of that back there in the hamper that still needs aired out." I Gibbs slapped him.

～～～～～～～～～～

"Bones! No! Wake up Bones!" He's lying there helpless on my front porch. I'm trying to get to him, but my body feels so heavy and I can't seem to drag my leg with any force. I see his tongue hanging out of his mouth, but I can't pull hard enough to get up the steps.

I feel this presence behind me holding on to my shirt. The more I try to drag myself the harder he pulls me back. There is this cackling noise that makes my hair stand up on the back of my neck and I hear the presence say, "You took something from me; I'll take something from you."

"No! Bones! Please don't hurt my dog!"

～～～～～～～～～～

I feel myself being lifted in the air and then curled around Chase. He's sitting with me on his lap again and I can feel his fingers running through my hair.

"You're safe, Sadey; Bones is safe, too."

I could barely focus on his words and my eyes felt so heavy.

"Open your eyes, Sade. Bones is right here with us. Come on, open your eyes."

I'm trying so hard; I barely get them blinking and it takes forever to hold them open and then focus. I felt something heavy holding down my good leg and I realized that it was Bones' head. I could feel Chase let out a big breath of air and realized that he was worried about me opening my eyes.

"Sadey; look at me." He gently put his hand under my chin and lifted my face to look me in the eyes.

"You're safe; Bones is safe. Were you dreaming about the dog on your porch?"

I could barely form the word "Yeah".

"Ok, try to relax; I know this sucks, but I've got you, ok. I will keep you and Bones safe."

He was still running his fingers through my hair and I felt him place a small kiss on the top of my head.

"Go back to sleep."

How am I going to go back to sleep? He just kissed the top of my head and my entire body just set off a four-alarm fire. Holy crap! And those muscles holding me? Wrapped up in his arms might be worth having a nightmare every night! Good grief, Sadey. Get a grip. He's just worried about you, is all.

It seemed to take me forever to truly relax and go back to sleep. I woke up in my own bed again and almost felt disappointed until I shook the stupidness out of my head and came to my senses.

When your mother asks, "Do you want a piece of advice?" it is a mere formality. It doesn't matter if you answer 'yes' or 'no' — you're going to get it anyway.

Old-lady scooter

Friday, September 28th

Friday mornings = staff meeting, and promptly at 8:00 a.m. Since I'm not dead, I was expected to be there – and getting there was proving to be more difficult than I intended. Bath time with mom was very early, because Chase said it was going to take a while to get me ready, and into the building in time for staff meeting. I hate to admit that he was right.

Mom and I decided to argue over what clothes I was going to wear to work this morning; arguments I used to have with her when I was seven, and thought I knew that pink polka dots and pink stripes should go together because they were both pink. Seemed logical to me at the time. However, mom just wasn't understanding that dress clothes and casts don't work well together.

I actually had to settle for a broomstick skirt – I hate dresses! However, if I am required to be dressed in my Sunday best, broomstick skirts are the only choice. At least they were flowy (I think I made that word up), and they weren't confining. I could still manage to sit in unladylike positions and not appear to be unladylike.

Mom did my clothes and hair; I did my make-up, one-handed. Shoes consisted of flip-flop like sandals I could slide on and off my noncasted foot without assistance. That process took a lot longer that I would have liked. Now I was completely exhausted and hadn't even started my day yet. Chase was standing in the doorway waiting patiently for me to finish this lengthy process.

"Are you ready for your first day back at work?"

"I guess we'll see. I'm already so tired; just getting ready has completely worn me out."

"How's your head?"

"I still have a mild headache, but it's not throbbing, so I think I'll be ok."

"Are you sure? I can call your boss if you'd like?"

"Remember how scary Cami can be when she's mad?"

"Yeah."

"So, multiply that by 10 and that's the wrath of my boss if you miss staff meeting. I'm not dead; therefore, I must attend. That's pretty much the way it works. On the bright side, there are always donuts."

"Well, ok. If you're sure. I had a wheelchair in the outbuilding that I put in the back of the Blazer for you. I expect that you will use it all day – no excuses. You can't get up and down and move around on your own, so you need to use the chair. It's nice and fancy and has the little knob on it that drives you around."

"So, it's basically an old-lady scooter, not a wheelchair?"

"Well…" I gave him that glare that he knew said I meant business. "Ok, fine. You win. It belonged to my grandmother. I wasn't sure it still worked, but I hooked up the battery and it started right up. It's better than me having to push you around your office all day, because you couldn't use a regular wheelchair with a cast on your arm. So, get over yourself, stop worrying about what you'll look like driving around your office in a scooter, and start thinking about all the people you can run over this morning."

"It's still embarrassing."

"More embarrassing than having two casts on your body and a greenish color bruise on your forehead?" He needed Gibbs slapped, but I was too tired to lift my arm to his head.

"I pretty much covered up the cast on my leg with my skirt, just for the record. But, ok, you're right. This is just really hard to deal with, you know. I hate relying on other people for anything."

"I know, so I'm not going to give you that speech about sucking it up because you're in a situation you have no control over. Your OCD is just going to have to deal with it. And if we don't get going, you're going to be late and I don't want to deal with anybody's wrath."

"You mean, besides mine?"

"I'm getting pretty used to dealing with your wrath. You're just a tiny pussycat in a world of lions. Now, stop arguing and let's go. I hope I got all your stuff."

The ride to the DHHR office was fairly uneventful. Getting me into the building was a whole other ballgame, though. Mark was still on the loose, despite Leland's best efforts. I felt like a prisoner being led through the back door.

Chase pulled around to the back side of the office where there's a door that's not used often, but opens up to my floor, luckily. He was met at the door by Matt and Jason, two of my colleagues. They got the scooter out of the Blazer, while Chase did his best to get me out of the car without embarrassing me too much. I was surrounded by three over-protective men.

I got comfortable in the scooter while being hovered over by my bodyguards. I managed to figure out the controls pretty easily and got myself in the door. Matt and Jason were on either side of me, and Chase was following right behind, carrying all my stuff. Poor guy. They got me to my office, and I noticed that my regular chair was gone and my office was cleaned and organized. Apparently, Chase had contacted my boss and had everything worked out. I couldn't ask for a better caretaker; too bad he's not marrying material.

Chase set up my computer and got all my files organized on my desk for me. My boss poked her head in the door, looked at me in my new scooter surrounded by my bodyguards, and just said, "I brought an extra box of doughnuts, and there's a large cup of chocolate milk sitting at your spot as well. I figured it would be a rough day."

Matt said, "I can't believe she expected you to be here today."

"She's not dead," Jason replied as he was laughing.

"I'm feeling like death warmed over; does that count?"

"Nope. Gotta be six feet under to miss a staff meeting. Hand me the files you want to take to the meeting. I don't want you trying to do two things at once. I might get run over," Jason added.

Chase kept giving Matt funny looks the whole time we were getting me situated. Finally, before he left, he looked at Matt and said, "Are you Matt Harper, WVU point guard?"

Matt gave him a funny look and said, "Yeah; I played all four years of college. Should I know you?"

Chase started laughing as he said, "I know you pretty well. March 17th, my junior year, blew out my knee from that foul you took me out with."

Matt got a horrified look on his face and then cringed as he said, "Marshall? '05?"

"Yep; that was me."

"Oh, my God! I'm sorry. That was a ruthless game."

"It definitely was."

"If it makes you feel any better, I came out of it with a jacked-up shoulder myself."

Chase laughed as he said, "Ok, maybe a little better. Just take care of Sadey, will ya?"

"No problem." So, Chase and Matt played basketball together in college; interesting. Matt was a solid 6'2" himself, but he looked long and lanky compared to Chase's solid, muscular frame. Matt and I met in college, where he was on a full ride for basketball.

Chase looked at me and said, "Looks like your bodyguards here will take care of you today. Better get to that staff meeting before Count Grouchula starts yelling."

"Thanks, Chase."

"No problem. Now let me see you work that scooter down the hallway."

As I rolled out of my office and rounded the corner, I heard Chase say to Matt and Jason, "Mark is still out there somewhere. She is not to leave this building under any circumstances, understand? Also, you personally check each of her clients as they come through the door. You have a picture; you know what he looks like. I'm not taking any chances. Got it?"

"We got it," they said in unison.

I stopped my new ride and turned around just as the three of them were coming around the corner. "You know I don't need bodyguards in here, right? This building is secure. Stop being the overprotective dad and go to work. You have clients to torment as well."

"Sadey, you know I like you, but I'm not going to argue with you about this. You don't leave this building without me. Period. End of discussion. Order lunch, torment your own clients, make phone calls, do paperwork, whatever you can do from inside this building. But you are not leaving here unless you are in the front seat of my car. Comprende? Now have a good first day back to work."

"What if I'd rather be in the back seat of the car?" My smart-ass side was coming out.

"Then you have to be naked." Well, then.

On that note, he rounded the corner and out the door he went. I had to pick my chin up off the floor and take both feet out of my mouth. Matt and Jason were bent over laughing. I headed into staff meeting and noticed once again that my regular chair at the conference table was missing and there was plenty of room for me to manage the scooter in there. There was also a large cup of chocolate milk sitting in my spot and the extra box of donuts, which just happened to be a combination of glazed and glazed covered with chocolate, were sitting right in front of me. This might just be a good day after all.

Let the bitch-session begin.

I'm on sale today ~ if you buy one sarcastic comment, you get another one free of charge.

An hour and a half later, I was back at my desk working and the phones were ringing off the hook today.

"This is Sadey."

"Good morning. My name is Shayna Reynolds, and I was contacted by the Big Brother/Big Sister program that you needed a Big Sister for a 10-year-old girl."

"Yes. Shayna, thanks. Do you have time to talk? I could give you a little background."

I hung up feeling a little better. I didn't get any new cases in staff meeting – probably since I can't drive to go do some investigations – and then Kasey got set up with the Big Sister program. My day was looking up.

I've realized that, while donuts are great while you're eating them, they don't last long in the system. It didn't take long for me to be extremely hungry. So, since my office is in a central location, I just decided to yell. "Is anybody hungry? I'm going to order food." It only took a second before my office was surrounded by hungry social workers. The consensus was pizza – always a good choice. A half hour later, I was devouring pizza and chugging a large Coke. Now maybe I can concentrate on work the rest of the afternoon.

I was able to kick out two custody disputes and catch up on all my documentation. Shayna stopped by to get the paperwork on Kasey and I liked her immediately. I think this will be a great experience for Kasey. Hopefully she can learn to be a kid again.

Chase showed up right on time. My bodyguards took me out the back door and loaded me into the Blazer. We were driving home comparing tortuous things we enjoy doing to clients, when I saw a familiar object flash in the side mirror. I immediately started shaking and tears were filling my eyes.

"What is it Sadey? What's wrong?"

"Mark. It's Mark. Look behind us." I couldn't stop shaking. "He's following us. He had to be waiting for me at the office."

"Calm down. You're safe in my car." He was talking and dialing at the same time. "Leland. I found Mark – he's following us. He must have been waiting at the DHHR and watching Sadey."

Chase told Leland where we were and then we decided to drive towards my house. Mark already knew where I lived, but he didn't know where Chase lived, and we didn't need to give him another target. As we passed the Dairy Queen, Chase looked over at me and started laughing. "I bet you'd really like to stop for a Blizzard right now, huh?"

"You think?" My sarcasm started flowing freely. So did my tears.

Chase reached over and put his hand on my knee. "Sadey, you're safe. He screwed up by following us – Leland will have him behind bars tonight." That touch – wow! How can I be terrified and my body tingling at the same time?

We headed to my house, slowly. I guess Chase was giving Leland time to get to us. It worked. We pulled into my driveway, with Mark right behind us, and Leland right behind him. Mark had us blocked in and Leland blocked him in. It only took a minute for Leland to pull him out of his car and slap on the handcuffs – and none too nicely, I might add. It didn't take long for Mark to be placed in the backseat of Leland's car, still swearing his revenge on me. I should have immediately calmed down and been relieved, but for some reason I couldn't stop shaking.

Got her! It didn't take long for Mark to find out that Sadey's new babysitter was indeed the brother of the cop that arrested him; well, he's actually the Sheriff, but semantics. He waited patiently in the back corner of the DHHR parking lot, until he finally saw the babysitter and two other guys loading Sadey in the car at the back door of the building; interesting.

He stayed a reasonable distance behind them, following them from the DHHR towards the direction of Sadey's house. For some reason, they were taking a longer route to get there, and he suspected that he might have been spotted; but they showed no signs of actually noticing him behind them. As they pulled into Sadey's driveway he very quickly boxed them in, but neither of them made a move to get out of the car. That's when he realized that the gig was up.

~~~~~~~~~~~~~~~~~~~~~~~~~~~~~~

Halfway through dinner Leland, Cami, and Chase were all still arguing about me.

"I don't know why she can't stay in her own house," Cami said.

"Cami, she still can't take care of herself," Leland replied.

"You guys do realize that I'm still in the room, right?" I tried to add, but nobody was listening to me or even admitting that I was sitting right beside them. So, I just kept picking at the French fries and trying to figure out what was really going on in my life.

This time last week I was living a normal life, in my own home, driving my own car.

This time last week I didn't have a cast on my arm and my leg.

This time last week the biggest problem I had in my life was trying to decide what to do about my relationship with my dad – of course this is still a big problem in my life that's been coupled with a few more problems.

This time last week I didn't even know Chase existed, let alone be living under his roof while he took care of me.

"Are we sure that Mark can't bond out?" I heard Chase ask.

"I will make the recommendation of no bail based on the fact that he assaulted a state employee and he's a flight risk, but, no, I can't guarantee it."

"Then she stays with me until we can guarantee it."

Cami jumped in. "Maybe we should actually consider asking Sadey what she wants since she's a grown adult and she's sitting right in front of us."

"Fine," Leland snapped, "Sadey, what do you want to do?"

I just kept staring into space. What do I say? Yes, I want to stay in my own house. No, I still don't feel safe. "Is there a happy medium?"

"What do you mean?" Cami asked.

"I mean…I don't know what I mean."

"You mean that you're still scared but you want to stay in your own house?"

"At what point will you stop reading my mind, Cami?"

"At the point that one of us dies. Sadey, it's ok to speak up. Everybody just wants you safe, that's all."

"I know. I just…This is my home, you know. I don't even feel safe in my own home. My grandmother's home. This was always the place I went when my life at home was in chaos; now it's my home and it's become my place of chaos. I don't want to leave here, but I'm scared to stay."

Cami scooted her chair right beside me and wrapped her arms around me. I was trying hard not to cry, again, but it wasn't working for me. As the tears streamed down my face, all I could say was, "Sorry. I'm a basket case and all you guys are trying to do is help, and all I can do is cry. Sorry."

"Don't be sorry," Chase said. "None of this is your fault. It is what it is, and we just have to figure out how to deal with it."

"We? It shouldn't be 'we'. It should be me. I don't want to have to rely on everybody else for help. I should be able to help myself, you know. Not to mention I've put all of you and my family in danger. That's not fair!"

"No, it's not," Cami replied. "But Chase is right; it is what it is, and now we just have to sort it all out and find the best way to fight it, ok."

"Yeah. Ok. But Mark's in jail for the weekend, right?"

"He won't go before the judge until Monday morning," Leland responded.

"So why can't I stay here this weekend? At least I should be safe for the weekend, right?"

"Ok, but somebody stays with you. You still can't walk by yourself and at least we can keep you from injuring yourself any further." Chase was laughing as he obviously made fun of me.

"Great; round-the-clock babysitters – my favorite thing. Now, if only I could get some cute guy to make me dinner and do my laundry, I'd be set." That got everybody laughing.

"So, I guess that makes me chopped liver, huh?" Chase asked. "See if I ever wash your sweatpants again."

"Queen of Sarcasm. Right here. You can't have the job, so you might as well stop trying. Now, who gets to take me to bed tonight?"

Cami jumped in quickly. "I hope you mean, 'who gets to put you in bed', 'cause I don't want to picture anything else in my head right now."

"Spoiled sport."

And so began my weekend.

Today I feel like lighting someone's face on fire and trying to put out the fire with a fork...or a machete. Yeah, definitely a machete!

The Replacements

Saturday, September 29th

I woke up Saturday morning to a cold, wet nose nudging my arm. I was hoping it was just the first nudge, because if I'd slept through the first nudge then there would soon be a 90 lb. dog straddling me and a tongue bath would soon ensue. I quickly yelled, "I don't know who is babysitting me this morning, but Bones is nudging me and he needs out."

I heard a familiar voice say, "I got it. Bones. Come on, boy."

Chase. He obviously has no life if he's willing to just keep taking care of mine.

"Morning, sunshine."

"You obviously have no life, huh?"

"Why do you say that?"

"Well, let's see. You are willing to take care of a handicapped girl, with two casts, slept on hair, no make-up, morning breath, with a 90lb. dog that has a deadly tongue. So, either you have no life, or I'm just pure entertainment."

"You forgot the most important part of taking care of you?"

"What's that?"

"Being able to quickly respond to 'eyes open, must pee'."

I couldn't help but laugh. "You think you're so funny, don't you?"

"I'm thinking about quitting my day job and going into stand-up comedy. Whaddaya think?"

"I'm pretty sure you shouldn't quit your day job. Now, about that gotta pee thing."

"Yeah, yeah. I know the routine."

It wasn't long before I was lounging on the couch munching on a chocolate pop-tart. Of course, I still had that bed-head hair, but at least the morning breath thing and the big dog thing were taken care of – oh yeah, and the peeing thing. I was just sharing the last piece of my pop-tart with Bones when the doorbell rang.

"Why is somebody ringing my doorbell?"

"I locked it out of habit. Don't get up – I've got it." Chase thinks he's just downright hilarious these days. "Well, my replacements are here."

"Replacements?" Just as soon as I asked the question, I had the answer. Through the door walked my sister, Noelle, and following her was my little-big-brother, Trey.

Trey Brayden Collins. My big little brother. 20 years old, 6'1" and a name that means 'Third born' and 'brave'. (My mom had a thing with names meaning something). He's had to be brave over the years; he was the brunt of most of my father's abuse. Dad never thought Trey was manly enough. He played the trumpet in the band, instead of being a star quarterback, like my dad thought all 'men' should do. I guess he thought he could beat the 'manly' into him.

My mom stepped in more than once and even pressed charges against dad once after a bad beating that left Trey bruised up with a broken arm. Dad spent a year in jail for that episode. Trey's in college now at WVU majoring in Music Education, and a member of the marching band. He's a good kid – turned out well in spite of my dad.

"Trey! What are you doing here?"

"I heard a rumor that I could torture the crap out of you and there was no way for you to fight back, so I jumped right on that."

"Funny guy, huh? Who told you that? Chase?"

"Um, well…"

"Traitor; you haven't known me long enough to gang up on me with my little brother!" He just gave me this cute smirk.

I looked back at Trey and said, "Seriously, what are you doing here?"

"Came home for the weekend and thought we could have a sibling day – Phase 10 and pizza."

"That sounds like a great idea. As long as you don't cheat."

"I never cheat. You're the one who cheats."

"Well, this sounds like a lot of fun. You kids have a good time. I'll be back in time for the next shift." At that, Chase left.

I haven't seen Trey in over a month, since school started. "So, how's the college life treating you?"

"It's cool. We're in the midst of football season so it's extremely busy. I love playing in the Marching Band, but I'm exhausted by the time the season is over. We had a bye week, so it gave me a much-needed weekend off. It's been pretty cool observing in some of the high school band classes around the area, though. There's some really cool band instructors out there and I can't wait to have that job myself!"

"I'm sure you'll make a great one. So, what else have you been up to?"

"Not much. You up for a game of Phase 10?"

"Yep. But I'm a little confused?"

"About what?"

"I have some broken bones, and yes, a mild concussion, but my powers of deduction are still working well."

"Sadey, you're talking in circles. Are you sure it was just a mild concussion?" I was going to attempt an eye roll, but then decided against it since it gives me a headache. So I just went with a direct approach.

"I'm sure. So, here it is. The last time both you and Noelle were in my house together it was to defend mom's decision to stay with dad after his last arrest. So…what are you two here for? Did mom send you?"

First, they just stared at me, then they looked at each other, trying to figure out who was going to be responsible for telling me the truth and enduring my wrath. "Speak up. One of you. Mom sent you, right?"

"Sadey, look…" It was Noelle that spoke up first. "Mom just doesn't understand why you're so angry and she…"

"Wants you to convince me that dad is still a great man and I should go see him again in jail?"

"Well, yeah, but…" Noelle tried to continue, but I think the evil glare I was giving sort of stopped her mid-sentence. Bones was now at my side with his chin resting on my leg, giving me that sideways look that was questioning whether or not I was ok. I reached down and started petting him to reassure him that I was fine, and he didn't need to move into protect mode. He settled onto the floor with a big flop and proceeded to sleep through the remainder of the argument.

"I've had this argument with mom already, but I wasn't expecting to have to defend myself to you guys as well. Why is it that he's the one that committed the crime and is sitting in jail, and I'm the one everybody is mad at?"

"Nobody's mad at you Sade," Trey replied. "But you know what it's like when mom gets something in her head, and right now you are her little project."

"I don't want to be anybody's project. I'm a grown adult and I can make my own choices. Why is everybody trying to make those choices for me?"

"Don't shoot the messengers. Mom just works so hard at keeping her 'perfect little family' together and right now you're not playing the game by her rules."

"Why should I play by her rules, Noelle? Why does she get to make the rules?"

"Because she's the mom, that's why. At least, that's what I always tell Blake and Abi when they argue with me." That got a small chuckle out of me. It's seems to be the standard 'mom' line – 'because I said so'. There was just no answer for that argument and you just did what you were told just because she said so. Seems like a stupid reason to a 27-year-old, but it worked when I was eight.

"You guys can't honestly tell me that you want to go see dad in jail. Neither of you have gone, right?" They both shook their heads 'no'. "So, then, why is everybody on my case?"

"Because mom already made us feel guilty, and our job was to pass that guilt onto you."

"Thanks, Trey. You guys are such pals."

"Sadey," Noelle piped in, "I know that this case you're working on…"

"Don't patronize me, Noelle."

"I'm not. I swear. But you tend to wear your heart on your sleeve, even when you don't want to. It's what makes you, you. I know you're angry with dad; we all are. But I also know that deep down you really love him. Besides, mom is going to drive us all crazy until we go visit."

"I did visit – not on purpose, but still…"

"So, then, how bad can it be to go visit again?" Trey asked.

"Have either of you ever been to a jail, ever? No, you haven't. So, you have no idea what it's like to go through all those metal doors, to be searched like you're the one who's committed the crime. The cameras watch your every move, because obviously if you're there to visit a criminal then you must be just as bad as them, right? It sucks!"

"Wow! Are you really angry with dad, or angry with the system and how it makes you feel, Sadey?"

"Look, Noelle, we can't all be as perfect as you, ok. I don't have a perfect marriage, with perfect kids, living in a perfect little house. I just can't pretend we had that perfect childhood. Apparently the two of you have some sort of memory lapse, because all I remember was years and years of dad making promises of trips and vacations, and us constantly being let down because he loved the drugs more than he loved us!" Now I was crying, but so was Noelle. "Oh, man. Noelle. I'm sorry; I didn't mean it. I was just mad, and…"

"No Sadey, you're right. Not that I have a perfect world, because it's far from perfect, but I guess I'm just better at suppressing the bad memories. I've worked so hard to make sure my kids are never disappointed; probably to make up for all those years that we were disappointed. I want them to have a better childhood than I did. But you know that mom has spent our entire lives trying to pretend that things were great when we all knew that they weren't. You can't fault her for just wanting some peace and harmony in the family."

"No, but I can fault dad. It's his fault! He's the one that cared more about the drugs than he did us. Good grief, Trey, he broke your bones. You obviously haven't forgotten that, right?"

"Sadey, we haven't forgotten anything. My childhood wasn't any better than yours when it came to dad. I was never good enough for him, you know. But I'm an adult now. We all are, and he's still our dad; no matter what his faults. And let's be honest, we've never been told the whole story when it comes to his problems; only what mom wants us to know. Wouldn't you like the opportunity to interrogate him? I know I would. Why not band together; us Collins' are a force to be reckoned with when we want to be – mom definitely instilled that in us."

"Ok, Trey. You've got me there. I wouldn't mind getting some real answers. Not the watered down 'mom answers'."

"So, we do it together. What's the worst that can happen? It sucks and we all get drunk afterwards? I could use a beer."

"Um, little brother, you're not old enough to drink beer, and I'm totally not getting arrested for contributing to the delinquency of a minor. It would be my luck that Leland would walk in the minute I handed you a bottle."

"Well, you can't blame a brother for trying, can ya?"

"So, mom wins, again. Doesn't mean I have to be happy about it, though. Keep in mind that I intend to bitch, moan, and whine the entire drive there."

"And that would be new and different how?"

"Easy little brother. I can smack you upside the head with my cast and put a nice bruise on your forehead too."

"Um, yeah, like you can catch me. I'm pretty sure I'm safe. So, Noelle, what's the plan?"

"Why are you asking me?"

"Because you're the big sister, so that makes you the one in charge."

"Thanks guys. Well, might as well get it over with tomorrow, then. I can schedule a visit for mid-afternoon, and you can head back to school after we're done," she said to Trey.

"So, it's a plan. Now, how long are you guys on duty today?" I asked chuckling.

"I'm just short-term; told Dane I'd be home for dinner."

"What about you Trey? Are you joining me for dinner, or do you have plans as well?"

"No plans – besides you. And I'd say we are ordering out for dinner because I'm not a great chef and I'm not allowed to leave you alone."

"Seriously! Whose rules are those? Cami? Leland? Chase?"

"Um, well…"

"Let me guess; all of the above?"

"Yeah, but don't tell, ok? Cami still scares me. Do you remember the time I undressed all her Barbies and 'washed' all their clothes in the toilet?"

Now I'm laughing so hard my sides are hurting. "I'd totally forgotten about that."

"Yeah, well, that sweet little best friend you had there gave me a swirly and threatened me with a wedgie. I had absolutely no doubt that she'd follow through with that threat and she still scares me. So, how about a pinky promise that you won't tell her I told you?"

"Too funny, little brother, but I can't do that pinky promise. I'll save your butt as much as I can, but keep in mind that she's been reading my mind for 27 years, so you may not be safe even with that pinky swear."

"I know; she's kind of like mom. She has ESP or something. And they're both pretty scary."

I spent the rest of the evening getting my butt kicked at Scrabble. Trey definitely got smarter in his college years; either that or I got dumber. Then we channel surfed until we came across "Heartbreak Ridge"; you can't go wrong with Clint Eastwood. But I think I fell asleep halfway through the movie, because I was jolted away by a couple of voices talking about me.

"I think Sadey's still ticked about it, but we're going tomorrow afternoon. I'll be here about 2:00 to get her, if that's ok," I heard Trey say.

"I assume your mom's coming by in the morning to get her ready?" I heard Chase ask.

"As far as I know. She fell asleep while we were watching the movie, so I just left her on the couch. If you're lucky, she'll sleep all night."

"If I'm lucky?"

"Yeah, she'll probably be a little irritable because she thinks that Noelle and I ganged up on her. Hopefully she'll be a tad more understanding tomorrow, but I'm not counting on it."

I really wanted to yell at Trey and remind him that he and Noelle did gang up on me, but I also wanted to hear what else they had to say about me, so I kept pretending to sleep. Only problem was, I had to pee, so I couldn't eavesdrop for too much longer.

"I don't know the whole story, but I do know this case she's working on is getting the best of her. And having this guy, Mark, after her hasn't done much to help her work through whatever's eating her. But she's actually doing pretty well, all things considered."

"Look, Chase, I don't know you at all, but mom is pretty appreciative of everything you've done for Sadey, so I guess that makes you somebody we can trust."

"Thanks, I think. Funny thing is that I've only known Sadey for a week, but I kind of like your sister. She reminds me a lot of Cami, probably since they share a brain, but she's a strong person. I don't have any other responsibilities, no other family besides Leland, so it's not a problem for me to help her out. Besides, I think Bones likes me better, but I can't tell Sadey because she'd accuse me of bribing him with food."

Ok, that's the final straw – I'm kicking both of their butts. Bones doesn't like anybody better than me, and nobody is going to bribe him for his love! I decided that I can get off this couch all by myself. I sat up just fine, then used my good hand to try and push myself up to a standing position. I felt like a baby deer, trying to stand up for the first time. I was wobbling back and forth on the edge of my casted foot, like one of those weeble-wobble wooden thingamajigs. I tried to fall backwards so that I'd land back on the couch, but that didn't work out for me. Instead, my weight shifted, I wobbled to the right, and I hit the floor with a very loud thud. Although I was hoping that the thud I heard was simply in my head and not a real noise, my hope was immediately dashed when Chase and Trey came running into the living room and dropped down to my side.

"Are you ok?" Trey asked.

"What the heck were you trying to do, Sadey?" Chase chided. "Don't tell me you were going to try and get to the bathroom on your own?"

"Um, yeah, well, I thought maybe I could…"

"Don't let her bright green eyes and batting eyelashes cloud your thinking, Chase. I'd bet my brand-new trumpet that she heard us talking and thought she was going to come in here and give us a piece of her mind. Am I right Sade?"

I just huffed. Why am I so easy to read? I've definitely got to find a poker face!

"How about if you guys just get me off this floor. I have to pee and now I have a headache again."

Chase looked at Trey and said, "She has this problem; every time she opens her eyes she immediately has to pee. Even if she just peed 15 minutes ago. I've even tried to dehydrate her and it doesn't do any good."

Now they were both laughing at me, which just ticked me off more.

"Get me off this floor! And stop talking about me like I'm not even in the room. I'm injured, not stupid. I could hear you boys talking about me."

I turned my anger towards Trey. "You and Noelle did gang up on me."

Then I focused on Chase. "And Bones still likes me better!"

I'm pretty sure I sounded completely stupid saying that, but I had to get in the last word.

They were still laughing at me while they got me off the floor, and then Trey gave me a hug and told me he'd be here at 2:00 tomorrow to get me; no excuses, my butt was going with him to visit dad. Chase led me to the bathroom and waited patiently for me to finish. He led me back to the couch, sat down on the other end and just stared in my direction.

"What?" I was still mad at him for conspiring with my brother. He wasn't fazed by my attitude; he just sat staring at me.

"Do you want to talk about it? I'm an objective third party."

"No, I don't want to talk about it! Why does everybody think I should talk about it? Just because he's my dad doesn't mean I can't be mad at him. All he ever did was break promises to me. I promise we'll go on vacation this summer, Sadey. I promise this Christmas will be different, Sadey. I promise I won't do drugs anymore, Sadey. I promise I'm clean, Sadey. Yeah, right! Promises, promises! But he never kept a single one of them! Yet, I'm supposed to just be all happy and pretend nothing ever happened. Just go to the jail and chat with him like we're old friends hanging out at the park. But we're not old friends – I don't even know him. He's spent as much time in jail as he did out of jail. But mom always defended him! Why did she do that? She never once just said, 'yeah, he's an SOB'. She always told us how much daddy loved us and how much he missed us, but he didn't miss us enough to stop getting in trouble. Why didn't he miss me enough to stay out of jail? Did he just not love me enough? Why not? I was a good kid; most of the time. Grandma always told me I was a good kid. She loved me; she even left me this house. But the only thing he ever left me was broken promises! So, why should I talk about it?!"

Chase just sat there and let me spew. Tears were streaming down my face, my head was pounding, and I was absolutely exhausted. He scooted over on the couch, put his arms around me, and just let me cry. He never said a word.

What the heck did I just do? I just poured my heart out to somebody I barely know. Good thing he's not the marrying kind, because I'm sure he thinks I'm a complete nutcase by now. I'm just sitting here crying and feeling sorry for myself. This is ridiculous. I'm a grown woman and I'm acting like a small child. Get a grip, Sadey!

"I'm sorry. I didn't mean to just go off on you. You've done so much for me in the past several days and all I've been is a pain in the hind end."

Again, he didn't say anything. He just sat there and let me cry on his shoulder, literally.

"Say something. Tell me I'm a nutcase. Tell me I'm being stupid. Tell me something, for crying out loud!"

"Do you feel better that you got that off your chest?"

"That's all you've got to say? You're not going to tell me how ridiculous I'm being?"

"No. You're not being ridiculous. Everybody has feelings. Feelings aren't right or wrong, Sadey; feelings just are. My third-grade teacher told me that. You can't help how you feel about something; you can only control what you do with those feelings. You're tired and you've had another emotional day. Why don't you just get some sleep, and you can start fresh tomorrow."

"My mom used to say the same thing about feelings. But don't you ever get mad about anything? You never get frazzled or upset or act like a basket case. Why not?"

"We can't both be crazy – one of us has to keep our sanity at all times. Right now, it's your turn for the nutcase act. I'll get some revenge on you at some point."

"Ha ha ha. You're right. I need some sleep, and some Tylenol; my head is pounding. Not to mention my face is swollen again from all this crying."

"Do you want some pajamas?"

"Yeah, but I don't have to have them. I don't want to put you in a weird position. I think I can get dressed on my own. Sort of. Can't hurt to try anyway."

"If you say so."

Chase got me to the bedroom and handed me a tank top and shorts. He turned and walked out of the room, like a perfect gentleman. I totally need to find me a man like this.

I got out of my shirt just fine and managed to get the tank top over my head, only getting my cast stuck on it a couple of times. Unfortunately, the shorts were a different ballgame. I sat down in the chair to keep from losing my balance and started pulling my sweatpants off my legs, even doing that kick your legs wildly thing that you do sitting on the side of a pool. It wasn't working. I tried to lean over and pull the sweats over the cast, but they were stuck, and I couldn't bend my leg to make it work. Dang cast! Seriously, my cast was caught in my sweatpants and I couldn't get them off, and I couldn't pull them back on either.

So, here I was sitting on the edge of a chair, in my underwear, with my sweatpants stuck halfway down my legs. Now what? I can't yell for Chase; I'm sitting here half-naked. Ok, so I'll just sit here all night. Mom will be here in the morning to help me bathe; she's going to dress me anyway. Not a great plan, but it's the only thing I could think of at the moment. So, I just sat there.

Apparently, Chase began to get worried. "Sadey? Are you ok?"

"Uh, um, well, yeah, sure. I'm fine."

"You don't sound fine. Are you having trouble getting dressed?"

"Well…"

"Do you have clothes on?"

"Some of them."

"Oh, man."

"It's ok. I'll just sit here. Mom will be here in the morning to give me a bath, and I can just get dressed then."

"Tell me you're not serious."

"Sure, I'll be fine."

"Sadey. Did anybody ever tell you what a pain in the butt you can be?"

"Yeah, all the time."

"Ok, well at least it's not new news. I'm coming in to help. Don't get all modest on me either. You can't sit in that chair, half-dressed, all night. Ok?"

"Like I have a choice."

He opened the door, slowly, like I might attack or something. He looked at me for a second, and then doubled over laughing.

"Stop laughing at me. Either help me or don't, but don't laugh at me, jerk-face."

"Sorry. You just look so helpless."

"Well, what did you expect to see? I'm not exactly Miss America right now, walking across the stage with perfect hair and makeup, in an evening gown, on 2-inch heels."

"I'm not even going to respond to that for fear of you knocking me upside the head with that cast on your arm. Now let's get you dressed."

Again, he was a perfect gentleman. Got the sweatpants unhooked from my cast and put my pajama shorts on me without even copping a feel. I don't know how I feel about that. Am I not good enough to cop a feel? Or is he really just that much of a gentleman? Wait; is he…No, never mind. I'm just seeing things that aren't really there; right? I mean, it's possible that he has the same feelings for me…Ugh!

No sense in dwelling on the stupid stuff. Time for bed. Tomorrow is going to suck soon enough; might as well try and get a little bit of sleep while I can.

Today's forecast: Mostly grumpy with a 60% chance of grouchy. High of mean/Low of nasty. A temper tantrum warning is in effect. Take immediate shelter!

The visit

Sunday, September 30th

I woke up to a pounding in my head; the kind that makes you have a heartbeat in your eyes. I've never wished a day to go away like today. I just want to get this over with; done; finished; kaput. Maybe I can go back to sleep, and when I wake up, it will be tomorrow. Sounds like a great idea to me. Only one problem – I already opened my eyes, and that can only mean one thing...

"Who's in charge of me this morning?"

"Unfortunately, it's me," Cami answered. "I suppose you need to go pee, huh?"

"Good guess. How did you get stuck with the morning shift?"

"It's Sunday – your mom went to church and none of the boys were willing to bathe you."

"Wow – that's a self-esteem killer right there."

"Well, let's see. Trey is your brother – ick. Leland is my fiancé – hands off. Chase is available, but he said getting you undressed and redressed for bed last night made you feel awkward enough that you probably didn't want him to see you completely naked. Therefore, it's me that gets the honor."

"I'm sorry Chase had to do that. I suppose he was falling on the floor laughing when he told you the story, huh?"

"Well, something like that. Except that he did feel bad for you because you felt kind of helpless; but he still found it somewhat funny. Now, I don't want to have to change your sheets as well as give you a bath, so let's get you to the bathroom and just get all this stuff over with at once. I hear I'm supposed to dress you in something besides sweatpants since you have a visitation appointment this afternoon."

"Don't remind me. Why did I agree to this anyway? I really don't want to go see my dad, even with Trey and Noelle."

"It's called guilt. Your mom's the master, remember? Just think, you don't actually have to talk to him. You have Trey and Noelle there, so let them talk. All you really have to do is sit there and look pitiful."

"I guess. I still don't want to go. Not to mention, I had a complete breakdown on poor Chase last night. I kind of feel sorry for the guy. I mean, he sorta got thrown into this situation; hadn't even know me for two days and all of the sudden he became my bodyguard and caretaker. Not really fair to him, you know."

"He doesn't mind, Sadey. Really. It's actually giving him something to do besides hang out at my house with Leland. Before you decided to go and tick off the drug dealer, he spent most of his time very absorbed in his work; he tormented the crap out of his clients. Don't get me wrong; he's good at his job and he has a big heart, like Leland. He actually cares for the people on probation, but he does make them walk the straight and narrow."

"He's taking good care of me and he's never judgmental. He let me have a complete breakdown last night and he didn't say a word. He just sat there and let me scream and cry. What kind of man does that? Shouldn't he at least tell me I'm being unreasonable, or to suck it up, or something? It's just weird, I guess."

"That is strange. Leland probably would have told me to get over myself, or something. But look on the bright side, he's not trying to play psychologist or anything. Is it too weird for you? I mean, we can work out other arrangements if you don't want him here. He wouldn't take offense to it; neither would Leland. He told me you've had a couple of nightmares."

"Yeah, but he calmed me down; and he didn't tell my mother, so he won brownie points for that one."

That made her laugh.

"Cami, can I ask you a question?"

"You just did."

"Ok, smarty pants. Is it weird that I don't mind having him around? I mean, I know he's not really marrying material or anything; but he makes me feel safe, ya know."

"It's not weird at all. And who says he's not marrying material?"

"Um, you did, remember? At your house – the cookout, like a week ago. I was apparently drooling the first time I saw him, and you made fun of me and then proceeded to tell me how much alike we were. That we'd eat each other alive, I think were your exact words. It's not like I'm looking for marrying material – you and mom are always looking for me some marrying material. I'm just saying – I don't feel weird around him or having him doing all this stuff for me. He'd actually make a good nurse."

"Well, I'm glad because his schedule's a lot more flexible than the rest of us, with the exception of your mom, and I have this fear that you two would kill each other if she moved in here with you."

"Yep! I love her to death, but death may be the end result if I'm secluded with her for too long."

"I'm going to fill you in on something, but you didn't hear any of this from me, ok."

"Sure. I love a good secret."

"Well, I'm not sure how good it is, but it's about Chase and Leland."

Now she had my full attention.

"When the boys were younger - while they were in school - their dad got drunk and beat the crap out of their mom, resulting in two broken arms. He then drove his car over a guardrail, down a big embankment, and died on impact. Nobody was sure whether he did it on purpose or he was just so drunk... The boys were told that their mom was in the car with him and jumped out before the car went over the hillside, and that's how her arms got broken. They had seen enough of the abuse to think the story wasn't true, but still young enough to not question the adults."

"Whoa. Wow. He fixed my hair the other day and told me he learned a good ponytail by fixing his mom's hair when she had a broken arm, but he didn't tell me any of that. No wonder he's so understanding."

"It's also why the boys went into law enforcement. Leland was going to put every drunk behind bars and Chase was going to clean up all those drunks so they never hurt anybody. Says a lot about their character, huh?"

"You know that when I had those nightmares, he just picked me up and carried me into the living room and then sat with me on his lap until I fell asleep. The weird part is that it didn't even make me uncomfortable to be sitting there."

"And?"

"And what?"

"And there's more to that story, so tell me what's on your mind."

Ugh! "Ok, well, the last nightmare he was running his fingers through my hair and then he kissed me on top of the head and told me to go to sleep."

She was looking at me with a crooked smile on her face and waited patiently for me to continue.

I rambled quickly. "That kiss and his fingers in my hair and those muscles I was wrapped in just sent like this major zing down through my body. Cami, I've dated guys for months and never felt that zing. I'm pretty sure I'm losing my mind. What the hell is wrong with me?"

"Well, we don't have time for that psychological exam…"

"Ha ha ha."

"And nothing is wrong with you; it's called being turned on. I realize that's a little new for you given your not-so-fabulous choice of men in the past, but…"

"Ok, fair enough, but still. I mean, I had just had a major nightmare; how the hell could I be turned on after that? I can only hope he didn't notice."

Now Cami was laughing hysterically.

"What?"

"He doesn't miss much. But, like I said before, if you're uncomfortable…"

"No, I'm not uncomfortable. I just need to get my head out of the gutter."

"Yeah? Let me know how that works out for you."

Chat time with Cami was way too short. I almost forgot to tell her about Shayna and the Big Sister program for Kasey. Then, right in the middle of one of those laugh until you pee yourself stories, Trey came through the door and ruined the moment. Any other time I would have been happy to see my little brother, but today he was here to deliver me into the depths of hell; for that, I didn't feel so welcoming.

Thanks to Cami, I was cleaned up, my hair was braided, and I was dressed in some loose-fitting capris that hopefully wouldn't get stuck on my cast when I got undressed this evening. Trey told me that Chase had let him borrow the regular wheelchair, not the slow-moving scooter, so that he could easily get me in and out of the jail, but that way I couldn't run away. But, still, I figure the corrections officers are going to have a ball trying to search me today. That thought brought a smile to my face and at least gave me a small chuckle.

The drive to the regional jail seemed to take longer than usual. I don't know if it was because I was dreading this trip so much, or because Trey spent the entire time trying to convince me that it wouldn't be as bad as I was making it out to be. I kept reminding him that I was just here a week ago and it wasn't a bowl of cherries then. He kept telling me to suck it up and get over it; that I was acting like a whining baby. I not so kindly reminded him that we were in an enclosed vehicle and I could easily put some bruises across his face with my new cast.

"Sadey, you can't stay angry your whole life. At some point, you just have to move on, you know, just let bygones be bygones."

"I can be angry for as long as I want! It's a woman's prerogative."

"You're not hurting anybody but yourself. You're the one holding a grudge and you're the one that's going to end up with ulcers. Why not just let it all out, lay it all on the table, and then just leave it there."

"Easier said than done, Trey."

We pulled into the parking lot and Noelle was already there waiting for us. Getting me into the wheelchair was a lot of fun, but I had to admit that I was learning to balance myself a little better, especially since my shoulder was feeling better; unfortunately, not better enough to let me try and use one crutch. Probably by the time I get it mastered they might actually remove the casts. Wishful thinking.

I was totally right about the searching thing. The officers had a ball with me; they were trying to figure out if I was hiding anything in the casts. Just about the time I was ready to say 'screw it' and turn around and leave, they finally gave up with interrogating me and let us through to the visitation room. I still jumped every time I heard those metal doors bang; this place gives me the creeps. Not to mention, I always feel like I'm being undressed with eyeballs in orange uniforms. Thank goodness Noelle was here today; she was looking great and I was just looking helpless.

Dad was already in the visitation room waiting for us. His eyes lit up, and then filled with tears, as we all came through the door. I will admit that I hate seeing him like this; he looks like he's aged 10 years since I saw him last week. It was obvious that he hadn't shaved in several days and his eyes seemed puffy, like he hadn't had much sleep either.

"I can't believe all of you came! You have no idea how lonely this place can be. Sadey, baby, are you ok? Please tell me you're ok. I swear I can find out which pod that guy is in and I can make sure he's taken care of, if you know what I mean."

"Dad, seriously, I'll live, and the last thing you need is to give these people a reason to keep you in here any longer."

"You're right, as usual; but I wouldn't mind knowing the SOB's name." He gave me a sly smile, but then it changed quickly as he said, "I didn't think you'd come back; you were so…well, when you left last week, I just wasn't sure…"

Noelle, the peacekeeper, stepped in so I wouldn't lose my cool on dad. "Dad, don't instigate her, please. Mom did the whole guilt trip thing to get us all here at the same time. Nobody wants to be here; we'd rather be hanging out at the house together, not hanging out here."

"I'm sorry. Really. I'm just so thankful that you guys are here. You have no idea. So, can we catch up some? How's college? How're the babies? How long do you have to keep the casts on?"

"Ok, dad. One of us at a time," Trey said. "College is great. We're in the middle of football season so I'm extremely busy with the band. I've been observing in some band classes at high schools around the college and I really like it." Trey's face just beams when he talks about band stuff – it's obvious he loves music.

"You'll make a great band director. I'm really proud of you, of all of you. I saw you on TV last year, during a football game. We were watching the half-time show and I saw you marching. The other guys thought I was a little nuts to cry during a football game, but I saw you, and you know, I just..."

"Yeah, dad, I know."

I thought Trey and dad were both going to start crying. Geesh, this is not turning out how I had planned. My goal was to come in here, chew him out, be ticked off the whole time, and storm out the door. Basically, I wanted to hate him, and I wanted to make sure he knew how mad I was at him. But, for some reason, that's not how the day went. Noelle got out pictures of Blake and Abi and then showed dad her latest ultrasound. This brought tears to his eyes, again. Good grief; I'm a sap.

I started actually feeling sorry for my dad; that wasn't in my plan. He started asking me about the casts, and who was helping me out, and I just started talking. Started talking like we were all sitting in the recliners at home, waiting on dinner to be ready, just like old times. We were catching up like old friends that hadn't seen each other in a while. Dad even asked about Bones, and he's never even met my dog.

Visits are limited to 45 minutes, so it really didn't take long for our time to be up. We all gave dad a hug, and I briefly registered Trey whispering something in his ear before we headed out the door. This time I was placed in Noelle's car, since Trey was leaving from there to go back to college. I was not looking forward to being confined with my sister in a car, especially when I wasn't the one driving and I couldn't control the speed. We weren't even out of the parking lot before she started in.

"See, that wasn't so bad. You know that dad loves us, right?"

"Don't start on me, Noelle. I know he loves us, and I don't want to discuss it with you."

"I'm not starting on you, Sade. But, for some reason, this is more difficult for you than for the rest of us. But you have to admit, this went better than you expected."

"Yeah, it did. That doesn't make it any easier for me to deal with, ok. Just lay off! I'll deal with it in my own time; not with you guys telling me how to deal with it. I just don't understand why it doesn't bother you that dad is sitting in jail, again."

"It does matter. It does. But I try to look at it from a parent's point of view; something you can't do."

"Oh, great. This is going to be one of those speeches about how you're better than me because you're a mom and I still haven't found the right man, let alone have children, right? I don't need your crap, Noelle. I am perfectly happy with my life, and not being a mom doesn't make me a bad person."

"I didn't say that. Geez, you're emotional today. I'm not putting you down, Sadey. I can just see things from a different perspective, ok. As a mom, I know that there will be times that I disappoint my kids and vice versa, but I won't love them any less, you know. I think that's how I deal with dad. Yes, I've been disappointed, we all have. But that doesn't make me love him any less; it actually makes me feel sorry for him."

"Feel sorry for him? Are you kidding me? It's his own fault that he's sitting in that jail cell. He made those choices, not us. And I'm not disappointed in him; I'm just plain ticked off, ok. I just hope that when I do have kids, that I won't ever let them down, won't ever make promises that I don't keep."

"What is it with you and the broken promises thing? Get over it. So we didn't take vacations; big deal. You can take vacations now anytime that you want."

"It's not just about the vacations, Noelle. It's about the fact that he constantly promised us family outings that never happened; they never happened because the drugs were more important than our family. So, no, I'm not going to just get over it. I don't want to argue with you all the way home; it's been a stressful day."

"You're right. I'm sorry. I just want some peace in the family."

"I'd like nothing more than to have a normal holiday, with everybody sitting around drinking eggnog and telling stories; unfortunately, that's just not the case with our family. Dad has made sure of that."

"Ok. Fine. Subject change. Let's talk about that adorable hunk of meat that's been taking care of you."

"Seriously?"

"Ok, come on, Sade. You can't tell me that you haven't considered him a fine piece of man candy?"

"Ok, I'll admit that he's pretty cute, and he always smells great, but it's not like he's marrying material, so what difference does it make?"

"Really? You've lost your ever-lovin' mind, little sister. If he was taking care of me, I'd definitely be taking every chance I could to get a peek at that fine body. Just sayin'..."

"Well, obviously he doesn't like what he sees in me because he had to help me get dressed last night and he didn't even cop a feel. So..."

"All that means is that he's a real gentleman. I would have used the opportunity to at least wrap my arms around him to keep from falling, especially with those bulging muscles."

At that I just doubled over laughing. This is my prim-and-proper sister telling me how she would feel up a guy. Not bad advice, just a little weird. Until I had my nightmares, I hadn't actually drooled over him since the first time I saw him walk out of Cami's back door. Now that image just popped into my head and I was having visions that would cause my mother to smack me upside the head.

"Ok. New subject."

"Again? I was kind of enjoying this subject, and the way that you're blushing over there sis…"

"I am not blushing."

"Yes, you are. Admit it Sadey; he's adorable."

"Ok, yeah, he's adorable. But don't you think it's a little strange that he just jumped right in and took care of me like he's known me forever?"

"Not if he's anything like Leland. Think about it, Sade. Leland may be a cop, but he's a cop with a heart. If Chase has a heart anything like Leland's then it wouldn't even occur to him that he shouldn't just take care of you. You're Cami's best friend; that's good enough for him. At least that's the vibe I'm getting from him."

I told her about the nightmares, in confidence, threatening to kill her if our mother found out. Then I described the kiss and my body zing, and she was smiling from ear-to-ear as she said, "See, told you so."

"Ok, let's just talk food. That's one subject I'm comfortable talking about. I'm starving."

"Apparently the Davis brothers are in charge of dinner tonight, because I was instructed to drop you at Cami's house; I guess they're grilling out."

"Awesome. Is it wrong of me to hope they are putting steaks on that grill?"

"Nope. Is it wrong of me to hope they are doing it without shirts?"

"Good grief, Noelle. What happened to my prim-and-proper sister? You're turning into me; that can't be a good thing."

"I'm married..."

"And pregnant."

"That too, but I'm not dead. I can still notice the finer things in life."

"Well, let's notice those finer things a little quicker. You're driving like an old mom in a minivan."

"Maybe that's because I am an old mom in a minivan."

Fifteen minutes later we pulled into Cami's driveway; Leland and Chase both came around the house to help unload me. I felt like

I was some kind of cargo – always being loaded and unloaded. I can't wait to at least get this cast off my leg.

"Who's watching the grill?"

"We are," Chase said as he was laughing.

"Great. I guess that means that my dinner is going to be burnt."

"No smartass. I haven't even put the steaks on the grill yet."

"Then stop wasting time getting me unloaded, because I'm starving."

"Man, you're awfully demanding for a girl that is relying on me to safely get her to the backyard, where the food is located."

"Safely? So, what's the danger here? Your cooking?

"Now who's being the smartass?"

"I'm allowed – Queen of Sarcasm, remember?"

"Well, maybe the Queen needs dethroned."

"You think you're so funny, don't you?"

"Sometimes. I don't think the wheelchair will be a good idea; the grass is still damp from yesterday's rain. Just climb on my back."

"You're kidding, right? I'll break your back. Not to mention I can't hold on very well with a cast on my arm."

"You're a buck ten soaking wet, so shut up and hang on."

I got myself on his back and wrapped my arms around his neck, reminding him that if he tries to drop me I can smack him upside the head with my cast. He just laughed at me and then pretended he was going to drop me. I started to kick him with my casted leg, but then he wrapped his arms around my legs tightly so I couldn't move. So, here I am, hanging off Chase's back, trying not to drool, and trying to keep my body in check for fear of that zing happening again. I looked back at Noelle and said, "Is this what you were talking about?"

Noelle started laughing so hard she was snorting. Chase was obviously confused but wanted in on the secret. No chance!

"Someone want to fill me in?"

"Nope!" Noelle and I answered at the same time.

My sister was right about one thing; I was starting to think about him without this t-shirt on. Not only did he smell good, but the muscles that rippled across his arms while he was holding onto my legs – yum. This is all Noelle's fault. Not sure whether I should Gibbs slap her or thank her. That thought made me chuckle.

"What's so funny back there?"

"Um, nothing."

"Yeah, right. You girls evidently have something going on that you're not going to inform me about, huh?"

"Well, maybe it's about you."

"Ah, so you've been talking about me? So, is it my charming personality or my amazing good looks?"

"Um, well…" Now I just made myself look like a complete idiot. Way to go Sadey.

"Hold onto my neck, tight. I don't want to drop you when I set you down."

"My pleasure."

I thought that I said that in my head, but obviously I said it out loud because Chase started laughing. Ugh – I'm a serious dork. Did I really just say 'my pleasure' to Chase? That settles it; Noelle is getting Gibbs slapped.

Chase set me down on the picnic table and headed for the grill. He put the steaks on the grill, and they sizzled; just like in the charcoal commercials. Cami came out the door with fried potatoes and hot rolls, but the only thing going through my mind was that I'm a dork. Ugh! Time to shake it off and get back to the subject at hand: food.

"I hope you made a lot of those, because I'm starving!"

"I used an entire bag of potatoes. Those boys over there are bottomless pits. I guarantee you that there won't be a single potato left in this dish, or a single hot roll, or even a small bite of steak. It's a good thing Bones isn't here; I couldn't afford to feed these two AND a dog!"

"Hey," I yelled over to Chase. "Are you going to get those steaks done anytime soon, or are you going to let me starve to death?"

"I don't know yet. How about you share that secret with me, and then maybe I'll consider feeding you."

"Fat chance, bucko."

"What secret?" Cami asked.

"I'll tell you later. Promise."

"Must be juicy." That made for an interesting evening. I glanced up from my steak just long enough to see Chase looking at me with this stupid smirk on his face, like he already knew the secret and wanted me to know that he knew. I blushed. Cami laughed. She knows me way too well; this is going to be a really long night!

Everything you do is based on the choices you make. It's not your parents, your past relationships, your job, the economy, the weather, an argument or your age that is to blame. You, and only you, are responsible for every decision and choice you make – and the consequences that come with those choices.

Nothing but a gentleman

Monday, October 1st

The day started out great. My boss told me only 2 days a week in the office until I was better, so I chose Wednesday and Friday. Since today was Monday, it meant no alarm clock. Yay me!

I was obviously exhausted because when I opened my eyes the clock said 10:17. There was no Bones nudging me, or slobbering on me, so obviously whoever was babysitting me this morning had already taken him out. Scary. I slept through it all.

I was just about to yell when Bones bounced through the door and took a flying leap on the bed. One of his very large paws landed square on my ankle, the already broken one. He commenced to licking my face up and down, dripping drool into my eyes and ears. I was screaming in pain; Bones just abruptly stopped and started giving me that sideways stare that either meant "Are you ok?" or "You better get moving before I decide to lick you again." I was hoping he was showing concern because if his tongue got a second chance, I was doomed.

"I'm sorry. I tried to stop him, but he's bigger than me."

Chase. And, of course, I was crying again. "Are you ok? Oh, man, what happened. I'm so sorry."

"It's not your fault," I said between sobs. "He's used to waking me up with kisses. He just stepped on my ankle."

"Oh my gosh. Let me see."

He came running to the bed, doing his best to push Bones off of me. He yanked the covers off me to check my ankle, obviously not giving a thought to what might be under the covers – or what might not be – like pajama bottoms. I vaguely remember getting hot in the middle of the night and doing that wild kicking thing to get them off; they happened to be lying on the floor at the moment. He very quickly covered me back up and turned about three shades of red.

"Um, sorry, I just assumed…"

"Yeah, it's ok. Cami actually dressed me before bed, but I got hot and managed to get them off. I didn't really think about who would be getting me up this morning. It's my fault."

He was absolutely embarrassed, and it was totally my fault. Geez. Now what? This is the second time he's seen me in my underwear.

"Sorry. This is the second time you've had to, well, kind of dress me. I know you didn't sign up for that part of the job."

"Well, at least it's a good view."

Now I was the one with the red face.

"Can you wait until later for a bath? Your mom called and she sounded horrible; said she didn't want to breathe on you and risk you getting sick. I can get Cami to come over after school if you want."

"How about if we just let me pee right now?"

"Oops. I forgot that your eyes are open."

"One of these days, when I can take care of myself, I'm totally getting back at you for trying to take over my job as Queen of Sarcasm."

"Yep. I'm sure you will. But for right now, I guess we better take care of your current needs before I'm forced to give you a bath."

"Forced? Really? I guess that would be the last thing you'd want to do, huh? See me naked? I wouldn't want to inconvenience you in any way. Why are you taking care of me anyway? You feel sorry for me? Is that it? Are you trying to fix me like you tried to fix your mom?"

He just stood there with a complete look of shock on his face. What the hell is wrong with me?! He probably hates me right now. He was joking with me and I totally went off the deep end. I absolutely win 'idiot of the year award'.

"Oh, man. I'm such a jerk. I didn't mean that, I just…I just wish I could take care of myself. I wasn't trying to…"

He didn't say anything. He just helped me out of the bed and led me to the bathroom. I just sat there and cried. Why am I so stupid? This guy barely knows me, and he's done so much for me and I was just so mean to him. Get it together, Sadey.

"Chase?"

"Yeah?"

"Are you still here?"

"Yes. Where else would I be?"

"I don't know. A thousand miles away from me. I'm sorry. I wouldn't blame you if you walked out the door and just left me. I didn't mean to be so mean. I'm sorry."

"It's ok. Are you ready?"

"Yeah."

He got me out of the bathroom and back to the chair in my room. He had some sweats and a t-shirt on the end table. He didn't say a word; just put the sweats on me, took off my pajama top, replaced it with the t-shirt, and proceeded to take me to the kitchen table.

"Say something, please. Anything. I'm sorry. I shouldn't have said that; any of it. You've been nothing but a gentleman to me and I've been such an ass."

"Sadey. I need to be honest with you. I guess I owe you that much."

"Owe me? Chase, I'm the one that owes you. You've put your life on hold to take care of me, somebody you barely know, and I've been nothing but a pain in your ass. I'm either bitching or crying, or both. I'm really sorry."

"It's fine. I swear. I actually haven't minded a bit taking care of you. You've given me some entertainment in my life." I'm not sure if that was a good thing or not. "I guess Cami told you about my parents and my wonderful childhood; I guess we have a little more in common than we'd like, huh?"

"Maybe why we're so absorbed in our jobs trying to the save the world?"

"That's kind of how I justify the hours I work. I'm trying to make everybody else's lives better than mine was. My mom died when I was 17, Leland had just turned 19. He took care of both of us. He had a scholarship at Marshall, but he stayed here in town for the first year just to get me through everything and then he went to Marshall when I went. He's an awesome big brother. But I have to admit that I was very jealous when he started dating Cami. Don't get me wrong; Cami is a wonderful person and if I had to pick out a wife for him, she's perfect. It's just that…"

"She replaced you."

"Yeah, I guess. That sounds horrible of me, doesn't it?"

"Not at all. He's the only family you have, and she kind of stole him from you. Not necessarily in a bad way – just different; now you just have to share him. I felt like that a little bit when Leland came along too; especially since my dating choices have always been so pathetic, and here Cami lands herself this dream of a guy, you know…"

"Yeah; I get that. I just threw myself more into my job; I was working 24/7, torturing the crap out of my clients. I spent more time at their homes than I did my own. When all this happened with you, it was like a nice distraction, you know. I don't mean that it was great that Mark ran over you, but you gave me something else to focus on."

"Glad I could distract you, and apparently entertain you at the same time."

"Queen. I get it."

"Now you're learning. I really am sorry that I said all that stuff. I've put you in a weird position at times, and you've never even blinked. Just did what you had to do to help me, and I've been a head case the entire time. I'm just not a good patient. I've been taking care of myself for so long that it's strange to have to rely on somebody else, not to mention sharing my house. I'm used to just walking around in a t-shirt and underwear, or whatever I feel like wearing, mostly with bad hair and no make-up. It's just been an adjustment."

"Well, for the record, it wouldn't bother me if you wanted to continue running around in a t-shirt and underwear; I'm fond of the view."

I'm pretty sure I just turned a few shades of red thinking about him thinking about me in my underwear. Then he quickly ruined the moment.

"Unfortunately, you're going to have to do that in my house instead of yours."

"Why? What's wrong?"

"Mark made bail. The judge set his bond at $75,000 cash only since it was a felony threat, but he apparently had that much cash because he's currently on his way back to the jail to be released. I guess the drug selling business is pretty profitable."

I think I had the deer in headlights look again. I was just stunned. How did this happen?

"Why me? What did I ever do to deserve this?"

"Nothing, Sadey. This isn't your fault. You just happened across a real live wire this time. An explosive one, at that. He has a court date set for the end of next week. We can only hope for the best. But, until then, my house is the safest place for you. I'm sorry."

"Me too. Now I'm totally invading your privacy."

"It's fine. Really. It's actually nice to have some company, and Bones doesn't seem to mind."

"Probably because you have a lot more woods for him to wander through. Not to mention, you do spoil him rotten."

"I gotta stay on his good side; I'm pretty sure he could get the best of me. We'll make this work; it'll be fine, you'll see. Now, let's get you packed and get out of here."

It didn't take long to throw my crap in a suitcase. Chase took it all out to the car and came back in to get me. We turned off everything, locked up and headed out the door, following Bones; he was already heading to the Blazer and had jumped in the back seat.

As we headed across the porch, that loose board that needs fixed jumped right up and tripped me again. I was already putting all my weight on Chase, and even though I tried to regain my balance, I immediately did my famous weeble-wobble act. Unfortunately, I never regained my footing, and I caused Chase to lose his. I went backwards, feet straight in the air, landing on my butt and falling onto my back; Chase followed, went down hard on his knee and elbow, and then landed on top of me.

We were nose to nose. I didn't know whether to laugh or cry, so I did both. Now my tailbone hurt on top of my leg, arm and head. Chase lifted his weight off of me, leaned on the elbow that he hadn't landed on, wiped some tears from my face, and said, "Please tell me you didn't break anything else."

I started laughing hysterically. Bones came bouncing back out of the car to make sure we were ok. He was staring at us, turning his head back and forth, looking at each of us with those brown hound-dog eyes, and proceeded to give each of us a face full of doggy kisses. This brought Chase to his feet immediately, using his arm to wipe the drool off his face.

"This weekend, the porch gets fixed. I'll provide the labor; you provide the beer and pizza."

"Deal. Now get me off this porch, please."

This has definitely been a traumatic morning. I was ready for a nap and I'm sure I haven't been up all that long.

We took the long way to Chase's house; going by way of McDonald's since I hadn't eaten yet today. Plus, Chase said he wasn't taking any chances of Mark finding his house, so we turned a 10-minute drive into a 30-minute tour of the town. Of course, Bones didn't seem to mind. He had his head hung out of the window the entire trip, his long tongue leaving a trail of drool flying in the wind. That had to suck for the people behind us. His favorite part of the car ride was the trip through the McDonald's drive thru. Chase got Bones his own box of chicken nuggets and some large fries.

"Are you sure he doesn't need an apple pie to go with it?" I asked sarcastically.

"You're right; he might." And then he ordered two apple pies; one for him and one for Bones.

"Seriously?"

"He's hungry. Nobody ate breakfast so he didn't get to mooch."

"I'm starting to think you love the dog more than me."

"Well, bathroom duty is a lot easier with him."

"Ha ha ha."

We finally got to Chase's house, after we drove around the entire city. He got my stuff set up in the spare bedroom and even put together a makeshift desk for me; he set up my computer and created a workspace. I even had a TV; the only thing I was missing was my own bathroom!

I tried to work on some documentation, but my mind just kept wondering back to Mark. I finally decided to make some calls and check up on some clients, hoping to put my focus on something else.

Janice was first on my list. "Hey, girlfriend! How ya feelin'? When are ya gonna invite me over again so I can stare at that fine piece of meat you have waiting on you hand and foot?"

"Seriously? You too? Noelle said the same thing yesterday, and then I was having thoughts and images in my head that probably shouldn't be there. You two are going to get me in trouble."

"Well, I hope it's a good kind of trouble. But I assume you didn't call me to brag about the fact that you're currently living with a 6 foot, blonde-haired cutie, right?"

"Ugh. No, as a matter of fact, I called to check up on Deborah. Is she doing ok?"

"For the most part. She's going through treatment just fine; she's even participating in the group sessions. Her only hang-up is Mark. This guy really seems to have a hold on her emotionally for some reason."

"He's back out on the streets again, too; as of this morning. Apparently, the drug business is extremely profitable for him because he posted a $75,000 cash bond."

"You're kiddin'? Wow, Sadey, we are totally in the wrong profession."

"At least our professions are legal."

"Well, there is that. Physically, though, Deborah is fine. She's secure in our building; no way for Mark to get to her. What about the girls? Are they ok?"

"Yeah, Kasey was supposed to go bowling this weekend with her Big Sister, Shayna. I'm going to call her later to see how that went. Karleen is on my list of calls as well. I need to go visit the girls at her house, but this body cast thing is holding me up a little."

"If you're lucky, that little cutie you're living with will help hold you up."

"Janice."

"Yeah?"

"I mean this in the most loving of ways, but you need to get laid." She was laughing so hard I'm sure she was snorting.

"Are you offering that little cutie to me or telling me to go pick one of my own out."

"I'd say option #2 is your best bet. My cutie is busy taking care of me. Now, can we get back to the business at hand, please?"

"Sure, change the subject, just when it's getting good."

I hung up with Janice feeling a little better about Deborah, but this day is going by so slowly, it's ridiculous. Only 1:30. Can't call Karleen, she's on the air. Can't call Shayna, she's observing in Cami's room. Can't call Cami, she's teaching.

I leaned back on the couch, with intentions of just chilling for a little while before I could make those phone calls. I woke up two hours later; Bones was stretched out on the couch with his head in my lap, and he was snoring. Snoring like a human! Uh oh – eyes open. Ok, maybe I can do this on my own. It's not fair for Chase to have to jump every time I need something; I've got to start trying to do things on my own.

Here goes nothing.

Slowly lift Bones' very large head off my lap; that was a workout. Lean left; use my good arm. Good leg on the floor; push off with good hand. Stand slowly, leaning on the arm of the couch with my good hand. Weeble-wobble; balance. I can do this. Really, I can. Ok, put casted foot on the floor and balance. Slowly, slowly. Ok, just hold onto the table – take one step. Weeble-wobble again. Balance. Ok, nothing to hold onto. Now what?

I heard laughing; it could have only come from one person. I look up and he's standing in the doorway of the hall, leaning against the wall, with a big smirk on his face. Damn, that smirk is hot!

"Thought you could do this on your own, huh?"

"I'm not doing too bad."

"True. But now what? You're standing in the middle of the living room with nothing to hold onto."

"I hadn't gotten that far. I was just trying to convince myself that I didn't need help to do everything."

"Yeah? And how's that going for you?"

"Well…"

"Let's get you to the bathroom before you injure yourself further."

"Good idea."

This sucks! I shouldn't have to rely on everybody to take care of myself. I can't wait 'til these casts come off. 18 more days until my doctor's appointment! Maybe, just maybe!

"So, is Janice coming over? She's great for my self-esteem."

"Your self-esteem doesn't need any help. It's just fine."

"Yeah, well, still…"

"I need to call Karleen and check on the girls. Do you think sometime this week we can somehow go over to her house? I really need to do another face-to-face with the girls."

"We can work it out. No problem. Let's just hope she doesn't have a lot of stairs. They tend to kick our butts."

"No kidding. Maybe after work on Wednesday? Since we'll already be out."

"Whatever. My schedule is flexible. Just set it up and we'll get you there."

"Thanks."

"Is Karleen cute?"

"What? Seriously? You're as bad as Janice?"

"Whaaatttt? I was just wondering."

"Good grief. Between you and Janice… Obviously you need to get laid, too."

"Are you offering?" Damn smirk!

"For real?! I'm going to call Karleen before this conversation takes a very bad turn."

"And here I thought it was just getting good."

"Out! Go fix me some dinner, or something!"

"Yes, your highness."

He still had a stupid smirk on his face when he left the living room; that smirk was getting to me. Now my heart was beating fast, and my cheeks were warm. The zing was back. What the heck is going on here? Time to focus on work!

I called Karleen and set up a visit at her house for Wednesday at 4:30.

Next call – Cami.

"Hey, give me the low-down on Kasey. Is she doing any better?"

"Hi, Cami. How are you? How was your day at school today? Really, Sade. You need a better introduction."

"Ok, smarty-pants. How was your day at school today?"

"It was great. Thanks for asking."

"Now that we've gotten the small talk out of the way…"

"Yeah, yeah, yeah. Kasey's doing great. She came in this morning and started talking about going bowling over the weekend. She would've talked all morning, so I told her to go in the library and write it all out into a story, with illustrations. She thought that was a great idea and she worked on it all morning. She was so excited!"

"Yay! Awesome! I can't wait to talk to her Wednesday. I just really want this family to succeed, you know? They need something good in their lives."

"And you're out to save the world; I know Sadey. You're on a mission. I'm just glad that there's a chance your mission is going to be successful."

"Thanks."

"On another note…I hear you're back to living with Chase again."

"Yeah, as of this morning. Apparently, the drug business is lucrative these days."

"Yeah, I know Sade. I'm sorry this is happening to you. But I promise you're in good hands. At least he can cook. You'll probably gain 20 pounds while you're staying there."

"That's just what I need. I can't afford for my sweatpants to get tight. He's in the kitchen right now fixing dinner – it smells good, whatever it is."

"That's one thing these Davis boys are good at – cooking. Well, there's something else that my Davis boy is good at, but I don't know about yours."

"You think you're funny, huh?"

"Sometimes. But seriously, he'll keep you safe. Oh, I heard that your mom is sick; would you like a bath tonight?"

"Yes, please, if you don't mind. I'm doing better at sort of cleaning myself up, but I can't do a real bath because of my arm."

"No problem. I'll be over after dinner."

It's not what you accomplish in life, but what you overcome that proves who you truly are.

Longest Day Ever

Wednesday, October 3rd

This has been the longest day ever at work. My butt feels completely numb, this scooter thing really sucks, and I'm tired of being on the phone and typing all day. It's definitely not as comfortable as lounging around on Chase's couch. I made arrangements to visit with Kasey and Lacey at Karleen's house at 4:30. It's only 2:00 and I'm pretty sure I'm not going to last another 2 ½ hours sitting in this scooter, staring at these very bland walls. I've decided that when I'm back to work full-time I'm definitely decorating; maybe some pictures of my niece and nephew on the wall. Anything but these blah and boring walls; they seem to be closing in around me today. Just about the time I was ready to find the nearest sharp object and gauge out my eyeballs, Matt popped his head around the corner and asked, "Are you going to survive the rest of the day?"

"Nope, I'm thinking of gauging my eyeballs out."

"Please don't. You'd just bleed on your desk, and then the boss would make me clean it up."

"I could really use a Blizzard about now."

"Please allow me to make your day, then." In his hand he held a large Chocolate Extreme Blizzard – with whipped cream! I wanted to kiss him.

"For real? Oh my gosh, I just want to kiss you."

"Man, I'd love to take the credit for this; unfortunately for me, Chase was the one who just dropped it off for you."

"I think I'm starting to fall in love with that man."

"You're really in love with the Blizzard, but I'd be happy to pass that message on to Chase."

"Don't you dare! It was just a figure of speech."

Matt wasn't buying any of it. "A Freudian slip? Yeah, right. I can see it in your eyes when he's around."

I stuck a large spoonful of that amazing Blizzard in my mouth, and then started in on Matt.

"What is it with you people? Just because he's drop dead gorgeous doesn't mean I like the guy. He's just jumped in and took care of me; for that I'm eternally grateful. But it's not like I'm going to marry him or anything."

"Ok, well, I'm going to go write that on my calendar so that one day I can prove you wrong."

"Ha, ha, ha. So, I can't believe I never knew that you and Chase played basketball together?"

"We didn't play together; apparently we played against one another. That was my sophomore year at WVU. It was a brutal game; I'd totally forgotten about that foul. It wasn't completely intentional; I mean, I didn't intend to hurt him, just to foul him. They took him out of the game, but nobody ever told me that I ended his basketball career. I feel really bad about that; he was really good."

"He doesn't seem to be holding any kind of grudge against you, so I'd say you're safe."

Just as I stuck another spoonful of Blizzard in my mouth, my phone rang again. Matt started laughing, and I was groaning as I picked up the receiver. "Hello. This is Sadey."

"Sadey – did you like the present I left you?"

I dropped the spoon on my desk; my hands started shaking, and I could feel my heart start beating out of my chest. Matt knew immediately that something was wrong and yelled for Jason. I mustered up enough air in my lungs to respond, "Why me? Why are you doing this to me?"

Matt gave Jason the quiet signal and hit the speaker button on my phone. I was absolutely scared to death. How did he know I was at work today? Why can't he just let it all go?

"Like I said before; you took something from me, so I took something from you."

"The dog? That was mean and childish. You've got a fight on your hands." At this point, there were tears forming in my eyes. I had a visual picture in my mind of that dog lying dead on my porch; somebody's pet. I had to stay strong; I couldn't let him know how scared I really was. Take a deep breath, Sadey; he can sense your fear.

He was laughing at me; more like cackling. It was the most evil laugh I had ever heard; just like in my nightmares.

"Just exactly how do you think you can fight me when you can't even walk? Do you really think a little piece of paper is going to keep me away from you? I owe you. You cost me $75,000; for that you'll have to pay."

My office seemed to spring to life, but silently. I've never seen men move like this without making a single noise. Matt was signaling me to keep him talking; obviously Jason ran to make sure the phones were taping. I'm sure somebody was calling Leland, but I didn't know how long I could keep this up without losing it. Tears were streaming down my face, but I had to be careful not to sound like I was crying.

"I didn't cost you that money, Mark. You did that all on your own when you decided to run me down with your car."

"You should be dead, bitch. Apparently, you're just one lucky broad; but your luck is about to run out. You've been warned."

I was now listening to a dial tone. I hit the button to shut off my phone, laid my head on my desk and cried until there weren't any tears left. My shoulders were heaving, and I couldn't breathe; I felt like the wind had just been knocked out of me. Matt pulled up a chair beside me and was doing his best to calm me down. There was a flurry of activity happening around me, but I couldn't tell you what anybody was saying or doing. I just kept hearing those words in my ears: *you should be dead; you've been warned.* I heard them over and over in my head.

I felt a familiar arm wrap around me. "It's ok Sadey. I'm here, and Leland's on his way. The conversation was taped; we've got him."

I just lost it. I still couldn't muster up enough energy to raise my head, but I was screaming.

"We don't have him, Chase! He's still out there threatening me. You should have heard him; he told me that I should be dead, and my luck had run out. Why isn't he in jail?"

"Because he obviously has enough money lying around to pay a $75,000 cash bond and somebody is helping him hide. This will rescind his bond, though, and put him back in jail. Leland will get him; don't worry, Sadey. You know he'll pull every resource he can to find this guy. But everything he said to you has been recorded. Playing that to a judge is going to cost him a lot of years behind bars."

"Just get me out of here, Chase. I can't deal with this anymore."

"I'm sorry, but we can't leave here until Leland assures me that it's safe. They are surrounding the building to make sure he's not out there waiting for you somewhere. We just can't take that chance, ok?"

"Don't leave me, Chase. Please don't leave me."

"I'm not going anywhere; I won't let you out of my sight. You're safe with me."

For the first time, I looked up and looked around me. Chase and I were the only ones in my office; everybody else probably left when I started yelling. I was scared to my toes, and he could feel it. He didn't let go of me and I wasn't sure how I would ever thank him.

"Chase?"

"Yeah?"

"How do you do it? How do you know just what I need at just the right time?"

He started laughing. "I don't know. I guess it's just a gift. I see you didn't get to eat that Blizzard I sent."

"I only got a couple of bites in before my world crashed again, but hand me that spoon..."

About halfway through the Blizzard, Leland walked in my office. He took one look at the Blizzard, grabbed my cup and spoon, helped himself to a spoonful of ice cream bliss, and then handed it back to me.

"Bad day?" I jokingly asked. That brought a laugh from Leland and Chase.

Leland said that they searched the building, the parking lot, and all lots around the building and didn't find him.

I just remembered that I was supposed to be at Karleen's in an hour. "Oh my gosh, Chase, we can't go to Karleen's today. What if he's out there following us? I can't take the chance of him finding the girls. I can't put them in danger."

"You're right. Just call her and see if we can come on Friday."

I was still shaking when I dialed Karleen's cell phone.

I hung up hoping and praying that she could keep the girls safe. I don't know why he's so fixated on me, but at least he's not after the girls. I sat around being a basket case for another hour before Chase said it was ok to leave. There were officers sitting outside the door to protect me while I got loaded in the car and Chase said there was another officer sitting up the road from his house just to make sure it was safe.

I was lying on the couch surrounded by pillows, like maybe if I just wrapped them around me it would make me feel safer. Bones was stretched out on the floor snoring, and my head was pounding so hard I considered asking for a pain pill. I didn't even turn on the TV or check my email. My eyes feel like they're twice their normal size from crying, and I was still shaky. I could smell Mexican food, so I was really hoping that Chase was making tacos. Thank goodness he can cook!

Thirty minutes later my belly was full of tacos and refried beans, and I was praying the two Tylenol I took would kick in soon. Chase cleaned up the kitchen and then he fell into the recliner across from me; he was looking pretty run down.

"You're tired. I'm sorry I've done this to you."

"Sadey, don't blame yourself. This isn't your fault; it's Mark's fault. You need to remember that you were only doing your job, and I now know you well enough to know that you'd do it again in a heartbeat because you love those families you're working with."

"Can I ask you a really huge favor, and it's ok if you don't want to or if it would make you uncomfortable..."

"Just ask, Sadey, whatever it is."

I took a deep breath and quickly said, "Is there any chance you would lay here with me on the couch? I mean, like, I just basically can't quit shaking and..."

Luckily, he didn't make me finish this awkward request. He just got up from the recliner, rolled me on my side and then climbed in behind me on the couch, basically spooning, but he hadn't put his hands on me. I think he was a little nervous, so I just reached back, grabbed his arm and wrapped it around my stomach. I needed the security.

What I got, instead, was the zing again and I'm hoping it wasn't noticeable, but all I was initially aiming for was some comfort.

"Does this make you uncomfortable?"

"No, not at all; well, define uncomfortable. Never mind. I just didn't want to cross any boundaries, Sadey, and have you mad at me."

"Being mad at you is the furthest thing from what I'm feeling."

"Yeah; me too."

Then it hit me why he said never mind earlier. Apparently, he had a zing as well; his was just a little more noticeable to me.

Is this what I wanted, like deep down, and I was just using the fear as an excuse. Or am I just testing him? What the hell am I thinking, anyway? I obviously made him uncomfortable; maybe in a good way?

He kissed the top of my head again – major zing – and then said, "Stop arguing with yourself. If this is going to make you too uncomfortable then I can go back to the recliner."

"No, I, um…I just didn't want to make you feel weird."

With a small laugh, he said, "Weird is nowhere close to what I'm feeling. Now, stop shaking, stop worrying and talk to me about today."

I took another deep breath. "I've never had this happen before, and I'm scared to my toes. I mean I get people mad at me all the time, but I've never had anybody try to kill me. I've had clients cuss me out, but this is a first for me."

I was definitely at ease with Chase; he was kind of like one of those big brothers that take care of the little sister. The only difference was that Chase was easy on the eyes, and he created a zing in my body that I've never felt before, and I have to admit that I like that he was affected by our spooning as much as I was. Oh, yeah, and he could cook – definitely a plus.

"You know what I really miss the most?"

"What?"

"Taking a bubble bath."

"Too funny. I thought you were going to say 'taking long walks with Bones to the Dairy Queen'."

"That too. Although truth be known, I prefer to drive there."

~~~~~~~~~~

You should be dead; you've been warned! You took something from me, so I'll take something from you. You're one lucky broad, but your luck has run out. You've been warned! You've been warned!

~~~~~~~~~~

"Sadey! Wake up!"

When my eyes finally came into focus, I realized that my heart was beating really fast, I was sweating, and I couldn't stop shaking. I was once again sitting on Chase's lap and he was rubbing my back.

"You had another nightmare. Was it from the phone call from Mark?"

All I could do was shake my head. Now there were tears flowing down my face that I couldn't stop. Chase wiped the tears and just held me tighter.

Instead of waking up in my bed, which usually happens after a nightmare, I woke up still on Chase's lap and wrapped in a blanket.

"Morning, Sweet Cheeks."

"Sweet Cheeks; really?"

"It fits. Feeling better?"

"Yeah, I guess. I've never had nightmares, ever, in my life. Sorry I'm going all psycho on you."

"I didn't mind having you sleep on my lap, so it's all good."

I couldn't even voice the fact that I enjoyed waking up on his lap, wrapped in his arms. I think I'm losing my mind, but the feelings I have for Chase are completely different than I've had for any man I've dated; even when I had been with them for several months. My heart and my head are having some huge arguments right now.

"Who's winning?"

"What? Oh, um, you are, as usual."

He gave me that adorable panty-dropping smirk as he said, "One of these days you're going to have to tell me what argument I'm winning, because when I try to imagine them it does bad things to me."

"Bad things?"

"Ok, so maybe not that bad."

There's that smirk again; damn!

If life is a highway, I wish someone would finish with the road construction already – I'm tired of the detours, road-blocks and potholes.

Drool

Friday, October 5th

I'm really starting to hate Fridays. Being in these casts really, really sucks, but I've gotten used to not having to get up early in the mornings. Fridays are the major exception because staff meeting is at 8:00 a.m., so that means mom is here way too early to get me ready. Of course, we had to argue over what I was wearing again this morning, because mom swears it's going to be cold all day, and I keep swearing that my office is stuffy hot. I just quit arguing and let her put me in a sweater; it just wasn't worth it.

"Are you ready?" Chase asked.

"No. I need a really big favor."

He looked at my skeptically, and then said, "Ok, what?"

"I need a new shirt."

"Why? What's wrong with the sweater that you're wearing?"

"It's hot in my office, and I have to sit there all day. I got tired of arguing with mom, so I just gave in. Please get me another shirt.

I'll wear a jacket to the office and back; I just can't deal with a sweater all day."

"Ok, fine, but if your mom finds out, I'm telling her you held me at gunpoint, ok?"

"Chickenshit. Just get me another shirt."

I've obviously gotten way too comfortable with Chase, because he was barely out of the room before I started trying to remove the sweater. I thought it would just be a smooth transition; sweater off, new shirt on. I was getting better at getting some clothes on and off; however, today wasn't that easy.

Much to the amusement of Chase, when he came back in the room, I had the sweater off the arm with the cast, but I was having trouble grasping the sweater with my casted hand to get it off the other arm. One arm out, one arm stuck, with the sweater only halfway over my head – that's all Chase needed to break out into fits of laughter. Not to mention, the bra I was wearing happened to be red lace; embarrassment at its finest!

"Stop laughing at me!"

"Let me get the camera first."

"You do and I'll kill you."

"You and what army? You have a cast on one leg, a cast on one arm, and a sweater stuck on your head. I'm not really all that threatened."

"Just stop laughing and help me out."

Chase got the sweater off my head, and at that point he noticed my bra, and he was staring directly at it. I assume he was staring at the bra; maybe he was picturing what was underneath. Either way, my face now matched the color of my lacey, red bra.

"Um...I need to go get a new shirt."

The shirt he was holding was white; definitely not going to work with a red bra. I'm not really sure who was more embarrassed at this point, him or me. Bones used this opportunity to climb up on the couch, straddle me with his paws, and lay his head right on my chest; typical boy. His nose was directly against my chin and he started with the snake kisses. His tongue just kept darting out of his mouth like a snake and my fresh make-up was now mixing with doggy drool. "Bones, stop! Get down!"

Chase freaked out when I yelled at Bones and came running back into the room, darting towards the 'maiden-in-distress' call. When Bones saw him coming, he jumped off the couch and headed for the door. Chase quickly let him out and then rushed back to me. I was sitting on the couch, my head shoved back into the pillows, in a red lace bra, with drool dripping from my chin, down my chest and settling into the under wires of my bra. This morning couldn't possibly get any worse, right?

"Can I have a washcloth now, too?"

"You obviously need a drool-free bra as well, huh?"

"That would be nice. Sorry."

Good thing it's only a 10-minute drive to work because this morning was not turning out as planned. Chase came back with a wet washcloth, a pink bra, a new shirt, and a red face. He was turning his head from side to side like Bones does when he's confused. I busted out laughing; Chase, on the other hand, was very embarrassed. He was just standing there holding a washcloth in one hand, a bra and shirt in the other hand, and he wasn't sure what to do with any of it.

"Just give them to me."

He handed me the washcloth and I started trying to wipe off the drool. The biggest problem was that the drool had now settled in my bra, in every part of my bra, and this would require a bra removal in order to clean me up. Chase sensed the problem and got a look on his face that said, "now what?"

"You want the truth?"

"I think I know the truth. The bigger question is, what is it that you want me to do?"

"I'm pretty sure you've seen boobs before, right?" He slowly shook his head 'yes' like he was almost afraid to admit it. I really wanted to bust out laughing, but I knew he was already feeling a little awkward, so I stifled it.

"Just unhook my bra; I'll clean myself up and you can redress me, ok?"

"Yeah, ok." He walked back behind the couch, sat me up a little, unhooked my bra and slid it over my cast, all while attempting to look in every direction besides my chest. I cleaned the drool from the underneath of my breasts, and Chase stood behind me trying to pretend this wasn't happening. At least I think that's what he was doing. There was something different about his face, like he was arguing with himself. Now I was embarrassed.

Why? Seriously, Sadey. You've been naked in front of other men, what's so different now? Maybe because I think I might like him. No, maybe because he's kind of like a big brother; that would make that major zing pretty creepy. No, maybe...Hell, I don't know. This is crazy; not only am I talking to myself, but I'm answering myself, too. That's the first sign of insanity, right? Yes, and the second sign is to not even notice that an adorable hunk is standing behind you, trying not to stare at your boobs, that are out there for the world to see.

Apparently, I had stopped cleaning myself off and I was just staring into space. "Um, Sadey, are you ok?"

"What? Oh, um, yeah...just having an argument with myself."

"Really? Who's winning?"

"You."

A strange look came across his face as I handed him the washcloth. He did his best to slide the new bra straps over my arms while situating it under my breasts. He got the straps on my shoulders, and I leaned forward on the couch, so he could fasten it in the back, but my girls weren't being very cooperative. I was able to corral one of them in place, but with the cast I couldn't get the other girl to fully cooperate.

Chase was standing behind me waiting patiently for me to make this work without any further help from him. By the look on his face, he was either really embarrassed, or really turned on, or both. I wasn't sure what I wanted his response to be, actually. I was sitting here thinking about how I wanted Chase to be thinking about seeing me half-naked, when I should have been thinking about how to fix the situation myself.

I finally gave up, on both thinking and trying, leaned back on the couch and looked up at him. No expression on his face now at all; I need a poker face like that. I had my head resting on the back of the couch, with a look of defeat across my face. Then he just smiled, or was it a slight smirk; hard to tell from this position.

Chase very slowly leaned over top of me, put one hand under my chin, covered my lips with his and proceeded to make the rest of my body tingle. While his mouth was busy with mine, he used his other hand to reach down and fix the girls, sending another tingle through my entire body. I'm pretty sure a groan came from somewhere deep inside of me, and my brain was trying a hundred different ways to justify what just happened, but my body had only one reaction: Wow!

When everything was properly situated, Chase gradually stood up, grabbed my shirt, and said, "I guess we need to get you dressed and to work before you're late for staff meeting."

I just nodded; My heart was pounding in my ears and, I could barely breathe, let alone speak. "I think... I might... want... to be late... for staff meeting."

Chase seemed to be trying to catch his breath as well. "I would love for you to be late for staff meeting, but..."

"Yeah, I know. I'm not dead, so I better be there, and on time."

Nothing else was said. I was dressed, make-up fixed, and loaded in the car. We ran through McDonald's so I could get a sweet tea to go with my staff meeting donuts, and then headed to work. My bodyguards were already waiting at the backdoor when we pulled in. Chase had always been gentle loading and unloading me, but today just seemed different; more intimate. My head was still swimming from that kiss, and then when he picked me up out of the car, my body started tingling again. It was going to be a very long day!

I made it with five minutes to spare. I got the scooter situated at the conference table and decided it might be a three-donut morning. Geez! My boss was rattling about a family that's being a real pain, and I was completely zoning out. I couldn't think of anything but that dang kiss, and those strong hands with such a gentle touch.

Matt smacked the side of my leg under the table to jolt me back to reality, and just in time, too. My boss was talking about Mark and the phone call and then asked for an update on the Sams' case. Thanks Matt.

Staff meeting lasted forever; well, it was actually an hour and a half, but it seemed like forever. Now I was stuck back in my office, with the blah walls, and I was almost wishing I was back in staff meeting; just so I could have some sort of distraction. I think I was just staring a hole into the wall, because Matt came into my office and I didn't even notice.

"So, if you stare at that wall long enough, will it give you all the answers?"

"Yeah, it told me that I shouldn't let you in my office anymore because bad things always happen when you walk in."

"Hey, that's not fair. I did bring you a Blizzard the other day. That should count for something."

"Correction. You delivered the Blizzard that Chase brought me."

"Ok, fine, whatever. You win as usual. Now, about this morning…"

"What about this morning?"

"You were completely distracted in staff meeting."

"So."

"So? Ya gonna fill me in?"

"Nope. I don't bare my soul to anybody but Cami."

"Was your soul the only thing you were baring?"

I picked up the eraser that was on my desk and heaved it straight at his head. I missed, of course, but throwing it made me feel better.

"Touchy, touchy. Ok, you don't have to tell me, I'll just use my imagination. That's probably better anyway."

"You're a pig." I was looking around for something else to throw at him, but unfortunately my desk had been cleaned off.

"Ok, never mind the porn. What's for lunch?"

"Um, that's for you boys to decide. I can't exactly run out and get us anything. I'm game for whatever; donuts just don't last long."

"How about Subway?"

"Are you thinking of the 6" or foot long?" My sarcasm flows too easily sometimes.

"Now who's thinking porn?" He was still laughing as he left to go find Jason. I love the fact that the guys in my office really like to eat. That means they are always on the go for food, so I never go hungry when I'm in the office. Subway was delivered and devoured; now I just have to occupy my afternoon until it was time to see Karleen and the girls.

Typing one-handed pretty well sucks, so I keep putting off my documentation; guess that's what I'm going to spend my afternoon doing. Three hours later, my eyes were crossed and my body was stiff from sitting in this stupid scooter. At 4:00 on the dot, my bodyguards came in and escorted me to the back door to be loaded in Chase's car. I keep trying to do more and more by myself each day, but I feel like a hopeless failure. I might as well just give up and let them do their thing; makes them feel big and macho anyway.

"How was staff meeting?" I think Chase was trying to make small talk, so I appeased him.

"It sucked, as usual. Then I spent all afternoon typing in documentation one-handed."

"Are we still going to Karleen's?" No emotion.

"Yeah, do you know where you're going?" Calm. Cool. Nothing happened this morning. Then why are your palms so sweaty?

"You gave me the directions the other day. We're good." Then the car was eerily quiet; like neither one of us knew what to say. This was weird and different; usually we were chatting, or I was crying. Chase finally broke the silence.

"Sadey, about this morning…"

"You don't need to say anything Chase; it's fine."

"It's just…I mean, I just saw you…"

"Chase, don't dig yourself in a hole. Truth is, well…I sorta…" I couldn't verbalize that he was still making my head spin and my body tingle.

"So, basically, we're both speechless?"

"Kind of like this morning, huh? All I can tell you is, I've been distracted all day long, thanks to you."

"Distracted in a good way, or a bad way?"

"A good way."

"So, I'm not in trouble?"

"Well, you might be in trouble, but you won't mind the consequences," I teased.

"Good to know. We should probably change the conversation before I end up making you late for this appointment too."

"I wasn't late this morning; I had five minutes to spare."

"Smart-ass."

This was more familiar ground; back to normal. Well, as normal as things can be when I'm still daydreaming about that fabulous kiss, and those amazing hands. Time to get my head in the game. We drove around the block three times before Chase pulled into Karleen's driveway; I'm assuming it was to make sure we weren't being followed, and not because he was lost.

Kasey talked and talked for an hour. I barely got to talk to Lacey or Karleen because Kasey kept jumping in. She was already a different kid; she was actually being a kid. She talked about going bowling with Shayna, and Karleen taking them to the movies on Wednesday; they went to see Alvin and the Chipmunks. Lacey really liked going to the YMCA, and she thought it was cool that she knew Shayna too. I told Kasey that I would see her again on Wednesday at her mom's visit. She actually gave me a hug when we were leaving; definitely a different kid. I was starting to feel better about this case.

Ships don't sink because of the water around them; ships sink because of the water that gets in them. Don't let what's happening around you get inside you and weigh you down.

Taking a chance

When we left Karleen's, Chase said we had to go shopping. We had to purchase the wood to build me a new porch tomorrow, and we needed food at the house.

I was very unexcited about having to use the scooter carts, but I made it through Lowes and Walmart without causing bodily harm, accidental or intentional, to another human being.

I felt sorry for Chase since he had to unload the groceries by himself when we got home. I did sit at the kitchen table and cheer him on; I thought it was the least I could do. He didn't think it was quite as funny as I did, but I cheered him on anyway. Bones was very excited to see us come home, especially with a car full of food. He was doubly excited to get fed since Chase bought him canned dog food; I'm cheap – he gets the Wal-Mart brand at my house, and it's the dry food. Apparently, Chase thinks I'm being abusive to my 90 lb. dog by not feeding him canned food; give him another week, and he'll realize that Bones' appetite will break his bank account.

"So, what's on the agenda for the rest of the evening?" Chase asked.

"Ice cream." That's always a safe choice, right?

"Besides ice cream? That's always on your agenda. How about a movie?"

"I'll search Netflix while you fix the ice cream. I need some comfy clothes and then get my butt to the couch."

"Yes, your highness."

I got situated on the couch and started searching Netflix, while Chase fixed me a bowl of chocolate chip ice cream with hard shell and whipped cream. He had just gotten to the couch with the ice cream, a bowl in each hand, when he realized the hard way that he should have fixed Bones a bowl first.

That adorable huge dog immediately jumped up on Chase with his massive paws to get what he thought was his share of dessert, pushing Chase down on the couch; one bowl went flying over Chase's head and landed behind him on the floor – it immediately belonged to Bones. But, in order to get to that bowl, he had to go around the couch, or through Chase.

In his attempt to jump over Chase and the couch to reach that bowl, his wagging tail caused the other bowl to roll out of Chase's hands and flip in the air a couple of times, which in turn made whipped cream and ice cream sail through the air and cover me from my nose all the way down my lap. At this point we were both in shock, and we were laughing so hard no one could even move to clean up the mess.

Bones finished the ice cream he'd thrown to the floor and came back around the couch to me. Chase got up to get some towels, and Bones used that moment to seize the opportunity to obtain more ice cream. His tongue was going a mile a minute; he was doing his dandiest to clean up every bite of ice cream that managed to land on my body. Normally I would be mad at Bones for this, but it was so funny that I couldn't even muster up a little bit of mad. When he was satisfied that he'd cleaned up every drop of ice cream he could possibly find, he headed to the bedroom to crash. His belly was full, so now it was bedtime.

Chase came back in the room to catch the tail-end of this spectacle, holding a couple of small towels. The big problem now was that I was head-to-toe sticky, which meant a wet washcloth, not a towel; but Chase hadn't even been scathed. There wasn't a drop of ice cream on him; I, on the other hand, still had a dab of whipped cream on the side of my face and I felt very nasty. Chase gave me the once-over, sat back down beside me and leaned over to lick the small spot of whipped cream off my face.

"Seriously? You just licked my face?"

"Bones missed a spot, and he's my new best friend," Chase said as he was still laughing.

"You're kidding, right?"

"Nope. First, this morning's drool netted me a fabulous kiss while I copped a feel, and now the ice cream. I'm pretty sure you're going to require at least a half-naked clean-up, maybe totally naked, and no way am I calling your mother this late at night."

He had a huge smirk on his face, and I knew I was in trouble. I tried to convince him that the only part of me that really needed washed was my face and my neck, but he wasn't buying it. His argument was that Bones had used his tongue on multiple parts of my body, inadvertently leaving drool in his wake. Of course, truth be told, I wasn't really putting a ton of effort into convincing him of anything.

With one arm under my legs and the other under my back, Chase lifted me off the couch like I weighed nothing. I could feel the bulging muscles of his arms, and I was doing my best to try and forget about those wonderful hands rearranging my girls this morning. He carried me into the bathroom and sat me on the counter with my casted leg propped on a stool.

He grabbed a warm washcloth and started with my face and neck. When he got to my chest, he laid down the washcloth and slowly lifted my tank top over my head; his eyes never left mine. At this point my heart was beating out of my chest, I could feel my face flushing and I lost all ability to breathe on my own.

But that feeling left as quickly as it arrived.

"You wanna hold up your breasts so I can clean under them?"

I don't know why that pissed me off, but it did; and I went on a hormonal spewing spree.

"So, what, like it was ok to touch the girls this morning, but not this evening? Maybe you weren't as turned on as I was this morning or you'd be jumping at the chance to get your hands on me again tonight! Or maybe that was all just an act in the living room just now!"

I was on a rampage and Chase was frozen in front of me with his mouth open in disbelief. But I didn't give him time to respond.

I could have landed a plane with my arms just going all over the place.

"And here I was completely distracted all day today thinking that maybe, just maybe, I'd found someone who actually gave a shit about me and wouldn't mind to have his hands on me and actually making me enjoy something for a change! I mean, seriously, seven guys, which is pathetic enough, but still, seven guys in my life and not a single one of them even bothered to see if I was getting anything out of the sex! All they wanted was to take theirs and run. I kept thinking, in the back of my mind, that maybe you'd be the one, the one to actually give me some kind of pleasure, to give me something that wasn't just crappy sex, but apparently I was wrong since you won't even touch my breasts tonight, let alone anything else!"

I was torked and rambling; I didn't even care what was coming out of my mouth at the time, or if it even made sense; Chase, on the other hand, was taking everything seriously and personally and finally stopped me.

He put a finger over my lips and somewhat sternly said, "Stop talking."

What the hell?!

"You don't have the right to tell me…"

The finger was gone, and he replaced it with his lips. He firmly, but still softly, put his lips on mine and kissed me with everything he had. My heart was back to beating out of my chest and I couldn't form a real sentence if I'd wanted to.

As he broke away from the kiss, he softly put his finger back over my mouth and quietly said, "I wasn't telling you to stop talking to be mean or in charge of you; I wanted you to stop because you were spewing things that I'm not sure you actually meant to say."

Now I was wracking my brain and trying to remember exactly what I said while I was rambling. He didn't let me think for long.

Chase put his hands on the countertop on either side of my thighs and softly said, "You said that nobody had ever given you anything out of sex and maybe I would be the one to finally give you some pleasure."

He tenderly lifted my chin up so I would look him in the eyes; I was trying to look anywhere but at him. I can't believe I actually said that out loud! Criminy, he probably thinks I'm completely crazy at this point.

"Sadey; look at me please."

I hesitated, but finally looked up at him.

"Tell me the truth, please. No guy has ever given you an orgasm?"

I shook my head 'no' and looked down at my fingers, which were fidgeting in my lap because I was so freaking embarrassed. I can't believe I let my most pathetic secret slip.

He took a deep breath, lifted my chin back up and said, "Ok; we're going to go fix that."

"Fix what?" I couldn't look him in the eye at this point.

"This lack of sexual pleasure you've experienced; I'm going to give it to you, if that's ok."

I didn't know what to say. My hands were shaking, I was nervous and embarrassed, and the only thing I could do was let my sarcasm flow.

"You just looking for some crappy sex, too?"

He didn't even bat an eye.

"No; I didn't say I wanted to have sex with you."

"What?! Seriously?! You're an asshole!"

His mouth was back on mine and his hands were in my hair holding me in place while he kissed away all my defenses and melted all my unreasonable anger.

As he pulled away from the kiss he very sweetly said, "I would be happy to make love to you all night long if that's what you wanted, but I'm never going to just have sex with you."

A total look of confusion came across my face.

"It's still having sex, no matter what you call it."

"No, it's not. There's a big difference between having sex and making love. Apparently, the only thing that you've experienced is having sex, and obviously crappy sex at that. But I'm pretty sure from your description that nobody has ever made love to you; nobody has ever cared enough to take care of you before himself."

I had no words for that; he was absolutely right. Even though I was never a one-night-stand kind of girl, I always managed to date losers and the 'wham-bam-thank-you-ma'am' kind of guys.

I finally found some words.

"Can we start over? You know, at the point where you were cleaning me up and I wasn't being a psycho bitch?"

He got that really cute smirk on his face, picked up the washcloth and said, "The only reason I was asking you to hold your own breasts is because I didn't want to make you uncomfortable or make you think that I was only cleaning you up in exchange for sex. Seeing you naked, maybe, but not just sex. However, I'd be more than happy to hold them up if you'd like."

Of course, his idea of holding them up involved softly squeezing them while running his thumb across my nipple and making some kind of groan leave my body. The whole time he was using his other hand to clean up the ice cream mess from my chest and stomach. I had no way of controlling the fact that my heart was pounding, my throat was dry, and my hands were shaking and sweating.

I wasn't sure I could form an answer when he asked, "Is it ok if I take you in the bedroom and give you that experience you deserve?"

I nodded yes. It was all I was capable of at the moment.

He still had my chin in his hand as he looked at me and said, "I don't know what you've ever done sexually, but if I do something that you aren't comfortable with then you need to tell me. That's important, ok. I will leave my shorts on; I don't want you to think that I'm doing this for some kind of quid-pro-quo. This is entirely for you and your pleasure, ok?"

Confused look again. "Then how are you going to…?"

"My hands and my mouth, if that's ok with you."

Well then.

He carefully lifted me off the countertop and carried me into his room, laying me softly on the bed. My shorts were removed, and my casted leg was propped up on a pillow. As he crawled back up the bed overtop of me, my nerves set in. He zeroed in on that right away.

"Sadey, you just tensed up. What's wrong?" I tried to look away, but he wouldn't let me. "Tell me, please; talk to me. Are you having second thoughts about this? I will redress you and we can go watch TV if that's what you want."

"No, no. I just…"

"Just what?"

"Well, um, what if I can't…you know…have one?"

"You will."

"What if I can't?"

He leaned down and softly kissed me. Then he slid his lips across my cheeks and in that sexy whisper, said, "You will; I swear." Major goosebumps!

As he started placing soft kisses on my neck he said, "Close your eyes; relax. I've got you."

I closed my eyes, but the relax part never did happen. His hands and his mouth discovered every part of my body and it wasn't long before I exploded into a feeling so intense it brought tears to my eyes.

As his kisses reached my face again, he wiped away the tears and said, "I hope those are happy tears."

I shook my head 'yes' and then could barely form the words, "Is it always that intense?"

"Well, that's always my goal."

My body went completely limp and all I could muster out was, "Holy Hell".

Chase kissed the tip of my nose and said, "Open your eyes, Sweet Cheeks; look at me."

My eyes were heavy, and it took a minute for me to completely open them. I managed to get out the word, "Thanks."

He kissed my forehead and said, "Anytime; all you have to do is ask."

I don't know why that statement struck me as odd, but I got a strange look on my face as I said, "Be careful what you say; I might start taking you up on that offer."

He rested himself on his forearms, that panty-dropping smirk back on his face, and he softly kissed my lips. His lips buzzed against mine as he quietly said, "I hope you do; all the time."

Really? Is that what I really want? I mean that was the most awesome experience and he was so careful and gentle with me, but he managed to make me lose myself in him. Why am I arguing with myself over this? I know I haven't known him that long, but never in all of ten years and seven guys has anyone made me feel what I do for him, physically or emotionally. All he has to do is touch me and my body comes alive with that wonderful zing. Obviously, what he just gave me had an effect on him as well because I'm feeling that effect against me, but does he feel the same zing and loss of breath and all that other stuff for me that I feel for him? Maybe I'm just overthinking this.

Chase brought me out of my argument with myself by kissing the tip of my nose and saying, "I hope I'm winning this argument you are having with yourself."

"You are; you always do."

"Good. Sadey, you do know how I feel about you, right? Actual emotions, not just sexually?"

I was stumbling over my words. "Yeah, I guess; I mean…"

"Have I been too subtle? I didn't want to push you into something you didn't want or weren't on the same page about. But sometimes it's difficult to hide those feelings from you or hide what you do to me."

"It's just…well…I'm having a hard time with this. If I admit to myself how you feel about me, then I have to deal with my own feelings for you and I'm not good at talking about affection and love and all that crap. I can do psycho bitch really well, but affection…"

"Ok."

I thought he took that as an answer, and we were done talking about it. Much to my dismay, he just rolled off of me to the side and then rolled me so we were spooning again.

"If you get too embarrassed looking at me and discussing this, then we'll do it so you don't have to face me." Ugh!

"Chase, I just, ugh…this is hard for me."

"Ok, then let me help. Can I assume that your heart and your head are arguing about the feelings you have for me?"

"Yeah. How did you know that?"

"Because my heart finally won that argument sometime last week."

"How?"

"It wasn't easy. My head kept telling me that we hadn't known each other long enough to have these feelings and my heart kept saying 'so what' and then discussing how easy it is to be around you and how you can make my heart skip a beat with just a simple laugh or bickering or being able to carry you around. It all just seems so…"

"Content."

"Yeah."

"That's how I feel with you, but then there's so much more. I feel kind of like that creepy stalker girl because I just can't wait until evenings when I can have you to myself. I like the normalcy of having dinner and just laying around watching TV. I like having you put me to bed and I liked that when I had nightmares that you just sat with me curled up on your lap. It's because you care; not because you feel like you have to do it, right?"

"I do care about you Sadey; a lot. Probably more than any normal man should feel this soon after meeting someone. But I won't do anything, and I mean anything, that would push you towards something you don't want or you aren't comfortable with. It would absolutely crush me if I pushed you away. If all I can ever have with you are dinners and nights on the couch watching TV and maybe giving you moments like this again, then I'll still be happy because at least I'll have you in my life."

It's how I felt as well. But... you want more?"

He let out a deep breath, rubbed his nose through my hair and softly said, "Yes; I want more, but..."

It made me smile.

"Me too."

He pulled my head back to him and said, "Really?"

"Yes, really. Why did you doubt that?"

"I don't know, I just...but then why are you still arguing with yourself?"

"These feelings scare me, Chase. Never in my entire life have I felt like this about somebody. I had my first kiss at 16; lost my virginity at 17. I've dated lots of guys, slept with seven. I've never told any man that I loved him because I've never had any man actually elicit those type of emotions from me; no man has ever made me feel anything, physically or emotionally. No man has ever caused my body to zing when they touched me."

I turned over towards him, and I could feel the embarrassment creeping up my face as I said, "You are an absolute Prince Charming; every girl's dream guy. Do you have any idea what you do to me when you touch me? Every time you carry me? Just grabbing my hand or putting your arm around me when I'm upset?

Even just holding me when I've had a nightmare? You just don't know what you do to me; the crazy things that my body does."

"I think I have a small idea." Smirk. "Can I show you?"

Damn. He didn't even touch me, and the zing started. I could barely form the word 'yes'.

His fingers lightly grazed across my belly before he brought them up to my hair. He placed a kiss on the tip of my nose as he said, "Your breathing becomes ragged."

Kiss to the corner of my mouth. "You can barely whisper when you try to talk."

Kiss to my throat. "You have a hard time swallowing."

He was completely right so far, and my body was reacting just as he was describing it. He skimmed his lips up to my ear as he whispered, "Your body is all flushed. Stop me if I get something wrong."

I obviously couldn't stop him; he just continued. He was barely touching me with his lips, but my body was on fire. He kept them going down my arm until he reached my wrist.

He placed a soft kiss on my wrist and said, "Your pulse is pounding, and your palm is sweaty." He said that while laying my hand against his face. He slowly laid my arm back down on the bed as he moved his mouth across my stomach and up my breastbone, laying soft kisses along the way.

I'm putty in his hands.

He laid his cheek on my chest as he said, "I can feel your heart beating out of your chest."

Of course he can, because it is!

As he moved his mouth to my left breast, his right hand had gathered the other one. I could feel the smirk on his face as he rolled one nipple with his fingers and pulled the other with his mouth. "And your nipples are hard and sensitive."

His right hand left my breast and started skimming down my body while he was still torturing the other one with his mouth. His fingers went down my leg and back up the inside of my thigh. I was pretty sure my body was literally on fire. I was on sensory overload.

As his hand came to rest between my legs he placed kisses up my chest, to my collarbone and then tugged on my ear as he said, "Do you want me to fix this problem that you're having?"

Um, YES! That was what I wanted to say, but the only thing that came out was some sort of moan. He rubbed his nose against mine, gave me that sexy smile and said, "Would you like the same treatment you just received or something different?"

My throat was dry, and the moan was back. He softly kissed me, creating another zing, and then waited patiently for my reply. I knew what I wanted, but somehow I had to form the words.

"Ch...Chase?"

"Yeah?"

"Will you…um…will you make love to me?" There, I said it; it was on the table, or actually the bed. Whatever.

His green eyes sparkled, but then they clouded for a split second; just long enough for me to think I may have gone too far. He finally put me out of my misery by saying, "I want to; more than anything. But I don't have any protection and that's not fair to you."

"It's ok, Chase. I'm on the pill, so I'm fine with it."

He ran his fingers through my hair and then the back of his hand down my cheek as he said, "Have you ever had sex without protection before?"

"No. Have you?"

"Only twice; same girl. So why are you ok with it now?"

"First of all, because I trust you. And second, because we're not going to have sex; you're going to make love to me." I gave my cutest smile.

A smile started to form on his face as he covered my body and kissed me until my toes curled. As he was removing his shorts, I realized that I had apparently been missing out on a lot of things before Chase; I was unaware those things came in that size! The only thought going through my head at the moment was 'I hope that thing fits!' It did, barely, and he made love to me, slowly and gently, until every bad memory I ever had with any guy had been thrown out the window.

I never left his bed.

God bless Bones!

Don't let the fear of taking a chance cause you to regret what could have been the best thing in your life.

A new porch

Saturday, October 6th

"Good morning." I woke to a kiss under my ear.

"You are too damn happy in the mornings. There is typically nothing good about them until after 10:00 a.m. and a large sweet tea; especially on a Saturday."

"I wouldn't mind changing that for you this morning."

I rolled over to face him as I said, "Not to sound too romantic or anything, but there will be no morning sex in your future until after I've peed."

He was still laughing when he deposited me in the bathroom. When we crawled back under the covers he snuggled back up to me and I was waiting for the roaming hands to begin. Instead, he tensed up a little as he said, "Sadey, I didn't mean to push anything on you so quickly. We haven't known each other that long and I know we had like a big heart-to-heart last night and all, but…well, I just don't want you to think that the only reason I've been taking care of you was for, you know, this."

"Are you finished sounding stupid?"

"Probably not."

"This is why I talk to myself. Then I can argue with myself and it only sounds stupid in my own head, not out loud. Nobody is going to justify anything, ok. We're both adults. At the risk of sounding stupid out loud myself, I just want to say that I have no regrets about the last day's events, and so neither should you. Well, maybe one regret: I never did get to eat that ice cream." That made him laugh.

"Ok. It's just that I helped out with you at first because it was the right thing to do, and you needed my protection. Then, well, I just wanted you to need me because I wanted to be around you. Then things got more intense, more scary, and I couldn't let my emotional guard down if I was going to make sure you were safe. Then well, there were those clothes issues, and well the drool, and…"

I rolled into him and started playing with his chest hair; I loved running my fingers through it. "Chase, I just want you to know that nothing you have done for me has gone unnoticed, by me or anybody around me. You've stuck your neck out for me when you had no real reason to; it wasn't your problem. At first this was all just a major inconvenience for all of us, but then, I just sort of fell into a routine with you, and I got way too comfortable. I let my guard down as well. If you want to stop this, any of this, even me staying at your house, it's ok. I've invaded your life and put you in an awkward position." This was a complete lie, of course. It would definitely NOT be ok if he tells me he wants this to stop, but…

"Sadey-baby, the only awkward position you put me in was how to maneuver around that leg cast in a way that didn't hurt you. The only thing I want to stop, is this stupid conversation." Thank God!

"Good, because I was pretty sure there was going to be some morning sex in my future before you decided to talk instead of kiss me."

This time he opted to kiss me; all of me.

When I could breathe again, I gave him my cutest smile and said, "Just so you know, this was my first experience with morning sex, as well."

"Seriously?"

"Yeah, well, I told you I only dated losers. None of them ever stayed the night, so there was never an occasion for morning sex," I said as I shrugged my shoulders.

He rubbed his nose against mine and asked, "So, how was your first experience with morning sex? Did you like it as much as evening sex?" That made me chuckle.

"Last night would be hard to beat, since, you know, it was like the first time, well…but, yeah, this morning was awesome as well. You know, though, it must be nice to be a gorgeous playboy and have all the right moves, because up until last night I had literally felt like a 27-year-old virgin."

Chase was instantly tense and began running his fingers through his hair.

"What's wrong? You just totally tensed up on me."

He took a deep breath and said, "Ok, well…um…I need to make a confession."

"Well, as long as you aren't going to tell me that you're gay or married, then I think it will be alright."

That brought half a smile.

"So…ok…well, I've never told anybody about this; not even Leland."

"I can keep a secret; whatever it is, I swear that I will never leak it."

He leaned in to kiss me and then started on what I thought was hilarious; him, not so much.

"I wasn't always a gorgeous playboy. Truth be told, I totally sucked at having sex." I wanted so badly to interrupt him and give him a hard time, but I realized that he was about to entrust me with something big and I needed to give him that respect.

"My first time was in my senior year; pathetic for a guy, I know. But Leland was really big on teaching me to be a gentleman and that meant no sleeping around or treating girls like they weren't worth more than a one-night stand. So, anyway, I wasn't sure I even made any time with this girl anything special and it really bothered me, but she never let on that I'd let her down in any way; I just felt like I had. So, I get to my freshman year in college and met this girl in my Sociology class. We went out several times and when we finally slept together I knew that I just wasn't very good at having sex; leave it to me to be horrible at something that's supposed to be wonderful. Not to mention, it was a total kick to the ego."

He gave me an uncomfortable smile, probably trying to see if I was judging him for any of this; I wasn't. He continued.

"There was this girl in my dorm, Jennifer, and she was basically known as the dorm slut; she would sleep with anybody and every guy wanted the privilege because she was supposedly the 'Queen of orgasms'." He winced. "Sorry, that sounded kind of crude, but I'm just repeating what was said."

He realized I wasn't fazed, even though I couldn't voice that word myself last night; ended well for me anyway, so whatever.

"So, here's the bad side of me. I paid Jennifer $100.00 to spend an entire night with me teaching me everything I needed to know about pleasing a woman; things that they liked and disliked." I was trying to hold back a laugh at this point. "Ok, Sweet Cheeks, stop laughing at me; this is embarrassing enough."

I reined it back to a cute smile; but I had to bite the inside of my mouth to keep from laughing.

"Anyway, the $100 was actually supposed to be money to keep her silence, not necessarily for the sex class. But, by morning, I actually felt like I could live up to my Davis boy reputation. I never told anybody, especially not Leland, because he would have been pissed at me for doing that. But at least the next time I slept with a girl I actually felt like I made it great for her as well."

I leaned in to kiss him as I said, "Best $100.00 you ever spent."

"You don't think that's creepy."

"No, actually it sounds pretty creative to me; and you're the first guy I've ever met that would even go to lengths like that to be good in bed. Most of them don't give a shit about whether or not they pleased a woman, as long as they got what they came for; mainly every man I ever dated. I promise to keep your secret."

"Thank you. By the way, my number is eight."

"What?"

"You said you'd only been with seven guys and said that was pathetic. Well, I've only been with eight girls, and one of those was Jennifer."

"Wow. I just assumed you had girls falling at your feet; you know that you're drop dead gorgeous, right? Plus, there's a rumor that you were a big basketball star as well."

He just laughed as he said, "I don't do one-night stands. But I'm now really fond of the morning after, and I'd totally love to show you some more of my moves right now, but we probably ought to get going so we aren't late meeting the Lowes truck."

I assured him that if we went through the drive-thru for breakfast then we had at least 15 minutes to spare.

We only beat Lowes to my house by 10 minutes, since my morning activities mirrored my evening activities, minus the ice cream and the emotional breakdown.

I had to convince my mom that I was able to give myself a bath now, minus washing my hair, but that Chase was able to do that in the sink for me. Lying to my mother is never a good idea; she'll figure out the truth soon enough, but it didn't need to be today.

We pulled into my driveway, and barely had the door opened before Bones went flying out of the car; he was excited to be back at the house, and he immediately went traipsing down in the woods out back looking for more chew bones.

The sun was bright and starting to warm the air nicely. There was a nice breeze blowing, which made it a perfect day to sit outside and watch some hunks build me a porch; I only had to supply beer and pizza, which was a pretty good deal for me.

I had to argue with Chase for several minutes before I could persuade him to let me sit in a chair outside while they worked on the porch. He kept giving me the speech about Mark still being loose, and how he couldn't protect me as easily if I was outside, in the open. Finally, he agreed to put up the EZ-up and situate my chair so that I could see the whole road, but he was still fussing and feuding about it while he was putting it up. And I had to admit, he was sort of cute when he was fussing about me.

Leland and Cami had perfect timing, showing up just as the Lowes truck was leaving. They stayed in the car for a minute and I saw them do a pinky swear; or most likely a bet.

Leland gave me the same speech about Mark, but Cami shut him up pretty quickly, and made him get a chair out of the trunk so she could sit beside me.

It wasn't long before a couple more hunks showed up to help out; they were apparently friends of Chase and Leland's, and Janice would be upset she was missing the show. Being the good friend that I am, I snapped a couple of pictures on my phone and sent them to her.

Cami got us some sweet tea and settled in the chair beside me. She looked at me kind of funny, with a small smirk on her face. I had an idea that she knew exactly what happened last night even without me saying a word; I have no idea how Cami seems to know everything, but she does.

"So, it looks like somebody had a good night last night," she said as a statement rather than a question.

"What makes you say that?" I tried to keep my voice steady, but I'm sure I was blushing.

"I can read you like a book, and the page I'm on right now says you had a very pleasurable evening, or morning, or both," she said with a smirk on her face.

"Um, well, it wasn't like, in the plan or anything; just sort of a Bones mishap."

"As your best friend, I'm pretty sure you're required to give me the details on how a 'Bones mishap' could lead to a night of, shall we say, unbridled bliss."

"I'm pretty sure Chase would kill me."

"Since he keeps looking over here with a big grin on his face, I think he probably already knows that I know, so just spill it sister." I was thankful that Leland and the other hotties were in the garage getting tools because I didn't need the rest of them seeing this exchange take place.

Since it was obvious that I wasn't going to get out of this, I proceeded with the 'R' version, starting with the morning drool, onto the evening ice cream and bathroom psycho breakdown that then resulted in the best night of my life. Cami was doing her best to stifle the laughing, but it wasn't working out well for her. She found most of my day quite hilarious and was actually excited to find out how well it ended, especially since she was aware of my crappy sex life and it's most important details. But I couldn't tell if she was just happy that my dry spell was over, or happy that it had been ended by Chase; either way, I didn't care because I was extremely elated with the circumstances.

Leland came out of the garage and looked over at the two of us laughing; he stopped dead in his tracks and gave Cami the raised eyebrow look that I find so cute on Chase. She simply smiled back at him.

"Dammit, little brother!"

"What?" At this point Chase had no idea why Leland was cussing him out. Leland didn't take long to remedy that situation.

"You just cost me a week's worth of giving full body massages; with happy endings."

It only took a second for Chase to figure it all out; and give his brother hell.

"I thought you liked happy endings."

"Yeah, when I'm receiving them; not when I have to work for them."

Cami and I were laughing hysterically. Cami couldn't help herself when she told Chase, "Ask him what he actually lost in that bet."

Leland was mumbling, or cursing, under his breath. He looked over at Cami and said, "Really? Must you kick a man when he's down?"

"Love you; mean it." Then to Chase she said, "He's just upset because he's not getting any happy endings in the car, while he's driving."

Chase smacked his brother on the back and said, "Ah...every man's wet dream."

"I thought that was a bus full of cheerleaders." I had to add my two cents to the fun.

Chase walked over, bent down to kiss me, and then said, "Those are for when all you want to do is to get laid; I've moved past that."

That thought made me smile. I was very happy with Chase's love making skills, and even happier knowing that they weren't just a one-time thing.

Leland attempted to take the focus off sex and lost bets and back onto the task at hand.

After that the day seemed to fly by and building me a new deck did not take as long as I anticipated, especially with four men working; four men who were definitely easy on the eyes, particularly when they started working without their shirts. Yum!

I had a new porch before sunset, and they had only devoured four pizzas and two cases of beer; that worked out pretty well for me.

There were no altercations with Mark, so it made for a smooth day, and thanks to a day of hard work, an early night to bed. The rest of the weekend was almost boring; a rainy Sunday turned into a movie marathon day, and two people and a large dog don't actually fit well together on a couch all stretched out, but we made it work.

I did the impossible and fell for you – it wasn't planned. My mind tried to talk my heart out of it, but my heart was louder and won.

Wednesday, October 10th

Wednesdays and Fridays were starting to become miserable days because they required me to get up early and actually go to work. The rest of the week, I could sleep as long as I wanted and then make phone calls at my leisure to check on clients and their progress, or lack thereof.

I was actually looking forward to this afternoon; Deborah was going to get a visit with the girls, and I was anxious to see how they would interact. Since Chase was going to be her probation officer, it made sense for him to go to the visit as well, so that made my life a little easier.

Chase picked me up for lunch, getting me out of the office earlier than I anticipated, which was good since I was getting cranky earlier than I anticipated. Chick-fil-a was a good choice on the way to Western Health. Nothing like some chicken butts, waffle fries, and a cookies-n-cream milkshake to get the afternoon off to a great start.

We got to Western Health a little early, so I went around tormenting all the other counselors and getting the scoop on my other clients. Chase was not as excited about all this movement, as it meant that he had to escort and assist in these endeavors. However, I was able to get some valuable information on numerous clients, thereby adding to the amount of documentation I must do, but also allowing me to get enough info to recommend closing a couple of my cases at staff meeting on Friday.

Janice had gone to pick up the girls for the visit and was running a little late. When she finally arrived, I noticed that Kasey was not the same bubbling kid that she was last week when I saw her.

"What's up kiddo? You don't look that happy to be here."

"I'm just nervous, Sadey. What if mom's not better and she's still mad at me for telling on her?"

"Kasey, your mom is not mad at you at all, and you didn't do anything wrong, ok. I just want you to know that. Telling the truth is always best; no matter what the consequences may be." She started to relax a little, but still had a worried look on her face. "Kasey, look at me a minute. Do you remember me telling you about my dad?"

"Yeah. Is he better?"

"Yeah, he is. And you know what else? I went to the jail and visited him a couple of weeks ago."

"Really? Was he happy to see you, because I told you that you shouldn't blame him, remember?"

"I remember. I also remember you telling me that you just wanted your mom to get better, right?" She shook her head 'yes', so I just continued. "My dad was very happy to see me, and even though he knew I was mad at him, he still hugged me and told me how much he loved me. I think that's going to happen with you today. Your mom knows that you love her and you want her to get better, and she also knows that it's her fault she's here, not yours. I just want you to remember that it was your mom who did the drugs, not you, ok? You have been very brave, and I'm extremely proud of you; so is your mom. Do you think you're ready to go see her?"

"Yeah, I think so."

"Alright. Let's go get Lacey and get this party started." She laughed at that statement and seemed to lighten up some. She even grabbed Lacey's hand before we went in.

Deborah took one look at the girls, and she had the same reaction as my dad; her eyes lit up and they also filled with tears. The girls took off running to their mom and there was a big group hug. The visit was off to a good start.

Janice, Chase, and I just sat off to the side talking about stupid stuff so that Deborah and the girls wouldn't think we were watching their every move. Kasey talked a lot about Shayna and the things that she gets to do with her, and Lacey talked about all the kids at the YMCA.

Deborah was happy and sad at the same time; I could see it in her eyes. It was obvious that she loved hearing how happy her girls were, but miserable that they were like this without her. Good. This is exactly the response that was needed. She needed to realize that it was her responsibility to give her girls these kinds of memories, and it was in her best interest to get her act together. She opened up and told the girls about the stuff she does in rehab, about the counseling sessions, and the other ladies that have the same problems that she has. It was actually good for Kasey to hear that there were other moms out there that were like hers; she didn't feel so alone in her struggles.

This is your double-standard, Sadey. Your dad is no different than the moms that are here trying to get over their addictions. You're telling Kasey how to act with her mom, but you're not giving your dad the same treatment. But it's not the same. Sure it is; a drug addiction is a drug addiction and everyone deserves the opportunity to get clean. They all need family support to do it, and you're not being very supportive. Yeah, but my dad didn't just do drugs, he sold them; that doesn't make him any better of a person than Mark. But your dad didn't try to kill somebody, either. This is ridiculous. I'm here to watch a visit and all I'm doing is arguing with myself. Ugh!

"You ok?" Chase had noticed me staring into space again. "Who's winning the argument this time?"

"Not me. I never seem to win when I argue with myself. I think I need some better arguments." Chase and Janice both chuckled at that, but they also both knew me well enough to know what I was struggling with.

As we were wrapping up the visit, Leland came in the room – not sure how he had any idea this visit was happening, but, whatever.

"I need to talk to Deborah and Kasey if that's ok." We all just shrugged our shoulders like, whatever, we don't care.

"I'm feeling like a total failure not being able to find Mark; it's been a week and I'm never this incompetent. So, I'm hoping you guys could give me some more information, like maybe someplace he could be hiding or somebody he's with; maybe somebody you've seen him around. I'll take any little thing at this point."

She was lost in thought for a minute before she said, "This is off the record and won't get me in any kind of trouble?" Her eyes were pleading with Leland. He was great with that.

"Absolutely; you're basically doing your time here, so anything you tell me will not come back on you."

She thought about that for another minute, looked over at Kasey, then back at Leland. She finally started talking.

"Ok, well there was this one time that he came to the house and he was bringing me more Xanax." She cringed when she said it, but none of us even blinked, so she went on. "He had this girl with him, young like maybe college age, and told me that she was a new dealer working for him. She was too strung out to be a dealer, so I figured that she was a client of his and his new play toy. Anyway, her name was Amber, and she was pretty tall, just a little shorter than Mark, with short blonde hair that was cut in kind of a spike on top. I don't really know anything about her other than that. He could be holed up with her; I don't know."

Kasey jumped in to say, "She drove a green mini-van, like dark green. It was one of those old ones that look kind of square and short."

Janice immediately jumped out of her seat and was moving fast to the door saying, "I know her; I know who that is."

She was only gone for a few minutes when she strolled back into the room with a couple of papers. She handed them to Leland as she said, "Ok, because of confidentiality, the only thing I can tell you…" The 'tell' was in quotes and emphasized. "…is that she walked out of the inpatient program after 2 weeks and you might want to check with Matt about a possible removal in the home."

I'm pretty sure those papers in Leland's hands were copied straight from the file, but nobody voiced it or acknowledged it. Leland kissed Janice on the cheek and took off out the door; hopefully with all the info he would need to catch this SOB.

Chase got me hobbled out to the car as Janice was getting Lacey buckled into hers. Then I heard Kasey holler at me, "Hey Sadey."

"Yeah?"

"You need to go visit your dad again so you can tell him that you love him."

"I did tell him that Kasey, and you shouldn't worry about me and my dad; you have enough worries with your mom." What is it with this 10-year-old kid, and why is she so wise beyond her years?

"Yeah, but you still blamed him and not the drugs. I'm being brave and helping my mom, so you need to be brave and help your dad." Then she just got into the car with Janice, and they pulled out of the parking lot.

I stood there kind of dumbfounded for a minute, and finally Chase touched my elbow and guided me into the car. We were barely out of the parking lot before I had tears welling up in my eyes. *Not now, Sadey. Don't cry now. She's just a kid; she doesn't know what she's talking about. Not that you would ever admit to someone else being right, anyway. You're too stubborn.*

Chase just reached over, grabbed my hand, and squeezed it. All he said was "Stop arguing with yourself and follow your heart. You have too big of one to let it go to waste."

Man, I just wanted to slap him right now, and that kid, and Deborah for making me feel sorry and want to help her, and my dad because it was his fault I was feeling like this. Why couldn't everybody just leave well enough alone? I'm perfectly fine! Which is why you are once again arguing with yourself, right?

"Sadey, I know you don't want to talk about your dad, and I respect that. But arguing with yourself over the situation is only going to make matters worse. You're going to have to make some decisions sooner or later."

"How about minding your own business?" I was not in the mood to be lectured. "Why does everybody else think they know better? It's my dad; it's my life. Just let me be about it."

Apparently, Chase decided that stomping all over my feelings was a fine and dandy thing to do today, because he responded with, "You're being bull-headed and selfish. He's your dad whether you like it or not, and one of these days you're going to have to learn to forgive and forget."

"Who died and made you God?" I yelled. "Did you forgive and forget with your dad? Huh? After what he did to your mom? And just how many times am I supposed to forgive? Tell me that! He ruined my childhood!" I was on a rampage now, and Chase was stuck in the car listening to me, being the brunt of all my anger. I should apologize, but I was too stubborn and bull-headed to admit I was wrong.

"Sadey."

"What?!" My temper was still flaring and tears were flowing down my face.

"He may have ruined your childhood, but are you going to let him ruin your adulthood as well?"

He has a point, you know. So what? It doesn't mean I have to forgive and forget what my dad has done to our family. No, but you can try to put it behind you and move on.

"When you're finished with this argument with yourself, how about telling me what you want for dinner."

I wanted to stay mad at him, but for some reason he always had a way to calm me down. No matter what kind of tirade I was on, Chase found a way to take it in stride and say just the right things to put me back on track. I was still in my own world when we pulled into his driveway; I hadn't even noticed that he was out of the car until he opened my door. He leaned in the door, unbuckled my seatbelt, and then very gently kissed my forehead, which quickly brought me out of my stupor. Man, I love those lips! And the rest of his body as well. He was just inches from my face when he said, "How about we go inside and you let me rub some of that tension out of your shoulders."

"I really want to be mad at you right now."

"I know. But I was thinking that we could go in the house and have some make-up sex. Then you could continue being mad at me while we eat some dinner, and then we could make up again."

Now I was laughing hysterically. He didn't waste any time helping me walk into the house; he simply picked me up and carried me. He was placing kisses around my face the whole time he was walking – multi-talented – and he even managed to unlock the door without taking his eyes, or his mouth, off me. The front door opened, Bones bolted out, and Chase kicked the door closed behind him. Forget the mail; forget the blinking message light on the phone; forget the foreplay. I was undressed in record time – Chase was getting proficient at removing my clothes around those pesky casts. The kisses continued; from my neck all the way to my...Oh dear heavens!

Dinner was quick and simple; grilled cheese and tomato soup. Chase cleaned up the kitchen and then came into the living room with me, where I was searching for something worthwhile to watch on TV.

"The light is blinking on the answering machine; you might wanna check that before you get comfy. And I don't think you took the time to get the mail either." That brought a smirk to his face.

He hit the button on the machine, and an all too familiar voice came over the line. "I found you Sadey, and that little bodyguard of yours doesn't scare me. Just remember, I owe you." Click.

"My number is unlisted. Shit!" I've never seen Chase so angry. He was immediately on the phone with Leland, and he was screaming throughout the entire conversation.

I was scared to my bones! Once again, tears were streaming down my face, and my whole body was trembling.

"Why can't they find him, Chase? Leland's good at his job; why can't he catch this monster?"

"I don't know, Sadey. I don't know. But hopefully all this new information will help. At least they have a lead that they didn't have before." Chase settled on the couch beside me, pulling me into his arms. He was holding onto me tight; he could feel my body quivering. "Leland's doing everything he can. He has so many people out looking for him; the guy must have a hide-out somewhere."

It wasn't long before Leland showed up, and he had some reinforcements with him as well. Chase's answering machine was confiscated for evidence, and his whole house was searched, inside and out, for anything that could have been dangerous. The house was all clear, and so was the yard. I had no doubt about this since Bones wasn't acting any differently. He may be a drool machine, but he's a great watchdog – he takes his job seriously. He was currently sitting at my feet with his head in my lap, protecting me from all the scary police officers that were running around the house.

After everything calmed down a little, Leland came back in the living room and sat down with us. "He's supposed to have his preliminary hearing on Friday; let's hope he shows. If he does, we serve the warrant on the charges of threatening a state official, and I'm doubling that charge after the message you just got, and that should be enough to revoke his bond and hold him until trial. Let's just hope the judge sees it our way. I talked to Galvin last week when he made the phone call to you at work, and he immediately got a warrant for that. The problem is that we can't find him; I've never had this problem. He's holed up somewhere, and somebody's protecting him; I'm hoping it's this girl Amber. I have Officer Dobe running down all the information about her. I talked to Matt and he said that her full name is Amber Reynolds, and he removed a newborn almost a year ago and placed her in foster care because the mom was too doped up all the time to even take care of herself. She never went through with the treatment plan and never even asked to see her little girl; she's currently in a foster home that's working to adopt her. But, Mark, he's starting to make mistakes, and that's going to get him nailed."

"I'm so tired of being scared." Chase just tightened his grip on me at this point. The next thing I know, my cell phone is ringing off the hook. Cami called to make sure I was ok; mom called to freak out, and Trey called to see if Chase needed any help kicking ass. Good grief. It was definitely going to be a long night.

My 4 moods ~

* I'm too old for this crap.

* I'm too tired for this crap.

* I'm too sober for this crap.

* I don't have time for this crap.

The fire

Friday, October 12th

Staff meeting was cut short for me since I had to go to court this morning. I managed to get a couple of investigations off my caseload, which helped ease the pain of that a little. Chase didn't even bother leaving the DHHR building; he just waited in my office for me to finish so we could head to the courtroom. When I rolled into my office, Chase was sitting at my desk with his feet propped up; but he appeared to be deep in thought.

I was so nervous. On one hand, I wanted Mark to show up so they could arrest him again; on the other hand, I didn't want to face him. Chase could sense my hesitation.

"It's going to be ok, Sadey. You'll be safe in the courtroom; there will be security everywhere, ok?"

"I'm nervous, Chase. Actually, truthfully, I'm terrified." He stood up, pulled me up from the scooter, and wrapped me in his arms. He lifted my chin, looked me in the eye, and then kissed me, hard. I wanted to melt, right there in his arms.

At this point he simply waltzed me out of the building and into the car. Or maybe he was just worried that if we stood there any longer we were going to be found in a compromising position in a state building and we would both lose our jobs; not to mention, we'd be late for court.

I had to enter the courthouse via wheelchair since there are so many steps. Another minor inconvenience, which also showed my vulnerability. I really wanted to walk right in the courtroom, no weaknesses, with a fight to the death attitude. Let's be honest; I didn't have it in me. I'm wearing two casts, being pushed in a wheelchair, and my hands were still shaking. Since the first two were obvious, I was hoping that nobody would notice the third thing.

When we entered the courtroom, I could see Galvin already sitting at the Prosecutor's table. Leland was up front talking to a couple of uniformed officers that appeared to be bailiffs. There was an attorney sitting at the defense table, but no Mark. Ok, so you've beat him here. Now he has to walk in on your territory, not the other way around. Gather some strength Sadey; the whole room is on your side. Court was set to start at 9:30, and it was 9:25; still no Mark. I wasn't sure how I was feeling about this. If he walked in right now, he'd definitely still see the fear in my eyes. If he didn't show up, it meant I didn't have to face him; but it also meant that he was still out there to cause more chaos in my life.

9:35 – no Mark.

9:45 – court called to order anyway. Judge Bangor asked about the defendant – Mark Kinders– and his attorney said he had no idea where he was, that he hadn't spoken with him since he first received the case last week. The attorney said that Mark had indicated that he would waive the preliminary hearing, but he was not here so that couldn't be confirmed. Judge Bangor listened to Galvin and the new information – namely the threatening phone calls – that had happened in the last week, and immediately issued a bench warrant for his arrest for failure to appear.

Just as the judge dismissed the courtroom, another bailiff came running into the room hollering at Chase. "Davis, there's a fire; I think it's your house."

A flurry of activity began immediately. Chase became frantic and he and Leland were discussing what to do – namely about me. "Chase, I'm going with you. Don't even think about leaving me with somebody else."

"Sadey, if Mark did this, he could still be around there watching. I don't want you in any danger."

"Dammit, Chase! Now is not the time to argue with me! Bones is at your house; get my ass in the car and let's go! Now!"

That's exactly what we did. I have no idea how we made it out of the building and into the car so quickly, but we were escorted to his house by lights and sirens – no red lights – no stop signs – no slowing down. It was full speed ahead and hold on for the turns, which is actually very difficult to do with a broken arm. I don't know whether I was more scared or more angry at the moment; maybe a strong combination of the two. Chase's house is on fire because of me. His house; my dog; I can't handle losing anything else. This is just all too much!

"This is all my fault, Chase!"

"No, it's not, Sadey. We don't even know yet what caused the fire. We're jumping to conclusions."

"We know damn well what caused the fire – Mark Kinders! And it's my fault; the SOB is after me and he just burnt down your house to send that message!" I couldn't hold the tears back any longer. I was crying in big sobs and I couldn't control the flood of emotions that were going through my head at the moment.

Chase is going to hate me; he'll never speak to me again. Bones had better not be hurt. Chase worked hard to buy that house, and now it's gone because of me.

We made it to Chase's house, or what was left of his house, in record time. We couldn't get anywhere near the driveway because of the fire trucks and police cars. Leland was already shouting directions about closing off the area and beginning a man hunt for

Mark. They were sure he would stick around to watch his handiwork.

Chase just stared in awe of the wreckage. His entire house was engulfed in flames – there would be nothing saved; nothing at all.

I just covered my face; I couldn't look at the damage. "I'm going to be sick." Chase immediately came around the car to get me out, and then had second thoughts. He opened the door, but then squatted down beside me.

"Sadey, I want you to stay in this car, with the doors locked."

"Chase, no! No! Don't leave me in here alone!"

"You can't walk. I have to go look around; I have to find Bones." At the mention of his name, I lost control again. I couldn't breathe; it was like a 1,000 lb. weight was sitting on my chest. Where is my dog? Was he in the house or out? I couldn't remember when we left this morning whether we left him outside or not. This can't really be happening, can it?

"Sadey, lock the doors and stay put. Let me go find Bones first and then I'll come back and get you, ok." I was scared out of my gourd, but I just shook my head 'yes'. He slowly started walking towards what used to be his house, and I could see him telling the firefighters about Bones and trying to figure out if the dog was in or out of the house when the fire started.

I had my eye on Chase the entire time; I never saw the rock that smashed out the passenger side window. Shards of glass flew into my face and neck as a large rock made contact with my head. I think I saw a shadow of something leaping through the air, but then I was out.

~~~~~~~~~~~~~~~~~~~~

All Mark could think about was 'that bitch ruined my life; I'm gonna destroy everything precious to her, and anyone that gets in my way'.

"They'll be in court waiting impatiently for my arrival, which will obviously not happen," Mark said to Amber.

"Ok, I get setting the fire; but sticking around afterwards is too dangerous."

"I want my chance at her. We both know she'll be there with him, so all I have to do is wait for the right opportunity and then 'lights out' for Miss Sadey Collins."

"How do you plan to not be noticed; the cops will be everywhere."

"So will the firefighters. I will be dressed like one of them milling around. It will be total chaos with so much smoke and fire that it won't be uncommon for the firefighters to have their shields down on their helmets."

"Just please be safe, ok."

"Yeah, yeah. Ok. Look, nobody knows about you so you can just be some onlooker driving by slowly to see what's going on. Just don't go too far because I'll need a ride out of there."

~~~~~~~~~~~~~~~~~~~~~~~~~~~~~

I woke up in the hospital, in the Emergency room, I assume. I could hear Chase's voice say something like, "her eyes are open", and I felt a huge weight on my body. Chase had a hold of my hand, and he was crying. "Sadey, Oh my God, Sadey. I'm so sorry. I promised to keep you safe and I didn't. Please don't hate me; I didn't mean to break that promise. I didn't see him, I swear. I'm so sorry."

Suddenly there was a large tongue on my face, obviously trying to clean whatever wounds I had. I realized that the huge weight I felt on my body was Bones; he was laying on top of me and licking my face.

There were nurses everywhere, running around doing things to monitors, tending to cuts on my face and neck, and doing something to Bones.

"What happened?" I could barely muster up enough strength to speak.

"Sadey, I'm sorry. I'm so sorry. I was only trying to find Bones; I didn't mean to not protect you." Chase was still crying, and I was still so confused. My big, strong protector had been reduced to tears. I remembered the fire; everything was destroyed.

"Chase –my God, your house, I'm so sorry; he burned down your house because of me. What happened to me? Why am I here?"

He sat up, trying to wipe the tears from his face, and regain his composure.

"I went to find Bones and I told you to lock yourself in the car. I thought you would be safe; I'm sorry. Mark was watching and waiting, just like we suspected, except nobody saw him because he was dressed like a firefighter. When he saw you were alone, he took a large rock and threw it through the window; it busted the glass and hit you in the head. You had small shards of glass in your face and neck that the nurses removed. I don't know where Bones was, but apparently, he saw Mark and ran at him full force. He knocked him to the ground; Mark hit his head on the concrete, and he was out cold. They took him by ambulance, but I don't know what his condition is."

He was crying again. "Oh Sadey, I'm so sorry. Please don't hate me. I love you. Please forgive me."

Whoa. What?!

I felt like I couldn't breathe. "Ok, back up. First of all, Mark is caught?"

Chase was starting to calm down, and replied, "Yes. Bones knocked him out when he knocked him to the ground."

"Is Bones going to be arrested for assault?" Apparently, I'm on some pretty good drugs because what I just said sounded really stupid.

It brought a chuckle from Chase and a couple of nurses. "No, he's not. As a matter of fact, Leland is getting him an award for bravery for saving your life. He has a broken leg, but it's just a small fracture, nothing big; they're not sure if he broke it getting out of the house or from the fall with Mark, but he's going to be ok."

"Is that why he's laying on top of me? Because I can't really breathe."

"Yeah, his leg is splinted up. I'll see if they can get him his own bed. Nobody could pull him away from you. He rode in the ambulance with us to get here."

That sounded good. He deserved his own bed; he was a hero now. I would definitely be feeding him canned food from here on out! My brain waves started firing again, and I realized exactly what Chase had said earlier.

"Second, did you just say that you loved me?"

"Um, well, yeah, I think I did."

I couldn't help but laugh a little at the look on his face. Best to move on or the drugs will start talking for me. "We'll deal with that when I'm not on drugs. What's the deal with your house?"

"It's completely destroyed. Nothing much salvageable, besides the garage, but it was all concrete. It was insured, so things can be replaced. He poured gasoline around the entire house and just torched it."

"I'm sorry about your house Chase. It's my fault. And we just bought all that food."

"Sometimes I really wonder what goes on in that head of yours, Sweet Cheeks. But it's not your fault Sadey – Mark burned down my house – not you. Stop blaming yourself, ok. This is crazy. But the bastard is in custody, that's all that matters."

"Chase?"

"Yes, baby?"

"I guess you're going to have to move into my house now. And it has a new porch we can sit on because all those cute guys built it in just one day. And we need to go to the grocery store again because we left the ice cream at your house."

They definitely gave me some good drugs. I heard Chase laughing, but I don't remember anything after that. I don't know how long I was at the hospital or even how I got home, but I woke up in my own bed and there was a lot of noise coming from my living room.

~~~~~~~~~~~~~~~~~~~~~~~~~~~~~~~~

Amber was sitting in the parking lot of the Go-Mart just up the road from the house that Mark was setting on fire. She saw the house go up in flames and it wasn't long before the fire trucks arrived; they were followed closely by the police and several other cars. She saw the girl Mark was after talking to the guy who owned the house; well, the charred remains of the house now. She kept her binoculars on the girl knowing that Mark would show up eventually.

As soon as she saw him go up to the car she pulled out in the road and drove slowly towards the house waiting for him to come running towards her. Instead, she saw Mark on the ground with a large dog on top of him and cops swarming towards him. She didn't waste any time, she got the hell out of there as quickly as she could, flying past a couple of uniforms and the local media. She headed straight to her mom's house; she wasn't taking any chances on anybody putting the two of them together and showing up at her house. She'd just lay low there for a day or two until the frenzy died down.

~~~~~~~~~~~~~~~~~~~~~~~~~~~~~~~~

Bones was sleeping beside me on the bed, and when I stirred it woke him up. He didn't bother nudging me; he just snuggled up closer to me and handed out a few doggy kisses. I could see that his front leg was bandaged up and he was not putting any pressure on it. He appeared way too calm, so I'm assuming they gave him some doggy drugs like what they gave me. I looked up and saw Chase standing in the doorway of my bedroom. He looked awful. I patted the bed, motioning for him to come over and sit down beside me.

"What's going on out there? Is the entire posse here?"

"Yeah, and then some. Cami; your mom; Noelle with Dane, Blake, and Abi – and they're adorable; Janice; Matt; and Trey has called me three times already. He was ticking them off on his fingers. Nobody will leave until they're convinced you're going to be ok. On the plus side, they all brought food."

That brought a smile to my face; food is a good subject.

"How are you feeling?"

"Like I got run over by a car."

"Well, this time it was a rock to the head, but some of the same results. You have a bad concussion and a lot of cuts that are bandaged where they removed the glass from your face. Do you feel like meeting with the crowd?"

"Maybe in a minute, after I pee." He busted out laughing, but then I ruined the fun. "Chase, I'm sorry about your house; really. It's my fault you were dragged into all this to begin with." He put his finger over my lip to shush me, then bent down and softly kissed me.

"Let's get you to the bathroom, and then go out and face the gauntlet; then maybe they'll all go home."

After ensuring that I didn't look in a mirror, Chase maneuvered me out to the living room where everybody immediately started hovering. My mom was trying to mess with the strips on my face and I had to bat her away. It took a minute to convince them all to back off a little. They meant well; they just wanted to make sure I was going to be ok, but they were in my bubble. After some long, drawn out conversations about taking care of me, I'd finally had enough and had to say something.

"Would everybody please just shut up for a minute? Please!"

They all looked at me a little funny, but the room suddenly got quiet.

"Thanks. I know that everybody wants to take care of me, and I love you all for that. However, if you try to start making out nursing charts again, I'm just going to have to kill you. So, let me make this clear to everybody. Chase is moving in here; he has no home, thanks to me and my stalker, so this is now his home. Don't give me that look, Chase, and mom, don't argue with me. He can handle the basics. Since I don't need round the clock security, then that makes things a little easier. Chase can go back to work and we can work out some of you coming by for a couple of hours here and there to check in on me, ok? Hopefully on Tuesday they will get me out of this cast and I will able to walk some on my own; that will help a great deal."

I was getting a few head nods, and a few strange looks, like they figured it was just the drugs talking. But I didn't care; this was my house and I was going to make the rules.

"You are more than welcome to send food; I've never turned down a good meal. But you can't hover over me anymore. I'm suffocating. I love all of you and I'm the luckiest girl in the world to have friends and family like you guys. But I need to deal with all this my own way, and I need to move forward."

Everybody just started looking around at one another; probably trying to decide who was going to speak up first and endure my wrath. Cami took the lead.

"Ok guys. You've heard her. She needs her rest, but they'll also need food and some random check-in times. Chase and I will work it all out and let you know what she needs. Is everybody ok with that?"

"No, I'm not ok with it." Of course my mother would be the one to disagree with everything. "That's my little girl and I'll take care of her if I want to."

"Mom, she's not saying you can't take care of me; just that I don't have to have somebody here round the clock now."

"Ok, but I expect to be the first one you call if you need something, understand?" She was still pouting.

"Yes, ma'am. Now all of you go home so I can go back to bed without all this noise. Oh, mom?"

She perked back up. "Yes, baby?"

"I do need some new clothes. I think most of my stuff was burned up in the fire; especially my sweatpants."

"I'm on it. Dane, take the babies home. Noelle and I are going shopping. She'll be home later this evening. Chase, I'll bring back some food when I bring over the clothes later; and we'll get you some clothes, too. Cami, I expect you to call me immediately if there's something she needs."

After mom finished spouting directions to everyone, and feeling needed again, they all started parting ways, slowly.

Janice got up from the chair, smoothing down her bright, multi-colored skirt, that only she can pull off, and started walking over to me; she stopped abruptly and looked over at Chase. With a huge grin on her face, she said, "Girlfriend – I still want to know where I can find me one of these hunks to take care of me. They just don't make 'em like this where I come from." That got a big laugh out of me.

"You can't have my hunk; check with Cami – maybe she'll give up hers."

"Fat chance you two. I had my hunk first; find your own," Cami replied. And just on cue, Cami's hunk walked through the front door. He obviously heard that part of the conversation, because he added, "They broke the mold with me, Janice, but I'm sure there's an extra semi-hunk out there somewhere that will put up with your southern accent."

"Ah hell no... You may be adorable, but this southern girl can still kick your grits."

On that note, everybody filed out except for Cami and Leland. Chase brought Leland and himself a beer and they both sat down and got comfortable; I guess Leland and Cami must be staying a while.

Just as he got settled, Leland's phone rang.

"What's up Fort?" Daniel Fort is an officer in Leland's inner circle.

"You know the girl, Amber, that we're trying to find? She was at the fire."

"Seriously? How do you know that?"

"I was scanning all the footage from the media and just about the same time that the dog took Kinders down, that green van was slowly coming down the street and then took off quickly, but she didn't realize that there was video being taken all over the place from the media. She was definitely supposed to be his getaway plan."

"Any idea where she headed?"

"The opposite direction from her house. Did we ever find out if she had family around here?"

"Hang on." Leland looked at me and said, "Do me a favor and call Matt. I need to know if Amber has family around here; I remember something about her mom, but that specific info wasn't in her file that Janice gave me. She was Mark's getaway at the fire; TV video caught her."

I called Matt, who said that she has a mother in the area, on the north end of town. "The mother isn't well; not sure exactly what her medical issues are, but she's sick enough that she couldn't take Amber's baby."

I gave Leland the address and he, in turn, gave it to Fort, who was most likely now on his way to finding Mark Kinders' accessory.

Two hours later we had covered everything from Mark, to the house fire, to Bones' bravery, to my injuries, to Chase's new living arrangements. They left with the promise that they would be back tomorrow afternoon to try out the new front porch and throw some steaks on the grill.

Turns out that Mark had broken his back in two places, had a broken clavicle and one hell of a concussion. Good! Serves him right. I really wish Bones would have just killed him, though; get this over with.

Bones came limping down the hallway and climbed up on the couch beside me. Chase settled in on the other side of me and wrapped his arm around me. He was sitting in the corner of the couch and I was leaning into him with one foot on the couch and the other on the floor. Bones apparently got a little jealous or something because he got up and climbed across me to Chase. He plopped himself down on Chase's lap and laid his extremely large head on Chase's shoulder. It had to be the cutest thing I've ever seen; wish I could get to a camera right now. It wasn't long before Bones was snoring and the whole situation made me feel like, despite everything that just happened, I was very happy at this particular moment and I didn't want that feeling to ever leave. I let out a big sigh, snuggled in a little closer, and realized that for the first time in my life, in spite of the pain, I was content.

When you hear a southern girl say "Ah, hell no..." you'd better run.

Dr. Appointment

Tuesday, October 16th

I woke up this morning hoping and praying that my doctor's appointment would go in my favor. I've been in these casts a little too long for my liking, and I'm hoping that x-rays will show some healing and I can get these babies removed.

The waiting room was fairly empty, and I got back to the room right on time; very unusual for a doctor's office. They took me straight to X-ray, and took pictures of my arm and my leg. But my payment for being taken back to the room so quickly was that I had wait forever and a day for the doctor to come in with my results. I was already feeling impatient, but now I'm starting to get a little cranky as well. Just about the time that Chase was ready to knock me upside the head, the doctor came in and saved me.

My arm was not completely healed, as it was broken in two places; my leg, on the other hand, was healing nicely and the cast could be removed. Unfortunately, the cast was being replaced by this leg boot/cast kind of thing that went all the way up to my knee, but I could walk with it. I was required to go to Physical therapy twice a week; I still couldn't drive, and he kept me on limited work release, but at least its progress. Not to mention, the doctor wasn't too thrilled with the new injuries to my face. I was able to walk myself out to the car with only minimal difficulty, but getting in the car was still a little bit of a challenge.

I couldn't wait to get home and take a real bath – and shave my legs! My ankle was still pretty weak, so I'll admit that I did need a little help getting out of the tub without falling, but I was pretty sure I could dry myself off. Chase didn't see it my way; he thought he should help out with the drying off process.

Wearing this boot-thingy meant that my ankle still had to be taped up and wrapped so that I didn't risk twisting it and causing more damage, like breaking another bone. This meant I couldn't walk on it until it was taped up and the boot-thingy was on my leg; so this gave Chase an excuse to carry me to the bedroom, naked. Of course, his excuse was that it was easier to tape up my ankle if I was lying down, and the best place to lie down was on the bed.

While I'm flat on my back, stark naked, I figured this was as good a time as any to bring up that conversation we started on Friday. "So, mister magic fingers, I think you still owe me some answers."

"Answers about what?" Chase was actually confused, which meant the ball was in my court and I was already in the lead.

"I know I was high on some sort of painkillers, but I know that I distinctly heard you say that you loved me. Wanna explain that?" Now I was the one with the smirk on my face.

"What kind of explanation are you looking for?" I thought I saw the corners of his mouth turn up, like he wanted to smile, but had to stop himself. He was still taping up my ankle and using it as a distraction to keep from answering my question; it was kind of cute.

"I'm looking for the one where you tell me whether you meant that statement, or whether you were just caught up in your emotions and the adrenaline from Mark's attack on me."

He finished taping my ankle, smacked me on the side of my ass and said, "Roll over."

"What? Why? So you don't have to answer to my face there chicken?"

"No, so I can rub your legs because we have to keep the circulation going. So shut up and roll over."

I did, but he wasn't getting out of the conversation that easily. "So, can you move your mouth and your hands at the same time?"

"I'm pretty multi-talented, if you must know. And I can see that you're gonna make me get mushy, right?"

"Maybe."

He stopped rubbing my legs and stared at some blank space on the wall. I was pretty sure he was arguing with himself, so I gave him some time, in hopes that I could win the argument he was having between his brain and his emotions. He eventually crawled up on the bed beside me and propped himself up on one elbow. Of course, this was only slightly awkward, since I was laying here naked as a jaybird, and he was fully clothed; but then I realized that I really wasn't all that embarrassed. He started stroking my hair and then leaned in and kissed me on the forehead

"I didn't mean to make you uncomfortable Chase. I just…well,…it's just that…the other night when you, me, and Bones were all cuddled up on the couch…well…I realized that it was the first time in my life that I was really content…like truly happy. You know?"

He didn't give me any funny looks or even break eye contact; he just said, "Yeah, I know. I've kind of grown accustomed to having you around all the time, and I'm just not sure I want that to change. Although it will definitely be easier having you around with your killer stalker safely locked behind bars."

That got a laugh out of me.

"I know it's just been a month since we met, but I've never, ever felt like this before. What you said about adrenaline, and maybe I'm just feeding off all this stuff that's happened with Mark…I don't think so; I don't think that's it. For the first time in my life, I care about something more than my job. All I think about is you; and each time something else happened, or you were scared, I felt it. I felt it like it was happening to me. I think I can honestly say that…that I love you, Sadey; I really do."

By this time, I had a few tears streaming down my face; but not sad tears, for a change. I couldn't have been happier; or so I thought. Because, as Chase wiped the tears from my face, he rolled me back over onto my back, and proceeded to make me the happiest woman alive.

An arrow can only be shot by pulling it backwards. When life is dragging you back with difficulties, it means it's going to launch you into something great. So just focus and keep aiming.

Monday, October 22nd

I was growing accustomed to being able to sleep in on Monday mornings; however, this was the first day of physical therapy and Chase insisted we be on time. I wasn't sure I was looking forward to this, but it's supposed to help make my leg stronger so I can eventually walk without the boot.

At first it wasn't so bad; the physical therapist, Mitchell, was massaging my leg, ankle, and foot. Unfortunately, I had to admit out loud that Chase was right about the circulation in my legs, because the PT just said the same thing. Ugh. But then he started making me do some pushing of a rubber band thingamajig, and that hurt like the devil. No matter how much I wanted to be ready to do more on my own, I was now physically aware of my limitations, even without the cast.

The PT made it clear that I was not to put any pressure on my foot without my ankle being wrapped and my leg being in the boot; major bummer. Apparently, I could easily rebreak my ankle, which would land me in a cast for several more weeks; that was not an option I wanted, so following the directions of the physical therapist seemed like my only alternative.

When we got back in the car, Chase started reiterating what the PT was telling me. "You heard Mitchell, right? He said no pressure, so stop trying to stand up by yourself in the bathtub, got it?"

"Admit it; you told him to say that just so you could get my wet, naked body out of the bathtub every day."

"No. I swear I didn't say a thing; but I'm definitely going to follow his directions to the letter." Of course, he said this with that cute little smirk of his on his face.

"Of course you are," I said chuckling.

Then he just went silent, and he was obviously arguing with himself, because his lips were moving but nothing was coming out.

"What's going through your head? You're obviously arguing with yourself. And you aren't very good at it."

"Says the girl that loses every argument she has with herself. But I'm trying not to be obvious about it; I sure don't want anybody to think I'm crazy, like you."

That earned him a punch to the side of his leg. "So, what are you arguing with yourself about this time?"

"I want to talk to you about something, but I don't want you to go on the offensive or yell at me."

"Am I that scary?"

"Sometimes." He said it laughing, but I knew whatever he wanted to say was serious, and he was battling how to say it to me. Guess I should just make it easy on the poor guy.

"Ok, spill it. I'll try not to yell and get scary. I swear."

"Here goes." He took a deep breath, and then a long sigh. "I want you to go with me to the jail on Thursday afternoon."

I took a deep breath so I wouldn't explode and yell at him for making such a stupid statement. I let out my breath, and calmly asked, "Why?"

"Don't yell, ok."

"I'm trying. Just explain yourself."

"While you were doing PT, I got a phone call from Galvin. He has apparently agreed to a reduction in sentence hearing for your dad."

"What's that mean?"

"It means that his lawyer has requested that he be allowed to finish the rest of his sentence on either home confinement, probation, or a combination of both. Galvin called me because in order for the sentencing to be considered, there has to be a pre-sentencing investigation done by the probation office. Because his conviction is for drugs that lands him in my office."

"You'd be my dad's probation officer? Isn't that against some sort of regs or something if you're living with me?"

"No. I asked Galvin about that and he told me that there's no conflict of interest because, for one, we're not married, and secondly, we are a small county with limited POs so it would be cleared by the judge."

"What if I wanted to marry you?" I said with a huge grin on my face, and in my best sarcastic tone.

He didn't miss a beat. "Then you just have to wait another month until after your dad's hearing."

"Ha ha, you're too funny. So, why do I have to go to the jail?"

"You don't. But you will get every answer you've ever wanted to hear, because he knows that if he's not 100% honest with me, he stays behind bars for another two years."

"I don't know, Chase. I really don't want to go see him."

"I know; really, I do. I'm not trying to make you mad, or even uncomfortable; I'm not trying to push you to do this big reconciliation thing either. I just know that, good or bad, you're going to hear a wealth of information. Some of it might set your mind at ease, and some of it might seriously tick you off. Either way, you'll get some answers; answers from him and not the cookie-cutter version from your mother."

"Ugh. This pretty well sucks. You know how much I hate that place."

"Just think about it, ok? My appointment with him is Thursday afternoon at 1:00, so you have until Thursday, noon, to make up your mind."

"Yeah. Ok. Fine; I'll think about it."

"Fair enough. Now, how about some lunch?"

"Are you buying?"

"Yeah."

"Olive Garden?"

"What if I had said it was your turn to buy?"

"We'd be going to McDonalds; I'm cheap."

"Ok, Olive Garden it is; just because you've had a rough morning."

My totally awesome lunch then led to an amazing two-hour nap. Physical therapy is apparently more exhausting than I realized, because I was out like a light in no time flat. I think the only reason I woke up was because I had to pee.

I sat up and swung my feet over the edge of the bed and started putting my boot on so that I could walk myself to the bathroom.

But, as usual, nothing ever works for me; I'm a complete failure. I was trying to grab the Velcro doohickeys to wrap around my leg, and the Velcro caught on my cast, which caused me to jerk my arm, which caused me to go head-first onto the floor.

It's like the same movie playing over and over in my life. This commotion woke up Bones, who had been sleeping comfortably beside me on the bed. He immediately jumped off the bed and began kissing my face with everything his tongue had to offer; at least his leg was doing better.

Apparently, the commotion was also heard by Chase, since he came running into the bedroom pretty quickly.

"Are you ok? What did you do?"

"I'm not telling you because you'd just laugh at me, and I can't laugh right now or I'll pee my pants. Just help me up."

"Got it – eyes open, must pee."

After a successful trip to the bathroom, with no more mishaps, I finally got settled in on the couch; and I had successfully stolen the remote from Chase. As I searched through the hundreds and hundreds of channels to try and find something worth watching, I decided to ask Chase the million-dollar question.

"Chase – can I ask you something? And I want you to be 100% honest with me. Ok?"

"Sure. I've never lied to you, and I won't start now."

"About your house…it really is my fault that your house got burned down."

"Sadey…"

"No, Chase, don't interrupt. Just listen, please. I feel really guilty about you losing your house. You worked really hard to buy that house, and it's gone, because you were protecting me. Are you going to wake up one day and hate me because I was the reason your house was burned down?"

"Can I talk now?" I just nodded. "Sadey, how many times do I have to tell you that it's not your fault, it's…"

"Yeah, yeah, yeah – it's Mark's fault. Seriously, Chase, if you hadn't been trying to protect me from Mark, your house would still be standing."

"And I wouldn't be sitting here ogling over how adorable you are in sweatpants and waiting patiently for you to tell me you want to take a bath."

"Seriously?"

"Seriously. Sadey, aside from the fact that Mark is an evil SOB that caused you way too much physical and mental harm, I am kinda thankful for the guy. Yeah, Cami introduced us, but Mark brought us together."

"Sometimes I think you're too sweet. How can you possibly just be this nice about something so huge?"

"I learned a long time ago that stuff can be replaced, but people can't. I'm willing to lose a house, if it means I get to keep you."

"I just mean…I just don't want you to…"

"Just stop, Sadey. Look at me. Please." He took his hand and gently held my chin. We were eye to eye and nose to nose. "I liked my house; I love you. I don't want to hear another word about the house. Ok?"

I simply nodded my head up and down. I couldn't speak; I could barely breathe. Looking in his eyes has some sort of paralysis effect on me – my heart races, my palms get sweaty, my body tingles, and my mouth can't speak words. Just as well, since he really didn't want to talk anyway. His hands left my face, and headed elsewhere…

One small crack doesn't mean that you are broken ~ it means that you were put to the test and you didn't fall apart ~ Linda Poindexter

Traitor

Thursday, October 25th

"I'm going, mom, I promise. Just please stop nagging me. It's not like I have a choice; between you and Chase, you guys are gonna make sure of it."

"I'm not nagging, Sadey. I love you. Just call me later and let me know how it went."

"I will; bye."

"Chase?!"

He came walking into the living room like a dog in trouble, with his tail tucked between his legs. He knew I was ticked.

"So now you're telling my mom on me?!"

"It's not like that Sadey. When I do a pre-sentencing investigation, I have to talk with other family members in the home; it's required to make sure that the person has a support system in their home. That meant that I had to talk to your mom, which meant that she knew I was going to the jail. You can piece the rest together on your own."

"I'm going, just because I already told you I would; but don't expect me to be happy about it."

"Fair enough. If I bribe you with a great massage, or a Blizzard, will you at least be nice."

"Hmm. That's pretty tempting. But I'm still mad at you."

The smirk was back on his face, which usually meant I was doomed. Good thing it was time to leave for physical therapy, or I would most likely be without clothing in about 2.5 seconds.

I was trying to pout and still be mad at Chase, but he makes it very difficult because he's so dang sweet. He helped me into the car, reached across to hook the seatbelt and brushed his hand against my breast.

"No fair. I'm trying to be mad and you're busy copping a feel. You're playing dirty."

He didn't even respond; just that stupid smirk.

Physical therapy was extremely painful today; so much so that the PT recommended that Chase give me a pain pill after I had some food in my stomach. I did argue with Chase on this, because I figure if I'm forced to go to the jail and see my dad, then I should at least have all my senses about me, and pain medication makes me loopy. We finally settled on 800mg Ibuprofen, for now. But since I'm required to eat before I can take any medication, lunch was definitely the next stop.

Since it was my turn to buy, we stopped and had the Pizza Hut lunch buffet. Plus, we didn't have a lot of time to waste, and it was a 45-minute drive to the jail. I argued that this was just enough time for me to eat a large Blizzard; Chase argued that I should have to earn the Blizzard by being nice and polite while we were at the jail. I did my best to convince him he was wrong, but since he was the one driving, I was just plain screwed.

"I can't wait until I can drive again; then I can stop and get a Blizzard anytime I want."

"You're also forgetting that you don't own a car right now."

"Oh yeah." After Mark decided to spray paint my car, I decided this was as good a time as any to get rid of it. It wasn't in bad shape, just needed a new paint job now, and it was full of bad memories. So, I sold it to the kid down the street pretty cheap; he said he could get it painted and it would make a great car for him to take back and forth to school.

"Well, as soon as I can drive, then we're going car shopping, and then I can get my own Blizzards."

"Until then, you're under my control." There's that stupid smirk again.

I was fine the rest of the trip, but the minute we pulled into the jail parking lot, it was like I lost my nerve again. "I really don't want to do this."

"Too bad; we're here so you can't back out now."

He turned towards me in the car and said, "Sadey, listen. You don't even have to talk if you don't want to; this is my appointment, not yours. So, let me and your dad do all the talking and you just sit and listen. Ok?"

"Yeah. Fine." I was still pouting, but I wasn't going to get my way. That was obvious; might as well make the best of it.

The search process was a little easier, but they did have to inspect my boot and make sure I didn't bring any drugs or weapons with me and hide them inside my new wardrobe. We were led back to the visitation area, through those awful clanging metal doors. Again, my dad was already waiting in the room when they brought us back. Apparently, he had no idea I was coming; he was thrilled. He jumped up and hugged me like he was never letting go; he was squeezing the life outta me.

"Dad, I can't breathe."

"Oh, sorry Sadey. I didn't know you were coming; I'm just excited. You got your cast off your leg? Does that thing feel better? What about your arm? Is it healing?"

"How about one question at a time, dad. My leg is doing better, but I have to go to physical therapy twice a week because my ankle and foot bones are still very weak. I can't walk without this boot thing, and I still sometimes need help with things. My arm is healing, but it was broken in two places, so I have to wear the cast longer. But I'm fine."

"I'm just so glad you're here; they just told me that the probation officer was coming to see me."

That was Chase's cue to get me off the hook. "That would be me, Mr. Collins. My name is Chase Davis, and I'm the probation officer that deals with drug cases."

"Great. Please call me Bryson; there's not anything formal about my life. So how did you convince my Sadey-bug to come with you?"

"I bribed her."

I started laughing because I knew exactly what the bribe was, but I wasn't sharing that information; not with my dad. Unfortunately for me, my dad may have spent his life doing stupid stuff, but he's definitely not stupid.

"Ahhh. I get it. You must be the guy that Kadira said was staying with Sadey. Does she know that you're sleeping together?"

"Dad!"

"Well, it's obvious to me; but if she doesn't know yet, I won't be the one to rat you out."

"I'd appreciate that. I've got too much going on to deal with her lectures right now."

"Ok, my lips are sealed. But you know she's going to find out sooner or later."

"Yep, but I'm all for 'later'."

"Are you two done, because I don't want to have to plead the fifth on this conversation if Kadira ever asks me?"

"Sorry. Maybe you should just do your PO thing and I'll sit over here and shut up." That got a chuckle from Chase and my dad. They were both aware that sitting off to the side and shutting up is not one of my strong points. It's weird, though. I just had a normal conversation with my dad, and it felt kinda good; at least there's no more tension in the air.

Except I just noticed his hands.

"What happened to your hands, dad?"

"Oh, nothing. It just met some concrete it didn't like."

"Spill it, dad."

He looked at Chase, then back at me, and then resigned himself to the fact that I wasn't going to let it go. He looked at Chase and said, "I'm hoping what I'm about to say doesn't get held against me, but I've done too much lying to her over the years…"

"Go ahead; you're good," Chase said.

Dad let out a deep breath and said, "Ok, well when I found out that it was Mark Kinders that ran you over then I was seriously in a fit of rage. I got back to my cell and was asking my cellmate if he knew Mark – he did – and he said that he was here. I was so pissed at the situation that I punched the wall in my cell several times; it was that or kill somebody. One of the guards put two and two together and had me put in solitary for a couple of days to calm down, and then they moved Mark to another cell block so that our paths would never cross."

Then a light bulb went off.

"It was Trey, wasn't it?"

"Trey, what?"

"That told you it was Mark Kinders. When we were here last time, I didn't tell you his name, but when we were leaving I saw Trey whisper something to you when he hugged you goodbye."

He fessed up and I swore to Gibbs slap Trey the next time I saw him. But Chase butted in to give dad more to fume about.

"Bryson, what I'm about to tell you is probably going to get you seeing red again, but I'm going to need you to promise me that you won't act on what you're going to hear."

"I'll try, but if it's about something else with Sadey..."

"Listen, Mark has been caught, again, and he's here in this jail somewhere. He set my house on fire the day of his last court hearing and then threw a rock through the window of the car at Sadey and that's what the cuts on her face are from. Bones attacked him and broke his back in a couple of places and broke his left clavicle. He's been caught and he won't be getting bail. But I need to know that you can handle him being in here with you without you doing something stupid; Leland has it all under control."

My dad's face was turning a few different shades of red and his leg was bouncing non-stop under the table. He finally took a deep breath, looked at Chase and said, "It might be best to put me back in solitary for a couple of days; I'm going to need to vent."

"Fair enough; do they have rooms with the rubber mats on the walls here?"

"Yeah; there are a few in solitary."

"Ok, I'll talk to the guard and see if he can give you a room for a couple of days so that you're not hitting concrete again. But you have to keep your anger in check or everything else we're about to do will just be a waste of my time, ok."

Dad agreed; he calmed down a lot and so Chase thought it was good enough to continue what we actually came here to do.

"Ok, Bryson, I don't know if you've ever done one of these pre-sentencing investigations, or not, but I have to gather a wealth of information about you. And I need you to be completely honest with me, or I can't help you, ok?"

My dad looked at me, then looked back at Chase, then back to me. "Sadey, are you sure you want to hear all this? You're going to hear my whole life history, and it's not pretty. I wouldn't blame you if you didn't want to stay."

"Dad, I'm here because I want to hear this information. I've spent my whole life trying to figure out how you could spend so much time in and out of jail, but at the same time mom's telling us what a great guy you were. Bad or good, I want to know the truth."

"Ok, Mr. Davis; let's get this started."

"You can call me Chase, Bryson. With me there are no formalities either, ok. My job here is to make sure you are capable of serving the rest of your sentence on the outside, without doing anything stupid that would land you back in here. I will also tell you that I'm a stickler with the drugs; I will test you often, and randomly. Ok?"

"Ok. I really want out of here; I'm tired of jail."

"Tired enough to make some serious changes in your life?"

"Yes. I promise." I sucked in air when he said that, and he immediately realized what he said. "Sadey, this isn't another one of those broken promises. I will prove to you that I am a different person now. It's ok if you don't believe me; but I'll spend the rest of my life proving it to you if I need to."

I didn't respond to him. A flood of emotions were going through me right now, and I was starting to think that I made a mistake by coming here today. *What was it that I was really after? A confession? Confession to what? Maybe I just wanted him to be miserable? Or was I trying to get back at him for all those childhood activities I didn't get to do? Whatever it was, I was stuck here now, so I might as well make the best of it.*

Chase realized that I was arguing with myself, so he put the focus back on him and dad.

"Bryson, why don't we get started with my questionnaire, and then maybe we can get some questions answered."

"Yeah, that's fine. Ask away."

Apparently, this is an extremely long process that Chase has to go through each and every time he gets somebody that's being recommended for probation. This part of his job has to really suck; I hate documentation, but his paperwork is definitely worse than mine. He probably spent 10 minutes just getting background family information from dad; all the stuff about his parents and family. This was boring information that I already knew, so I sort of zoned out again.

How did he know that Chase and I were sleeping together? Does mom really know and she's not saying anything? Now I'm kind of embarrassed.

I zoned back in when Chase asked, "So tell me about Trey. I know there was an incident of domestic violence."

"Yeah. One of my lowest of moments. I grew up in a world where men were tough, and never showed emotions or pain. I really thought that's how all men should be, you know? Trey wasn't the sports kind; he was more into the band and the smart kids' clubs. I was never a smart kid, and I really didn't understand why he didn't want to play football; why he was a band geek. That's what they called themselves; I didn't just call him that. Anyway, I was high, and we got into an argument about buying his own trumpet instead of just using the one at the school. I thought it was a waste of money, but he stood his ground. He told me I was being an asshole, and I just lost it. I slapped him across the face, and when he raised his arm to hit me back, I grabbed it and twisted it around his back. I threw him against the wall and broke his arm."

My dad was crying as he was telling this story. This was the summer before I started college, and Trey was just in junior high. I vaguely remember this incident, but it was never talked about; mom just said that dad lost his temper. Nobody ever mentioned that dad was high when this happened. Dad kept talking.

"I think one of the neighbors called the cops when they heard all the yelling and stuff, because they showed up pretty quickly. Kadira said she didn't call them, but she did press charges against me for abuse on Trey. She didn't say anything about the drugs, but apparently it was obvious that I was high. I landed quite a bit of time behind bars for those combined charges."

Dad started talking about stuff that has never been mentioned in my home. "The thing is, Kadira told me that she loved me, gave me a kiss, but then left me sitting in jail. I was so angry. I just kept thinking this was all Trey's fault because he instigated it by calling me a name. Nobody came to see me for two weeks. It took me that long to realize that I really was being an ass, and Trey was just a kid; my kid. I broke my own kid's arm because I was high; that's the real truth. When Kadira finally came to see me, she didn't apologize for having me arrested. Instead, she told me that she left me here so I could calm down enough to realize I was wrong; and she was hoping that I would realize how bad the drugs were for me. She's the smartest and strongest person I know."

Dad never stopped crying. He was actually pouring his heart out to Chase, and to me. I was starting to see my dad as a real person, not just a dope head.

Chase can read people almost as well as Cami can. He just seemed to know exactly what questions to ask to make dad spill his guts. And never once did he judge or criticize my dad for anything he was talking about. I realized that I really did love him; and I loved my dad as well. For the next half hour Chase had dad talking about all the drugs he had used and sold, and about this latest incident that landed him sitting in this jail right now. I couldn't believe how open and honest my dad was being, and how much it affected me to hear him talk about all his crimes.

"I screwed up big time. This is the first time in my life that I realized what affect this had on my family. I've never had a close relationship with my kids, and that's because of the drugs. When Sadey was here the first time…"

He was crying hard at this point, and Chase didn't push him at all. He sat so patiently and waited for dad to get control of himself and begin talking again. This time he started talking to me. "It just hit me hard, Sadey. You kept telling me how I had broken all these promises that I'd made to you. The truth is, I didn't have a clue I was doing that. The only thing that mattered was getting that next hit; being high. Your mom took care of everything, and I just let her. It didn't even occur to me that what I was doing had any effect on you kids; your mom made sure you were well taken care of, so I never even noticed. I can't take it back, and I can't even apologize enough for you to even think about forgiving me. My stupid drug habit caused you an unfathomable about of pain, and I was clueless. I'm so sorry, Sadey. I can't tell you that enough."

At this point, I was crying too. Chase put his hand on my knee and squeezed; just showing me he was still here for me. I got up and hobbled around the table; I leaned down and gave my dad a big hug. He stood up and hugged me like he was never letting go.

"Thanks, dad. Thanks for just being honest."

"Sadey-bug, I love you. I've always loved you; I just let the drugs be my first love, instead of my family. I'm so sorry I've put you through all this; I hope you can eventually forgive me."

I sat down beside my dad for the rest of the interview, and I started thinking about all that lost time we had as a family because of the drugs. I deal with so many families that are going through these same issues. Even though I spend a lot of time trying to get these people in rehab, I need to spend more time with them together as a family, helping them to put the pieces back together again. Now I need to put together the pieces with my own family. Trey and Noelle seem to be able to move forward; now it's my turn.

"Are you arguing with yourself again, Sadey?" I must have been in that zone again, and Chase can read me like a book.

"Um, well, sort of. I just realized that I'm the only one who's not been willing to move forward, and maybe it's time I do." My dad got a big smile on his face, and so did Chase. I looked at my dad and said, "This won't be a quick and easy process for me; I won't lie. I've spent a lot of years being angry with you, but I really want to put our family back together. We need to have holidays with everybody sitting around the table, together, sober. I want those memories."

Dad grabbed my hands in his, turned and looked me straight in the eye. "Sadey, from this moment forward there will only be happy memories, and no more broken promises. I will work hard to make this happen for you. That's a promise I'm not going to break."

Chase piped in at this point. "Bryson, I hope for your sake, and Sadey's, that everything you just said is true. As your PO, I can put you back in jail for any slip-up; but if you break this girl's heart again…"

"I get it. I get it. I swear to both of you; from this point forward, no more drugs, and no more broken promises."

I hugged my dad and left the jail with tears still streaming down my face.

As we got to the car, Chase pinned me up against the door, tucked my loose hairs behind my ears, then leaned in and kissed me.

Here we go again; my palms are sweaty, my body is tingling, and I can't control my breathing. All I can think is, I'm the luckiest woman in the world! Well, that, and ice cream.

"Chase?"

"Yeah baby?"

"Did I earn that Blizzard?" He busted out laughing.

"I'm ready to toss you in my backseat and rid you of your clothes, and you're asking for a Blizzard?"

I was still having trouble with that breathing normally thing, but I managed to whisper in his mouth, "Blizzard now, reward for you later; too many cameras here. And you owe me a full body massage because I was nice."

"Ok, you win. But I'm holding you to that reward, and you'll get that massage," he whispered back. One more extremely hot kiss that made me melt; and I got in the car.

I got my Blizzard, a large one, and Chase got his compensation as well. A very rewarding day, if I should say so myself.

The pity train has just derailed at Suck it up street, crashing into We All Have Problems, before coming to a complete stop at Get the Hell Over It.

Family visit

Friday, October 26th

My phone is ringing as I'm headed into staff meeting: Leland.

"I need a favor."

"I'm listening."

"Do you know what today is?"

"The Friday from hell?"

"Besides that?"

"Ok, not off the top of my head." Lightbulb. "Oh, God, Leland. It's been so crazy that I totally forgot. I have staff meeting but then I can have someone run me over there and I'll spend the rest of the day with her."

"Thank you. I saw her put some Bailey's in her coffee this morning; not a good sign. She did pretty well last week about her dad, but she and her mom were tight, and she struggles on this date every year. Thanks for doing this; it's not me that she needs at times like this – it's you."

"No problem; and thanks for calling to remind me."

I wasn't late walking into staff meeting, but I was pushing my luck, especially when I told the boss that I needed the rest of the day off. She got a little huffy until I reminded her this was the anniversary of Cami's mother's death and she goes off the deep end every year.

Matt called Chase and told him that he could drop me off since he was going out to do some home visits, which Chase was happy about since he had a busy day, but said he'd go get me later since we would probably all go to dinner.

We stopped on the way and picked up a pizza at Pizza Place since it was Cami's favorite and a stop at the liquor store for two six-packs of pre-made Mudslides; the plan is to be intoxicated before the boys get home.

As I walked into Cami's living room, I could tell this was going to be rough. She was sitting in ragged sweatpants similar to mine, with an old Motley Crue t-shirt; hair hadn't been touched and I'm assuming that a shower was never taken.

I came in with the pizza and Mudslides and forced her to eat and drink. Then we sat on the couch watching the QVC channel – never a good idea for me. Every so often, just randomly, something on the show would remind her of her mother and I would sit and hold her while she cried.

Cami's parents were in a car crash several years ago on October 18th. Her dad was killed instantly, but her mom remained on life support for 8 more days before she died. Cami tends to take the day her mother died extremely hard because she sat by her bed day-in and day-out for 8 days just willing her mom to come back around. At the point she was showing no brain movement, Cami was the one who had to sign off for them to take her off the life support. They lost her 4 hours later. October 26th haunts Cami every year.

By the time the boys got here, Cami and I had devoured all 12 mudslides and we were basically straight-up drunk; the boys were less than thrilled. Apparently, they were planning to take us out to eat, but we were a lost cause. They fired up the grill instead and gave us steaks and baked potatoes to help ward off some of our alcohol intake; it sorta worked.

There is something about losing your mother that is permanent and inexpressible ~ a wound that will never quite heal.

Wednesday, October 31st

I woke up to a tongue in my ear, and it wasn't Chase. Yuck! "Bones, seriously, is the bath really necessary? Go find Chase; he'll let you out."

"I already did. And he's had breakfast. That tongue lashing probably means that he's ready for you to get up."

"What if I'm not ready to get up yet?"

"I'm pretty sure that Bones will argue with you. And then you'll be covered in drool, which means you will need another bath, which I'll gladly assist with. But, if you're very adamant about not getting up, I can put Bones outside and give you a reason to stay in bed. Of course, you won't have all those clothes on for long. Either way, it's looking good for me."

"You two are starting to gang up on me; it's not fair. Bones used to love me before you moved in."

I used this as my cue to get out of bed; otherwise, I was going to be naked, either in the bathtub or on the bed. Plus, I had to pee. And I smelled muffins!

"What are you baking? It smells awesome."

"Apple cinnamon muffins. Did you know that your mom just makes them from this Martha White package mix?"

"No way. Uh-huh. She makes them from scratch."

"Nope. Go taste my muffins; I'll prove it."

I sat down at the table and slathered the butter on Chase's muffins. They were awesome! And they tasted just like my mom's! She's so busted.

"I'm totally busting her when she gets here tonight. On the plus side, this probably means that I can make my own muffins, right? I swear I'm going to learn to really cook; it just may take you a while to teach me. I mean, I know how to cook a few things pretty well, I just don't do it much because cooking for one pretty well sucks and isn't really worth the effort. Maybe with the two of us then it might be worth learning some good recipes."

"Ugh, guess I'm in this for the long haul, 'cause that won't be an easy job."

"Ha ha, you're so funny. But I'm planning on dragging out the process for approximately 70 years; I'm a slow learner."

"And adorable when you're trying to be coy and funny."

"Even with bed head hair?"

"I love bed head hair! Especially if I caused it." I hate that dang smirk! "So, who else should I be expecting for dinner and trick-or-treat chaos tonight?"

"Just mom, Noelle, Blake, Abi, me, and Bones. I have the best trick-or-treat neighborhood and it's usually a safe place for the kids, so we get a pile of them here. And it starts at 6:00 so we need to plan dinner and get a couple pumpkins carved because I have to have them at the end of the driveway with candles lit in them."

"Is that some neighborhood rule or something?"

"Not really a rule; more like a tradition. It's just what everybody does to make sure that kids know which houses they can go to, and it makes sure their walkways are lit. Plus, this was my grandma's house, and she did it every year. So, we might wanna get busy."

"You finish breakfast, and we'll go get the pumpkins your highness. Well, after you get rid of that bed head hair, brush your teeth and put on some real clothes."

It only took an hour for that process to occur, and then we were out the door and headed to the pumpkin patch. I love the pumpkin patch; I'm like a kid in a candy store! Of course, there weren't as many pumpkins available since today was Halloween, but I still had plenty to choose from. It was a slow process since I couldn't walk easily, but I insisted on walking around the whole pumpkin patch to find just the right ones. My mouth was going a mile-a-minute as well; I'm sure Chase was ready to kill me.

"You know what? From now on I'm going to decorate my house for all the holidays. Next year there's going to be tons of fall decorations across the porch; I love this season."

"I think the smell of the pumpkins is making you high."

"You're not funny. But starting tomorrow, lots of fall decorations are going to be half off. I could load up and store it all in totes. I can put the totes in the garage. This is going to be great. I could act like a real homeowner and learn to cook and everything."

"How about we take it one step at a time. Pick out the dang pumpkins and we can take them home and carve them. Then tomorrow you can go shopping and buy some fall decorations, ok? I'm sure your mom would love to take you."

"You don't want to go shopping?"

"I'd rather slit my wrists."

"Party-pooper. Ok, mom loves a good sale, so I'm sure she'll take me. Unfortunately, she can't maneuver me around, so I have to use those scooter things at Wal-Mart. That'll suck."

"I'm sure you'll live through the ordeal. Let's get these pumpkins home before we run out of time."

Chase wasn't sure it was a good idea to give me a sharp knife, but I assured him that I wouldn't try to kill him with it. Again, another eye roll; I've got to start practicing my eye roll, because right now I'm losing, and I don't like to lose.. We finally got the pumpkins carved and lined up along the sidewalk. I was a mess. I had pumpkin seeds all over the table, and pumpkin goo all over me; Chase on the other hand, was perfectly clean.

"How do you do it?"

"Do what?"

"Stay so clean all the time. No matter what I'm doing, I always seem to wear most of it."

"I'm a man of many talents."

"So you say. Exactly what talents do you have?"

The smirk was back; wrong question. He walked around the table behind me and leaned down to whisper in my ear. "For one, I can make your heart beat fast just by doing this." Then he started kissing my neck, and dang was he right; my heart was beating out of my chest and I was already starting to catch my breath.

"I can feel you trying to take deep breaths when I'm doing this."

Maybe that tank top I put on to carve the pumpkins wasn't such a good idea after all. His hands started moving gradually down my chest; the tank top was no match for those magic fingers that very slowly made their way inside that fabric; they only stopped long enough to realize that the bra I was wearing clasped in the front. Not anymore. Wow!

I tried breathing normally; that didn't work. I tried rubbing my hand on my pants to relieve the moisture on my sweaty palm; that didn't work either. There wasn't anything I could do about the hand in the cast, so I was doubly doomed. I'm pretty sure he was winning this talent contest, and I didn't stand a chance of even competing in this competition. I tried to speak, but I could barely form the words.

"Ok. You win."

While his hands moved further down to the elastic of my sweats, he leaned closer to my ear and whispered, "Not yet. I still have a few more talents that I need to show you."

My breathing was even more ragged, and my body was tingling all over. I managed to respond, "Don't you think I should get all this pumpkin goo off my body?"

A few more kisses on my neck, and I was officially putty in his hands. It only took a second for him to lift me off the chair and lay me across the table. I was covered in pumpkin gunk to start with, and now I'm laying in it as well. But, at this particular moment, I don't even care. He quickly rid me of my sweatpants; and those strong, amazing hands, with the magic fingers, made their way slowly up my body as he stared directly into my eyes. I am very thankful for a sturdy, solid oak table.

An hour later, I had officially lost the talent competition, had a bath, lost another competition, and was trying to regain my composure so I could straighten up and help with dinner before my mom and sister got here with the kids. I had managed to clean off the table and rid it of all the pumpkin goo, and I had officially lit every candle I could find in the house.

"Why are you lighting all the candles?" Chase was obviously clueless to the perceptions of my mother.

"Are you kidding? It smells like sex in here and my mother will be here in half an hour."

"I'm cooking spaghetti and garlic bread. Won't that be enough?"

"Nope. You obviously don't know my mother and her powers of perception."

"It won't matter. You have sexually exhausted just painted across your forehead."

"Thanks. You're not helping."

We had just placed dinner on the table when the kids came running through the door, followed by Bones; he can smell dinner from a mile down the road. Bones helped do the dishes, and we only had 10 minutes to spare before trick-or-treat started; good thing my sister purchased those plastic, already put together costumes for Blake and Abi. Blake was dressed as Superman and Abi was Wonder Woman.

Chase and I handed out candy while mom and Noelle took the kids trick-or-treating. He was giving me a hard time about my candy expenses, but I assured him that I was the coolest house in the area.

"Chase. Look." Walking towards my house down the road was a punk rocker, and a princess. "I think that's Kasey and Lacey." I saw Karleen and knew I was right. They came running up on my porch and gave me a hug.

"You guys look adorable."

"I'm not adorable. Lacey is adorable; I'm punky."

"More like spunky." Chase gave them double the candy and they headed onto the next house. As Karleen turned to walk away, I said "Thanks for bringing them by, Karleen. It's great to see Kasey being a kid."

"She's doing great, Sadey. I think the counseling is helping, but Shayna has been a Godsend for her. She's really helping Kasey be a kid again."

When they left, I told Chase that he was a big sucker. "Why?"

"Double candy. Really? Admit it, you have a big heart."

"I'm not admitting anything; I'm totally pleading the fifth. But you do know what this means?"

"What?"

"Since this was a face-to-face, you have to document it. And you better mention the fact that I gave them double the candy."

"And if I don't?"

"I'm telling your mom the real reason for the candles."

"You play dirty."

And just on cue, mom and Noelle came back with the kids. I gave Chase an extremely dirty look, and he just smirked. Dang, I hate that smirk!

A great attitude becomes a great mood, which becomes a great day, which becomes a great year, which becomes a great life.

I Hate Mondays

Monday, November 5th

"I just want to know how you can get out of bed in such a good mood every day, and so early. I seriously wait for Bones to get almost to his 3rd nudge before I even think about rolling out."

"Apparently Bones and I don't require as much beauty sleep as you do."

"Ok, funny guy. How much time do I have?"

"We have to leave in an hour."

"An hour? Seriously? I could have slept at least 15 more minutes."

"Not with that hair, you can't. If you're lucky, you'll get that cast off your arm today, and then maybe you can actually fix your own hair."

"You are not starting out your Monday morning very good mister. I'm thinking about just cracking you over the head with this cast before they remove it."

"You'd have to catch me first. Now get your butt moving, or you won't have time for breakfast."

I threw some Pop-Tarts in the toaster while I persuaded Chase to do the ponytail thing with my hair. I plopped down on the couch to watch the news while I ate, but just as I got comfortable my cell phone rang. Since I had left it in the bedroom, it required me to roll off the couch and hobble down the hallway to answer it. Janice was calling to tell me that Deborah was set to be released from rehab on Friday; that's great news! I sent a text to Cami so she could be prepared for Kasey this week and headed back to the couch.

"What the…" When I walked in the living room, Bones was sitting on the couch in the seat I just vacated, and he was helping himself to my Pop-Tarts. "Bones? Seriously? That was the last chocolate Pop-Tart!" Like he really understands what that means. All he cared about was that there was food left unprotected on a table; in Bones' language, unprotected food equals a doggy snack.

"What's the commotion?"

"Bones just ate my Pop-Tart; and it was the last chocolate one. This day is not starting out very good; I hope that's not an omen for things to come because I'm very tired of this cast."

Chase was trying hard not to laugh at my unfortunate circumstances; probably because I definitely had on my best pouty face. "Come on, grumpy. Let's go, and I'll run through Tim

Horton's on the way to the doctor's office." That brought a smile to my face.

"That's the nicest thing you've said to me all morning."

I hate Mondays! The only good thing about this Monday morning is that I'm getting the cast off my arm today – hopefully. Chase was true to his word, and I ate a box of Timbits on my way to the doctor's office. As I was popping the last one in my mouth, it occurred to me that they would probably weigh me when they called me back.

"Dang!"

"What?" Chase was giving me a puzzled look.

"You just let me eat an entire box of Timbits, and they're probably going to weigh me. If I gained 10 pounds, I'm blaming it on you."

"Um, babe, I hate to inform you of this, but if you've gained any weight it's because you've been in a cast for the last month and you can't get any real exercise. It will not be because I allowed you to eat Timbits this morning."

"I have to blame somebody and you're lookin' good for it."

"Well, I am lookin' good…"

"Ok, never mind. Let's just go convince the doctor to remove this cast."

"Sounds good to me."

We sat forever in the waiting room. When they finally called my name, Chase whispered in my ear, "Do you wanna make some sort of wager on how much weight you've gained?"

"No! And if you say another word, I'm cutting you off!"

He gave me a pouty look, but he didn't say another word. Smart man! Luckily, my weight gain was only 2 lbs; which still depressed me, but not enough to stress over it. I just keep convincing myself that after all my casts and boot thingys are removed then I can exercise. Not that I'll really do it; exercise makes me sweaty and I don't like being sweaty. Not to mention, I'm just plain lazy. I was just about to start arguing with myself when the doctor walked in; he saved me from myself.

"X-rays look better. Both breaks are healing nicely, so I'm going to remove the cast." I got really excited at that point, but then he quashed my excitement a little when he said, "However, your wrist is going to have to be taped like your ankle, and you'll have to wear a brace on your arm until the physical therapist thinks you're not in any danger of fracturing it."

Chase piped in and asked about what limitations I still had. I didn't ask this question because I didn't want to know the answer. I just wanted to be thrilled that the cast was off and then do whatever I wanted to at this point. Chase made sure that didn't happen. Party pooper!

"Obviously you still can't drive because of the boot. I don't want you putting any pressure on the wrist except in physical therapy. You need to wear it at all times, except when you're in the shower. I know you'll just want to be all gung-ho on getting your life back to normal, but you've got to be careful. Too much stupidity and you'll be back in a cast."

I shook my head in understanding, but my brain was still thinking about all the things I could do by myself now: shave my legs, wash my hair and fix it into a ponytail, type… Chase, of course can read my mind, and he looks over at me and says, "I know what you're thinking, Sadey, and I'm not letting you overdo it." Then he looks at the doctor and asks, "What about work? Can she do 5 days again or is she still on restriction?"

That was a good question; one I wasn't even thinking of. But I didn't like the answer.

"She can do 3 days now since she's doing 2 days of physical therapy. On PT days, she needs to be resting."

The nurse wrapped my wrist, showing Chase exactly how to do it properly, and then she put the brace on my arm. It wasn't too bad; at least now I could use my fingers some, so that will make things a little easier. I kept wiggling my fingers and Chase found that extremely funny.

"Why are you laughing at me?"

"You're just kinda cute; especially sitting over there wiggling your fingers."

"Let's get out of here. I want to go home and shave my legs and wash my hair; with my own hands."

"I like it better when we're using my hands. But I'll still be supervising."

The nurse was finding us very humorous. I definitely didn't like the fact that she was siding with Chase on this. "Sadey, as much as you want to be Miss Independent right now, the truth is that somebody still needs to be helping you out until your wrist is stronger."

When we got home, I decided to try out my new fingers and type some documentation. It wasn't too bad. I struggled a little, but I figured I could work through it; at least the cast was gone. I called Karleen to discuss plans for Deborah coming home on Friday, and then Janice filled me in on Elaine's progress; she'll finish the AA program on Friday as well. So, I made another phone call to Elaine's mom to make plans for Sampson coming home over the weekend as well. It's looking to be a good weekend.

However, my day just took a turn for the worse. I heard Chase on the phone, but I couldn't hear anything he was saying, and I didn't really care until he came back in the living room looking pale.

"What's wrong?"

"Sadey, I don't know how to tell you this, but, you know that Mark's preliminary hearing was today, right?"

"Yeah; so what? We didn't have to be there since his lawyer said he was going to waive it."

"Well, as they were transporting him back to the jail from the courthouse, there was a wreck - an intentional wreck. Somebody t-boned the transport van, killing the driver and injuring the other Corrections Officer." He tensed up completely and could barely say the words, "Mark escaped."

"What?! No way! Shit! Who hit the van? How did this happen? Deborah and the girls are coming home on Friday; this isn't good."

"I don't know the details of the wreck, yet. Leland just called to tell me about Mark so that we could be on guard; again."

On the menu for today: a large serving of irritated with generous sides of frustration and angry, with pissed off for dessert.

~~~~~~~~~~~~~~~~~~~~~~~

Mark couldn't believe how his luck was changing for the better. He thought that hearing was never going to end and the drive back to jail was unbearably long. But just as they were crossing the intersection back onto Rt. 50 a car came flying into the side of the van. The guy driving the van was straight up dead; right away. The other officer was hurt pretty badly and he himself was in massive pain.

The sling on his shoulder wasn't doing a damn thing to help his broken clavicle and all they did for his back was to wrap some tight gauze around his midsection, they kept him in a cell in medical, and the strongest pain medicine they gave him was ibuprofen. He couldn't wait to get a hold of his own stash; a few Xanax and good smoke of pot would help considerably with the pain. And now he has another bump on the head from bouncing off the side of the van.

But no time to focus on the bad. The cheap-ass transport van didn't have a separation panel which meant he could stretch himself almost to the driver's seat. Luck was on his side again; the driver was leaning over the side of the seat just far enough that with a little extra stretch he was able to grab the keys from the dead guy and use them to get his cuffs off before the other officer could do anything to stop him. He got out of the van as quickly as he could; the woods were on his right side and he wasn't slowing down. When he was safely out of sight, he turned around to look at the wreckage and was surprised to see who was driving the car that hit them.

Janelle Reynolds; Amber's mom.

She's been sick; she never drives.

And she hates him. Then it occurred to him that she did this on purpose; she was hoping to kill him when she hit the van. How did she even know where he was? Nevermind; Amber's in jail and she would have called her about his hearing.

That stupid bitch turned on him the minute they put the cuffs on her; trying to hide out at her mom's house was the dumbest thing she could have done. Although, truth be told, she was never that smart; she was just a fine piece of ass.

He figured he had about a 15-minute head start on the cops. He was too far away from his own house and they'd have that surrounded in half a second.

He made a split-second decision that he hoped he wouldn't regret.

He headed to the house of his rival – Jesse Murphy; it would be at least a 3-mile hike through the woods, but hopefully the end result would be some decent drugs to take the pain away and maybe one of his crew would give him a place to crash for a few days.

Stupid people should be required to wear shock collars until they are properly trained for life.

Weekend be damned

Friday, November 9th

Staff meeting was the longest ever. It seemed like everyone had lots of things going on in their cases; but most of it was good news, so at least it wasn't a depressing meeting. After staff meeting, I had an MDT (Multi-Disciplinary Team) meeting for Deborah, and we all discussed her progress and where she goes from here. Everyone involved in her case was at the meeting: Janice, Galvin, Timothy Weston – her attorney – Melaney Gavison – the Child Advocate – Shayna, Chase, and myself.

Janice updated everyone on Deborah's counseling and drug rehab program; the team all agreed that she would continue to attend group counseling every two weeks, and individual counseling once a week. Everyone was happy with Kasey and the Big Sister program, and I made it clear that Deborah was to work with Shayna to continue this program once the girls were home. The girls were to return home tonight, and I told Deborah I would be there sometime over the weekend to visit and make sure things were in order.

Chase took me out to lunch, and I realized how much I hated to have to come and go through the back door again; at least I didn't have to use that stupid scooter anymore. I spent the rest of the afternoon in my extremely boring and blah office; which reminded me that I needed to decorate.

The shopping trip absolutely exhausted me! I definitely overdid it today; but I was a woman on a mission, and the mission was accomplished. So the rest of the evening was spent lounging on the couch watching movies and eating popcorn with Chase and Bones. But the relaxing evening went out the door quickly with one phone call.

"Sadey, its Kasey."

"What's wrong and why are you whispering?"

"Mark's here and he has a gun. He's waving it at mom and screaming at her about all the trouble she's caused him."

"Crap! Ok, listen to me carefully. Can you and Lacey get someplace safe right now?" I looked at Chase and said, "Call 911 and then call Leland. Mark's at Deborah's and he has a gun."

Kasey replied, "He's in the living room. We can get to the bedroom."

"Ok, good. Go to your room, lock the door and then both of you hide in your closet, ok. Help is on the way."

This was the fastest I've ever changed clothes; especially with the boot and arm brace. Bones was obviously aware that something was wrong, so when we headed to the car he was right there to jump in; and he wasn't taking 'no' for an answer. No time to argue with the dog.

~~~~~~~~~~~~~~~~~~~~

Deborah pulled in her driveway after six long weeks of treatment, detox, counseling sessions and far too much time separated from her girls. She looked in the rearview mirror and saw Kasey and Lacey safely buckled in their seats; she couldn't believe that it was only six weeks ago that she was choosing the drugs over these two beautiful little girls. She swore to never make anything a priority over her girls again; they needed a mom and she vowed to be the best mom she could be to them.

The girls grabbed their duffel bags and headed around back so they could dump their clothes and shoes in the mud room. Deborah walked up on the porch with her mind still on how lucky she was that Sadey had seen the good in her and gave her the opportunity to start over. As she grabbed the door handle, the hairs on the back of her neck stood up and she felt like something was wrong but shrugged it off as the nerves of her new start.

She opened the door and froze. There was a gun pointed at her temple and the person on the other end, with his finger on the trigger, was none other than Mark Kinders.

The girls! Where are the girls?! Oh, God, I just got them back. No! No! This can't be happening!

"Welcome home Deborah. I've missed you; jail can get a little lonely at times."

Don't give in to the fear. With gritted teeth she asked, "What do you want?"

"I can't decide; I'm not sure if I want to torture you first, or just go ahead and kill you."

Deborah thought she saw Kasey in the kitchen, but it was such a quick movement; maybe she was just seeing things. Her brain is a little foggy right now with a gun pointed at it.

Please go hide! Please, please, please.

She was just willing the girls to hear her, to hear Mark and know that she was in trouble.

"So," Mark said, pulling her out of her own thoughts, "Where are the girls?"

She was visibly shaking now. She could barely get out the words, "Sadey is picking them up and bringing them home; they'll be here soon, so whatever you plan to do to me, just go ahead and get it over with."

Mark was so distracted with her that he didn't notice the girls running from the kitchen down the hallway.

Please, please, please. Don't turn around. Don't turn around. Go hide, girls.

She tried to keep him distracted and focused on her.

"You know that I didn't turn you in, right? I never said your name or told them where I got the drugs; the officer that arrested me found out that information on his own."

"I almost believe you; almost." He slapped her in the face and said, "You sold me out, and I've lost everything because of you." He slapped her again and started to yell, but…

"Leave her alone!"

"Kasey; no, baby, no!"

"I'm the one that told them how you've ruined our lives."

Mark whipped around to point the gun at Kasey and Deborah immediately gained a strength and resolve that she'd never had in her life. She threw herself full force into Mark knocking him to the ground, sending his gun sliding across the room.

As Deborah was wrestling around with Mark, Kasey grabbed the gun, pointed it at Mark's head and said, "I know how to pull the trigger and it will all be self-defense." She looked at Deborah and said, "I called Sadey."

As if on cue, help arrived.

~~~~~~~~~~~~~~~~~~~~~~~~~~~~~~~~~~~

Leland plowed through the door with his gun drawn. He was on Mark in half a second. As he slapped on the cuffs, making sure he was none too careful with his shoulder, he said, "You've met your match with that little girl over there. You're lucky I got here first or she might have pulled that trigger; I almost let her just so she could get her revenge for what you've put her through in the past few years."

Leland secured the gun as Chase and I came through the back door. Kasey went running straight towards me.

"You were so brave, Kasey; I'm very proud of you, and I'm sure your mom is too. Where's Lacey?"

"She's hiding in my bedroom closet."

Chase took off down the hallway and was back in a second carrying a very scared 3-year-old who still had tears in her eyes.

Deborah had been in complete shock, and she had just fallen into the couch. Chase brought Lacey over to her as Kasey sat down on the couch and was hugging her mom.

"Kasey, you have no idea how thankful I am that you're such a brave little girl. I'm so proud of you. Thank you." Deborah was holding her girls tightly, still traumatized from the thought of never seeing them again, just as she got them back.

Leland had Mark up and taking him outside, with Chase and I following right behind him. Then I heard the creepiest growl that had ever come from Bones. I realized at just that moment that I had been in such a hurry to get to the house that I left the door open and Bones was still sitting in the front seat; well, he was, until he saw Leland come out the front door with Mark.

The rest just happened in slow motion.

Bones came bounding out of the car running full force towards Leland and Mark. Leland couldn't move fast enough to save Mark from the wrath of Bones. My 90lb dog went airborne and never slowed down as he landed with front paws directly on Mark's chest with enough force to send him backwards into the front window. Leland landed square on his butt as Mark sent glass flying in all directions.

A loud shriek snapped everybody back into focus. Mark was now lying in the living room floor, with large shards of glass embedded in several parts of his body, and a large dog standing on top of him; a large piece of glass was sticking out from the side of his neck and he was bleeding profusely.

Luckily, Chase's call to 911 earlier had paramedics there pretty quickly. I gathered all the girls in the kitchen to keep them away from the madness, as Leland was squatted down beside Mark trying to stop the bleeding in his neck. It was increasingly difficult with Bones standing directly over Mark still growling. He refused to move and even Leland couldn't push him out of the way.

It took me, Chase and Leland to get Bones off Mark so the paramedics could tend to him. Jake Farnsworth, my Chemistry partner in High School, was the paramedic that showed up to the scene of the attack. He got an IV started and began wrapping gauze around the neck wound. He didn't remove the glass for fear of him bleeding out before he got him to the hospital.

Jake and I caught up for a minute, long enough for me to tell him whose life he was attempting to save.

Jake and his partner, Mike, got Mark loaded into the ambulance and headed for the local hospital.

Leland walked around snapping a crap-ton of pictures and took off to the hospital to check on Mark. Chase and Kasey began cleaning up all the glass while I kept Deborah and Lacey in the kitchen, trying to calm them down from everything that just happened.

I called Janice to relay the events of the evening and she agreed to come over and hang with Deborah and the girls for a while to try and help them deal with everything they just experienced.

Chase drove to the hardware store and bought some plastic wrap to cover the broken window.

My phone was ringing just as Chase got finished with the window.

"Sadey, its Jake. I have some news for you."

"Lay it on me."

"Mark died on the way to the hospital. The glass was too loose and even with the wrap it fell out and he bled to death before we got him in the door."

"The glass was loose?" I'm pretty sure he was feeding me some kind of bullshit, but the end result made me pretty ecstatic.

"Um, yeah. I tried to hold it in place with the gauze, but it didn't work. So…anyway…I just wanted to let you know."

"Jake?"

"Yeah?"

"Thanks." He knew that 'thanks' was for the lack of effort to save Mark as well as for the phone call.

I spread the good news, handed Deborah and the girls over to Janice, and then Chase, Bones and I went home with a stop at Dairy Queen for very large Blizzards that we figured we owed Bones for his heroic effort.

Karma is like a rubber band; you can only stretch it so far before it comes back and smacks you in the face.

Saturday, November 10th

Chase and I decided last night that we'd go over to Deborah's later this afternoon to check on her and the girls and so Chase could replace her living room window for her; Cami was expecting us at her house for dinner at 6:00 sharp, so we had to go out no matter what. The only problem was that it was a yucky fall day. It rained all night and my beautiful 70-degree days had been replaced by low 50-degree days. I had absolutely no desire to get out of bed this morning; unfortunately, my eyes were open, which meant only one thing: gotta pee. I reluctantly crawled out from under the covers and I realized that Bones and Chase were cuddled up together, snoring. I did my best not to wake them, but it didn't work.

"Why are you walking on that foot without your boot?"

"Because I had to pee."

"Why didn't you wake me up?"

"Because I'm tired of not being able to do things for myself. Plus, you and Bones were all cuddled up nice and cozy; I didn't want to wake you." I tried to give it my best smile, but he wasn't buying it. I was only a step away from the bathroom by this point, so there was nothing he could do about it. But when I opened the door to come out, he was standing in the doorway to block my exit.

"Nice try, Sweet Cheeks." He scooped me up and carried me back to the bed. I started to argue, "I'm getting stronger; I think you should let me..." He kissed me before I could finish the argument. "I thought you were mad at me for walking without the boot." Then he kissed me again, with that stupid smirk on his face. Just as I opened my mouth to say something, he kissed me again.

"It's the best way to shut you up." Chase was still smirking as he sat down on the side of the bed with me on his lap.

"So, if I keep talking, will you kiss me again?" And his answer was...he kissed me again – with plenty of tongue. Then his hand started moving up the side of my leg, over my hip and slowly made its way under my t-shirt; there was easy access to his destination since I don't sleep with anything on under my shirt. That familiar tingle started moving through my body, and it was only a short time before I was relieved of all my clothing. As his kisses made their way up my body, I tried to speak through the groans I couldn't control. "If I walk without the boot tomorrow, can we start our day this way again?" I was answered with another kiss, and...

I spent the rest of the morning doing absolutely nothing. Bones curled up beside me on the couch, and we ate donuts and watched cartoons. Chase had been down in the basement doing who knows what; but he wasn't thrilled when he came upstairs. "When was the last time you were in that basement?"

"Um, I don't know. I never go down there. I turned the small bedroom into the laundry room because I really didn't need the basement. It just came with house. Why?"

"There's a water leak in the back corner that we need to fix. I was thinking we should fix up the basement and make it into a nice hanging out in room. But we're gonna have to fix that part of the floor first."

"So, basically you want to turn my basement into a man cave." He got a look on his face like he wasn't sure how to answer that question, so he was just standing there with his tail tucked between his legs. "You're downright adorable when you're backed into a corner."

"Ok, well, it's just that it's sitting there empty and maybe it could be useful; plus, I feel kinda useless around here."

"You are far from useless, Chase. But, about the basement, I don't really care. If you want to do something with the basement, be my guest. Living here by myself, I really didn't need it for anything."

"Well, as long as I'm kinda using your house, I thought it would be nice to have a little 'man cave'."

"Using my house?"

"Well, it sounds kind of weird to say I've moved in, you know, 'cause we've only known each other a couple of months."

"Ok, right now I just want to smack you for saying that out loud, but since you're so cute acting like a kid in trouble, I'll let you out of it. But I'm just gonna say one thing, and you better listen." He was nervously moving from one foot to the other, anxiously waiting for me to get him out of the mess he was currently in; it was adorable. But, then again, he's adorable.

What did he really mean by 'using my house'? Does he not want this to go anywhere, or is he just using me because he's using my house? Do I want him to stay here? For good? It has only been two months, but I could see myself living with him the rest of my life. So why, then, am I arguing with myself? I've never felt like this about anybody. I want him to stay; yes, for good.

Chase obviously sensed what I was doing, because he can read me like a book. Sometimes that's not a good thing. He came over and squatted down in front of me on the couch, took my hands in his and said, "Are you going to continue to argue with yourself or tell me that one thing that I'm supposed to be listening to?"

I took a deep breath. "Ok, the truth is that I'm better at arguing with myself than I am at expressing my feelings out loud. So, I'm just going to jump in with both feet." I took another deep breath and then poured my heart out. "I want you here. I don't think I want you to leave. Ever. I've never felt so at home with somebody as I do with you. I don't feel like you're a visitor here at all. You belong here; with me and Bones."

I paused, and then just kinda blurted out, "I love you."

Tears started forming in my eyes. It's the first time I've ever said those words to a man. I'm not very good at expressing affection. Don't get me wrong, I'm good at being emotional; but affection is something totally different. I think Chase knew that what I just said was a really big step for me.

"Sadey, baby, don't cry." He crawled up on the couch beside me and pulled me into his arms; a familiar place that I've grown to love. As he was stroking my hair, he turned my face towards him and proceeded to kiss me until I melted. With my eyes still locked on him, all he said was, "I love you, too."

We sat there on the couch for several minutes, not saying a word. It wasn't even awkward; nobody speaking. I really think that's why I'm so content with him; we can just sit and cuddle and nobody has to say a thing. I could have spent the entire day just sitting there in his arms. Unfortunately, we had things to do today, which meant getting me bathed and ready to go.

"I could sit here all day, just like this."

"Me too. Unfortunately, you need a shower and some real clothes on so we can go pay a visit to Deborah; that was a rough homecoming for her."

"But the bastard is dead; that's what matters."

"Truth is, now she and the girls can move on with nothing from their past holding them back."

"She deserves that; she's worked hard these past few weeks. Oh, dinner at Cami's; were we supposed to bring anything? She didn't say."

"No, she's making lasagna and she said she had everything she needed. All we have to do is show up."

"Sounds good to me."

"Now, let's get you in the shower and dressed in some normal clothes."

An hour later we were in the car, headed to Deborah's house. Chase fixed her window while I chatted about the events of last night and convinced Deborah she was headed in the right direction.

The steeper the mountain, the harder the climb, the better the view from the finishing line.

When we got to Cami's house, she was in the kitchen finishing up dinner, and Leland was standing in the doorway with a beer in his hand, pretending to help. He was happy to see us walk in; it gave him an excuse to get out of the kitchen and hide in the basement. He handed Chase a beer and they escaped quickly, leaving us girls alone.

"How ya feeling?" Cami asked me.

"I'm tired of all these rules, but otherwise, I'll live."

"Yeah, you never were one to follow the rules," she said with a big smile on her face.

"I know there's a reason why I can't walk without the boot yet, but it drives me crazy that I can't even go from the bed to the bathroom without my bodyguard jumping all over my case." I did a nice eye-roll as I said that.

Then Cami got a weird grin on her face as she responded, "Well you sure don't mind him jumping all over the rest of you."

I think my cheeks turned red, because she started laughing at me at that point. She was right; that's one thing I didn't mind at all. I still wasn't sure what to make of our conversation this morning, or the fact that I just blurted out to Chase that I loved him, and I never wanted him to leave. Was I actually ready for that?

"Sadey? What is it?"

"Huh? What?"

"You just spaced out on me for a minute, and that usually means you're arguing with yourself. So just spill it."

"Ugh. Some days I wish you couldn't read me so well."

"Too bad. Now what's on your mind?"

"Am I crazy?"

"Certifiably."

"Gee thanks."

"I'm kidding. Why do you think you're crazy, Sadey?"

"I've only known Chase for two months, and this morning I told him that I loved him." Cami got a shocked look on her face. "See, even you're shocked."

"I'm not shocked that you love Chase; I'm shocked that you said it out loud. You're not one to easily talk affection, Sadey. You're quick to share your opinion, but not your affection. So, what's up? That's the first time you've ever said that, right?"

"Yeah, but I don't know, Cam. It's like I'm so content with him around; like he just belongs there. This morning he said something about using my house, and I felt the urge to slap him. I actually told him that I wanted him to stay there forever. Have I lost my mind?"

She was taking the garlic bread out of the oven, and as she set it on the stove she paused, and then said, "I don't think you've lost your mind at all Sadey. If you remember correctly, I fell that hard and fast for Leland, and I really can't imagine my life without him. Maybe it's just a Davis brothers' skill, but you have to follow your heart."

"Following my heart is easy; following the arguments I keep having with myself is the hard part."

"Ok, so if your heart is telling you that you're in love, why the heck are you letting your brain argue with you?"

"I don't know. I just keep questioning my heart. I've honestly never felt like this before. Even when I'm mad at him, I can't be mad for long. He just has this way of always turning something bad into something good; not to mention, he has this smirk that sort of makes me melt."

"Yeah, I know that smirk well. It's a Davis brother quality. Leland just has this look and, no matter how mad I am at him, I just turn to putty."

"Yep, that's the one. So, I'm not completely crazy then?"

"Not really. Just make sure you know what you want before you jump in with both feet; I would hate to have to beat up my future brother-in-law. Not to mention, then I would have to find somebody new to be Leland's best man, and that would be a pain in my butt."

Now I was laughing. "I dated Justin for almost a year, and never did feel exactly what I feel now with Chase. Is that weird?"

"No, because Justin was a horses' ass. Chase is a gentleman."

"No kidding. And he can just pick me up like I weigh absolutely nothing. Where do those muscles come from?"

"Didn't you know that he had a full gym in his basement at the house?"

"No. I was obviously never down there, and he never said anything. Come to think of it, he never says anything about the house at all. Shouldn't he be mad at me, or at least blame me because Mark set fire to his house? I mean, he lost everything; he's never once complained."

"He wouldn't; he's not that kind of guy. These boys are not complainers. They grew up hard and fast; and they know how to take care of themselves. To them, material things just don't matter."

"This morning, Chase was down in my basement, and when he came upstairs, he told me I had a water leak. But that was actually just his way of bringing up the basement and saying that we should do something with it. That's what actually began the whole conversation when my heart exploded."

"Boys like to have a man cave, Sadey. It makes them feel all important and manly-like. He probably misses having that gym and just being able to escape."

"I feel really bad, Cami. I had no idea about the gym stuff, and I'm pretty clueless about the man-cave thing. But the truth is, I would let him redo my entire house if he would just stay there forever. Now I'm sounding all sappy and crap, but I am the most content I've ever been in my life. Being run over by a car was actually the best thing that's ever happened to me."

"Now I think you are certifiably insane. We better holler at the guys before dinner gets cold." She didn't even have to say their names; they were already walking into the kitchen. Neither Cami nor I said a word, but it was pretty obvious that they'd been listening to our conversation; I didn't know whether I should be embarrassed or just pretend not to notice.

Dinner was awesome; Cami is the queen at making lasagna. I think we covered every topic from obnoxious parents to unruly clients to idiots out on the street. We talked about Cami and Leland's wedding next summer, that they still hadn't set a date, and who they were considering for the rest of the bridal party. About the time we got deep into the wedding conversation, Leland and Chase started cleaning off the table and rinsing the dishes; they were obviously trying hard to get out of helping with the plans. Oh well, at least the dishes were getting done.

Chase didn't say a word about mine and Cami's conversation all the way home. *Maybe they didn't really hear it all; maybe we just imagined them getting there so quickly. What did it matter? I mean,*

I didn't really say anything more than I told him this morning, right?
Or did I? I can't remember. But, really, does it matter what he
heard? I didn't say anything I didn't mean.

"Am I winning?"

"Huh? Oh, uh, yeah. You usually do. Just once I'd really like
to win an argument I'm having with myself."

"Nah. That'd be boring."

"How do you always know when I'm arguing with myself,
anyway?"

"You just have this look about you."

"Wow, that's helpful."

"If it's any consolation, I think you're absolutely adorable when
you're arguing with yourself."

"Gee, thanks."

"So, what argument did I win this time?"

"None of your business."

"That's not fair; I should at least know what I won." He got that
pouty look on his face that's so cute; but I'm still not telling him. I
tried to just ignore him the rest of the way home, but he kept making
idle conversation just to keep me talking; probably in hopes that I'd
spill the beans about my argument. Not gonna happen.

When we opened the front door, Bones came flying out;
obviously we've been gone a while and he wasn't happy about the

amount of time he'd been locked in the house. I got comfy in some sweatpants and a t-shirt and headed for the couch.

"I'm thinking we should have some ice cream." I was trying to talk about anything but that conversation with Cami, or the argument I had with myself. But he responded, "Not until you fess up."

"Fine. I'll get my own ice cream." So I turned around and headed for the kitchen instead of the couch; I was bound and determined to be completely stubborn. I was standing at the counter trying to hold the carton with my braced hand and dip the ice cream with the other. It wasn't working out that well for me, but I wasn't about to give in. Then Chase came up behind me and whispered in my ear, "Need some help, Sweet Cheeks?"

"No. I can do it myself." I was using my best stubborn voice, but I wasn't really all that convincing. Then he wrapped his arms around my waist and proceeded to slide one hand up under my shirt, while kissing my neck. I was now breathing hard and having trouble holding on to the ice cream scoop. He nibbled on my ear a little and whispered, "You still wanna be stubborn or ya gonna fess up?"

I was doing my absolute best to stay stubborn. As his hand slid around the waistband of my sweats, he said, "I can always stop this if you'd like."

No fair. He wasn't playing by the rules; he can't just get me all heated up like that and just stop. That's just wrong! I really didn't want to replay my whole conversation with Cami or myself, but I also didn't want those magic hands to stop what they were doing either. I could only muster up enough breath to say, "Cami doesn't think I'm crazy."

I could feel him start to laugh, but then all I was feeling was the number his hands were doing on my body. Another few kisses on my neck, and he said "Yeah, and?"

I obviously wasn't going to get out of this so easily, especially if I wanted him to continue exploring my body with his magic fingers. My heart was beating rapidly, and I was having trouble controlling my breathing, but I managed to respond, "And, it's not fair that you overheard our conversation and you're still making me repeat it."

That brought a full chuckle from him, but he was relentless. "I only heard the part about sappy and content. I was hoping you'd fill me in on the rest of it."

His hands never stopped working my body over the entire time he was talking. I was about to lose total control at this point; I managed to barely respond, "You're not playing fair. You know that, right?"

"Yep. But I'm pretty sure I'm still winning." That was it; I was mush. He slowly lifted the ice cream scoop out of my hand and laid it on the counter, then picked me up and proceeded to the bedroom, where he reminded me of one of the reasons I never wanted him to leave.

Needless to say, the ice cream melted.

True love is a friendship that catches fire.

Sunday, November 11th

Sunday was just as gloomy as Saturday; it was pouring down the rain and cold. It made for a great day to stay on the couch and do nothing all day. I had my laptop out and I was looking at workout equipment on the internet while Chase was showering. I didn't know what all he'd lost in the fire, but I wanted him to have it all back; he should get something for all the trouble he's been through with me. If that meant I needed to turn my basement into a man-cave, then that's exactly what I was going to do. And the bedroom that was piled with junk needed to be turned into an office. This is a 4-bedroom house, and I was only one person, with one dog; we didn't need all this space. Obviously, my grandma wanted me to make use of this home she'd left me, so that's exactly what I'm going to do.

"Whatcha doin'?" Chase plopped down in the recliner, hair still wet from the shower.

"Can I ask you something? And you have to be completely honest with me?"

"Ok. Shoot."

"Why didn't you tell me that your basement was full of workout equipment, and you lost it all when the house burned down?"

"Cami?" I just shook my head. He knew where I got my info from; that's just a given. "Sadey, it's just stuff, ok. Stuff can be replaced; people can't."

"That's true, but why didn't you tell me about the stuff? Chase, you've spent all this time taking care of me, and making sure I have everything I need; never once have you talked about what you lost or the things you need."

"Sadey, its fine; really. I'll get around to replacing things. I had insurance, so I have money to buy what I need."

"It's not about what you need, Chase. You have the right to be selfish, you know." He just kind of shrugged his shoulders like it didn't matter, but I knew better. He's just a tough guy; but deep down he has a heart bigger than anyone can imagine. "Ok, so here's the deal: if you aren't going to be selfish, I'm going to be selfish for you."

"No, you're not, Sadey. I'm just fine."

I put my laptop down, and carefully got myself up off the couch; I wobbled over to the recliner and sat down on his lap. He was not escaping this conversation. "Give me your hands."

"Why?"

"Just do it." He reluctantly put his hands in front of me and I held them tightly in mine. "We're going to talk, and you're not getting out of it by using your magic fingers to get me all hot and bothered. So, I'm holding on to your hands until I'm finished talking, ok?"

Chase thought I was absolutely hilarious, but I knew him well enough to know that if he could find a way to get me naked instead of having a heartfelt conversation, that's exactly what was going to happen. Not that I'm against being naked, because he always makes that worth my while; but this time he had to earn my nakedness with some conversation.

"Ok, big guy; this is what's going to happen. Are you listening?"

"Whatever you say, Sweet Cheeks. If I'm a good listener then can I get you all hot and bothered?"

"We'll see." Of course he was smirking, but I was totally gonna win this time. "Now, here's the deal. First things first: we are cleaning out the garage so you have someplace safe to park the Camaro. I know it's still sitting in your garage and it's not safe over there because nobody is living on the property. So that's the first thing."

"Yes, your highness; I can live with those terms."

"Next, we are remodeling the basement. You need a man-cave and we're going to create one. We'll buy new gym equipment and a big TV and couch and whatever else you might want. Even a beer fridge."

"I don't need all that Sadey." He started to argue.

"It's not about what you need; it's about things you want. You've lost a lot lately and all you've done is take care of me; so now I'm going to take care of you. No arguing. So, tomorrow after PT, we're going to Lowes and to Sears. Got it?"

"Yeah, I got it. So, can I get you all hot and bothered now?"

"Good grief."

Any plan I had today of being a productive member of society, I am officially throwing out the window. I intend to be as useless as the G in Lasagna.

Man Cave

Monday, November 12th

Physical therapy was painful, as usual. I was starting to dislike Mondays and Thursdays; Friday morning staff meetings aren't usually as painful as this. Well, actually, I probably have a different opinion on Friday mornings when I'm sitting in staff meeting, but seeing as how this is Monday morning…

We were on our way to Lowes, and Chase reached over, grabbed my hand and squeezed. "You ok?"

"Yeah. I'm just starting to hate physical therapy. It hurts more and more every time."

"No pain, no gain."

"You're so funny; it almost made me laugh."

"I know it sucks Sadey, but it will be worth it once you're healed up."

"Yeah, yeah, yeah. So you keep saying. I think that you and the PT are ganging up on me – trying to see who can cause the most pain."

"Now see, you have this all wrong. He inflicts all the pain and then I get to be the good guy and make it all go away." He had that little smirk on his face again.

"So, it is a conspiracy; I knew it. You're totally cut off."

"We'll see about that." Stupid smirk!

We argued the whole way through Lowes; I obviously had no idea how to design a man-cave, but I was doing my best to pretend that I did. We were in the paneling section, the Lowe's guy was trying his best to be helpful, and he wasn't even getting frustrated at my six thousand questions; Chase on the other hand, probably wanted me to disappear. He and the Lowes guy were discussing which paneling would work best and how much we needed; of course, I kept trying to interject my opinion into the conversation. I started to say, "Are you sure…", when Chase leaned over and kissed me. As I opened my mouth again, he kissed me again. Point taken. The Lowes guys was giving us Bones' infamous head sideways look, when Chase explained, "It's the only way to shut her up." Mr. Lowes Guy thought this was comical, but he didn't say a word, especially since he saw the look on my face.

"I was just trying to be helpful," I said as we got in the car.

"Sweet Cheeks, if you're this helpful in Sears, I'm locking you in the car."

I tried to be good in Sears; I didn't ask a lot of questions and I didn't question the Sears guy like he didn't know what he was talking about. I figured this good behavior had earned me a Blizzard. I mean, I don't do 'quiet' well, so I figured it should earn some sort of prize. Plus, when we were looking at the TV's, I noticed that there was a bigger one with a mail-in rebate that made it actually cost less than the one Chase was originally looking at – that had to earn me some points right there.

"A Blizzard? Really? We haven't even had lunch?"

"That's your fault. You were too busy shopping for your man-cave to stop and eat lunch. Plus, I was really good in Sears and I got you a bigger TV for less; that should count for something. And, also, we don't have any ice cream at home because you made it all melt the other night."

"That wasn't my fault."

"How do you figure?"

"If you'd just told me what you and Cami were discussing then I wouldn't have had to use my magic fingers to coerce it out of you; then the ice cream wouldn't have melted."

"You weren't playing fairly, and you know it. You guys were spying on us, and you heard everything I said; you just wanted to torture me."

"Did it work?"

I was just about to tear him a new one when his cell phone rang; saved by the bell. I don't know who he was talking to, but it sounded like business, so I zoned out and started working on a response to his last question in my head.

No, of course it didn't work; I let you win. He wouldn't believe that. No, it didn't work because I wasn't tortured at all. Crap. Ok, so he did win. And he did torture the crap out of me with those magic fingers. Crap. I was still arguing with myself and didn't even realize he was off the phone.

"Might as well give up; I win the arguments every time."

"You don't win every argument I have with myself."

"I win most of them. Anyway, that was Galvin. There's a hearing scheduled for Friday afternoon for your dad; it's the sentence reduction hearing."

"Explain that to me again."

"Next week, your dad will have spent 28 months of a 60-month sentence in jail. Normally, once a third of the sentence has been served, he can ask for a sentence reduction; meaning he can ask that he be able to serve the remainder of his sentence on home confinement and/or probation. That's why I did that interview with him. Galvin will make a recommendation to the judge that your dad be able to serve out the rest of his sentence at home."

"Something I don't understand is this; he's been in jail lots of times, but he's never asked for one of these before. Why is this time different?"

"Do you want my honest opinion?" I shook my head yes. "I think it's because of you."

"Me? Why me?"

"Because, for the first time in his life he's realized that his drug habit has had an effect on his family; namely, you. You opened up to him and told him how you truly felt, and it hit him pretty hard; he had absolutely no idea you felt that way. He's ready to make some changes in his life; not just serve his time and get out. That's the way I'm reading him anyway."

"So, if the judge agrees to this, when will my dad come home?"

"I would have to look at his exact arrest date…"

"July 21st."

"Then most likely it would be November 21st. Normally he could have asked for the reduction a couple of months ago, but there was a stipulation on his arrest because it was selling to an undercover, so he actually had to wait until now."

"So, he's not guaranteed this until the judge rules on it Friday?"

"Yeah. It's just like a sentencing hearing. He will have to answer a lot of questions by the judge and he may even have to talk about the original crime like he did with us that day. It depends on the judge. But anybody can be at the hearing; it's open. You don't have to go, but…"

"But I should, right?" He just nodded his head. He knew I would spend enough time beating myself up and arguing with myself about the situation that he didn't need to add his two cents as well.

Men go shopping to buy what they need; women go shopping to find out what they want.

Friday, November 16th

"I don't know why staff meetings can't be on Monday mornings. I mean, everybody already hates Monday, right? So why not torture us then. Fridays are supposed to be what you look forward to in a work week. No, not us. We dread Fridays because they always mean staff meetings. And 8:00 a.m? What the heck? The least she could do is let us sleep in a little bit!"

"You gonna gripe and complain all morning?"

"Probably."

"Ok. Just wanted to make sure what kind of day I was in for."

"And why do I have to dress up just to go sit in a damn meeting? Whose stupid idea is that anyway?"

"Your boss. And you look fine. We should probably get going soon before you end up being late."

"Can't I just call in dead today? This whole day already sucks. Why make it worse?"

"Ok, here's the deal. If you want to bitch, moan, and whine all day, that's fine with me. If you're doing it because you just woke up on the wrong side of the bed, then I suggest that we go back to bed and start all over; I could make it worth your while."

"Your cute little smirk isn't going to work on me this morning. I'm just grumpy."

"Are you grumpy just to be grumpy, or are you grumpy because you're arguing with yourself about your dad's hearing today?"

"What difference does it make? And why can't I get my hair to do anything this morning? I should just go back to bed." I threw the hairbrush down on the counter and just stared into the mirror.

Chase came up behind me, wrapped his arms around my waist, and leaned his chin on my shoulder. "Sadey, I know you're still battling this situation with your dad; this can't be an easy day for you. But taking it out on the world today isn't going to solve anything, you know that, right?"

"I'm not taking it out on the world; just you."

"Good thing I put on my Superman UnderRoos then. Wanna see 'em?" That brought a smile to my face.

"Superman UnderRoos?"

"Well, they're really just UnderRoos; the Superman is what's under them." Of course he had to say this with a stupid grin on his face.

"Is that a fact?"

Then the smarty pants answered me in his best Western voice, "Well, yes ma'am. I can prove it if you'd like." One hand was now sliding up under my shirt, while the other hand was going through the waistband of my broomstick skirt. His lips were moving across my neck planting kisses along the way. That all too familiar groan was working its way through my body. My heart was racing, my breathing was out of control, and his fingers were turning me into mush. It was all I could do to breathe out the words, "If you keep this up, I'm gonna be late for work."

"Well, I guess we better hurry this up then," he said with that fabulous smirk that makes my heart melt. He turned me around to face him and the kisses began again. His hands were gathering up the material in my skirt until it was all around my waist. I was quickly relieved of what little bit was under the skirt, and the countertop was cleared off with one sweep of his arm.

I made it to work with 5 minutes to spare, minimal make-up and hair in a ponytail.

Staff meeting lasted forever. At least I didn't have any bad news to report on my cases this morning, but I couldn't say the same for the rest of the staff. It was definitely a major bitch-fest this morning.

11:30 – hearing starts at 1:30. That gives me a total of 2 hours to stress out. *Why am I stressing out? I mean, my dad's done over half of his time, and he's admitted his guilt. Good enough, right? He'll still be on supervised probation, and under Chase's control. That's good. So, what's my problem with it? Do I really have a problem with it, or is it just easier when he's in jail? I mean I don't have to worry about dealing with the problem when the problem's locked up. What the heck is wrong with me? He's my dad; I love him. Shouldn't I want him home with the family? That's one of the things I yelled at him for; being in jail and not being home with the family. Good grief, Sadey.*

"You ok?" Matt was standing in my doorway.

"Yeah, I'm fine. Just a rough day."

"Good. Let's go get lunch. And don't argue. It's my job to have you at the courthouse by 1:25. That gives me plenty of time to feed you and change your attitude."

"My attitude? Who the hell..."

"Do I think I am? Your friend, that's who. Now shut up, get your purse, and let's go."

"What if I don't want to?"

"Are you always this damn stubborn? How in the world does he do it?"

"Who? And do what?"

"Chase – and live with you. Quit being a brat and let's go eat lunch. I'm hungry."

Matt dropped me off at the courthouse 15 minutes early. I walked as slowly as I could to the doors, which is easy to do with this stupid boot still on my foot; I was trying to waste time and convince myself that I was happy to be here.

This could be a great day for our family; my dad could be coming home. So, what the heck is my problem? I should be jumping for joy, not completely stressing out. This is ridiculous Sadey. Time to man up (or woman up)!

It was close to 1:30, so I opened the door to the courtroom slowly, hoping not to interrupt anything. As I gradually pulled the door open, I could see Galvin at the front table, but the judge wasn't on the bench yet; at least I wasn't late and making an entrance. I could see my mom and sister sitting behind the defense table; my dad's attorney was there, but dad wasn't at the table yet.

Chase was up front talking to the bailiff and he turned and headed towards me as I came through the door. He was smiling as he wrapped his arm around my waist and whispered, "I'm glad you're here." He planted a kiss on my forehead, and we headed up front to the bench with my mom and sister.

The side door opened, and a bailiff came through escorting my dad. Mom took one look at him and her eyes immediately filled with tears; she looked at him with such a longing. When dad came around the table, he leaned over the railing and kissed mom like there was nobody else in the room. Time just stood still. It was if they were the only two people for miles around, kissing for the first time; they just looked in each other's eyes, with a yearning, a hunger, more love than I could ever imagine.

Up until this moment, I had never really understood the love that existed between my mom and dad. It never occurred to me that someone could have that much adoration and affection for another person; that no matter what happened in their lives, that spark would always be there.

I looked over at Chase, and in that instant, I realized that the genuine love between my mom and dad was something I felt as well. I love Chase like my mom loves my dad; there is absolutely nothing in the world that Chase could say or do that would change my mind. I get it; I understand. I reached over, grabbed Chase's hand and just squeezed.

I swore at that moment that nothing in this world would ever be more important than family.

After an hour of questions and answers, heartfelt apologies and promises to change, the judge agreed to let my dad serve the rest of his sentence on probation, under Chase's supervision. There were a lot of stipulations, of course, but dad would be released at 9:00 a.m. on November 21st; the day before Thanksgiving. My mom cried throughout the entire hearing, and it was all I could do not to follow her lead. My heart felt like a ton of bricks; all the anger I had been harboring seemed to pile on my chest. It was time to let go; time to unload this burden. I hugged my dad before we left and told him that I loved him. Tears were filling my eyes as we left the courthouse.

I didn't say a word the entire way home; Chase never pried.

Anyone can fall in love; but if you fall in love with the same person over and over again, that's when you know its true love.

A Little stubborn

Monday, November 19th

Thanksgiving week.

Chase and I decided to take the entire week off and do something constructive. Of course, it's not like I've been doing all that much work lately anyway; 3 days a week with only minimal home visits. But Cami and Trey were both out of school this week, and Leland took vacation as well, so we decided it was a good time to remodel the basement.

Lowes delivered everything bright and early this morning. I didn't realize they were going make the delivery at 8:00 a.m. on a Monday morning, but lucky for me Chase took care of everything and let me sleep in a little. However, with all the commotion that he and the delivery boys were making, I didn't really get any extra sleep.

I had no idea what time Trey and Leland were coming over, but I figured it would be best if I wasn't running around in just a t-shirt when they arrived. So, I showered and got dressed before Chase could come up and yell at me for walking around without my boot – my ankle was getting stronger, so I just kept pushing my luck a little more each day. Jeans and a t-shirt, bowl of cereal for breakfast, and I was ready to face the day.

Cami came waltzing through the front door about 9:30, just to find me sitting in the recliner, with Bones curled up on my lap, chewing on a rawhide bone that Chase bought him over the weekend.

"Morning sunshine."

"You are very chipper for a Monday morning, there Cam."

"Thanksgiving break! Every teacher in the county is happy this morning. I see you're working hard this morning."

"I showered; what more were you expecting?"

"Yeah, about that shower…I've been instructed to check your ankle and wrap it properly, so prop it up here girl."

"How does he do it?"

"What? Know everything? It's just a gift." I gave her that look like she'd lost her mind. "Oh, ok, truth is that he heard the water running; he's in the basement babe – the hot water tank is down there. Duh!"

"Ugh. Sometimes I just wanna smack the whole lotta you."

"Admit it; you love us."

"Yeah, yeah, yeah. Just wrap the dang ankle so we can move on to another conversation."

Turns out that I hadn't done too bad of a job, except for the fact that my ankle was swollen; probably from the fact that I balanced on it getting out of the tub and then walked on it for about 5 minutes without it being wrapped.

"Um, Chase is going to be ticked."

"Don't tell him."

"Like he won't notice? Seriously, Sadey, he knows every freckle on your body. He's going to notice that your ankle is swollen. Let's at least ice it."

"You're kidding right?"

"Kidding about what Sade?"

"That he knows every freckle on my body?"

"Are you smoking crack?" Now I was the one with Bones' head turned sideways stare going on. "You're serious, aren't you? Do you not have any idea how much this man worships you?"

"Oh, well, yeah, I just…" I think it sort of embarrassed me, and I'm not sure why.

"What is it Sadey?"

"The boys are downstairs, right?"

"Yeah, can't you hear them?"

"Well, the last time I thought they were downstairs, they overheard an entire conversation and I paid for it the rest of the night. The ice cream even melted."

"I don't know whether to laugh or just be grossed out."

"What? Wait! No, it wasn't like that. We left the ice cream on the counter. Never mind. Anyway, here's the thing. Promise you won't laugh at me, ok?"

"Sadey, really? I'm your best friend; of course I'm going to laugh at you. Just talk."

I took a deep breath and then laid my heart out on the table to Cami. "Ok. You know my dad went to court on Friday, right? Well, when my dad walked in the courtroom, my mom just had this look on her face that said my dad was her whole world. He was in an orange jumpsuit, in handcuffs, being led in the courtroom by a police officer, and it was like nobody else was around for miles. It was right then that I got it, Cami; I really understood. I know that I've only known Chase for two months, but that's exactly how I feel. There isn't anything he could do or say that would change that for me; does that make sense?"

I could feel tears forming in my eyes and I really didn't want to cry. "I think I owe my mom an apology, Cami. I've been so hard on her because I just didn't get it; but now I do."

Cami took the ice off my ankle and just hugged me; that's what makes her such a great friend. She didn't have to say anything; she just listened. Cami wiped the tears from my face, looked at me very seriously, and asked, "So, do you want to tell me about the melted ice cream?"

Now the tears were flowing from laughing so hard, and from behind me, I heard, "We do not share secrets in this house. Maybe you should find a guy capable of making your ice cream melt." Dear heavens – Chase overheard us again; now I'm in big trouble.

"Shut up Chase. She has a guy hot enough to make her ice cream melt; you're just jealous." Good grief – Leland was right behind him.

"I'm not talking about leaving the ice cream in the car Leland," Chase retorted.

"Hey, those are my sisters you're talking about, so both of you boys better watch it." My baby brother was here to save the day; or not. "What's wrong with your ankle sis?"

Crap! Up until now the guys had just passed behind me going from the basement to the kitchen; now Chase came flying into the living room like someone pushed the panic button.

"What the...? Oh, God, Sadey, were you walking on it?"

"I'd like to plead the fifth." I was trying to sound cute and innocent, but I don't think it was working.

"Chill out, Chase. I've been icing it for the past few minutes. The swelling is going down." Cami tried to save me.

"The swelling has gone down? How bad was it?"

"Leland, get him out of here, back to the basement. We don't need you boys hovering over us. We're fine." I love Cami.

Chase was still messing with my ankle and rubbing the side of my leg; like if he rubbed my leg long enough then the swelling would magically disappear in my ankle. "Sadey, why didn't you holler for me? I could've helped. You know you shouldn't be walking on it; your ankle's not strong enough yet."

"Leland! So help me, if you don't get your brother out of here, you are permanently cut off!" I'm pretty sure Cami just used her teacher voice. I wasn't sure whether I should laugh or be worried about detention. Leland, of course, did exactly as he was told and literally pulled Chase out of the living room and down the basement stairs. Needless to say, nobody emerged again until Cami yelled and told them it was time for lunch. Then, all three guys walked into the kitchen like they were walking on eggshells; scared to say or do the wrong thing. It was actually kind of cute.

"Make your own sub; there are chips, macaroni salad, baked beans, cookies and brownies. Plenty of beer in the fridge." They were watching Cami talk and looking back and forth at each other like they were daring each other to make the first move. Finally, I couldn't take any more.

"If you boys are going to walk around all day with your tails tucked between your legs, I'm letting Bones eat first. At least he's sitting here wagging his tail."

Trey just shrugged his shoulders and started grabbing food; he didn't have anything to lose. None of the women in the kitchen would be cutting him off if he said the wrong thing. He piled his plate full, grabbed a bottle of Coke (because he was still, unfortunately, too young to drink), and headed for the table, where he claimed a seat next to me. "So, sis, wanna fill me in on the ice cream story; Chase won't share his dirty secrets and I could really use some new material for my wet dreams." I just punched him in the arm; but at least it lightened the mood.

Cami and I spent the afternoon discussing plans for Thanksgiving; of course, as is the norm, mom had invited her and Leland over for lunch since neither of them had parents still alive, and Cami has just been an adopted member of our family for so long anyway. The difference now is that she doesn't have to cook Thanksgiving dinner for Chase since he'll be at lunch with all of us now. Then we worked on wedding plans; she was still battling on how she wanted to go down the aisle. We ordered pizza for dinner and the boys gave each other a hard time about who had done the least amount of work for the day.

Trey left after dinner so he could spend the evening with mom, so the four of us popped some popcorn and watched Lethal Weapon. Bones ate half a bowl of popcorn himself and kept trying to drink Chase's beer. It would have been completely relaxing if Chase hadn't still been freaking out about my ankle; he had my legs propped up over his the entire evening, icing my ankle on and off the whole time. Chase knew better than to say anything to me about my ankle while Cami was in the house, but the minute their car pulled out of the driveway it was the first question out of his mouth.

"Are you sure you're ok? Why did you take a bath without me? All you had to do was yell and I would have been there to help. Why do you have to be so stubborn?"

"Which question do you want me to answer?" I tried to be cute when I said it, but it only halfway worked.

"Seriously, Sadey, sometimes you really worry me. You are so stubborn; you saw how swollen it was today. What would have happened if you'd fallen or something? You scare me to death some days."

"Sorry. It's just so aggravating being dependent on people all the time. I really felt like I could do it by myself for a change; you shouldn't have to wait on me hand and foot 24/7."

"I don't, but I would. I would do anything for you, and it drives me crazy that you won't let me." I really felt bad, but I didn't know how to make him understand things from my point of view.

"I will admit that it's just one of the many things I love about you. But, what if the tables were turned? What if I had to take care of you? How good of a patient would you really be?"

There goes his amazing eye-roll again; I've got to work on perfecting mine. "You win; this time. I just don't want you to injure yourself anymore, ok."

"Fair enough. Now let's talk about something besides my injuries."

"Ok, fine. What's the plan for Thursday?"

"Lunch at my mom and dad's is at 1:00; everybody is supposed to be there."

"And what are you in charge of bringing?"

"Stuffing and gravy; that's always my job. I think it's because they are the things I complain about. I like my stuffing crunchy, not squishy, so mom makes me cook it myself so I can't complain about how it's cooked."

"Your mom's a smart woman."

"Yes, she is." *I really needed to talk to Chase about Friday afternoon, but I didn't want to push anything on him or put him in an awkward position. But not telling him would be the same as lying to him, and I refuse to do that either. Ugh. How should I bring this up?*

"What is it Sadey? You just went into argument mode with yourself."

"It's not fair that you can read me like a book, you know that, right?"

"Well, maybe not fair for you; but definitely good for me. Now, what's bothering you?"

"Ok, again, I'm not good at this laying my heart out on the table thing, and I just don't want it to make things awkward between us."

I was nervous. *What if I poured my heart out and it seemed like I was pushing him into something he didn't want? But I think he feels the same way about me, but, still, what if I'm...*

"Sadey. Look at me." I was still sitting with my legs across his on the couch, and he just lifted my chin up towards him so I was looking him in the eye. He's just such a gentle giant. "I love you, Sadey, and nothing you say right now is going to change that; I don't want you to ever worry about hurting my feelings or feel like you can't tell me the truth about things."

Deep breath. Might as well lay it all on the line; he either runs or stays. At least this way I'll know.

"Ok. Friday, in the courtroom, when they brought my dad in, the look on my mom's face just struck me; you know. I mean, Chase, really, he was like in an orange jumpsuit with handcuffs on, and my mom just had this look on her face that said he was the most beautiful person in the world, and that she absolutely adored him. When he leaned over to kiss her, the rest of the room disappeared. They didn't care that they were in a courtroom; it was like that moment, that first kiss, when nothing else mattered. I remember that moment with you, and how my insides just turned to mush."

He hadn't said a single word and didn't take his eyes away from me while I was talking. He just kept intertwining our fingers and the more I talked, the more comfortable I felt telling him how I feel.

"I don't want you to think I'm crazy, Chase, but up until now I thought my mom was a complete idiot for standing by my dad's side through everything. Now, I get it. When I saw them in that courtroom, I thought of you. I don't know how to say this without it sounding corny or anything, but I feel like that with you. Like nothing else matters, like there's nothing you could ever do or say that would change my mind about how much I love you. I'm sure there are people who think I'm completely crazy; I've only known you for a couple of months. And I don't want this to sound pushy, or make things awkward between us, but when I saw my mom with my dad, I saw myself with you."

We sat in silence for what seemed like eternity, but he never took his eyes off mine. I had no idea if I had just said something wrong or something right; his poker face never gave away a thing. Finally, he smiled. He moved his hands away from my hands and up to my face. For a second, he held my face completely still and looked directly into my eyes. Life was moving in slow motion. Gradually, that smile on his face began turning into his sexy little smirk; that's when he finally spoke.

"Screw that rule about how long you have to know one another in order to fall in love. I love you with everything I have, and nothing is going to change that. Ever!"

A second later, he was unbuttoning my jeans. He slowly slid them down and off my legs and proceeded to move back up my legs with carefully placed kisses along the way. The process began again to remove my panties; again, the kisses continued back up my body from the tops of my feet, to my shins, my knees, slowly to the tops of my thighs, my legs slowly being parted and the kisses finding their way to the insides of my legs and on up until I felt like I would explode.

I was complete putty at this point. Chase was lying on top of me continuing to place kisses across my face, when all of the sudden he screamed, "Holy shit!" and fell off the couch. It only took me a second to realize what had just occurred, as I then saw Bones sitting at the foot of the couch.

"Damn his nose is cold!"

The best moments in life are the ones that make you weak in the knees.

Tuesday, November 20th

Everybody showed up early this morning to continue working on the man-cave. Mom, Cami, Noelle, me, and Abi went grocery shopping to get everything we needed for dinner on Thursday. Blake stayed at the house with Trey, Chase, and Leland for a little male bonding and to help them with the basement. I'm not sure how helpful a 7-year-old can be, but he was pretty pumped that he got to hang out with the big boys today, so it worked out great for everybody.

Three hours later we were back at the house, fussing and whining about the amount of people that had waited until the last minute like us to do their shopping. Blake had apparently been having a good time with the boys because he refused to leave when Noelle went down to get him. Of course Trey, being the great uncle, volunteered to bring him home when they were finished for the day, so Blake was on cloud nine.

Mid-afternoon, Bones and I were sleeping comfortably on the couch when Blake came running up the steps. "Aunt Sadey, Uncle Leland and Uncle Chase want a beer; where are they?"

"There might be a couple in the fridge in the kitchen. If not, check the garage. I hope you're charging them for doing a beer run."

He looked confused, so I filled him in on a secret. "When I was a kid, and Grandpa wanted a beer, I used to charge him a quarter each time I got one; I made quite a killing when he had friends over."

Blake got a huge smile on his face and I just winked, like it was our little secret what he'd just learned. I heard him go back to the basement and tell Leland and Chase that they each owed him a dollar. I can't wait for him to tell his mom this story; I'm sure I'll be in the doghouse, but it's an aunt's prerogative.

Did he just call him Uncle Chase?

I only have two drinks at the bar ~ the first one and the last one; the others don't count ~ they are just refills.

Thanksgiving

Thursday, November 22nd

Thanksgiving Day

Nothing like cramming 11 people in a house to cause some chaos in a day. Four women and a 3-year-old huddled together in a kitchen, while the men watched the Macy's Day parade, patiently waiting for football games to start. Blake, boy genius, got a camera for his birthday, and he was going around taking pictures of everybody and everything. Dad was back in his recliner, Leland and Chase on either side of the couch, Dane and Trey sharing the loveseat. It's the best chaos a girl could ask for; hands down.

Blake convinced Abi to come into the living room so he could take pictures of her sitting on everybody's lap. At least the men were being a good sport about it.

Back in the kitchen, the turkey was taken out of the oven, I was adding more butter and sugar to the green beans every time mom would turn her back, and Noelle was putting rolls on the pan waiting for space in the oven to free up; mom needs a bigger kitchen.

Noelle and Cami decided to go work on setting the table for 11 people and locating the appropriate number of chairs from odd places throughout the house. Mom and I were alone in the kitchen; this is as good a time as any for a mother-daughter discussion.

"Mom, I owe you an apology."

"What for, baby?"

"I've been a real, for lack of a better word, horse's ass, to you when it came to daddy. I just didn't get it. I only saw the bad things and the pent-up anger I had, and it never occurred to me how you could possibly back him up with all that's happened."

Mom stopped carving turkey and just looked at me curiously. I've already jumped in with both feet; might as well continue. "Last week, in the courtroom, I saw the way you two looked at each other. You were just like a young couple who'd just found love for the first time; you kissed each other like there was nobody else in the room. I got it; I felt it."

"Sadey, baby, you don't have to apologize. You can't help how you feel, and you can't choose who you fall in love with; your heart does. And feelings aren't right or wrong; they just are. I've told you that before. I love your father very much."

She wiped her hands on her towel and turned to face me. "Do you remember that movie 'Valentine's Day'?" I shook my head 'yes'; it's one of my favorites. "Do you remember that scene in the graveyard when Estelle tells her husband, 'When you love somebody, you have to love all of them. You love the good things and the bad things'."

"I know you have mixed feelings about me and Chase; we've only known each other a couple of months. But I get that feeling; I understand that now. You know that moment, right before a kiss, when he looks you in the eye and you're immediately breathless? It's better than the kiss itself. I saw that in your eyes and in daddy's eyes, and I have that feeling with Chase. Falling in love with him, I hadn't expected that. But being in love with him, that's something I couldn't stop, even if I tried. I just want to tell you I'm sorry. I've been a childish brat. You're the strongest woman I know, and if I can give Chase even half the love that you give to daddy..."

Mom came around the island and just hugged me. Tears were forming in my eyes; I felt like that bond between me and my mom was back. "I love you mom."

"I love you too baby. You know, at first, I wasn't keen on the idea of Chase and you living in the same home; you know my feelings on that. But I saw the transformation; I saw him go from a caretaker to a lover. I didn't like it. Don't get me wrong; I like Chase. He's a great guy; but I was worried about you. I didn't want you to throw your heart into a man that was just there to take care of you and would essentially go home at the end of the day. Does that make sense?"

I just shook my head yes. I understood what she meant. "But I've watched him; and you. I see the way you look at each other. I see the light in your eyes, the gentleness in his touch, and how protective he is of you. I don't really have mixed feelings anymore. Love happens, baby girl. And I think it might have hit you with a car." That brought a laugh out.

I hugged her again, and just said. "I'm sorry, mom."

"Don't be sorry baby; just love Chase with all your heart and you'll find a way to grow old together." Then just as she turned around to go back to the turkey she said, "And give me some more grandbabies; your sister is way ahead of you." Ugh.

Dinner was elbow-to-elbow. Eleven people crowded around one table definitely made for some togetherness. Blake, of course, had his camera at the table and randomly took pictures of us eating; I'm sure he'll use them for blackmail later on. Yes, he's that smart. He also had plenty to say during dinner.

I couldn't help but look around the table in amazement. There was a smile on everybody's face; the whole room was happy. Dad sat at one end of the table, and mom at the other. Every now and then Chase would just place his hand on my knee and squeeze; it was just a small gesture of contentment. There was just nothing better in the world than having your entire family in one room, happier than we've ever been.

Conversations ran the gamut. It flowed from college football, to interest rates, to the upcoming baby, to everybody being happy to have dad home. But the most awkward and maybe most interesting conversation centered around Leland and Cami's upcoming wedding. Blake had to input his opinion.

"Aunt Sadey, I think you and Uncle Chase should get married at the same time as Aunt Cami and Uncle Leland; then Grandpa can walk both of you down the aisle at the same time."

Noelle jumped in to try and thwart the awkwardness of that statement. "Blake, Leland and Cami are engaged, but Sadey and Chase just started dating."

My brilliant nephew had a response that made everybody catch their breath. "Doesn't matter mom. If Uncle Chase can make Aunt Sadey's ice cream melt, then they love each other enough to get married, because Aunt Sadey loves ice cream so much that she'd never let it melt. She'd call it ice cream abuse."

Cami and I immediately looked back and forth from Chase to Leland to Trey, trying to get somebody to fess up to who discussed that topic with Blake in the room. All three of them hung their heads, trying their best not to laugh. My brother-in-law, of course, had no knowledge of the conversation since he wasn't fortunate enough to be on vacation this week hanging out in my basement making the conversion into a man-cave.

"Somebody want to fill me in?" Dane asked.

Cami and I both yelled 'No!' at the same time. But Blake thought he was a wealth of information and felt the need to explain.

"See, dad, the other day Aunt Cami and Aunt Sadey were talking in Aunt Cami's kitchen and Uncle Leland and Uncle Chase were spying on them."

My face was thirteen shades of red; but the boys were trying their dandiest not to crack up laughing. He just kept talking, much to the dismay of the rest of us.

"Apparently Aunt Sadey wouldn't tell Uncle Chase what they were talking about, even though he already knew. So, Uncle Chase had to force it out of her, and their ice cream melted."

At this point I was ready to crawl under the table; Leland, Chase, Trey and dad were laughing so hard they couldn't breathe; my mother was trying to figure out if this was a funny story or if she should be appalled; Cami and Noelle were speechless, and Dane was quite interested in the details, while giving me a look of mere enjoyment at the laughter at my expense.

Noelle, the good sister, tried her best to steer the conversation another way. "Blake, sweetie, don't you think that Aunt Sadey having to clean up a mess of melted ice cream is something she doesn't want everybody to know about?"

"What's the big deal mom? I mean it's definitely not as bad as when she laid on the table in a bunch of pumpkin goo after they carved pumpkins for Halloween."

That's it; I'm so never showing my face around here again. At this point everybody in the room, with the exception of me, is laughing so hard they can't even think about taking a drink for fear of something spewing out of their nose.

"How 'bout we go back to the conversation of Leland and Cami's wedding?" Noelle thought she was helping, but she was really just giving Blake more things to talk about.

"I still think Uncle Chase and Aunt Sadey should have a double wedding with them," Blake just couldn't keep his mouth shut.

"Ok, Blake, since you clearly have an opinion on everything, why don't you explain why you're so adamant that Sadey and Chase get married with Leland and Cami." My dad just had to egg him on.

"Did anybody think to maybe ask my opinion on the matter since you're talking about me?" I decided to throw in my two cents since I was clearly the object of the conversation.

"Look, Aunt Sadey. I don't want to be rude or anything, but the only person in the room smarter than me, besides my dad, is Aunt Cami, so I think you ought to think about what I'm saying. Here's my reasoning…"

"How old are you again?" I thought that 10-year-old Kasey was too wise for her age, but my 7-year-old nephew is making me feel stupid.

"I'm 7 ½ Aunt Sadey. You should know that." He was rolling his eyes at me. Good grief. "Ok, so back to what I was saying. First of all, Uncle Chase and Uncle Leland are brothers, so that makes sense. Plus, Aunt Cami and Aunt Sadey are the bestest of friends, so that makes sense too. Plus, Aunt Cami doesn't have a dad anymore, so Grandpa can be her dad and Aunt Sadey's dad at the same time and Grandpa wouldn't have to buy a suit twice. I think it makes perfect sense; I'm not sure what's wrong with the rest of you."

At that statement, Blake pushed his chair back, grabbed some dirty dishes and started walking towards the kitchen. It was eerily silent in the dining room. Everybody was just sort of looking around trying to figure out what the heck just happened and how we all got put in our place by a 7-year-old. What the hell…

"Well, since today is all about Sadey, does anybody else have anything they'd like to add to my life? Obviously I'm pretty entertaining, and fairly stupid, according to my genius nephew, so…anybody…?"

Chase and Leland were cracking up at me. Mom decided to help Blake clear the table. Everybody else was just trying to look in every direction besides mine. Finally, Chase got up, leaned down and kissed me, then said, "Well Sweet Cheeks, I guess you better go shopping for a wedding dress." I punched him in the arm.

"Very funny. Don't you have a football game to go watch?" That gave the men all the leverage they needed to move to the living room and get comfy on the couch to prepare for a lazy football watching afternoon.

I was exhausted by the time we left, and I didn't say a word to Chase all the way home. He might be downright adorable, but I was still mad that he was telling stories on us in front of Blake. Ugh. I'll never live that down!

I headed to the bedroom and changed into sweats and a t-shirt, forget the undergarments. Next step was the couch, with a pillow, blanket, and the remote control. It had been a long day and I had no intention of doing anything constructive the rest of the evening.

Chase apparently had the same idea because it wasn't long before he was donning a pair of sweats (and I'm thinking not much else considering the view I was getting) and had settled in on the other end of the couch. He was trying to play footsies, so I'm guessing he was doing his best to suck up.

"Are you planning on staying mad at me all evening?"

"Yep."

"Ok. Just checking."

I found some NCIS reruns and figured this was a good way to waste the evening. A half hour went by, and Chase scooted closer on the couch.

"Still mad at me?"

"Yep."

"Ok. Just checking."

"Are you going to do this all evening?"

"Probably."

"I can't believe you told them about the ice cream and the pumpkin gunk. It's not like I want our sex life broadcast to the world; especially not to a 7-year-old."

"Ok, I admit that Blake is brilliant beyond his years, and I was completely clueless. But we weren't just discussing our sex life, per se. Leland and I were kind of trading, um, funny stories, and Trey was, um, taking lessons." He said this with a weird look on his face, like he wasn't really sure how to explain his stupidity.

"Let me get this straight. You and Leland were basically giving my brother some ideas on how to get lucky creatively, with a 7-year-old in the room?"

"You make it sound so dirty. And in our defense, Blake was upstairs watching TV most of the time and running back and forth doing errands for us. He just happened to hear some of the good stuff on you; that's all."

"That's all? That's the best you can do." I was so totally trying to be ticked off at him; but it's hard to stay mad. It's not like he was telling our dirty secrets to a kid on purpose; he's just male, thinking with the wrong part of his body. "Just for the record, I was thoroughly embarrassed this afternoon."

"Sorry about that. But, for the record, I was kind of humored by Blake's suggestion that we get married with Leland and Cami. He's quite an interesting lad."

"Too smart for his own good; that's for sure. You've gotta give him credit; he has definitely given this a lot of thought. But I'm trying to figure out where he got the idea from originally."

"Um, well, um…"

"Spill it, mister. What did you do?"

"Nothing; I swear! It wasn't me; it was Leland. He said it jokingly the other day. He was talking about the fact that Cami was going to ask your dad to walk her down the aisle, and then the conversation just went crazy from there."

"So that part was actually true; she's really going to ask him to do it. We were talking a few weeks ago about how she was going to go down the aisle, and she mentioned that she wished my dad was out of jail because she would ask him; but that was before he was even given a court date. We haven't really discussed it since then. I think that would be pretty cool, though. I mean, we grew up like sisters."

"So, am I even slightly forgiven?"

"Maybe a little."

"Does that mean I can share your blanket?" I lifted up the blanket a little so he could scoot over on the couch.

"This doesn't mean you're off the hook big guy. I'm just feeling generous tonight."

"How generous?"

"Sharing the blanket is as far as you're getting. I'm lusting over Gibbs tonight."

"Dang." That didn't stop him from trying. Every so often his hand would try sliding up my leg, or he'd lean over to act like he was going to pet Bones and his hand would 'accidently' brush across my girls. He finally gave up and I thought I was in the clear, but no luck. He started his 'sweet guy' act again, which I have trouble resisting.

"So, did anybody ever tell you how cute you are when you're attempting to be mad?"

"Give up; you're not getting any."

"What about if I do this?" Then he started kissing my neck, slowly, from my collarbone up to my ear, where he started nibbling. I had to admit that goose bumps were starting to form. But I was trying hard to stand my ground. Trying to control my breathing, I replied, "Nope, sorry."

"What about if I do this?" He started sliding his hand up under my t-shirt, stopping only briefly to give me that magnificent smirk when he realized that the girls were hanging out freely. Then the magic fingers started doing their thing. Dang.

Controlling my breathing was getting more difficult, but I tried again to convince him it wasn't working. "Still…not…working. Sorry."

"Ok, I have more tricks." Then I officially lost control. He slid to the floor in front of me and the sweats were slowly removed and replaced by his mouth. I didn't even bother trying to respond; I couldn't control my breathing or the groans escaping my body. I was officially putty in his hands, and he knew it.

Ok, yeah, I'm going to marry this man!

A guy should be able to handle me in sweatpants before he deserves me in a wedding dress.

Moving Forward

Friday, November 30th

Staff meeting was the usual obnoxious hour and a half. I definitely ate more than my share of donuts and drank an entire large sweet tea by the time the meeting was over. Fortunately, the day got better from there. I just hung up the phone with my mom, trying to work out the details of Christmas, even though it's 25 days away; she apparently wanted to get a head start. I no sooner laid the phone back in its cradle when it was ringing again.

"This is Sadey."

"Girlfriend, have I got some news for you." Gotta love Janice and her southern accent. "You are NEVER gonna believe what just happened."

"I don't actually have to guess, do I?"

"Not today. This has been the weirdest mornin' of my life; hands down."

"I realize things happen at a slower pace in the south, but I hope you're gonna get around to telling me sometime soon."

"Ok, don't get your panties in a wad. So, I'm working on paperwork this morning; a nice quiet morning. All of a sudden James Michaels walks into my office, and he's got this guy by the shirt collar." I'm not sure where this is leading, but I'm definitely not going to interrupt her. "Actually, he was more like a kid, only 19. Anyway, James drags him into my office and literally plops him down in a chair. He had Kara with him, and she was standing almost nose to nose with the guy giving him the cutest glare I swear to peaches I've ever seen. I was pretty sure that fireballs were gonna shoot outta her eyes at any moment. Then he proceeds to make this guy tell me why he's in my office. So, long story short, apparently the guy is his neighbor and James caught him outside the apartment selling weed. He was on his way to walk Kara to preschool, so she saw it."

"Oh, no. That's not good."

"Just you wait, sugar; it gets better. So apparently James grabs this kid by the shirt collar, puts himself, Kara, and this kid on the bus and drags him into my office. The kid didn't even argue with James; just did what he said. So, James does the Gibbs slap on this kid and forces him to tell me all about it. Then he made him give me the rest of the weed and forced him to apologize to Kara for what she saw."

"Wow."

"There's more. Then he marched him to the front desk and forced him to make an appointment to join the drug counseling group. Told me he uses and sells the stuff."

At this point I'm sort of awe-struck. It's always a good feeling when clients actually start making good decisions. I was going to ask what happened to the drugs, but I didn't have to.

"It doesn't end there. About that time Leland walks through the door; Ima guessin' James called him on the way over here. Leland reads the kid the riot act and tells him that James saved his ass today by making him give me the weed, because otherwise he would have arrested the kid for possession with intent to sell. The kid was scared out of his gourd. It was all I could do not to laugh."

"So, basically, James is doing great these days, huh?"

"No kidding. I've never seen anything like it, and I've been doing social work most of my life; here and in South Carolina."

"You just made my day; maybe I can get in a visit with him next week and work on closing his case. It would be great to lower this caseload a little bit."

"I hear that girlfriend. My caseload just gets bigger and bigger; kinda like my backside, come to think of it."

When Chase picked me up after work, I relayed Janice's story to him. Since James is still on probation, I thought Chase would like some good news. We decided to stop by on our way home just to tell him how proud we are of him and get me some documentation to possibly close his case.

I knocked on James' door and heard little feet running across the room – Kara. Just as she opened the door, the drug-selling/using neighbor poked his head out of his apartment; probably just being nosy about who was visiting James. He did a double-take when he saw Chase; he undoubtedly thought he was seeing Leland again. When Kara opened the door for us, she saw the neighbor poking his head out his door. The wise-beyond-her-years little girl looked at Chase and said, "Are you a cop too? Because that dummy guy right there thinks it's ok to sell drugs with me in the building."

The guy started to close his door when Chase hollered at him, "Hey, dummy guy. Come over here."

Janice was right – he looked like he was just a kid. The kid didn't even hesitate when Chase hollered at him; just did what he was told. Chase grabbed him by the shirt collar, just for effects, I'm sure, and told him to hit his knees. The kid dropped to his knees immediately and then looked up at Chase like 'now what?'

"What's your name dummy guy?"

"Franklin."

"Ok, Franklin. This little girl here saw you selling drugs this morning, is that right?" Chase was in interrogation mode. So cute. "So, what are you going to do about that?"

"Um, well, James already took me to see that lady and I have to go to drug classes, or I'll get arrested and go to jail."

"Well, dummy guy, that sounds great; however, you made a 4-year-old girl see a drug deal. That's probably the dumbest thing you've ever done; hence the name dummy guy, right?" This was getting fun; I need to take Chase with me on home visits more often. James was in the doorway now, in sweatpants, with wet hair – I'm guessing he was in the shower when we knocked. But he was enjoying the show with dummy guy.

Dummy guy – aka Franklin – was still on his knees in front of Kara, and obviously still confused as to why Chase had him on his knees. Years of social work made me understand; when you talk to a kid you do it on their level; dummy guy has probably never even heard of social work. Chase continued his interrogation.

"I'm thinking that you probably owe Kara here an apology, dontcha think?"

"I said I was sorry this morning in that lady's office."

Chase Gibbs slapped him. "First of all, the lady's name is Janice; she will either be your best friend or your worst enemy, so think about that. Second, just saying I'm sorry is not an apology."

Kara was standing in the doorway with her arms crossed giving dummy guy a stern glare; she'll make a great teacher someday. When Chase gave his explanation of an apology, Kara decided she would add to it. "Yeah, dummy, my daddy here told me that if you're really sorry for something then you have to tell the person why you're sorry; otherwise, it doesn't count." Kids are way too smart these days!

"Ok, ok, ok. I get it. Little girl..."

"My name is Kara."

"Ok, Kara. Look, I'm sorry you saw me selling drugs this morning. It's a bad habit I have, and your dad is forcing me to get help, so I won't be doing it again. Ok?"

"You promise?"

"Yeah. I promise."

"Good. Hey dummy guy, do you have any kids?"

"No, why?"

"It's a good thing, because if you had kids then Miss Sadey would take them from you until you stopped being a dummy-head. I guess you got lucky."

Dummy guy didn't really know what to do next; he was just sitting on his knees looking back and forth from Chase to Kara and back to Chase. Chase grabbed him by his shirt collar and stood him back up. "Ok, dummy guy, I'm done with you. The next time I see you it better be in the midst of some kind of community service; got it?"

"Yes sir. I got it."

"Good, get outta here."

You didn't have to tell him twice; Franklin was hightailing it back to his apartment and closed his door behind him. After dummy guy left, we went in James' apartment and chitchatted for a while. I told him I was going to work on closing his case now; he was doing a great job with Kara and what he did this morning showed real character. James gave us an update on Kara's preschool, and she showed us where she was learning to write her name; she was extremely proud of her accomplishment.

Don't let your past hold your future hostage.

Monday, December 3rd

I never look forward to doctor appointments, but today was different. Today there's a very good chance the doctor is going to tell me I can get rid of the boot on my leg and brace on my arm. I keep giving myself this pep talk, telling myself that I've worked hard in physical therapy. That's only partially true since I hate PT, and it always hurts to go there. But, nonetheless, I was hoping for some good news this morning.

"Are you about ready?"

"No. I can't get my hair to do anything. I swear if I don't get this brace off my arm today I'm going to knock somebody out with it."

"I hope that somebody isn't me. Would you like some help with the hair?"

"I suppose. It's probably the only way we're gonna get out of here on time, huh?"

"Probably. So stop being Miss Independent and just let me help you."

"I'm just so tired of you having to help me do everything. It's frustrating."

"Only for you; I don't mind. I have to admit that we've had lots of quality time together because of these broken bones; I'm totally not complaining." He said this with that cute little smirk on his face.

"Don't make me hit you with this hairbrush, mister."

"Man, last time you threatened me I had to go put on my Superman Underroos. Should I go get them now?" Stupid smirk.

Ok, dilemma. First of all, I have an appointment in one hour; on the other hand, it's only a fifteen-minute drive. Second, I love his Superman Underroos; but it will require me to get redressed. I could argue this matter all day; unfortunately, I have a doctor's appointment in an hour. So...

"If you keep arguing with yourself, then I'm not going to have enough time to ravage your naked body."

"Just for the record, my body isn't naked right now."

"That's ok. I can change that." And he did. Not to mention, he's getting pretty good at clearing off the counter with one sweep of his arm; practice makes perfect.

We made it to the doctor with 10 minutes to spare; pretty good, if I should say so myself. We then waited almost a half hour in the waiting room, and I was starting to get extremely grumpy. They finally called me back and took me straight to x-ray. Then I was placed in the little room, with the too tall table that's covered with paper. And they allowed me to sit there for another 20 minutes. We were finally blessed with the doctor's presence and he was holding my x-rays in his hand. It seemed like he was moving in slow motion putting those films up on the light board. He stared at them for a couple of minutes, then he finally turned around and said, "Wrist is good, ankle is not. Did you reinjure your ankle somehow?"

I was in total shock. "Wh-what? What's wrong with my ankle?"

"There is a hairline fracture right here in the front. I don't need to recast it, but it will require something stronger than just taping it." At this point my mouth was on the ground.

"This sucks!" That's pretty much all I could think of to say at the moment. I was trying to stop the tears that were filling up in my eyes. I couldn't make my voice work, and Chase was quick to see that.

"So, doc, what kind of nursing do I need to do now?"

"Well, basically you're going to need to tape her up from mid-foot to 3 inches above the fracture; I'll show you here in a minute. Then she'll have an ankle brace – it's an Aircast Air Stirrup brace. If her ankle was just sprained, then she could actually just walk on it wearing a shoe. But since there is a fracture then she'll still have to wear the boot when she walks."

"Um, boys, you do realize I'm still in the room, right?"

"Yes, but I know darn well that you won't listen to my instructions; so I figure if I tell Chase then he'll make sure you do what you're told. And, just for the record, how do you think you fractured it?"

"Well, I was, um, well..." Crap.

"She decided to shower and get dressed while I was in the basement working. I don't know what she did, but her ankle was extremely swollen when I came upstairs."

"Ok, young lady. Doctor's orders: No pressure on your foot without the boot – period. Make Chase give you a piggy-back, or sit in a wheelchair, or whatever you want; but no pressure without the boot. If you follow my instructions, then maybe we can get you out of this before Christmas. But at the rate you're going you'll be booted up into the New Year."

"Ok, fine. I got it." This royally sucks! At least my hand is free, and I can do my own hair and type normally again. But I'm seriously tired of all these limitations on walking. Ugh!

"Good. Now how's the pain after physical therapy?"

"Awful. It's tolerable on my wrist and arm; it seems easier to build my strength back up there, even though there were two breaks. But my entire leg hurts when I'm finished."

"It's supposed to hurt some, but how long does the pain last?"

This time Chase answered for me. "At least a couple of hours; sometimes more. She tries not to show the pain because she wants me to think she's alright, but I can see it on her face."

"Is that true Sadey?"

I just gave them both an evil glare, which of course told them he was right, but I didn't have to say so. Now I was really grumpy; something Chase is quickly getting used to. The doctor gave me a prescription for pain medication and told me to take it 30 minutes before I went to therapy; this would cut down on the pain. I pouted all the way out of the office, especially since this new brace they put on makes my leg feel like it's three times its normal size. Taped, braced, and booted!

We got to the car and I realized how heavy my leg really was when I required help to get in the Blazer. I'm past grumpy; at this point, I'm just a straight up bitch. And Chase doesn't even blink. How can he do that?

"I just want to know how you can always be so even keel all the time. You don't get wound up or throw fits or even pout. You only have two temperaments: happy and horny."

He just looked over at me and smiled; I wanted to smack him. I was trying very hard to be grumpy and he's just happy-go-lucky. Seriously, what the…

My moods don't just swing – they bounce, pivot, recoil, rebound, oscillate, fluctuate and occasionally pirouette.

Third Time is a Charm

Thursday, December 20th

Here we go again – doctor's appointment. Hopefully the air cast and boot will be removed today, and I can walk normally again; that would be an awesome Christmas present.

I was just finishing my hair and make-up when Chase came up behind me. "You know, the last two times you had a doctor's appointment we cleaned off this counter and you got at least some good news. So, I was thinking, maybe the third time would be a charm. Whaddya say?"

"Are you serious? Is there ever a time that you're not horny?"

"When I'm sleeping, maybe. Well, I guess that depends on what I'm dreaming of at the time, so…"

"So, basically you're just horny 24/7?"

"You could say that. But, in all fairness, I didn't have this problem until you came along. However, today I'm actually offering my services. I mean, I would hate for you to get to the appointment and the doctor tells you you're stuck with this boot for a while longer; then I'd blame myself for not starting your morning out properly." Gotta give him credit for that explanation.

"So, really you're just doing your civic duty?"

"Yeah, something like that. Now, are you going to waste time arguing with me, or are you going to let me make your morning a little nicer?"

"The biggest problem I see here is that I'm actually having a good hair day."

"No problem – can't touch the hair on your head; got it." Less than a minute later I was back on the cleaned off countertop, minus my pants. Good news – I mean besides the obvious – was that not a single hair got harmed in the process. I'm thinking this is going to be a good morning.

I started to get a little antsy, though, when the doctor stared at my x-rays longer than usual. But when he finally turned around, he was smiling.

"Good news. Looks like you're all healed up." I squealed with delight; the doctor and Chase just rolled their eyes at me. Then of course he had to go and taper my enthusiasm. "However, Sadey, you're not 100% in the clear. Your ankle is still weak, so running is out of the question."

"I can assure you doc that the only running she does is to the bathroom." Chase and the doctor found that quite humorous; and Chase was smart enough to say it while standing beyond my reach.

Even though that wasn't a restriction that was of any concern to me, he had to continue with more little rules. "You still need to continue physical therapy; if Chase feels confident enough to do it with you, then you can do it at home. Either way you still need to build up the strength in your ankle. One more thing, and I'll say this beyond punching distance, you still need to make sure someone is around when you're getting in and out of the shower; for safety reasons, until you've regained all your strength."

"Ugh. Fine. But I think this is a conspiracy between the two of you." The doctor and Chase just kind of looked at each other and shrugged their shoulders; I knew it.

"I want food."

"You usually do."

"What's that supposed to mean?"

"It means you were busy doing other things this morning besides eating breakfast, so I'm sure you're starving by now."

"That's your fault; you know that, right? That means that you're buying."

"I think that this morning's extracurricular activities were definitely worth the price of me buying lunch. So, I suppose we're not going to McDonald's; am I right?"

"Cute and smart; I like that in a man."

"You know, we could skip lunch too and practice some more extracurricular activities."

"Ok, hot stuff, here's the deal; I love you and I love sex with you, but if I don't get some food soon then I'm going to pass out and sex with you will be completely out of the question."

"Point taken. Where to?"

"Something Mexican."

"Your wish is my command."

"That's the man I love. Now that I no longer have this boot on my foot, it's time to do some shopping."

"I thought you already finished your Christmas shopping?"

"Not Christmas shopping for gifts; we need a Christmas tree. Oh, and I need a new car. Well, actually a used car is fine; nonetheless, I need a car."

"One thing at a time – food first, then tree. Let's wait on the car thing until after Christmas. A couple of days before the New Year and car salesmen will make whatever deal they possibly can not to be stuck with cars on the lot at the end of the year. We'll get a better deal."

"Ok – fine with me. I like saving money."

"No, you like spending money as long as what you're buying is on sale; there's a difference."

"Splitting hairs; let's just get me fed first."

Chicken quesadillas, chips and white cheese sauce, strawberry margaritas – good lunch. Christmas tree shopping was not that easy. Chase wanted a real tree; I said fake was fine. Plus, if we had a real tree in the house, then Bones would probably consider it his own personal fire hydrant. After a trip through Lowes, Wal-Mart, and Kmart, we still hadn't found an artificial tree that would satisfy Chase. So, we spent another couple of hours finding all the live Christmas tree sellers in the entire city. After I had walked what felt like miles and miles and miles, we ended up back at the first place we stopped. Ugh! But Christmas tree shopping was finished; now we just had to rearrange the living room and get it set up; all while we convinced Bones that if he peed on the tree then I would have to kill him.

Another hour later, the tree was in the living room and I was laying on the couch in the 'I'm too exhausted to breathe' pose.

"What about decorations?"

"Tell me you're kidding, right? It took the entire ding-dang day just to get a freakin' tree. Decorations can wait until tomorrow."

"Let me rephrase; do you own decorations?"

"Um, well, I have a few, I think. Did we see any decorations when we cleaned the garage last month?"

"Sweet Cheeks – you do know how much I love you, right?"

"Enough to give me a pain pill because if I take one more step my ankle is gonna break in half."

"I guess we're shopping for decorations tomorrow. Do you want a side of ice cream with that pain pill?"

"I'm pretty sure you fell out of heaven."

"No, I'm just using you to earn my way into heaven." On that note, he left in search of my ice cream and pain pill.

The 'Circle of Life' is not measured by the size of your circle...but by what is inside it.

Friday, December 21st

We found one large tote of Christmas decorations in the garage; ornaments that my grandmother had saved over the years from all of us kids. While Chase was kind enough to do the Wal-Mart run without me to get lights for the tree, I sat in the middle of the floor going through this tote ornament by ornament. Every single ornament told a story; some by me, others by Trey and Noelle. She even had ornaments from when my dad was a kid; snowflakes, snowmen, and felt angels. Grandma made sure that every ornament was dated and who gave it to her, even if she had to put a tiny sticker on the back with the information.

I was only a third of the way through the tote, on an emotional roller coaster, when I heard the front door open. I knew Chase hadn't been gone that long; but then again, maybe I'd just lost track of time. Bones was sleeping soundly on the floor beside me, and when the door opened he got up to make his greeting. His tail was wagging, but his entire butt was wiggling; he was obviously happy to see whoever just walked into my house.

I turned around when I heard, "Sadey-bug, would it be ok if I helped you hang decorations today?"

"Dad? What are you doing here?"

"Well, Chase called and said you'd found a tote full of grandma's ornaments, and I thought maybe a trip down a good memory lane would be a decent way to spend the day."

I didn't know what to say. I was a total wreck; my face was already streaked with tears. After staring at my dad for at least a full minute, I finally patted the floor beside me. I figured he might just grab a chair, but he didn't. He sat down right beside me on the floor and my emotional roller coaster day took a few extra flips and turns.

Dad picked up a felt handprint and turned it over. On the back, in grandma's handwriting, was written 'Bryson – age 6'. Tears started to fill my dad's eyes. "I remember this. I was in the 1st grade and my teacher traced all our handprints on the felt and then we cut them out and decorated them. I was a good kid back then."

I had no idea how to respond to that, but I figured this trip down memory lane was going to be a little rocky. There was a snowman shaped picture frame; the bottom of the snowman had a picture of Noelle, the middle had a picture of me, and the top of the snowman was a baby picture of Trey.

Dad held the frame in his hand, just fingering the pictures so gently, like he thought his simple touch might cause them to disintegrate.

"Trey was only 5 months old when your mother made this. She was always so sentimental; it's the one thing that Kadira and my mom really bonded over. They both knew how important it was to keep memories alive. I love that about your mother."

Dad and I went through every ornament in the box together. We told each other stories about what we could remember. Time just stood still; I was eight again, sitting on my daddy's lap while he told stories about his childhood. We shared some laughs, and some tears. I was so engrossed in the feelings of nostalgia that I didn't even hear Chase come in the door. He walked into the living room and saw me and my dad sitting on the floor surrounded by ornaments. A huge smile came across his face; he squatted down beside me, lifted my chin, and wiped away a few tears. He looked over at dad, and then kissed me on the forehead and said, "I'll be at Leland's. Here are the lights; we'll put the angel on the tree later."

Dad just nodded and responded, "I'll bring her over when we're finished here." That was all they said. Chase left and dad and I continued where we left off. He helped me put the lights on the tree and then we hung each of the decorations, gently, still sharing stories and memories as we put each of them on the tree. I swore at that moment that the only memories worth remembering were the good ones; just focus on the positive and the rest will fade into the background. We worked for at least another hour putting everything in just the right spots on the tree.

"Last one Sadey-bug." We just stood there gazing at the tree. Dad reached over, grabbed my hand and just squeezed; I broke down in tears. I hugged my daddy with more love and emotion than I can ever remember; a bond that will never be broken.

"I love you daddy."

"I know Sadey-bug. I love you too." I have no idea how long that hug lasted, but it was a moment in time that will be ingrained in my memory forever.

Dad dropped me off at Cami and Leland's house about an hour later. I did my best to cover my tear-streaked face with some makeup and create a product that Chase wouldn't mind taking in public. Of course, I've looked worse in public with him; but not on purpose. Chase came out the door when we pulled in the driveway.

"Cami's getting dressed; we're gonna go get some dinner, if she ever picks out something to wear. I'll be in in a minute; I just need to talk to your dad." I started walking to the door, but I kept turning around to see what they were discussing. They were talking too low for me to hear them, but there was no doubt in my mind that the conversation revolved around me. They shook hands like old friends and Chase came back into the house. I stopped him in the entryway.

"Thanks."

"For what?"

"Don't play stupid, Chase. This was 100% your doing. I don't know how you do it; but somehow you always manage to…"

He didn't let me finish; he simply leaned down and kissed me –
to shut me up I'm sure. "When I saw the tote of decorations, I
realized that it was full of wonderful memories, and you needed
some of those with your dad. I just made a simple phone call, that's
all."

"I love you."

He kissed me again; it was all that needed to be said.

*Good memories start with a smile, an empty slate, and "Remember
when..."*

Christmas

Tuesday, December 25th

Christmas Day!

"Morning Sweet Cheeks. Merry Christmas!"

"This is the only day in the world that I wake up happy at 7am."

"What about Black Friday?"

"That was 3am – big difference."

"So what's first – open presents or morning sex?"

"If you don't stop being such a happy morning person I'm going to have to trade you in for an older model that sleeps longer."

"So… I guess that means we're opening presents first? That's probably best anyway since I'm anxious to see the look on your face when you open your presents."

"I love presents!" Only took me a minute to get my act together. Opening presents is one of my favorite pastimes; probably because I never really grew up.

I stepped into the living room and I was completely awe-struck by the Christmas tree. The lights illuminated the entire room and

Chase had purposely left all the lights off, I'm sure, so that it would have this effect. It was like every ornament was perfect on the tree, and the tree itself just seemed flawless. I was frozen in place, frozen in time, again. I didn't even hear Chase come up behind me until I felt his arms wrap around my waist.

"It's the most beautiful tree I've ever seen; absolutely perfect."

I leaned my head back on his shoulder and said, "That's because it's the first tree I've ever decorated with love instead of just decorations." We just stood there together, wrapped in each other's arms for what seemed like an eternity; an amazing eternity.

I was brought back to reality by a nudging against my leg – Bones. I reached down to pet him thinking to myself, Sadey Nevada Collins, you are the luckiest woman in the world.

"How about we open some presents?"

"Great idea. What is that scratching noise?" Bones ran over to the tree and sat down beside this one box, just nudging it and whining. "What the heck is he doing?"

Chase had a stupid grin on his face, but he responded, "I don't know. Maybe you should go check out that box."

It wasn't wrapped normal; the lid and the box were wrapped separately. It only took me half a second to realize what the scratching noise was. I lifted the lid off the box and was greeted with a wagging tail and doggy kisses. She was a reddish-brown mix of rat terrier and Chihuahua, and she had the softest, velvety ears

I've ever felt. I picked her up and she immediately laid her head on my shoulder, but she was shaking terribly; she was probably scared being in that box, or scared of Bones. Either scenario would have made sense to me. But then Chase explained.

"She was an abused dog. One of my clients called last week and said that he'd rescued this dog, but he wasn't allowed to have animals at his apartment and wanted to know if I knew somebody who would take her. So, I figured that since Bones likes me better I would even up the stakes in the house."

I ignored that comment and asked, "Is that why she's shaking?"

"Yeah, she's easily frightened. But she's definitely a loveable dog; she just needs a loving mom, and a name."

"How about 'Holly'? She's wrapped up in holly berry leaves paper."

"Sounds good to me. Now, how about we open some more of those presents that are under the tree."

Apparently, Chase and I were on the same wavelength; I forgot to even drop hints about an iPad, yet it was the first thing I opened – well, except for Holly. He was absolutely thrilled about the Wii and couldn't wait to hook it up. It only took a minute to convince him that if he took the time to hook up his game system then he wouldn't have time for morning sex before we went to my mom's. It only took half a second before he'd made his decision, and less than a minute before I was out of my clothes. Luckily, we had given Bones a doggie stocking for Christmas, so he had some toys to play with to entertain him; Holly just followed his cue. It was a very successful start to my Christmas.

We took Holly and Bones with us to mom's house; she has a fenced in backyard, that's in serious need of an upgrade, and I didn't want to leave Holly alone with Bones in her first day at her new home. Might as well introduce her to the chaos of the whole family anyway.

When we walked in the door at mom's, Abi came running to pet Bones and then realized I was holding another dog in my arms. She immediately went crazy and I tried to explain that we couldn't be rough with Holly because she would be scared easily, but Abi was clueless that I was even talking. She grabbed Holly out of my arms and took off for the living room. I followed as quickly as I could so I could save my dog, but it was too late. Abi was already on the floor with Holly on her lap and the dog was giving her some serious tongue lashings. I guess I was worried for nothing; apparently Holly doesn't find 3-year-olds as dangerous as I do. After Abi had wollered Holly to death, I took her and Bones out back to ensure that no surprises ended up on mom's carpet. Chase came out back with me to ensure that Bones didn't eat Holly at the first chance, but he wasn't paying any attention to her. He was walking all around mom's fence, stopping frequently to lift his leg on a fence post.

"What the heck is he doing?" I asked Chase.

"Marking his territory."

"Really? He's been here before, why's he doing that now?"

"There's a new dog; a new scent. He has to make sure that any other dog in the near vicinity understands that he's the male in charge around here."

"Cute. So how do you grown men mark your territory?"

"We have our ways." He gave me that stupid cynical grin that meant 'I'm not giving away my secret'.

Brunch was served promptly at noon, and it consisted of scrambled eggs, biscuits and gravy, hashbrown casserole, cinnamon rolls, bacon, and sausage. Basically, it was the one day out of the year that calories didn't count and eating biscuits and cinnamon rolls in the same meal was perfectly acceptable. The hashbrown casserole was my job; I'm picky, so just like the stuffing at Thanksgiving, I either had to make it myself or I couldn't complain about how somebody else makes it. Trey was in charge of biscuits and gravy; he should actually be a chef instead of a band director, but at least we had him to fix it for us.

Christmas dinner was a lot better than Thanksgiving dinner because Blake didn't have any new secrets to share about me. After the dishes were cleared from the table, the gathering moved to the living room where the Christmas tree had piles of gifts under it. I will admit that I brought several of those gifts with me; I've got this cool aunt thing down to a fine art. It's tradition that mom hands out

all the gifts, slowly, one at a time. This drives Blake and Abi crazy
but this way we actually get to see what everybody got for
Christmas. It used to make me nuts when I was their age; but it's
something she's done for my entire life, so now I'm used to it.

This was the most awe-inspiring Christmas I've ever had. It was
late afternoon when we finally left mom and dad's house. I was
totally exhausted but full of more wonderful memories; this was the
year for positive memories to be made. We spent the rest of the
evening celebrating with Cami and Leland. I didn't think life could
get any better than this.

Chase and I shared the bed with Bones and Holly. Bones took
up his usual amount of space, but Holly was a tad stranger. She
crawled under the covers and positioned herself in the crook of my
legs. It was very odd, but something I guess I'll get used to. Chase
figured it was a security blanket for her; a way for her to feel safe at
night. Time to get a bigger bed.

*Sometimes it's the smallest thing that makes the greatest memories –
something that money could never buy.*

Monday, December 31st
New Year's Eve

Party at our house tonight. I'm excited, but there's still a lot of
cleaning that needs done. Chase and Bones have spent most of the

day in the man-cave while Holly and I have spent too much time on the couch watching NCIS reruns. Now it was crunch time.

"Chase?" I'm yelling down the stairs because I'm too lazy to run down there to talk to him.

"What?"

"Um, just wondering when you were planning on going to get the chicken bites?"

"They said to pick them up at 5:00. What time is it?"

"4:45. I should have bought you a clock for the man-cave."

"Ha ha. I'll go get them now. What's still left to do?

"Clean the entire house in 2 hours."

"No problem; got this totally under control."

"Meaning, you'll go get the chicken and I'll dust and run the sweeper."

"Sounds good to me. I'm taking your car." We went car shopping Friday, and I bought a Hyundia Santa Fe. It's a used car, but it's new to me and there's plenty of room for me, Chase, and 2 dogs. Plus, its all-wheel drive so winters should be a little easier. But the best thing about the car is that there are no bad words spray painted on it.

"Why, because there's a full tank of gas in it?"

"Yep. Be back in a jiffy."

"I'll be here cleaning when you get back."

And that's just what I did. I dusted the living room, ran the sweeper, did a quick bathroom wipe-down and loaded the dishwasher. I decided to just close the door to the laundry room and the office – no need to clean places no one is going to see tonight. Everybody was coming over at 7:00 and it's now 6:30 and Chase still isn't home. I was giving thought to calling his cell phone and chewing him out when he came through the door. He was carrying the plate of chicken bites from Chick-fil-a and a couple of Wal-Mart bags filled with chips & dip and beer. It's a good thing I had already purchased everything I needed to make strawberry daiquiris.

Dane and Noelle were the first to show up, and I noticed that Noelle was starting to get that pregnancy waddle now, but I wasn't stupid enough to mention it out loud. "What'd you do with the kids?"

"Mom and dad have them. I was going to hire a babysitter, but dad insisted, so I didn't argue."

"Free childcare is always good."

"Yeah, and they're staying all night – double bonus."

Cami and Leland came through the door carrying more bags of junk food; that's why she's my best friend.

The boys grabbed a bunch of junk food and headed to the man-cave. We gathered our snacks in the living room and began a gossip fest while we watched 'The Replacements' and drooled over Keanu Reeves.

We had time for one more movie before we changed over to Dick Clark's Rockin' New Year's Eve. We settled on 'Valentine's Day'. So what if it's New Year's Eve; it's a great chick-flick with a happy ending. The boys were not thrilled that we forced them to join us for the chick-flick, but they did what they were told for fear of not getting lucky on New Year's Eve; Steve Holy got it right in his song when he said 'men buy the drinks, but girls call the shots'. Our men are smart enough to know which shots will be called off first; they were easily trainable.

Beer and daiquiris all around; chips and dips were being devoured at record speed. Chase and I shared the recliner, and Dane, Noelle, Cami, and Leland all piled on the couch together; I'm thinking I need to invest in a loveseat or at least another recliner. Bones and Holly were laying side by side on the rug in the middle of the room chewing on the chew bones that Chase bought them; the dogs are spoiled rotten. Time Square was overflowing, and the countdown was less than 5 minutes away. Everybody refilled their glasses or grabbed another beer, with the exception of my prego sister who had been drinking apple cider all evening and pretending it was beer.

Less than a minute to go; everybody was on their feet, ready for the countdown, wrapped in each other's arms. Glasses held high – 10 seconds to go – 9 – 8 – 7 – 6 - 5 – 4 - 3 – 2 - 1. Happy New Year!

Glasses clinked; there were New Year's kisses all around the room. Then time just stood still.

Chase laid his beer on the end table, then grabbed my glass and set it down as well; I assumed so that we could sit back down in the recliner without spilling it. But then he just got this look on his face – the same look that appears when he's about to talk me out of my clothes.

I noticed that the room went eerily silent and everybody was looking at me. Before I could even comprehend in my brain what my eyes were seeing, Chase went down on one knee in front of me and opened a box with the most beautiful diamond ring I've ever laid my eyes on. I'm fairly sure it cost him an entire month's salary, but I wasn't focusing on that at the moment. Tears were filling my eyes as he said, in typical Chase humor,

"I would like to change my Facebook status to 'is married to Sadey Nevada Davis'. Will you accept my new status request?"

I was crying and laughing at the same time. I couldn't come up with a witty comeback; I could barely form an answer. What came out of my mouth was almost cheesy, but it was the best answer I could formulate at the moment. With tears streaming down my face, I managed to say, "I would be happy to accept your new status on one condition."

"Anything for you Sweet Cheeks."

"You have to legally adopt Bones; I mean, you are the only father he's ever known."

The entire room erupted in laughter and Cami and Noelle were squealing.

Chase stood up and looked at me with such affection in his eyes. All I could think was *'the only thing better than the kiss, is the moment right before, when he looks into my eyes and leaves me completely breathless'*. He slowly placed the ring on my finger and kissed me like it was the very first kiss. As we broke apart, while I was still trying to control my breathing, Chase formulated his best smirk and said, "I'm just marking my territory."

At that same moment, Bones stood up, hiked his leg, and peed on Holly's back, apparently marking his own territory.

Time to get him fixed.

In this life, we are all just walking up the mountain. We can sing as we climb, or we can complain about our sore feet. Whichever we choose, we still gotta do the hike.

Child Abuse and Neglect

If you suspect a child is being abused or neglected, please call your local Department of Health and Human Resources and report it right away.

You can visit https://www.childwelfare.gov/ to find all the resources you need to make sure someone can take action on behalf of our children.

If you see something, say something!

A child's life may depend on it.

Enjoy this book?

If so, please go to the site where you purchased the book and leave a review. It can be as short or as long as you wish.

Reviews, good and bad, help authors to know what you, the reader, are enjoying or not enjoying about their books. It makes us better writers — even if we don't like what you have to say.

Reviews also help us sell books (which is always a good thing). They help potential readers know what other readers enjoyed or didn't enjoy about the books.

That being said — be honest. Please. When I'm looking to purchase a book, the first thing I do is read the summary. The second thing I do is scroll down to the reviews. Just because a book received a bad review doesn't necessarily deter me from buying it, but it does help me know what others liked and didn't like about the book I'm thinking of buying.

So, please, take a moment and review this book (and any others you have read recently)

About the Author

Christy Wilson is the author of the CPS series, which follows the life and cases of Child Protective Services worker Sadey Collins. Although her degree is in Elementary Education, with a Master Degree in Reading, Christy spent several years working in social work. She started as a Homefinder for a foster care agency, before spending several years working for Child Protective Services. Investigating the abuse and neglect of children is mentally taxing and she has experienced first-hand the many challenges, and few successes, that are experienced by CPS workers.

Christy lives with her family in the mountains of Ritchie County, West Virginia. They have three children, five grandchildren and three large dogs who believe they are children (and are treated as such).

While spoiling her grandchildren is her favorite activity, writing comes in a close second. She also enjoys cross-stitching, scrapbooking, and reading everything she can from her favorite authors.

Other Books by this Author

The CPS Series ~

Broken Promises

Amongst the Debris

A Balancing Act

Off the Deep End

The Ties that Bind

Crossing the Line

A New Beginning

The Romantic CPS Series ~

Promises

Debris

Visit Christy's website at http://www.authorchristywilson.com to purchase books, sign up for her newsletter, and stay informed of important information.

Made in the USA
Middletown, DE
21 January 2022

59339715R00249